CW00952284

VANITAS

*Escape from
Vampire Junction*

Also by S. P. Somtow in Gollancz Horror

The Vampire Junction novels

VAMPIRE JUNCTION

VALENTINE

MOONDANCE

VANITAS

Escape from
Vampire Junction

S. P. Somtow

VICTOR GOLLANCZ

LONDON

First published in Great Britain 1995
by Victor Gollancz
An imprint of the Cassell Group
Wellington House, 125 Strand, London WC2R 0BB

A catalogue record for this book is
available from the British Library.

ISBN 0 575 05655 X

Photoset in Great Britain by
Rowland Phototypesetting Ltd
Bury St Edmunds, Suffolk
Printed and bound in Great Britain by
Mackays of Chatham plc, Chatham, Kent

to the *real* David Giler

VANITAS

a kind of still life, popular in seventeenth-
century Flemish painting, in which common
household objects are used to symbolize man's
mortality

VANITAS

an art gallery in Los Angeles in the late
twentieth century, owned by Native
American PJ Gallagher, ex-shaman, friend of
ex-vampires, dedicated to the Neo-Gothic
school of art, named after

VANITAS

the title of Timmy Valentine's last album, his
only album since his return from the Other Side;
critically perceived as empty, devoid of
passion; Timmy Valentine's first flop.

Part I

THE PRINCE OF NEO-GOTHIC

I heard the murdered woman
Singing in the rain
She too is beautiful
She can't feel any pain

I saw the murdered woman
Dancing in the mist
I touched her moist blue lips
Unfeeling and unkissed

Timmy Valentine

1

OVERHEARD AT A GALLERY OPENING

vanitas

She lay in the gutter with her long hair streaming in the torrent of sewage. She was—

vanitas

'But what does it mean, *Vanitas*?' said the blonde woman with the pierced lip and the mirror shades. 'Like, I just don't get it. It's something to do with the Neo-Gothic movement, I guess, but what?'

vanitas

She lay on the beach, her thin summer dress stretched flat against the sand with boulders, her nipples blue and hard; she was—

vanitas

'It's Latin.'

'*Coolness*! I love foreign languages,' she said, furtively piling a toast point with beluga. 'But what does it mean?'

'It means vanity. Not as in conceit or self-importance . . . but as in *emptiness* . . . the void . . . the great nothing . . . also, it's a kind of seventeenth-century style of painting. They were

depictions of everyday objects . . . household utensils . . . fruit
. . . and then somewhere in the middle of the painting . . . a
skull. A worm. Death. You see? The emptiness of our existence.
Vanitas.'
    'Oh, I get it. Downer.'
    'Oh! Excuse me for interrupting. Downer, you said? Would
you care for one?'

vanitas

She lay half in, half out of a storefront window, the neon cocktail
lounge sign strobing against her pale skin, the glass-shards
sprouting from her flesh like a crystal garden; but she
was—

vanitas

'Is it true that Timmy Valentine is coming to your gallery opening, PJ?'
    'When's he due to arrive, PJ?'
    'How does he feel about the returns on his new album, PJ?
Is he disappointed? I mean, it went platinum and all but . . . I
mean, compared to the sales on Vampire Junction and the
soundtrack album of Valentine – the Motion Picture . . . but then
again, that was all old stuff, wasn't it? I mean, who is this new
guy anyway? You knew Timmy Valentine, didn't you? Before he
disappeared, I mean. How can you go along with Stupendous
Pictures' charade?'
    'Oh, shut up,' said the blonde with the pierced lip and the
mirror shades. 'It really is Timmy Valentine. He went through
some kind of hormone treatment that made him like, permanently looking like a child. I know, it was in the Weekly World
News.'
    'Or was it the Enquirer?' someone said snidely.
    'No, no, the Enquirer said he hasn't aged because he was
abducted by a UFO and like, frozen in time. He was kept in
like, an ice locker along with Elvis and the Kennedy brothers.

But that's bullshit, isn't it, PJ? I mean, you *know* him and all, know about the hormone treatments.'

'Look! I think that's his limo now . . . they're going insane outside! . . . someone alert the crowd control guys.'

'*Vanitas*. I like it. A gallery for the '90s. A monument to the vacuity of contemporary artistic expression. It's like one of those sugar-free no-fat desserts . . . you know, with Simplesse and Nutrasweet . . . or one of those diet sodas, nothing but water and carcinogens. Oh, and it's in the Valley, too. A nice touch. A no-cal dessert in the midst of a cultural desert.'

'Is that what you're going to say in your *Times* article?'

'Oh, shut up, shut up, just scarf the beluga.'

'But really, PJ, don't you think the subject matter's a little macabre? I mean, for the very first show in your new gallery, don't you think you could have picked a slightly more *uplifting* theme? Or a better known artist than this Lauren McCandless?'

'PJ's wife is rather partial to this painter. And you know, it's his wife's money. So why don't you lay off that line of questioning?'

'Where's his wife now?'

'In Thailand. She's *loaded*. Granddaughter of a prince, I'm told.'

'Why are we whispering?'

'More champagne?'

'But to *seek out* those poor murdered women like that! It gives me the creeps.'

'*Coolness!*'

'Is that Timmy's limo now?'

'Wow. The Prince of Neo-Gothic himself.'

'A bit of a faded prince if you ask me.'

'That limo must be a whole block long.'

'Someone clear away those fans! Give the guy some breathing room!'

'It's not Timmy Valentine. It's someone else. Looks like it might be Sigourney Weaver.'

'When's *Timmy* coming?'

'He'll be late. I mean, he's the guest of honour. I mean, the gallery's named after his album and all.'

'Get a load of *that* painting!'

vanitas

She lay spread-eagled against a trash heap; she had no eyes. A cockroach darted from her parted lips. Apart from a tiny smear of crimson on one cheek, she was—

vanitas

'Could you tell us a little more about the artist, PJ? Who is this Lauren McCandless and why is he so *morbid*?'

'Well . . . my wife discovered him, actually. He was born in Pasadena, but he ran away to Thailand in the late '60s to escape the draft. He'd been hiding out in a temple in the hills in the north of the country, middle of nowhere, painting and learning to meditate from some ancient monk . . . been sending his canvases down to Bangkok, exhibiting them at the Bhirasri . . . no one had ever seen him until my wife sought him out, brought him out of hiding, convinced him it was safe to come back to civilization . . . then he went wild. Likes to paint dead women. Then, OK, there's this mad slasher, you know, a serial killer, preying on young sex workers in the red light district of Bangkok, driving the police crazy, frightening the tourists, and our friend becomes obsessively fascinated, and he starts this series of paintings of murdered women . . .'

'Maybe *he's* the killer.'

'Yeah. Maybe. But he always has an alibi.'

'So why didn't he come to his big LA opening?'

'Oh, I think he's gone back to the jungle.'

'Listen! Another limo out there . . .'

'I think it's him this time.'

'So, PJ, what's your position on the Timmy Valentine thing? Is he a fake or is he real?'

'No comment.'

'Hey, hey, get a load of *that* painting!'

'Why are they always so pale? Aren't most of them like, Oriental or something?'

'There's a reason they're so pale . . . you see . . . that was what attracted McCandless to them in the first place . . . there is this strange, translucent, anaemic quality to their skin . . . look how he's reproduced it . . .'

'Stop talking! I want to get a look at Timmy Valentine! He's stepping out of his limo now. He's smiling a little for the cameras. He's stopping in front of the gallery now. He's shorter than I thought he'd be. He's dressed completely in black. He's talking to the lady from *Entertainment Tonight*, you know, what's her name, I forgot.'

'The most curious thing about this particular serial killer . . . you'll *love* this! . . . is that, when each of the corpses was examined, every one of them was discovered to be—'

vanitas

'I'm standing here at the star-studded opening of the Vanitas Gallery in Studio City, California, a stone's throw from Universal Studios. Everybody's here tonight to gape at the gargantuan, gory canvases of Neo-Gothic painter Lauren McCandless . . . paintings that show, in horrifying photorealism, the victims of a modern-day Jack the Ripper who is stalking the sex clubs of the mysterious Orient. This is the first time McCandless's works have been shown in the US. A busload of protesters from Youth For Moral America has been waiting since this afternoon, but that hasn't stopped the celebrities from flocking to the show – it's the coolest place to be tonight! – and fashion mavens should note that the look tonight is definitely black; black on black, black with black, black-studded black, black, black, *black*. Here's rock star Timmy Valentine. Let's ask him what he thinks of it all . . . considering that music critics blame his groundbreaking album, *Vampire Junction*, for creating the Neo-Gothic movement in the first place . . .'

'Hi.'

'What do you think of all this? Gallery owner PJ Gallagher's a personal friend of yours, isn't he?'

'We go way back. And yes, I'm paying the mortgage on this joint.'

'Timmy, you disappeared almost a decade ago, then suddenly got resurrected just in time for the blockbuster motion picture

about your life . . . and you *still* haven't reached puberty! What
do you make of all that speculation about hormone treatments,
UFO abductions, or your just being a plain old hoax on the part
of Stupendous Entertainment Corporation?'
  'No comment.'
  'Are you prepared to say that you're *not* a hoax?'
  'Everyone who knew me then has testified that I'm me.'
  'But Timmy, word has it that your new album, *Vanitas*, has
had rather disappointing sales domestically . . . one musicol-
ogist has published an article claiming that you're a pretty face,
a double for dead Timmy Valentine, and that you're just dub-
bing an electronically sampled synthetic version of the dead
Timmy's voice . . . is that true?'
  'I'm not Milli Vanilli. If you'll excuse me . . .'
  'That was Timmy Valentine, folks. While we're waiting for
the next celeb to show up, we're gonna run a little video on the
Bangkok Butcher whose victims have been the subjects of
Lauren McCandless's morbid paintings . . .'

  *. . . they were working girls, the most beautiful girls that Bangkok's
all-you-can-eat sex industry had to offer. One was found in Pattaya
Beach. Another in a ditch next to one of the city's famous canals.
Another in a pile of garbage outside a McDonald's, lying on a heap of
half-eaten Big Macs. Although the crimes have not yet been solved, the
victims attracted the attention of Neo-Gothic artist Lauren McCandless,
who spoke to us from his current home, a houseboat docked on the Chao
Phraya River, across the water from the fabulous Temple of Dawn
and right beside the Oriental Hotel, made famous by Somerset
Maugham . . .*
  'What is it about these murdered women that fascinates you so
much?'
  'Ah, yes, those fabulous "dead yellow women" . . . that's a famous
story, Fiction, I mean. I don't suppose you've read it? Before your
time. Dashiel Hammet, you know. But they're not exactly yellow, you
see. Their skins have a certain pallor. You can see the delicate tracery
of the tissues beneath. They possess this quality because of the killer's
modus operandi, you see . . . every single one of them has been completely—'

vanitas

. . . completely drained of blood.

2

PORTRAITS OF MURDERED WOMEN

music of madness

Listen. Listen.

It comes at first out of the empty air, down an empty hallway, across an empty space; it comes through air-conditioning vents, through airtight windows of passing limousines, through the dense, polluted air itself. It jangles in the earphones of a jogger. It buzzes from a boombox beside a graffiti-strewn wall. it is everywhere, though it is nothing but air itself, agitated, constrained into rhythmic resonating. Of itself, it is emptiness. Yet listen. Listen.

It has made people's fortunes. It has made people destitute. It has driven men mad. It has given life, and it has drained life away. It has stolen men's souls. Yet of itself, it is emptiness. In itself, it has no soul. It is less substantial than the dust into which God once breathed life.

But listen. Listen.

Can you hear it?

This is what it says:

There is a light more luminous than love; there is a darkness more profound than death.

gallery

'Turn off the music,' PJ said. And it was gone.

In Los Angeles, glamour nights are early nights. Everyone who *is* anyone works in the industry, and industry people – the ones who are working, that is – have a tendency to get up early.

They have to use every second of available light. It's up at five,
into makeup by six, then on to the set where they wait around all
day for something to happen.

By one in the morning, to PJ's relief, the celebs had all
departed. All except Timmy Valentine, who, in spite of having
recently metamorphosed into a human being, still found it
sometimes trying to behave like one. It must be very hard, PJ
thought, to spend two thousand years without a soul, and then
to acquire one all of a sudden. Timmy hadn't spoken much
all evening; of the hundreds of overdressed guests who had
crammed the gallery, he had been the only one who genuinely
seemed interested in these paintings. Oh, the others had drifted
by, making their prefabricated, pretentious comments as they
dived into the caviar, listening to the various critics pontificate,
shuddering deliciously when some moral majority types had
attempted to gatecrash the party, chanting 'Pornography, pornography,' much to the delight of the television crews. By and
large, though, the glitterati knew that it was they, not the paintings of a middle-aged, psychotic ex-flower child, who were the
real centre of attention here; the cameras would not otherwise
have been there.

Not Timmy, though. He stood for half an hour at least in
front of every one of those paintings; stood quite still, almost
as though he didn't have to breathe . . . just like the old days,
the days when he had been one of the undead. It was uncanny
to watch him. In the sea of vacuous conversation that raged
through the gallery, he did not speak at all, but gazed with
concentrated serenity on McCandless's images of beauty and
depravity. Timmy's image had changed a little, as befit a
creature of the '90s; but beneath the close-cropped, sculpted
hair, the oversized black clothes, the black baseball cap worn
backward and the studded Doc Martins, there was still the
same two-thousand-year-old body of a prepubescent child, the
same sensual, yet asexual features that could be found on a
Roman bust in the Getty Museum, on the image of a celestial
eunuch in a Sung Dynasty Chinese codex, on the face of an
angel in a painting by Caravaggio. One could never forget those
eyes. A year ago, when *Valentine – the Motion Picture* had raked
in more money than *E.T.* and *Batman* combined, those eyes had

graced the cover of *Time* magazine; just the eyes, staring out from a black background; 'The boy with the billion dollar eyes,' *Time*'s reporter had rhapsodized.

PJ watched the boy watching the paintings; one by one, the lights in the gallery were dimming. Someone was vacuuming up the débris. Outside, through the glass doors, PJ could see that the crowd had dispersed; there was only a lone homeless man squatting by the mailbox on the corner.

'You want me to put on some music?' PJ said.

Timmy didn't answer him. PJ went over to the stereo console, cleverly concealed inside a *faux* Corinthian column, pushed a few buttons; it was Timmy's own voice that filled the air. The words of the song were about a murdered woman. Its rhythms were angular, industrial; laid over those harsh sounds was a subtly shifting synth pad that might almost have been New Age if its harmonies had not been so quirkily disturbing. Timmy's voice wove in and out of the two incongruous textures, somehow melding them together. The voice soared, sighed, arced as it always had before, but there was something about it that was different from all of Timmy Valentine's previous recordings.

'Yes . . . you notice it too, don't you?' Timmy said softly. 'But you can't put your finger on it.'

'I guess so.'

'They say the bits and pieces of the voice are me, but the sum total isn't; they say that some clever engineer has chopped up old voice tracks and sampled them and rearranged them to make new sounds. But I know I sang them. I was there, in the studio. My producer will say so, *has* said so, but they just keep running the stories about me faking myself.'

'Yes,' said PJ. 'But you must admit that it's hard for the average person to take, I mean the idea that you disappeared and, almost ten years later, you just pop back into existence, unchanged . . . and what about the big Timmy Valentine look-alike competition to find the kid who would play you in the movie? People's memories are short, but a lot of people still realize that the kid who won the contest was named Angel Todd . . . not Timmy Valentine.'

'Yeah. I know.'

The portrait was of Victim Number Seven. She was the youngest of the victims, probably no more than fourteen or fifteen. She was the one who had been artfully laid out over a trash heap outside a McDonald's. Only the contents of the trash, captured in vivid photorealism by the painter, gave away the fact that the setting was not Anytown, USA; for amid the candy wrappers and Coke cans and french fry buckets were decaying garlands of jasmine and burnt-out joss sticks and banana leaves, and newspapers covered with an alien script. The girl, of course, was beautiful, and quite, quite bloodless.

'You can't put your finger on it, PJ,' said Timmy, 'but I can.'

'What do you mean?'

'They can hear me breathing.'

'Breathing?'

'When I was one of the undead,' Timmy said, 'I didn't have to breathe to sing.'

PJ remembered. He was a child himself then, a half-Shoshone half-delinquent ragamuffin from a hick Idaho town named Junction. Junction had burned down and PJ's whole past with it. PJ thought about the past as little as possible. After the conflagration, PJ had gone back to the reservation, tried to relearn the ways of his mother's culture; he had done his vision quest; he had fought the great darkness that had threatened to overwhelm the world. Sometimes he still had nightmares, but they were fading. Any wound can heal if you really put your mind to it.

'I remember what your songs were like, in those days,' PJ said.

'Not human. The phrases just plucked out of the clear air. It's ironic, isn't it? Now that I'm human, and I have all these wonderful things to sing about . . . I can really *feel* the pain, the heartbreak, and the joy . . . I'm losing my voice. And they *know* it. I could feel it tonight. In the old days I'd have been able to smell it; I could sniff out all the pheromones of human emotion. It *sucks* that I have to actually try to listen to people, to feel them out. But the way some of my co-celebs were looking at me, I could really sense it. I'm a has-been. At thirteen years old.'

'You mean two thousand and thirteen. Give or take a century.'

Timmy smiled. 'I was a real boy once. For twelve years. And then . . . they tell me it was in AD 79 . . . I stopped being real. Until Angel Todd traded his soul for my immortality. That makes me thirteen, just thirteen. Thirteen and fucking over the hill. I hate myself.'

'Pinocchio, one year later. Was it worth becoming a real boy?'

'It's high-concept. Make a great sitcom.'

'Maybe you can sell it. Attach yourself as the star. You're still hot enough to get a television deal.'

'Yeah, yeah. But . . . but seriously . . . I overheard some execs talking tonight. They didn't know I was nearby. I'm still pretty good at lurking even if I can't change myself into a cat anymore.'

'What did they say?'

'That maybe it's time to can me, quit while the going's good.'

'They can't! They've spent too much on promoting you.'

'I know. But they've seen the returns on *Vanitas*, and they're starting to squirm.'

Abruptly, Timmy had had enough of gazing at the girl in the trash. He moved on to the next painting, the one on the beach. a strand of seaweed twisted about her private parts; another crossed her lips; one of her hands, open, held a sea-urchin. She might have been merely asleep, except for the gash across her abdomen, from which protruded a delicate tendril of intestine, almost perfectly camouflaged in a mound of coral and sea shells.

'Jesus,' Timmy said softly, 'she reminds me of someone.'

'Lisa Zottoli,' PJ said. 'You killed her in the swimming pool of your old mansion in Encino. When she came back from the grave she was always draped in seaweed.'

'I don't remember.'

'She was an abused little girl, your fan; she'd run away from home, snuck onto your estate; you turned into a were-shark and ripped her apart.'

'If you say so.' Timmy often claimed to have forgotten things that had happened during his centuries of vampirism. It was probably true. Surely the brain of a human boy couldn't contain the details of hundreds of past identities, thousands of grisly killings, trauma upon trauma. It was better not to remember, no doubt; but it disturbed PJ that he was so often called upon to be Timmy's memory. He didn't want to think of the past either, but unlike Timmy, he had not been blessed with amnesia.

'Did Lisa look anything like this girl?' said Timmy.

'No, she wasn't Asian; she came of Bible-banging redneck stock, I believe.'

But they did have something in common. They had both been completely drained of blood.

'Are you thinking what I'm thinking?' Timmy Valentine said.

'No!' PJ cried. 'There are no more vampires.'

But Timmy only smiled a sad little smile, and he kept staring at the painting, as though he was willing himself to remember what could not be remembered.

PJ remembered:

He was thirteen then himself. The fire ran down the main drag of his home town. Vampires in flames rolled down the steep, snowy slopes. The old men who had pursued the boy vampire to this desolate place were all dying too. It was all over.

Another fire. Ten years later. They had rebuilt the town of Junction as a movie set. They were replaying all those scenes from his childhood. But this time they had made the colours brighter. The snow was bleached cornflakes and the mansion of Timmy Valentine that straddled the hillside was just a façade. Behind the celluloid illusion, a quite different war was being fought . . . with a witch woman and a mad preacher . . . a war for the world's soul. That too was all over.

There was no more magic. Timmy Valentine was just an ordinary boy now. The darkness had been exorcised.

It's all, all over, really over, PJ told himself. And now I'm well-off, and I got me a beautiful, aristocratic wife, and the monster who caused all my troubles has become human, has become my friend.

'Are you thinking what I'm thinking?' said Timmy Valentine again.

'No,' PJ lied.

Timmy moved closer to the canvas. The dead woman, larger than life, dwarfed him. 'She's got the marks,' he said. He pointed to her neck, to two dark pinpricks, half obscured by the shadow of a strand of seaweed.

'Could be just a coincidence.'

'Could be.'

There was a time . . . when he'd been gifted with the vision, when he had been a *ma'aipots*, a sacred man-woman, that he

could have reached out with his mind, sought out, touched the
presence of unseen spirits. But since that second conflagration
in Junction, Idaho, he had seen no more visions, never entered
the other world, lived a life of enviable normality. Now PJ could
feel a familiar dread. He had not felt it in a year. It sat in his
stomach like a wad of blotting paper.

'You *do* feel it!' said Timmy Valentine.

'No. I feel . . . that I *can't* feel. I feel an emptiness.'

'*Vanitas.*'

'Yeah.' He laughed nervously.

'I could be wrong,' Timmy said. 'I mean, I've lost my ability
to sense things clearly. Just as you have.'

'Yeah. But now I'm spooked. Let's get out of here. I'll call
Chit in Bangkok, make sure she's all right.'

'OK. We'll take my limo. That way we can catch ourselves on
The Hollywood Minute.'

dissolve: rituals

Lady Premchitra was in the middle of performing a *kae bon* ceremony when her cellular phone began beeping from the depths
of her Louis Vuitton shoulder bag. It was not an opportune
moment and she hoped it would stop ringing soon; it was probably her mother, still checking up on her as though she were a
schoolgirl in a blue uniform and pigtails. She had been meaning
to perform the ceremony for months; one could never be too
careful in one's dealings with the Erawan shrine.

Traffic screeched all around her. There were tourists everywhere . . . shoppers thronged the two huge shopping malls,
cattycorner from one another, here at the busiest intersection in
Bangkok, which just happened to be the site of one of the most
revered shrines in the city. The sun was merciless. The smells of
human sweat, of jasmine garlands, of incense, of the perfumed
dancing girls that were even now moving slowly around the four
faces of the shrine with their slender hands delicately twisting in
the arcane gestures of Thai classical dance, mingled and clashed
in olfactory cacophony. I should have come at night, Chit
thought. She wondered whether the driver had been able to find

a parking place. Maybe in the basement of the Regent Hotel. She had to concentrate. She clasped the seven lit joss-sticks in her hands, bowed her head in reverence to Brahma, and tried to set herself adrift. Despite the jostling crowds and the constant thrum of motorcycle exhausts, there was a certain serenity to be found here, if you let yourself float.

If only the cellular phone would stop ringing . . .

At last she decided she might as well answer it. She put down her incense sticks and pulled the phone out of her bag. 'Mother,' she said, 'give me a break.'

But it was PJ, calling from Los Angeles.

'Darling,' she said, 'right now I'm in the middle of thanking the gods for hoodwinking my relatives long enough to let us get married without me getting disinherited . . . I meant to do this months ago . . . you know the deal. When Brahma grants your wish, if you don't fulfil your part of the bargain, something will happen to jinx it.'

'What did you promise to do?'

'I promised seven elephants and seven sets of dancing girls. I won't be through here for a while; there's a line a mile long for the dancing girls. What are you guys doing? Oh . . . the exhibit opened today, didn't it? Jesus, I forgot. Time seems to stand still in Bangkok. Either that, or it moves twice as fast.'

'We're getting back from it now. We're watching ourselves on *Headline News*, actually.'

'You're with Timmy?'

'Yes. Listen, Chit . . . there's something that's been bothering us a little . . .'

She moved out of the way as the dancing troupe came by. Sweat was making their makeup run, pouring down their heavy, spangled costumes, drenching the edges of their tall pagoda-like headdresses, but they smiled and kept time to the syncopated pounding of drums and marimbas.

'Bothering you?'

Now came Timmy's voice. 'It's those Lauren McCandless paintings.'

Then there was a lot of static, followed by PJ's voice . . . 'completely drained of blood.'

'OK,' Timmy said. 'It sounds like a line from a cheap horror movie. But, but . . .'

'Oh, come on. Lauren's just one of those eccentric American expatriates . . . the city's teeming with them. He's morbid, he's obsessed, he's *not* a vampire. I had lunch with him yesterday. In broad daylight. With genuine silverware. Sterling. My grandmother's. *And* I glimpsed his face in my powder compact.'

'So you *have* been worried about it . . . to the extent of having lunch with him . . . so you could test him?' Timmy said.

'Yes,' she admitted. 'But you know as well as I do that he's not a suspect. His alibis are airtight. And, well, he's a great artist, for God's sake! Of course he's crazy.'

'OK,' said PJ. 'But be careful. Come home soon.'

'Love you. You too, Timmy.'

'Love you.'

'Love you.'

She tucked the phone back into her bag. Then she dug out the celadon elephants, each one carefully wrapped in newspaper, that she'd ordered from her favourite pottery shop, way upcountry in Ayudhya. Each one was about an inch long, with tiny little zircon eyes and tusks of genuine ivory, and covered with the delicate blue-green glaze so prized in ancient times. Carefully she counted them. Counted them a second time because she thought she might have counted one twice by mistake. Seven elephants. That was the bargain she'd made with the god.

She set them down one by one on the offering table in front of Brahma's northern face. Then she purchased four seven-coloured flower garlands from the nearest vendor, lit a new set of seven joss-sticks, and began her slow clockwise circuit of the shrine, stopping in front of each of the four-faced god's altars to lay down a garland and murmur a prayer of thanksgiving, carefully threading her way through a jumble of Japanese, brandishing camcorders and jabbering.

She thanked the god for bringing her PJ. PJ, a creature so exotic even her relatives were too astonished to carp; half white, half red, half urban, half savage, half man, half woman; PJ, the vampire slayer. Of course, she thought, he's not as exotic as he used to be, now that the family's set him up as a bourgeois gallery owner in Studio City. And he doesn't fight vampires anymore, except, perhaps, in half-remembered nightmares. Their stay in Junction seemed more and more to have been woven from the fabric of dream: the forest burning . . . making love in the pelting rain and the mud . . . the men in flames lunging through the artificial streets . . . Oscar night at the Lennon Auditorium . . . what a farce that had been! They were thinking of moving it back to the Chandler after that terrorist thing. The images of that tumultuous year were all fragmented now, assembling and reassembling themselves into nonsensical collages; she was glad of the opportunity to forget.

Let me forget some more, she prayed to the four-faced Brahma. She was standing at the western face now, in the shadow of seven-foot-tall carved elephants. Suppliants kneeled, rubbing the teakwood with little sheets of gold leaf, murmuring their prayers. The dazzling sunlight, the flames of the incense-lighting torches, the closeness of the crowd . . . she was being roasted alive. She couldn't wait to go back into the air-conditioned comfort of the Sogo shopping mall, just a few yards away. She pressed her palms harder together, trying to squeeze herself into the tranquillity of *samadhi*, but it seemed to elude her now. Forget, she told herself, forget.

But as she turned the corner of the shrine and walked once more past the offering table by the northern face of the god, piled high with offerings of teak and ceramic elephants and baskets of fruit, she saw, in her peripheral vision, her own offering, seven sea-blue miniature sculptures with glittering eyes . . .

She stopped. Nervously she put down her incense sticks. There were only six elephants after all. She counted them again. Perhaps one of them had been knocked off the altar. No one would have walked off with one, surely; to steal from this holiest of shrines would be the worst possible karma. Although you never knew, some of these tourists . . .

Lady Chit was about to kneel down closer to the shrine so she could get a closer look. But a group of schoolchildren, in white and khaki uniforms, came breezing in, chattering, each with an armful of elephants, flower garlands and food offerings, and they were laying down their offerings all over the table.

She couldn't see the elephants at all now, and her cellular phone was ringing once again.

It was Lauren McCandless, asking for news of his big gallery opening.

'You could have gone, you know,' she said, as she walked away from the Erawan shrine toward the escalator that led to the second storey of the Sogo shopping mall. Already she could feel the air-conditioning.

'I know,' said the artist's disembodied voice, 'but lately I seem to have developed a phobia about crossing big bodies of water.'

'Maybe my husband's right.'

She was indoors at last. Away from the suffocating sunlight. She found a seat in one of the many coffee shops that overlooked the atrium of the mall, ordered an iced Blue Mountain, fanned herself with the silk-bound menu.

'Right about what?'

'He thinks you're a vampire,' she said. She'd meant it lightly, and her own accusatory tone startled her. 'You know . . . bodies of water . . . and all that.'

'Don't be silly, Chit . . . I'm living in a houseboat. Hey, I'm supposed to be the paranoid artist around here . . .'

She laughed. 'No time for paranoia now, Lauren. We're making you famous.' She suddenly thought of the missing elephant. Was it possible that she *had* miscounted after all . . . that the *kae bon* ceremony had been aborted . . . that everything was now about to go terribly, terribly wrong? Wasn't the *kae bon* business just another of those superstitions that one had to pay lip service to – a nice, comforting bit of tradition to cling to in the midst of the relentless technophilia of modern Bangkok? But her hands were trembling as she set down her Blue Mountain. This gnawing dread hadn't just come from nowhere. PJ had taught her to trust her feelings. 'And rich,' she added, filling in dead space. Glancing around, she noticed that every one of the *faux* Louis Quinze divans held an overdressed businessman or woman, and that each was speaking earnestly and ostentatiously into his or her own cellular phone; she longed to go back to America, where the rich were not so in your face all the time; she missed PJ, even though they had only been apart for a couple of weeks; at least there'd be someone here to share this sense of dread with.

'I don't know if I'll enjoy being rich,' said McCandless, 'after all these years of bucking the establishment and dodging the draft and all that . . .'

'Oh, you'll make do,' said Chit, 'we all do.'

'I'm so glad that morbid is *chic* this year. We all have *Valentine – the Motion Picture* to thank for that!'

An insistent *ping* from the depths of her shoulder bag made all the other coffee shop patrons look up at the same time. 'Damn,' she said, 'it's my *other* cellular phone.' She retrieved it from the depths of the bag. The other customers watched furtively. At least I've managed to one-up everyone else around here, she thought, putting the phone to her other ear. 'Hello, Mother.'

angel

Vampires! he thought. The phone conversation he'd had with Lady Chit that afternoon had certainly inflamed his paranoia. Not even the two joints he had smoked since then had managed to calm him down enough to get back to work. Now it was past midnight and Lauren McCandless didn't want to go to work at all yet, wasn't ready to stoke up his brain to the adrenalin level he needed in order to do battle with those intractable enemies of his, pigment, oil, canvas. He lay on the deck of the houseboat, on a straw mat, studying the photographs he had taken of the latest dead girl. He hadn't begun the painting yet, of course; he would have to absorb the photographs, internalize their details so that he would never have to refer to them in the course of the painting; once he was ready, days or weeks from now, he would storm into the studio at the back of the houseboat and work, feverishly and furiously, not eating or drinking, not even taking drugs, until it was finished. That's how it was for him . . . he'd described it to the guy from *People* Magazine as 'the eternal cycle of constipation and diarrhoea.'' Not a quote they'd used. Actually, he'd been whittled down to about two column inches in the *Picks and Pans* section. Fuck 'em.

Vampires! But that's what he loved about the Thais. Even the most sophisticated ones . . . the ones with fancy Ivy League

educations and billion-dollar Hong Kong bank accounts . . .
they were all superstitious as shit. Upcountry, people talked
about ghosts and demons as though they were just regular old
folks; but even in the city, with all its boomtown frenzy and
old-world ennui, people thought nothing of interrupting a board
meeting for a quick exorcism. It was wild. It was a close-to-the-
edge kind of society . . . a society that teetered perpetually at
the interface between genius and psychosis. Like Lauren
McCandless himself – the mad, draft-dodging artist who had
unexpectedly been singled out as a Metaphor for the '90s.

Of course, he'd never have been drafted, back in the '60s . . .
not with a certified diagnosis of paranoid schizophrenia in his
medical records. And of course, with the amnesty, he could
have gone back a long time ago. But he hadn't come to Southeast
Asia in order to run away from anything. No. He had been a
seeker, not a refugee. But draft-dodging was a politically correct
thing to have on a wild and crazy artist's résumé.

In the distance, a jazz quartet was playing. The night air was
heavy with Bangkok's dissonant odours: the pollution, the
night-blooming jasmine, the sewage, the incense, the succulent
fumes from dozens of open-air noodle shops and *saté* stands,
the fragrance of ripe mangoes. Lauren smiled as he leaned
against the headrest, holding up the photos in the light from
the Oriental Hotel where he was docked.

Beautiful. Bloodless. Dead.

He debated whether he should light another joint. No. Why
overdo it? The night was perfect. He stared into the eyes of the
dead girl. He felt himself drifting. Maybe it was just the movement of the houseboat. Or maybe he was entering that strange,
half-dreaming state of consciousness where his creative pro-
cesses took place. He couldn't yet tell. He stared into the dead
girl's eyes. Was she calling to him? Was it her voice he heard,
floating across the dark water?

He smiled. A sampan was drifting past. Some kid, dark and
doe-eyed, squatted by the bow with a radio in his arms. It was
Timmy Valentine he was listening to, that song about the murdered women, the song inspired by *his* painting . . . from the
album that had *his* painting on the cover . . . what fucking seren-
dipity . . . the world is playing the soundtrack to my life . . .

delusions of grandeur! It's good to be a schiz. I should lay off the Prozac for a while, really get into my craziness a little more.

The sampan moved downriver, out of earshot. The eyes of the dead woman held him, seduced him; he imagined himself embracing the bloodless flesh, felt the beginning of an erection.

And then, abruptly, there came the cold.

A shadow. Someone standing over him. The pool of darkness swallowed up the photograph. He couldn't hear anyone breathing though.

The shadow was slender, boy-shaped. He was afraid to look.

'Krai maa?' he asked in Thai. The houseboy had the day off, but maybe he had got himself in trouble and needed a place to crash.

The shadow didn't move at all. It blocked out the warmth of the night. Lauren shivered.

'Lauren,' the voice said. It was a child's voice. The voice came out of the cold and dark; it was not from the world around him, the world where the wind was warm and even the night was bright with neon. It called to him from some other place.

'Am I dreaming?' Lauren whispered.

'You decide if you're dreaming or not,' said the voice. Oddly, it seemed to have a Kentucky twang to it. 'Where I come from there ain't no dreaming.'

'Why do I know your voice so well?'

'C'mon . . . stop looking at those photographs. You want to see the real thing, don't you? You want to see the flesh grow cold . . . the blood run dry . . . you know you do.'

A hand touched his shoulder. Cold, ice-cold.

'I got something to show you, Lauren. C'mon, c'mon. No more farting around now. We're gonna go places, see things. You and me. Get up.'

Lauren turned and saw the angel.

3

ANGELS OF DEATH

dead yellow women

The angel bore a slight resemblance to Timmy Valentine . . .
but it wasn't him. No. His hair was blond, not dark; his lips
were a little fuller, his eyes a little wider apart; and Lauren knew
it was an angel because the glow about him came from within;
the light that haloed his features was not merely the chance
confluence of distant neon, but came absolutely from within.
His skin glistened with the phosphorescence you find in limestone caverns. He seemed no more than a child, but that was
only natural; 'suffer the children' and all that.

Lauren's madness was, after all, mostly for show; but in his
more lucid moments (others would perhaps not call them lucid)
he knew with a searing certainty that there existed creatures
from other planes of reality. This was, after all, the main reason
he loved living in Thailand so much; other people took this
knowledge for granted, did not view it is as some kind of with-
drawal from the world. I *do* hear voices, he thought, I *do* see
visions. And I haven't even taken any 'shrooms today. I *knew* I
could be a madman if I set my mind to it!

'Come,' said the angel.

'Where?'

'You know.'

He had a feeling that he did know. But he did not know what
he knew, but he knew that he knew. This, he thought, is what
being an artist is all about.

'Follow.'

OK. I'm following, he thought. The angel stepped lightly over
the side of the houseboat, hovered above the brackish surface,

turned, beckoned with an impish smile. I'll fucking drown, Lauren thought. I'm not *that* crazy! He leapt onto the plank that spanned the three feet to the pier.

The angel's laughter was like the buzzing of mosquitoes.

'Hurry! Hurry! Or you'll miss the show.'

'You almost drowned me. Who do you think you are . . . the angel of death?'

'Not *your* death, Joe.'

'Don't call me Joe! I had it legally changed.'

The angel laughed again. Now he stood on the bank. Behind him was the alley that led to Silom Road. How had the angel known his real name? That proved it was a vision of some kind. Lauren leaped off the pier onto the concrete. The angel beckoned again. Lauren followed. Yes. There was a kind of *déjà vu* at work. I've done this before . . . seen the angel before . . . maybe I was the one who told him my real name. In another vision that I've repressed.

And all of a sudden a whirlwind of images swept his consciousness:

. . . the woman in the gutter with her long hair streaming in the torrent of sewage . . .

. . . the woman on the beach with her thin summer dress stretched flat against the sand with boulders, her nipples blue and hard . . .

. . . the woman half in, half out of the storefront window . . .

Yes! He saw them not as the police photographs he had got from Police Inspector Singhasri, not the grainy black-and-white 8×10s surreptitiously faxed to his cellular fax from the Klongtan station, but in garish, overripe colour . . . the nipples a vibrant cobalt . . . the summer dress a pale cerulean spotted with alizarin crimson . . . the skin white, with a deep blue tracery, with a clear, cracked glaze, like Ming porcelain . . . and the lips deep Prussian blue.

He followed the angel.

Silom Road: a business district by day, by night jammed with souvenir stands that sprang up miraculously around twilight. The sidewalk reduced to an alley barely wide enough for one big Caucasian to squeeze through; the dark children scurrying, the merchandise stacked up in kaleidoscopic heaps: pirated videos, records, tapes, CDs, clothes, jewels, figurines, bongs, batik, shadow puppets, silverware, Rolexes, skewers of peanuty pork *saté*, noodle dishes being whipped up and wrapped in banana leaves, and the angel moving swiftly through them all, porous almost, now and then so translucent you could see the neon signs of the sex bars flashing through the pale flesh, drifting, not touching the paving . . . he followed. It was hard to keep up. Street urchins stepped aside, sensing the obsession in his eyes, not pausing to tout their sisters or themselves. The tourists, bulkier and more odoriferous because white people sweat profusely in the tropics, not understanding the rhythm of the street, blocking his way, staring at the wild-eyed aging hippie as he elbowed them aside.

He followed the angel. Now and then, at a corner, stepping between brash bright neon and dark shadow, the angel stopped, turned, smiled. They threaded through Patpong, thronged and cacophonous, the bar girls beckoning from between the stalls of souvenir hawkers. Though the noise level was obsene, the prostitutes and pimps called out to him in soft voices, each one reaching out with delicate gestures and demure glances, speaking to him as though he were alone with them in a thousand disparate, quiet, private universes; for every Thai, he had learned, has a genius for being beautiful, no matter how sordid the surroundings.

Another corner; another alley; suddenly the cacophony dropped to a whisper; no neon here, no pounding techno music. From an upper storey, the brittle music of a marimba. The angel was more opaque now, merging with the shadows. He stopped moving; he waved; from the darkness stepped a woman. A girl, really. Her skin was the colour of coconut curry; her eyes were dark and wild and perhaps surgically widened; she wore only a batik *panung* wrapped tightly around her narrow breasts, flattening her silhouette into androgyny. She had long, blue-black hair. When she smiled, the crookedness of her two front teeth was the flaw that lent personality to her otherwise perfect features. She did not seem to see the angel; she only saw Lauren. 'Oh,' she said, 'sir, sir, not many come down into this little *soi*; but come, I make you happy, sucky-sucky OK if you want, room upstairs, I tell my little brother stop practising the *ranaat* if it disturbing you.' Truly she was new to the oldest profession; she should have known there was no need for words. 'You want we go up now? But you must buy condom. I sell you one, package deal.'

'Shh,' said Lauren, 'don't say another word. You're too beautiful.'

She giggled. Cliché No. 4,517 down the hatch, he thought.

She took him by the hand. The angel stood to one side, haloed in the red glimmer of a distant Coca-Cola sign. She did not seem to see him. They walked toward a doorway, up a flight of unfinished concrete steps . . . the angel going before . . . the girl pulling him, walking backwards, never glancing at where the angel floated, always laughing.

The room was not air-conditioned. She flung open some shutters; through the mosquito gauze he could see out over the press of people. She held his hand to her bosom and he untwisted the knot that clasped the waxy fabric flush to flesh. Sweatsheened, the skin refracted neon, glittered. Just standing there, giggling again, she was driving him crazy. These girls were all alike. Primal. Mindless. All that was sensual and mysterious bundled together and compressed into a single slender slippery slip of a creature.

The angel stood on the bed, behind her, his arms spread wide. At the foot of the bed was a dresser with a mirror, but the angel cast no reflection.

The girl looked up and saw something . . . perhaps a shadow on the far wall. Perhaps not. Movement. 'Cold here,' she said. He cupped her breasts in his hands, trying to warm them with the fever of his lust. Her hand reached down, teased, unzipped, freed him from spandex and denim . . . but he was already ejaculating . . . pumping into her hand . . . oh yes . . . too many calluses . . . a farm girl. 'I'm sorry,' he said.

'You no buy condom yet,' she said.

'Can we try again?'

The girl's neck arched; she shuddered; she closed her eyes.

Then the angel swooped down and popped the girl's head like the cork of a champagne bottle. Blood spurted in a twisty fountain as the head thudded, bounced on the squeaky, saggy bedsprings. The arms flailed . . . slow motion . . . with the easy

grace of the dancers at the Erawan Shrine . . . slow . . . slow
. . . slow . . . waiting for time to catch up with them . . . blood
rained on him . . . congealed on his face, his arms, his chest,
his lips . . . while the angel fed. Slowly . . . now and then beating the air with leathern wings . . . slowly, drop by drop bounc-
ing on the tongue, wax beading on velvet, red on red, blood in
a dense mist, droplets dancing in the humid air, dancing and
the tongue . . . slowly . . . slowly . . . in and out of the small
mouth framed by silvery fangs . . . slowly. Slowly. Slowly. The
tongue darting in, out, in, out of the lubricious crimson. Oh,
the million reds that painted the dark air – Lauren's eye caught
the colours one by one, remembering . . . sable strokes on the
bedsheets, dry brush spattering the wall, scarlet pinpricks stippling the torso that whitened as the blood was drained away.
And the angel, through it all, smiling; not his thin lips, which,
drinking their fill, were ever severe and unappeased, but his
eyes; the eyes smiled, illumined from within.

And having fed, the angel wavered, melted, funnelled away
through the open window into the crowd.

Lauren sat on the teakwood floor with his arms wrapped
around the torso. The blood was thickening to the texture of
semen. His arms were slick with it. The girl's head stared from
the bed. A single vertebra protruded from the side of the neck.
The face was bloodless, the hair matted, the eyes gazing down
with an incongruous serenity.

This isn't happening, he thought. Too many drugs, too much
pretending to be crazy; actually pushing myself over the edge.
Get a grip. Get a grip.

He screamed.

dissolve

. . . angels . . .

Daylight. The houseboat rocking a little as one of the tourist
boats came splashing by. 'And over there, on the left, houseboat
of eccentric 'melican painter name Laulen McCandless . . .'
Who gives a fuck.

The houseboat rocked a little harder. Someone was coming

on board. Lauren reached for a bottle of Mekong that wasn't
there. He sat up, trying to squeeze the daylight out. The footsteps were light, shoeless; it must be a Thai.

'Pete,' he murmured.

'I've been looking through your studio,' said Inspector
Singhasri. 'You started a new painting last night, didn't you?'

'I don't know, Pete. It was one of *those* nights.'

'Get up, Lauren, I really want you to take a good look at some
photographs. Good stuff, Lauren, *real* good stuff. The kind of
thing you like, you know, sick.'

'OK, OK.'

'I've already turned on your coffee machine, all right?'

'Yeah.'

Pete pulled him up by the wrists. It couldn't have been later
than ten in the morning, but the sun was already almost too
intense to bear. He kept squinting until they were inside the
cabin.

There was, indeed, a new canvas on the easel.

The severed head stared up from the bloodstained sheets.
Not much detail yet: a single vertebra jutting from the back of
the neck, and the eyes, deep and browny and shiny as a smoky
quartz. The blood just lightly suggested with a little crimson
drybrush. A splotch of white over the red, like a wad of semen.
'Beautiful, ain't it,' said the inspector in his weird accent, half
Thai public school and half Kansas police academy. 'Lifelike.
Too lifelike, even.'

Lauren hadn't remembered beginning a new painting last
night. He'd had a lot of memory lapses lately, hadn't he? He
would have liked to think it was merely all part of being a
genius, but somehow . . .

'I was drunker than I thought I was,' he said.

'OK, you've seen the damn picture. Now you take big breath,
buddy, now you look at this.' And he pulled out an 8×10 from
a manila folder.

girl's head stared from the bed a single vertebra protruding from the
side of the neck the face bloodless the hair matted the eyes gazing down
with an incongruous serenity.

Lauren looked away.

'You might even say uncanny,' said the inspector.

'Are you saying I—'

Not saying anything for now. You got a good lawyer? You mind giving a sperm sample maybe, analyse, maybe match semen stains on sheets? We can clear up whole thing pronto.'

'Jesus fucking—'

'Yes, yes. Have you had breakfast? Let's go somewhere.'

'So this *is* a social call.'

'Well, Lauren, this is Bangkok, not some hick American backwater. We do things civilized around here. Even I arrest you, we still friends.'

They caught the ferry over to the Oriental Hotel, walked through air-conditioned marble corridors with bellboys in exotic uniforms. Lunched in a riverside coffeeshop on Phuket lobster, a delicate Moselblümchen, airy chocolate soufflés and iced *latte*. It occurred to Lauren that the cost of the lunch probably exceeded Pete's weekly salary, but he paid it, in crisp thousand-baht notes, without a murmur. It would have been far too rude to inquire about the inspector's secret source of income. In Thailand, as Lauren had discovered, one did not discuss such things. Perhaps Pete's family had always been rich; perhaps they had fingers in many pies.

Lauren did not pay much attention to the food. One of the perks of being a famous expatriate in Bangkok is that one rarely had to pay for a meal, and he had become almost inured to the lavishness and variety of Bangkok's many cuisines. When he looked down at his plate he saw other things: the lobster simmering in its sauce resembled the innards of a disembowelled woman; the soufflé had the texture of a human brain; the white wine ran like the pus from a woman's lymph nodes.

It was only after the *latte* had been cleared away, over the postprandial Remy Martin, that the inspector carefully steered the subject back to the one that had been consuming Lauren all this time.

'I'm under a lot of pressure, Lauren,' said Pete.

'Pressure?'

'You know. To solve the case. You always have airtight alibis . . . except, this time, maybe you slip a little bit, huh.'

'I didn't do it.'

'I know, you know. But it kind of suspicious.'

'You think a sperm sample will prove something? I'll give you a fucking sperm sample if you want. Perhaps you care to suck it out yourself.'

'Temper, temper!'

'Well, what then?'

'Something else.' The inspector gazed across the brackish waters of the Chao Phraya River. On the far shore stood the Temple of Dawn, its towering pagodas, studded with a million shards of Ming pottery, glittering like dragonskin in the scorching sunlight. 'You know that this town is not like other towns.'

'Damn straight.'

'I mean, yes, we have the traffic and the skyscrapers and the fax machines of modern metropolis, but underneath that, something very different, a dark kind of spirit. You believe in ghosts, demons?'

'What do you mean?'

'I think the murderer you, maybe not you, but not important. Something else here, using you maybe. Have you ever visited a *mo phii*?'

'You mean one of those spirit doctor charlatans? Shit, no.'

'You ever lose your memory? I mean, holes in memory where cannot remember something . . . just big empty thing.'

Lauren began to feel a distinct unease. It was true that he sometimes felt inhabited by an *other*. And then there was the angel. What angel? The image surfaced only for an instant. There had been an angel. 'What am I supposed to tell you?' he said. 'That a dark angel woke me from my slumber and led me to the scene of the crime?'

'Angel, huh! Describe him.'

'Describe? Describe?'

'Something supernatural? Maybe a dazzling white light?'

'You're trying to prove I'm crazy?'

'No. Actually . . . let me have the sperm sample. It will get me off the hook maybe. Prove I'm pursuing my leads you know, with, American-style, relentless vigour or whatever. What you have to lose, buddy? You innocent, ain't that so?'

'Innocent? Of course.'

'Another cognac?'

'Actually I rather feel more like a few stiff drugs.'

'Ha. Entrapping a police officer.' Pete laughed. 'I'll have some delivered to your boat; we just did a big drug bust, German tourists, you know the score. But no, that not the main thing; the main thing is catch that killer. Or, at least, make him not be in the news all the time. Big high profile arrest maybe just the thing. You can help me.'

'By having you arrest me?'

'No, no . . . well. Later, maybe. If you innocent, worry about it later; for now, make look like problem taken care of, not fucking up tourism anymore. You'll cooperate?'

Lauren could not figure out what the inspector was trying to tell him. The inscrutability thing was a real problem with Thais. They always seemed to take both sides of an issue at the same time. 'I'll cooperate, I guess.'

'OK. I'll make an appointment with the spirit doctor.'

'*That's* how you want me to cooperate? By going to a shaman?'

'Maybe he awaken your memories. 'Cause you know, that painting, this picture . . . this *prove* you know something. You my friend, buddy; I don't *want* you to be killer. I really lose face.'

'All right. If you say so.'

'OK. Here's something for you . . .' Pete reached into his shirt pocket and pulled out a smoky-glass vial. He handed it over diffidently. 'You know. The sample. I collect tomorrow. You have a refrigerator on your houseboat?'

Lauren laughed. 'You're not gonna have someone making sure it's me? I could amble down to Patpong and pay some hustler to jerk off into the bottle.'

'Do what you want,' Pete said. 'It doesn't matter.'

It was clear that Pete Singhasri really had no interest in whether the sample would be incriminating. He was just going through the motions of collecting his data. He believed something else entirely was afoot. Spirits and demons. With the Thais, it always came down to spirits and demons in the end.

They spent another hour or so in the riverside café, but the subject of the murders didn't come up again. Before Lauren had started living in Bangkok, it would have been hard for him to believe that pleasantries could be exchanged for so long, but he was used to it now. He knew that Pete's mind, too, was on other things.

It was evening before he made his way back to the ferry; he had spent the afternoon listlessly barhopping. By the time he reached the houseboat, he was already beginning to dissociate. He poured himself another shot of Mekong and sat down in front of the painting he couldn't remember starting. It was still there, still undeniably his; there was no one on earth who could do blood the way he could, thick, dark blood that oozed along the knotty imperfections of the canvas, blood real enough to drink. God, but the woman was beautiful. Even if there *was* only her head. Lauren lay back on the floor cushions. The houseboat rocked. Back and forth, in time to the breathing of the river. There was sex in the air. Something about the stickiness of the tropic night . . . the lubricious perspiration of the very air . . . god, but she was beautiful. He imagined her with such vividness that it seemed almost to be a memory. Staring at the half-formed face, he found himself masturbating in a frenzy. It was over in less than a minute. What a fucking mess. Some of it had even got on the painting itself. Jesus fucking Christ, he thought. I didn't even collect any of it in Pete's little bottle. What a goddamn waste.

He got out his brushes and went back to work.

4

PINOCCHIO'S PASSION

executives

There was a Lauren McCandless painting on the wall behind the executive's desk. It was, of course, one of the latest, newest series, one of the Dead Yellow Women series from Bangkok. That it was not McCandless's *very* latest picture was, for the particularly observant, a clear indication that the Stupendous Entertainment Corporation was finally feeling the pinch. The executive himself was not, as his perfectly capped teeth, Versace jacket and diamond-studded Rolex amply demonstrated.

When the boy who had once been a creature of the night came into his office, all the others were already present. He could tell right away that they had all come prepared for a slaughter. He remembered how it used to feel himself, haunting the night, sniffing the perfume of panic in the air; he remembered how they sometimes tried to run from him, how they could never quite get away; had he not been his victims' own terror, made flesh by the force of their own collective darkness? No one can escape from a vampire. A vampire is one's own shadow, nothing less.

Timmy Valentine wasn't a vampire anymore. But he could still make out the pheromones of predation, even through the blast of air-conditioning and the hum of an ionizer.

'You're going to dump me, aren't you?' he said.

One by one, the lesser executives looked up at the one who sat at the mahogany desk. A secretary, who had the British accent, real or assumed, that all executive secretaries in Hollywood must have, spoke up quickly, trying to fill the abhorred vacuum with mellifluous blandishments. 'Well, Mr Giler, what

you had in mind *was* just a wee bit more attractive an offer
than a mere dumping, wasn't it? I've got the details here, if Mr
Valentine would care to glance through them, and of course,
the lawyers and agents are all on call—'

'Shut up, Alicia,' said David Giler, Undisputed Shogun of the
Stupendous Entertainment Corporation. He smiled at Timmy.
Yes. Quite, quite predatory. 'Offer them some wine or something,' he went on, 'don't just sit around blathering intermi-
nably; you know the boy can see through all this bullshit; he's
a professional, damn it, even if he *is* only some dickless wonder
from the sticks.'

'Of course, sir,' Alicia said, hastening to comply. She was so
flustered that her accent became polluted with the unmistakable
tones of Teaneck, New Jersey. Timmy laughed. The executives
did not; not, at least, until Giler deigned to laugh first.

'None for me,' said Timmy.

'Of course,' said Giler, 'he never drinks . . . wine.'

The executives laughed; Timmy did not.

They drank; they munched on canapés; Timmy had a Diet
Coke. Food and drink really had little taste for him yet; on a
good day he could just about distinguish a steak from a potato.
It was slowly coming to him, though. And when it did, it made
him fell so, so alive . . . well, not quite *alive* . . . so, so, un-
undead.

Forgetting himself for a moment, he salted his Diet Coke. Salt
makes soda all fizzy, he thought. They probably think it's an
obnoxious childish thing, like blowing bubbles in it or gargling
it. In a year, he probably wouldn't have to use as much salt.
With a whole lot of salt the shock to the arteries was a faint
reminder of the taste of fresh-killed blood.

'Making you nervous, am I?' said Giler.

'No,' said Timmy, but he put the salt shaker down.

I'm a real boy now, he told himself. *Get real.*

'No need for nervousness,' Giler said. 'We're all grownups
here. Even if some of us have had to grow up a little . . . fast.'

Laughter.

'Shall we have some music?'

Alicia bustled about. The strains of *Vanitas* filled the air.
Timmy's voice. So familiar. But – as everyone in the room was all

too painfully aware – it wasn't like the voice in *Vampire Junction*. 'Showtime,' said Giler. He pulled out a copy of *Rolling Stone* from the crystal magazine rack on his desk. 'Cover story: *Who is Timmy Valentine?* A few choice quotes: "It looks like Peter Pan has finally had his first erection; what a shame he had to go fuck himself in the ass." Oh. Here's a good one. "Who are Stupendous trying to fool? We all know about Angel Todd. And we all know David Giler's no angel." Thanks heaps, Timmy – or should I call you Angel?'

'I'm not Angel Todd,' said Timmy Valentine.

'I know. Alicia?'

The British accent was back now, 'Mr Giler, I was paid $425,000 by a certain newspaper which shall remain nameless—'

'Enquiring minds to the back of the bus!' said Giler.

'—to pull Timmy's dental records and compare them with those of Angel Todd from Dr Witherspoon back in, wherever it was, Hangman's Holler, Kentucky – and Timmy is absolutely *not* Angel Todd. The canines, I'm afraid, were a dead giveaway; Angel's were fake.'

'Jesus! What's next, a fucking blood test?' said Timmy. 'Care for a semen sample?'

'I'm afraid we've already done that,' said Alicia. 'The ah, blood, that is. You don't seem to have ejaculated recently.'

'I *can't*,' said Timmy Valentine.

'We know,' said Giler. 'Look, Timmy, the point is that we've furnished all this material to everyone, and they're just not buying it. Which would be fine, except for Exhibit B.'

Alicia pushed a button on some kind of mega-remote-control, and the Lauren McCandless painting ascended slowly up into the flies, revealing, behind it, a 60-inch video monitor on which were scrolling up an endless series of names, factoids and figures.

'*Vanitas*,' said Giler. 'Day One - it actually edges Michael Jackson out of the Number One spot. Day Two – it's Number Seventeen. Well; maybe it's some freak factor no one figured on; maybe half the computers are down; maybe someone assassinated the president so no one went to the store. Who gives a shit. Now look at Day Seventeen. It's trailing a fucking Mantovani remix, for fuck's sake! I don't care if you're Timmy Valentine. You could be Elvis for all I care. Madonna in drag. The man in the moon. The main thing is that we are being fucking *slaughtered* out there. There's only one possible solution.'

'Hey, David,' Timmy said (a few of the executives gasped at the presumption implicit in that *Hey, David*), 'I understand. It's business. Stupendous is perfectly free to dump me; it's clause 29, isn't it, paragraph 3a? The one about the option to discontinue if the ratio of sales volume to the index of chart plummeting is equal to or greater than the terminal velocity of a falling turd?'

Giler was the only one who laughed. 'Kid should have my job,' he said. 'Cool under pressure. Like he's been doing this for a couple of thousand years.'

'I have.'

'Now don't start believing your own press releases.'

'Actually it was the *Weekly World News*.'

The executives all nodded. Their secretaries had all read the story at the checkout counter: the one that read *Timmy Valentine used to be a vampire; switched bodies with an ordinary Kentucky boy: Modern Day Pinocchio 'just wanted to be human'*. The article had relied on 'exclusive' interviews with 'valentologists' – yes! that word had finally made it into the CD-ROM version of the latest supplement to the Oxford English Dictionary – especially that Joshua Levy guy, the one who'd appeared on all the talk shows, who had claimed to have found likenesses of Timmy Valentine all through history, from the paintings of Caravaggio to Chinese vase paintings. Well, some of that had been true. But the brain of an ordinary mortal boy cannot contain two thousand years of memories. The new Timmy's memories were crystal-clear back to about a year ago, when he and Angel Todd fused, melded, and came apart, as the fire raged about them on a movie set in the town of Junction, Idaho . . . but before that, it was chaos.

'Ah yes,' said Giler, 'the *Weekly World News*. Oh . . .' He acknowledged Alicia's anxious gesticulating with an impatient flick of his forefinger. 'I do believe Alicia has a few more facts and figures for us; and these are even more interesting than the ones which seem to be triggering the implementation of our very own Clause 29.'

'It's the overseas figures,' Alicia said. 'Well, they simply don't seem to be quite as bad. In fact, the further east you go . . . the better it gets. By the time we hit Singapore, Bangkok and Tokyo, the indices are actually brightening a smidgin.'

'You see, Timmy? It could be a lot worse.'

The predator odour was definitely stronger now. I wish he'd just get it over with, Timmy thought. Better a clean beheading than this cat-and-mouse business. 'I take it you're going to offer some kind of parachute,' he said, 'golden or otherwise. But I notice that you didn't invite my agent to this afternoon's gathering.'

'In fact,' Alicia continued, ignoring all the deadpan sparring, 'our research does seem to indicate that the Asian market in particular is actually *buying* the idea that Timmy has somehow been reincarnated in the body of Angel Todd, or whatever daft idea it is we're hyping at the moment; after all, they *are* a little more superstitious than we are; you know, Tibetan gods popping up in the flesh every five minutes, shamans getting possessed by the dead, those bizarre Filipino fellows who do open-heart surgery without scratching the skin . . . all sorts of things like that, in the Orient, you see; Timmy's just another oddity.'

'Are you beginning to get the nature of your golden parachute?' said Giler. 'Good money after bad.'

'An Asian tour?' said Timmy, surprised at last. 'Or Eastern Europe, too? They still have vampires and werewolves there, don't they? Or did the Berlin Wall thing do away with them?'

'We're calling it a victory tour,' said Giler. 'It's going to cost millions, and we'll lose every penny of it. That's the beauty of it all, though; we have a safety net of insurance, tax breaks and goofy off-shore corporate labyrinths that will actually cause us to make money off every penny we lose. In fact, we're going to get out the buzz right away that this tour is doomed; people will stay away in droves; the bath Stupendous will take is gonna be, well, *stupendous*; after which we can safely move on to the next thing, you see, which is not going to be twelve-year-old fake vampire rock stars at all, but something quite, quite different – *thirteen*-year-old fake vampires? Eleven-year-old fake were-wolves? My unerring sense of timing tells me that the flavour of the month is about to change.'

'So you're going to kill me by drowning me in money?' said Timmy.

'It's even better than that!' said Giler. 'At an appropriate, predetermined moment in your *Vanitas* tour – in some wonderfully sleazy yet superbly photogenic location, such as Bangkok, so that we can get it on *Hard Copy* and *A Current Affair* – you're going to disappear – *again!*'

At that, there were cries of 'Brilliant!' 'You've done it again!' and 'Bravo.'

'Again?'

'Yes! Again! Perhaps we'll have one of those shaman, fakir-type Tibetan monk people handle it. We do have a few of those on the payroll, don't we? And I don't mean Shirley MacLaine – not that she wouldn't do, at a pinch, but she's just not *ethnic* enough. You, the archetypal being, conjured up out of the primordial chaos by forces beyond our control, are going to return to the vortex whence you came. On television, yet – magic of special effects and all that – kind of like the number we pulled when you "reappeared" at the Timmy Valentine look-alike contest that re-launched your career.'

'Stunning,' said Timmy Valentine, who was actually stunned. 'I think I'll have some of that wine after all.' It appeared in his hand almost by magic. 'You're not going to card me, are you?'

dissolve: gallery

'. . . and that,' said Timmy Valentine, 'is what happened at today's meeting. You should have seen Giler's face! He was really enjoying himself. I could smell it. I can still smell things, you know. Yeah. Sometimes I can.'

The gallery closed at midnight; it was around two o'clock, and Timmy was still drinking. PJ watched him, not quite sure what to do about it. After all, the kid was two thousand years old. He had killed. It didn't seem right somehow for him to say, 'All right, Timmy, you've had enough,' but he finally said it anyway.

'Yeah,' Timmy said, 'you're so fucking right.' He drained the

glass to the very last drop, reached for the bottle, but PJ pushed
it away.

'I have to lock up,' PJ said.

The Lauren McCandless canvases looked down from the
walls: dead women, pale, stony-eyed.

'Come on the tour with me, dude,' Timmy said. 'Hey, we're
stopping in Thailand . . . I'm even gonna play in that new
amphitheatre they built near the site of Prince Prathna's old
palace of iniquities . . . talk about nostalgia.'

'I would be able to join Chit sooner than I expected,' PJ said.
'But – I dunno.'

'You don't want to be part of the Neo-Gothic entourage. You
don't want to be part of Timmy Valentine's travelling three-ring
circus. That's it, isn't it? I've made you rich, and you won't even
hold my hand anymore.'

'It's not like you to act so—'

'Immature? Can't help it! I'm a fucking kid now! A kid with
no balls. I'm a freak. Yeah, I was a freak when I was a vampire,
but at least I had class! Now I'm just *Weekly World News* material.
Gimme some more of that wine.'

'Timmy—'

'Please, PJ.'

'That's why I don't want to go. I'm not cut out for babysitting.'

'Babysitting! I remember when you were a kid, PJ . . . a
grungy hick kid, half Irish, half redskin, in that one-horse town
in Idaho. Jesus, I scared you then. Don't I scare you anymore?
Don't you ever get the slightest feeling that I'm gonna swoop
down on you in the night wind and bare my fangs and suck
you dry? Am I just another fucked-up showbiz kid to you now?'

PJ said, 'No, Timmy; you still got fangs.'

Timmy laughed. 'You want to know what it feels like, me,
Pinocchio, a real boy after two thousand years of wishing?
Dude, it feels like shit.' PJ couldn't help noticing that Timmy
was trying hard to affect the mannerisms and even the accent
of the young people in the San Fernando Valley, trying to lose
that alienness of speech that had once set him apart. But it
wasn't altogether successful. Timmy had to work at being
human; it just didn't come naturally to him yet. PJ suddenly
realized that Timmy probably would succeed in talking him into

going along on the tour with him. After all, most of those who had known him since before the changing were dead now – Timmy's victims, directly or indirectly, one way or another. 'Why is it so hard to be real?' Timmy said. 'Why is it so hard to feel anything? Touch me, PJ.'

PJ balked.

'Gimme a break, I didn't say *molest* me.' They looked at each other across the marble coffee table; then PJ got up and put his arm on Timmy's shoulder. 'I don't feel that,' Timmy said. 'Isn't there supposed to be some kind of warmth, some kind of tingling, when a human touches another human being?'

PJ said, 'Come on, Timmy; you should go home, lie down and all that.'

'Yes. I sleep now.'

'You slept before.'

'But I didn't dream. It wasn't really sleeping. It was being dead.'

'You're incoherent. Come on, you've had a tough day.'

'Yeah.'

dissolve: streets

She stood at the entrance to the freeway, a little girl all in white, next to a white wall criss-crossed with taggers' writings.

'Stop the car for a moment,' Timmy said. It was Rudy Lydick who was driving – the faithful Rudy, who had managed to survive both Auschwitz and the fiery disaster at Junction, who had guarded the Valentine fortune during the seven years when Timmy had been in limbo, trapped by the witch woman's spell – lean, cadaverous, ancient.

'Yes, Master Timothy,' said Rudy.

PJ looked out of the window and saw the girl. There was something about her that reminded him of one of Lauren's paintings. She was spooky. Her eyes were vacant and the moonlight gave her face that whiteface, zombie-movie look. 'Timmy, don't stop,' he said. 'You can't deal with anyone now.'

Timmy vomited on the limousine's white leather upholstery. On the television, Madonna's *Like a Prayer* video was playing –

it was an MTV twenty-four hour Madonna retrospective mara-
thon. 'I said you wouldn't be able to hold all that wine,' PJ said.
'You're not supernatural anymore, you fool.'
'Fuck,' said Timmy miserably.
'Back to the estate, Rudy,' PJ said.
'No, goddammit!' Timmy said. 'That girl – something about
her—'
Her face was pressed against the window now. She smiled a
little. How old? PJ thought. Twelve, thirteen? Standing in the
street at three in the morning? This one had been around the
block.
The girl knocked.
'Come on, Rudy,' PJ said, trying to swab up the mess with a
sheaf of napkins from the limo's bar. Thank God the limo came
so well equipped. Full bar, ice, icepick, tongs, television, cocktail
glasses, swizzle sticks . . .
'Come in,' Timmy said loudly.
'Drive the fuck out of here, Rudy!' said PJ. But he was not
Rudy's master.
And she was in.
Without opening the limo door. Without so much as cracking
the window. Nervously, PJ shrank a little further into his seat.
He fumbled in his jeans pocket. He always kept a silver dollar
on him, a lucky piece. Sometimes silver worked, sometimes it
didn't. Vampires were quirky creatures; as the world's faiths
crumbled, so did the rules that kept them in their place.
'I didn't know there were any of you left in Los Angeles,'
Timmy said softly.
'Homeless,' the girl said, 'hungry.' But there was more to it
than that. The air now held the unmistakable odour of decay.
'Turn up the air-conditioning, Rudy,' said Timmy. Why
wasn't the boy afraid? PJ wondered. Didn't he understand that
he was just as vulnerable as any other mortal now, that he
couldn't just funnel away into a pool of shadow, transform into
a black cat, skitter away into the night?
'Hungry!' said the girl. She was hollow-cheeked, her eyes
were sunken and yes, quite, quite dead. A year ago there had
been a lot of vampires in the city. That was when Terry Gish
had come back from the dead, when PJ had been forced to

kill his best friend not once, not twice, but a final time. Had the plague *still* not been wiped out? Or was this some new manifestation?

'Who made you?' Timmy demanded. 'How long have you been haunting the streets?'

The motor was still running, the limo still stopped, the neon signs of Ventura Boulevard still flashing in the rear-view mirror, streaking the dead girl's white face in garish hues of turquoise, chrome, vermilion.

'Don't know,' said the girl. 'Just hungry.'

'You got a name?' Timmy was all intense now, concentrated; hard to believe he'd been an incoherent, puking wreck just minutes before.

'Cristel,' she said. She didn't look at people. Even though she'd crossed over, she still had the shifty, obsequious mannerisms of the homeless. 'Dunno when this happened to me. I fell asleep. On my way to the shelter. A couple days ago. Or maybe last year. Don't know time, don't *feel* time anymore, don't know why; like, I'm *hungry*.'

Timmy said, 'And do you know who *I* am, Cristel?'

'Sure I do. You're Timmy Valentine. I was waiting for you . . . outside the gallery . . . 'cause you understand. I know. It's in your songs. Messages. For people like me.'

'I don't have messages.'

'Yeah you do. Because you know what it's like.'

'Like?' said PJ.

'To be dead,' Cristel said. 'To be hungry. To be alone.'

As PJ watched, unsure of how afraid he ought to be, Timmy searched the limo's bar for a paring knife. He made a tiny slit in his left index finger and squeezed out a single drop of blood. He held it to the girl's lips. 'This what you want?' he said softly.

She nodded.

PJ watched, fascinated, as she sucked on his finger. There was something disquietingly erotic about it. As she gazed at Timmy the twin abysses that were her eyes seemed to brighten. The blue-white lips reddened a little. The gaunt cheeks pulsed. Timmy winced but did not cry out. Pain is a new sensation for him, PJ thought. Maybe he likes it.

Timmy glanced back at PJ, at the icepick.

'Now!' he shouted. He pulled his finger loose.

PJ grabbed the icepick. Timmy moved back and PJ slammed the icepick into the girl's chest. It cracked the sternum and went straight for the heart. For the tiniest moment the girl looked human: her eyes showed a sense of awe, pain, and finally betrayal; then, once more, they dimmed. A sluggish, dark blood oozed from the cavity. Her bones, brittle, were shattering. 'Calcium deficiency,' Timmy said softly.

For a moment Timmy seemed quite detached from all that was happening; then, abruptly, he began to vomit again. 'God, I'm so drunk,' he groaned.

That was when PJ decided that he would go with Timmy after all. Even now, so human, so terribly vulnerable, Timmy still had about him the glamour of something supernatural. PJ understood that. He himself had gone through transformation – from a grungy small town half-breed boy to a *ma'aipots*, a sacred man-woman of the Shoshone, who had been the medium through which a cosmic war for possession of the soul of mankind had been waged – and then he had become human again. I'm the only person Timmy's ever encountered who did that, he thought, go from a boy to some archetypal hyperbeing then switch back to human in all its frailty. Of course, Timmy went through two thousand years of it; *I* went through the whole arc in just a few. But I'm the only one who has even a clue what it must be like for him.

Timmy was trying to swallow some ice water now. The pieces of the young girl were all over the limousine. 'Jesus,' Timmy said, 'how much longer do we have to sit in this?'

Softly, Rudy said, 'I'll shampoo the upholstery in the morning, Master Timothy, and I'll dispose of everything . . . the usual way.' PJ wondered what that might be.

'It's *not* the usual way,' Timmy cried. 'It's the wrong way round . . . she was supposed to kill *me!*'

PJ held out his arms to the boy. He hugged him as he sobbed, childishly and inconsolably. 'That fucking studio head,' Timmy said, 'fucking made me feel like *shit!* and after he skimmed a second Rolls off my royalties. Fuck, fuck.' There was blood everywhere, and the car stank of puke and putrescence. To think, he thought, that once the idea of getting this close to

Timmy Valentine would have probably made me shit my BVDs
in terror. And now . . . he's kind of my best friend.

They turned onto Mulholland Drive.

He tried not to remember his last best friend, Terry Gish . . .
beating the crap out of him on the ninth level of Bloodsucker at
the arcade . . . fleeing the burning town of Junction with him
and Brian Zottoli, through the snow . . . burying him . . . seeing
him, bright-fanged, in the window in the smoggy moonlight
. . . trying to bury him again . . . and again.

The nightmare was creeping back into their lives. This time,
PJ thought, I'm never going to let anything happen to one of
my friends again. No matter what.

'I guess the gallery can run itself for a couple months,' he
said.

'Course it can. Those McCandless originals just sell themselves; lotta morbid people around town.'

'Yeah,' PJ said.

He poured himself a straight Johnny Walker as the gates to
Timmy's estate swung open and the limo glided slowly uphill,
to the crenellated mansion perched at the very crest of the Santa
Monica Mountains. Timmy had fallen asleep, curled up, sucking
his thumb, the vampire's blood still clinging to his clothes, his
cheeks, his lips.

Timmy's latest music video, an animated version of a six-
teenth-century Flemish *Vanitas*, started to play on the limousine's television set as they drove down the palm-lined driveway
toward the castle on the hill.

5

VALENTINE'S SHADOW

night creatures

They pulled into the circular driveway. Timmy was still fast asleep, so PJ helped Rudy move him into the house, into the huge bedroom with its marble floors, stuffed animals, Super Nintendo patched into a wall-sized television monitor, and a rack of electronic keyboards that communicated through MIDI with a studio on the second floor. PJ and Rudy wiped away the last traces of vomit, undressed him, laid him on the king-sized waterbed. Then they went downstairs to dispose of the vampire's body.

There was a supply of holy water in the refrigerator, and PJ realized that Timmy had been preparing for this eventuality ever since he had achieved mortality.

The limousine was parked by the front door, in a covered portico flanked with Doric columns. Rudy sprinkled the water on the corpse to break it up a little. It hissed as it began to crack, like a hot glass coffee pot suddenly thrust into cold water. Then he got busy with the vacuum.

'Where am I going to put these pieces?' said PJ. He was sweeping the fragments of Cristel's body into a trash bag.

'Master Timothy's arranged a place,' said the old man. 'In the back. Behind the lanai, there's a deep pit lined with charcoal. You'll find the lighter fluid and other appurtenances all to hand.' He frowned. 'You won't betray him, will you? It would be awful for him to lose . . . his . . . I mean to say, I have been with him a very long time; once, in a terrible place called Oswieçim, he gave me the will to go on living.'

PJ assented, and Rudy immediately answered his unspoken

question: 'If you don't mind, I'd rather not watch the burning of the body . . . that would, you know, bring back bad memories.' It was then that PJ remembered that Oswięcim was the Polish name for Auschwitz.

He found himself dragging the garbage bag full of dead meat back to the lanai by himself, laying it down in the pit, dousing the body with lighter fluid, and watching the macabre barbecue all by himself, breathing in the sweet sizzle of the charring flesh, the acrid odour of the plastic, the ammonia-laden stench of burning hair. The back yard – more than a back yard really, because there was so much land, so landscaped as to lure the eye into imagining fantastic forests – looked out over the teeming San Fernando Valley; tonight the millions of lights shone bright. PJ remembered other fires: the fire set by the pyromaniac Stephen Miles, driving the vampires from their hiding places in his old home town of Junction, now a ghost town . . . the fire that raged through Junction a second time, only this time it was a false Junction, a movie set, a flimsy thing of plywood and paint erected in a soundstage thrown up over the ruins of the old Junction . . . would the fire never end? Was it as eternal as the flames of hell itself? The fact that there was a vampire hitchhiking by the side of the Boulevard implied that there must be others. Somewhere, somehow. How many? PJ tried to reach out, to send his spirit soaring out over the city as he had once been able to do, but he could not; his shamanistic powers had been spent in that great confrontation in Junction . . . the power of the sacred man-woman had been granted to him only for the purpose of defeating the false messiah who had almost pushed the world into perdition . . . since that day he had had no visions, seen no totemic animals. I've got a lot in common with Timmy Valentine, he thought. I wanted to become a normal human being, and when it finally happened, it wasn't all it was cracked up to be.

Somewhere in the city there had to be other vampires. Vampirism was as pervasive as AIDS . . . its seed transmitted in the love-bite of the living dead . . . a disease that did not kill, but condemned its victims to a perpetual twilight. But what was PJ to do? Cruise up and down the Boulevard with a stack of stakes and a croquet mallet?

The flames were dying now. How long had he been out here, lost in this depressing reverie? He wondered whether he should call Chit. It was probably still afternoon in Bangkok, wasn't it? PJ turned around and started back toward the house.

In the living room, Rudy was reclining on a contemporary Southwestern-style chaise longue. The room was gloomy, lit only by the wash of light that rose up from the city below. Rudy's eyes stared out through the bay window over the million twinkling city lights. PJ was about to ask him to fetch him the portable phone when he noticed that the old man had blown his brains out. Rudy's hand still gripped the old forty-five, and his lips were slightly rounded as though about to give fellatio. The back of his head was ripped open, and the far wall smeared with congealing blood; there were a few pieces of grey matter speckling the Persian carpet in a Jackson Pollock-like splatter.

PJ tiptoed past the corpse. I guess I should go and wake up Timmy, he thought. Past the sweeping staircase, down the muffled corridor, through the studio with its piles of MIDI gear and jumbled cables . . . up one more flight to the gigantic bedroom. Timmy was exactly as they'd left him an hour ago. He didn't even seem to be dreaming. PJ pulled up a chair and sat beside the bed. A night light plugged into a wall socket – shaped like E.T. – and the lights of the city below through half-shuttered windows. Asleep, Timmy Valentine was a very angel. PJ could not bear to wake him, even though a man lay on the couch below them in a pool of blood. He felt disoriented in a way he hadn't felt since his childhood in Junction.

A Mickey Mouse phone chirped on the bedside table.

Glad of any excuse to delay having to wake up Timmy and tell him of his faithful retainer's suicide, PJ picked up the phone.

'Timmy . . . Timmy . . .' It was a deep voice, with a hint of Kentucky about it . . . and the faint static of long distance. 'I didn't know who else to call.'

'Jesus! It's not the Reverend Damien Peters? Guess I shouldn't have said *Jesus* like that, you shocked me.'

'Now you know I done lost my faith a long time ago, PJ Gallagher,' said the voice of the man who had once ruled over a multi-million dollar televangelical empire, and who had been humbled by the forces of darkness . . . and the IRS. 'What are you doing in Lord Valentine's Castle? Hanging around waiting for a handout? A-searching for the almighty cookie jar so you can finance a brand-new art gallery in Beverly Hills?'

'I'm surprised you recognized my voice,' PJ said.

'It's kind of a knack,' said the preacher-turned-movie star, 'you learn it early in the preaching business. The client whose name you can remember will always be a repeat customer.'

'But Damien, you're calling Timmy's at three o'clock in the morning, or something.'

'And *you're* a-picking up his private phone that only rings in his bedroom, at three o'clock in the morning. You traipsing around in a dress again?'

PJ laughed in spite of his nervousness. 'I'm no longer a sacred transvestite,' he explained. 'The vision quest giveth, the vision quest taketh away.'

'Yeah,' Damien Peters sighed. 'We all three of us had magic in us once, didn't we now. And then we went and got ourselves cured, and damned if we ain't wishing we were sick again, and whipping ourselves into a fine lunatic frenzy and feeling that old adrenalin racing and—'

'They're back,' PJ said softly.

'I know,' said Damien. And the room went very cold.

'That's why you called, isn't it?'

'Yes.' More a choke than a word.

'When did you – I mean, where—'

'Tonight. Oh, God, I—'

'Rudy killed himself.'

'Fuck! Fuck!' It was disconcerting to hear that word from the lips of the ex-televangelist. 'I have to talk to Timmy. I don't have time for bantering right now, because I'm up to my neck in vampires.'

'So are we.'

'You don't get it. I mean, this room is swarming with them. I've been staying at the Pink Motel, you know, and now I'm holed up in the bathroom and the bitches are partying up a storm on the waterbed.'

'Bitches? Damien—'

'OK, I was frustrated . . . didn't get the part in *Hell Hath No Fury* . . . so I picked up a couple of live ones on the strip . . .'

'You're consorting with prostitutes nowadays, Reverend?'

'Give me a break! I'm a-sitting here on the crapper with my silver belt buckle jammed under the door and I'm *shitting* myself, and if all you can do is crack jokes about my fall from grace—'

'I'm coming right over.'

'It's room 666. I know, I know . . . picked it out myself . . . thought I'd be cute. Jesus fucking Christ! I wish I still believed in him.'

When PJ put down the phone, Timmy was sitting up on the bed and watching him solemnly. 'Do you think Rudy felt a lot of pain?' he said softly. 'I don't think I could bear it if—'

'I don't think so,' said PJ.

'Better turn on the espresso machine,' Timmy said softly. 'We've got vampires to kill. Look under the bed.'

Beneath the bed, in contrast to the Bauhaus rigidity of the bedroom, there was a veritable magpie's nest – old pieces of HO scale train track, dirty laundry, guitar strings and even a rolled-up Chagall lithograph – not one of the bigger ones, probably only worth about ten thousand bucks, PJ thought – and there was also a coffin.

'Yes,' Timmy said. 'In the coffin. Come on, pull it out.'

It was a short, squat wooden box, black, inlaid with a silver filigree of skulls and bones. Child-sized; even Timmy probably wouldn't have fitted in it; he'd shot up at least a couple inches since his transformation.

'A relic of my childhood,' Timmy said. 'Go on, open it.'

PJ said, 'No native earth?'

Timmy laughed. 'Never believed in it. But I keep it there for old times' sake. It's almost like a security blanket, knowing it's there.'

In the coffin were about a dozen stakes, sharpened, and a couple of mallets; two silver crucifixes; some vials of what had to be holy water. 'Why do you keep this stuff around?' PJ said. 'Some kind of secret suicidal tendency?'

'You know this stuff never worked on me,' Timmy said. 'But maybe you're right. I do have a death-wish after all. Let's get the fuck out of here. Where's the Reverend staying?'

'The Pink Motel.'

Timmy rolled his eyes.

'What are we going to do about . . .' PJ began. He thought of Rudy, downstairs, dead.

'The dead,' Timmy said, 'are a lot more patient than we are.'

The Reverend's voice squawked. 'Didn't hang up yet,' PJ said. 'We're coming right over,' he said into the mouthpiece. 'Can you hold out for a while?'

'Sure,' said Damien, 'as long as the buckle's in the doorway.'

Timmy said, 'We'll grab coffee first.'

'Coffee? I heard that . . .' said Damien Peters.

PJ said, 'You have to be patient with him. He's new to all this . . . I mean, the shifting metabolism, the constant fluctuations of hormones . . . he *has* to have stimulants and depressants and all that stuff . . .'

'Yes, yes, hurry.'

'We can't take the limo,' Timmy said. 'Too conspicuous—'

'But it has a coffee machine,' said PJ.

'All right, then.'

dissolve

We pull up to the hotel in the dead of night, PJ's driving and I'm gulping down coffee in the back seat still trying to get used to how my body wrenches from mood to mood, the dark thick slush raking the alcohol from my blood, trying to bust myself out of an eternal present, feeling the ebb and flow of being a mortal, being at all. That's the hardest part of all, knowing each second slips away, doesn't linger in the mush of eternity like a dust-mote in the smog, knowing that time's not a pile of Jell-O quivering in the cold palm of your hand but a clear fast stream that jets right through and never is seen again; that's what I love most about not being dead anymore, the transparency of it.

We're here, Timmy.

OK. A couple stakes apiece should do us. We'll just walk right in with them, no one will notice; it's LA.

Why no one at the front desk?

Don't know.

My heart is pounding. Weird. In the old days I could hear every heart but my own. My heart did not beat; it sat inside me like a lump of lead. Now, listen to it thump!

The elevator.

Made it. No one saw.

Sixth floor.

The door to 666 was slightly ajar. PJ and Timmy stopped and listened. To his human senses, the world was perpetually muffled. Now and then Timmy thought he could hear a hint of what he used to hear: a rivulet of sweat oozing down PJ's neck; the pitter-patter of the cockroaches in the walls; the roar of a man's blood as it coursed beneath his flesh . . .

There it is. Damien Peters. I hear his blood rushing. He must really be scared for me to be able to detect it at all. And I can hear the two women inside the bedroom too. Their blood barely moves at all. What I hear is the empty pockets where sound should be, where the air is still and cold.

Two of them, Timmy whispered.

Yeah.

They must have heard me! How clumsy I feel because I can't just funnel into the airstream that spews out over the threshold!

We'd better go for it, said Timmy.

Yeah.

They did not move.

Until, finally, they heard the scream.

Kicked the door open, the two of them, at once. There were two vampires. Young women, no more than girls, Timmy saw. Circling each other on the waterbed. Scowling. One raven-haired, the other a redhead. Dressed in the black uniform of the Neo-Gothics. Dark and empty eyes. On the bed was the desk clerk, a young man in a shredded uniform. There was blood everywhere. They had clawed him all to pieces. They circled, hissed, pounced . . . lapped the blood up . . . the bedside phone was off the hook, and the young man's eyes lay next to it, on top of a Gideon Bible. The red-haired girl was uncoiling the intestines from a gash in the dead man's side.

Casually, the two girls looked up.

We've come to kill you.

Don't I know you?

No.

But I do, we both do, we totally know you. You're the one that sings. Once I heard you in my coffin. Some kid's all walking through the cemetery with his Walkman. Sun just gone down. It's our kind of music. Children of the night—

What music they make.

Who's your friend?

We've come to kill you.

Kill us? How can you kill us, dude? You *made* us!

. . . I don't think so. I don't remember. I would have remembered. *But I know all too well that the memory has deteriorated almost to the human level; a mortal brain can't hold two thousand years of eidetic images, no it can't, maybe I did create those vampire girls and maybe . . .*

But if I made you I can kill you.

Holy water splashing the bed now. Blue-black lacerations across the girl's face, the dry skin peeling, the blood squeezed out, dead blood, congealed and sluggish, purple as a smoggy sunset.

How could *you* do this to us? Don't you remember what you are?

No, said Timmy Valentine.

Lying.

Quick, Timmy. While they're immobilized.

They jumped the two girls as they writhed. Stakes pinned them down. The bed was springing a leak. The holy water was mingling with the fabled Los Angeles tap water . . . the girls thrashed now, the water burned them, the water was fire . . . curious how the entire bedful of water seemed to partake of the qualities of the holy water . . . was it some kind of homeopathic thing, the part overtaking the whole? . . . welts bursting open under the pancake makeup and the rouge, too much rouge, piled onto simulate the bloom of the living . . . and the desk clerk sinking slowly into the pulpy mush of warm water and cold flesh . . .

The girls grew still.

You want to come out now, Damien?

Slowly the bathroom door swung open.

Holy motherfucking shit. If you'll pardon my French. I done *shat* myself in there! Are you sure they're dead?

They're dead, Damien.

Jesus, look at them. This whole thing was a damn fool idea.

I should have stayed home. At home I got silver ingots buried in the walls, and a cross carved into the lintel of every damn doorway and window, and you think I'm paranoid. Serving Mammon has its dangers but it sure is a lot less hypocritical than serving God. Will you just look at them! They're not quite dead, look, one of them's quivering, the way you got her pinned down with that stake, shaking like a bowl of cherry Jell-O. It had to have been a trap. They got it in for the likes of you and me, PJ, because we've fought them or something; I don't know about you, Timmy, but maybe they reckon you're a turncoat, and they're persecuting you with extra zeal, like that Salman Rushdie feller with the Aye-ranians. But I got to thank you for coming. There was a time when I'd have stood right up to them, all my myself, with nothing but my Bible and my big mouth. But now the power's gone right out of me. No charisma in me at all. Can't even do a simple audition for a bit part in a Z-grade movie. And I was a natural for it too! Did you see the script? It's a small-time ripoff of *The Timmy Valentine Story* – you ought to have your attorney look at it, kid, betcha anything it's actionable. Look at that one's skin! Sloughing off of her arm like a goddamn banana peel. And the flesh beneath it all hard and jaundiced. And the smell . . . a refrigerator gone bad . . . Jesus fucking Christ. I should have stood up to them.

Damien . . .

It's like I told PJ on the phone, Timmy. The three of us have lost our magic. There was a cross we had to bear for being what we were . . . PJ had to straddle the boundary between man and woman and I had to wallow in boundless venality so I could have power over innocent people . . . and you, Timmy, you had to be a vampire. And we're lost now. God, where's my bottle of Jim Beam?

It's empty.

I know what he's saying is true. I was a creature of shadow once, but in my own realm I was real. Angel Todd took all that away. He even took the music from me. They're right about that new album. There's no blood, there's no flesh to it. The flesh, the blood, the guts are all inside me now, so that I no longer need to magic them into being. I've relinquished my power to a shadow's shadow. Why did I think I could be human? What's so good about being fucking human?

We need something, said the preacher-turned-actor. Some kind of renewal. We need to go into the forest and bang drums and rediscover our savage roots.

I already *am* a savage, PJ said. All right, I've turned in my leggings and my war bonnet for an Armani suit and a cash register, but I won't stay on no reservation. Ask Timmy to go with you. With his money, you could probably hire that Bly guy as your personal scoutmaster.

The vampires melted into the holy water. They laughed and laughed, the three of them, but laughter did not ease their pain.

He's out there somewhere, Timmy thought. *Darting between undead and unalive. He sucked my deadness out of me and maybe now it's too late for me to enjoy being alive, maybe I just know too much, even though what I know is shrinking every day, it's like each day I lose a year out of those two thousand years . . . why do I feel this way? Is it just puberty? How can I have puberty when I don't have any balls? Wasn't that a pimple I squeezed an hour ago, on my way down the stairs, as I was dashing past the corpse of Rudy Lydick? Why am I so numb about the death of a man who's been so true to me for fifty years? Is this what it's like to be into denial?*

Timmy. Timmy.

I—

You look like you're far away, little brother.

I was.

I've been telling the reverend all the gory details. About Giler and Stupendous and sending you on the tour to try to salvage the bottom line. I told him I was going with you, I'm the new babysitter. I think he wants to come too. We may make snide comments about this Robert Bly male bonding banging on drums and retelling old myths but you know, we all need some kind of renewing. We have to come face to face with our own shadows once again. We all need to recapture our personal magic. Isn't that so, reverend?

Sure is. Why, Timmy, you're a-crying.

I cry all the time these days. You know, it's a real pain, crying. I couldn't, you know, before. I mean, since around AD 79. Jesus, this feels weird.

Lordy, you get more human every day.

Somewhere out there, my shadow's still alive. He wants me to find him again. My future is pulling me toward my past.

Cry, boy, cry, cry your heart out. Crying ain't so bad. But what are we going to do about these goddamn corpses?

We'll manage. I've got a gold card.

6

WHERE LOVE AND DEATH ARE ONE

magician

The sperm sample, they told him, matched. One hesitated, however, to place someone of the stature of McCandless in a Thai prison, or even to have him formally arraigned – not only because he was an important foreigner, but also because he had powerful friends among the aristocracy. Nevertheless, he had to be kept under observation and prevented from running off. That was how Lauren McCandless ended up as a compulsory house guest on Lady Premchitra's ancestral estate. He was a sort of a prisoner – nothing official, of course – the sole occupant of a marble pavilion at the far end of a mango orchard. There was a guard on him, but it was *very* discreet. And he could still go anywhere in the city he chose, as long as the guard came with him.

Still, it was nerve-wracking. Even the nightly dinner-parties, with their high-echelon guests and exotic gourmet dishes, had become tiresome after only a week or so. And Lady Chit was always taking away his drugs. She wanted him to have his mind clear for his painting. She could be such a fucking do-gooder sometimes.

But tonight, there was a new kind of diversion – a magician.

He came with Pete Singhasri, so Lauren knew the real reason the shaman was here; it had to have something to do with the murders, and with *him*, the prime suspect. But of course they would have to endure the entire dinner party first – that was always how it went.

Tonight's do was in the east pavilion of the estate, a building of teak and sandalwood that partly overlooked a canal, one of the few *klongs* that hadn't been filled in to build highways. There weren't as many guests as usual, but the ones who *were* there were about as *crème* as you could get. There was an ambassador, a cardinal, several Hollywood people (incognito, in search of kinky sex), and, of course, *he* was one of the night's main attractions, but these guests were far too polite to mention the fact that he was believed to have committed the most notorious murders since Si Ui, the liver-eating paedophile serial killer of the 1960s.

Now and then, though . . .

Take Lady Chit's mother, for example, who was even now ploughing full sail through the throng, braying away in the upscale British English much favoured by the ruling classes in this country. 'Ah, Mr McCandless,' she said as she hove into view, 'have one of these canapés; beluga, you know, so much cheaper now that they've disbanded the Soviet Union.'

'I'm not a big fan of fish eggs,' said Lauren.

'I don't suppose you would be. But I was just in Russia, you know; my emerald set is missing a few stones, it's those beastly servants, and it *is* the best place to buy them, and it was so wonderful there, except there was all this ghastly talk of that awful man they've just executed, the one who killed all those children, you know, pried their eyes out, raped them . . . oh, have I said the wrong thing?' And all the while she was studying him carefully, as though he might betray himself with a telltale twitch or a Norman Bates-like shiver of the Adam's apple.

But Lauren said simply, 'Didn't do it,' and turned to take a Thai stick from a uniformed servant who stood, impassively, with a silver tray of them. Lady Chit's mother soon tired of pursuit and plunged back into the crowd.

It was at that point, however, that Pete Singhasri showed up, shaman in tow. He had brought the best. Lauren had seen this one on television, in fact, on the most popular talk show in Thailand, *Si Thum Square*. His name was Sonthaya, but people referred to him, in reverential tones, as *Ajarn* – professor.

Lauren could tell how respected he was by the way the crowd parted for the slender, old man in his motorized wheelchair and dark glasses. The ajarn waved away several trays of canapés and bore down on the putative serial killer, waving a gold-handled cane and muttering as Pete struggled to keep up. Meanwhile, the guests were far too polite to stare, but Lauren could tell that he was the centre of attention.

'They treating you all right?' Pete said.

'I suppose so.'

'Hey, I pull a lot of strings for this. Otherwise maybe you rotting away in a prison cell, you know that? So many things, so many evidence, nothing adding up. Tonight, if you do the right thing, maybe you can go home.' Inspector Singhasri looked steadfastly at the floor.

'So . . . they'll take the testimony of a witch doctor that I didn't kill those women?'

The ajarn cleared his throat. When he spoke, it was in a trebly, childlike voice. It struck Lauren that maybe he was one of those natural eunuchs – or perhaps even an unnatural one. 'I'm hardly a witch doctor! Cannot lie to me,' he said. 'I see through flesh all the way through to heart, like another man see through glass. You no hide from me.' Slowly he took off his dark glasses. He had no eyes. 'Ah! You surprise!' he said. 'On television, I don't take off my glasses. People not very sophisticated. In the country, maybe they think I some kind of monster. Wait a minute.'

He reached into a pants pocket, then covered his eyes for a moment; when he took away his hands he did have eyes after all, eyes whose irises glimmered like obsidian. 'Not so scary now,' said the ajarn. 'I have a big collection of glass eyes. You want to see a few others?'

'Well, actually, I—'

'Indulge me.' Ajarn Sonthaya giggled abruptly – a childish, incongruous laugh. He reached into the Central Department Store tote bag slung across his shoulder, covered his eyes again, and then snatched his hands away to reveal a pair of clear blue eyes. 'These I order from Switzerland,' he said. 'The irises are polished aquamarines. Very nice, no?'

'It is somewhat macabre.'

'Aha! A case of, how you say, pot calling the kettle black.' The ajarn, eyeless again for a moment, grinned like a skull. 'But I am great admirer of your work, Mr McCandless. I have big collection – not originals of course – I cut them out of museum catalogues. My daughter has made several into T-shirts, she selling them in street market, perhaps I shouldn't be telling you this . . .'

'Oh, don't worry about it,' Lauren said. 'What's a copyright or two among friends?'

Pete and the ajarn laughed heartily; Lauren did not.

'We'd better get started,' said Pete. 'Is there a private room somewhere?'

'For a moment I thought I was going to be the floorshow,' said Lauren.

'Heavens, no. Someone from the Bangkok *Post* is hovering in the background, though. We not afford this kind publicity.'

dissolve: shadows

When Lady Chit saw the three men moving off toward the maze of rose bushes – which had once encircled one of her grandfather's notorious gardens of sexual delight – she decided she had better tag along. She put her champagne glass down on a passing servant's tray and hurried down the pathway. She was quite sure that her mother was firmly in control of the party and would deflect any other curious people.

She knew the maze better than they did, of course – she had played hide and seek in it in the days when she was still a little girl going to the Ursuline convent school – and so she took a short cut, past a disused well, through a gazebo where a troupe of nude albinos had once performed before her grandfather – and she cut them off at the steps to the stilted teakwood house which had once been a secret meeting place for her grandfather's occult society, the Gods of Chaos – which had started as student highjinks at Cambridge and ended in bloody tragedy for all its members.

'You're looking very guilty, Pete,' she said. 'I don't want you doing *anything* to my precious famous artist, do you hear? If you do, when my husband comes home—'

'We're just going to have the ajarn go into a trance,' Pete said, 'dig into his memory a little. Why don't you go back to the reception? This might not be for the fainthearted.'

'Not only is Lauren McCandless innocent,' said Lady
Chit, 'he doesn't know anything about who killed those
women.'

'How do you know? Did *you* do it?'

It was rapidly getting dark. She could hear the mosquitoes
whining. One could almost choke on the scent of night-
blooming jasmine as it mingled with the fumes from the traffic
just beyond the walls of the estate. 'You'd be surprised at how
much I know,' said Chit. 'I've studied the paintings.'

'So you believe the paintings have something to do with all
this?' Pete said.

'I do. But not Lauren.'

'So he's a conduit of some kind, a supernatural mirror of some
demonic—'

'Perhaps. Look, I've seen things before. Things you've never
dreamed of. Like my own grandfather after his death, transformed into a *phii krasue*, trailing his entrails behind his decapitated head—'

Pete appeared sceptical only for a few seconds. He may have
been educated into America, but he had not lost touch with the
spirit world that terrified and nurtured every Thai soul. 'You
saw such a thing?'

'Oh, don't give me a hard time,' she said at last. 'I've got the
key to the teak house. If you do this out there, the mosquitoes
will kill you.'

Meanwhile, Sonthaya, who had put his dark glasses back on,
was sitting quietly in his wheelchair, palms folded, utterly still;
perhaps he was already entering the state of *samadhi* from which
he would be able to probe Lauren's unconscious mind.

Through this whole exchange, Lauren was strangely silent,
distracted somehow; he had a tendency to slip into some alter-
nate universe when reality got to be too much; and Chit had
hidden most of his drugs.

'Come on,' said Chit.

She led the way up the polished teakwood steps. The old
man was lifted up, still in his wheelchair, by the other two. The
house was very old; she was not quite sure where it had come
from, only that her grandfather had had it taken apart, beam
by beam, and reconstructed here in his secret pleasure garden.

The door was unlocked, and this annoyed her. She thought it had been sealed since the death of the wayward prince. It pushed open easily, as though it had recently been oiled; and there was a flickering light in the antechamber, as though from a kerosene lamp further into the building.

Looking around her she saw the murals that had once frightened her as a girl – Buddhist paintings representing the various hells to which those of bad karma could be sentenced for a time. The images were as horrific as anything out of Bosch, and as bizarrely two-dimensional – naked men being flayed alive, women with their breasts torn off with pincers, children with their tongues on fire – and in the midst of it all the Buddha, sitting in the lotus position, one palm gently upraised, gazing at the horror with compassionate eyes. Inspector Singhasri murmured something; perhaps it was the *namodasa*, a prayer Thais are apt to whisper when confronted with a supernatural presence. There was something here, indeed. Was it merely the memory of Prince Prathna that oozed from the oiled wood, souring its scent with a faint odour of decay? She wondered. A *jingjok* darted across the Buddha's face in pursuit of a dragonfly. She thought his eyes were following her, laughed a little. I'm a big girl, she told herself. A college graduate, for God's sake! And I've seen a lot worse than this.

On the wall, a demon leered . . . a many-headed *yaksha* stabbed a screaming old man with a trident . . . and fire flickered. The *frisson* subsided as she pushed her dread back down inside herself. I won't be afraid, she thought.

Lauren McCandless showed no emotion.

'There's another room,' she said, 'inside. I seem to remember some kind of furniture – couches, chairs. We'd be more comfortable. I could even have some ice tea sent up from the kitchen.'

The others didn't answer and she realized she was running on out of nervousness. She led the way through a bamboo curtain. Stopped for a moment. There was something else here. Heavy breathing from deeper within. Or was it just the bamboo links clinking in the dusty air? There, a shadow, something moving, the flickering light—

Eyes.

Lady Premchitra screamed.

But it was only two of the servant children, lithe little brown bodies scurrying out of sight.

'I'm overreacting, aren't I?' she said softly. 'Hey, you two come back!'

A shuffling sound as they came back, on their hands and knees now, their eyes downcast as was proper for the household staff in the presence of a member of the upper classes.

'We're very sorry, *khunying*,' they both mumbled.

'No one is supposed to come here. Aren't you afraid of the prince's ghost? Don't you know he became a ravening monster after he died?'

Their eyes widened, and she smiled a little. 'Go tell the cook to do us up some ice tea. And put your uniforms on before you come back, you're both practically . . . what were you doing, playing doctor?'

When they realized they weren't going to get into trouble, they giggled softly and backed unobtrusively away.

The inner room was a *hong phra*, a room for meditation and prayer, a room full of powerful Buddha images set up on gilt-fringed plinths, smelling of old incense. It was a good room; the sense of dread which permeated the rest of the antique building did not seem to penetrate here. 'I feel many presences,' said Ajarn Sonthaya in Thai, ignoring their American guest, 'many spirit-beings crowding about us. But they are not malicious ones. We are protected. Lady Chit, perhaps you would care to light some incense. Ordinarily one would not do this kind of ceremony in a place like this – for the world of the Buddha is on a plane far removed from the doings of a few ghosts and demons. But I do not think the Lord Buddha will mind. After all, he knows that none of us – none of all these things you see – though I do not – exist. It is my excellent karma to have been born blind. I don't see, cannot even really imagine what seeing is; I am less prone to the temptations of the deceitful Maya, spinner of illusions. We are nothing at all, and these feelings, these senses that rage through our minds, have no more substance than the echo of a decaying neutrino.'

'You sound very scientific, Ajarn,' said Pete.

'I was once a guest at a seminar on particle physics. In

California, you know. I'm considered quite the guru there –
whereas here, I perform parlour tricks for the rich.'

'Ajarn Sonthaya,' Chit said, 'do you really think so poorly of
us?'

The ajarn merely chuckled, and took a sip of the ice tea that
had materialized during his lengthy speech; the servants who
brought it had already vanished. He switched to English. 'Mr
McCandless,' he said softly, 'please lie down now. This very
dangerous. You lie down, you not get hurt.' Lauren lay down
on the cushions laid out in front of the altar area as Chit lit three
joss-sticks and placed them in the incense burner. Then she lit
a dozen white candles. As the glow spread through the room she
sat on the floor in the *phab phieb* position as she had been taught
to do by her mother, her knees together, her feet politely pointed
away from the puissant images that looked down from the many-
tiered altar: there were big Buddhas, tiny ones, Buddhas made of
jade, ivory, and bronze, and a beautiful reclining Buddha image
of solid gold that a great-uncle had plundered from a Burmese
temple a hundred years ago. The smell of incense, the oily scent
of polished teakwood, the fragrance of night-blooming jasmine
and the ever present hint of gasoline and decay melded into a wild
olfactory mélange that was pure Bangkok.

'What are you going to do now?' Pete whispered.

'Call forth the soul from the body,' said the shaman. 'Then
we will follow . . . we will see where it goes. Now, help me out
of the wheelchair. I have to assume the lotus position. You'll
have to help me into it.'

Pete and Chit helped the old man down from the chair. Once
on the floor, he manoeuvred himself easily into position. He
took off his dark glasses, rummaged around in his tote bag and
swapped his eyes for two dark cabochon star sapphires. Then
he said, 'This is what I'm going to do. I'm going to speak a few
soft words to him, powerful mantras which will put him into a
profound and dreamless sleep. His soul will be released from
his body. He will then be in a precarious situation, for if he is
somehow jolted from his slumber, his soul may not be near
enough to be reunited with his flesh, and then he will be trapped
for ever in a state of not-quite-living. That's why you and Pete
must watch him carefully.'

'You're going to hypnotize him,' said Chit. 'That's all this is, isn't it?'

The ajarn smiled. 'It doesn't matter what we call it. Magic or science, it's all in how you look at it.'

Pete had taken out his notebook and was getting ready to write things down. 'You'll follow him then,' said Chit, 'this vagrant soul.'

'And tell you what I see. Or who knows? You may see something yourself, if you are sufficiently in tune with the universe within. And he will speak. Though that which animates his flesh may not be himself, but another entity. We will see. And now, let me begin to recite—'

'Look!' said Pete. 'He's already—'

Gone. It was true. Lauren McCandless lay preternaturally still. He did not even seem to be breathing.

'Just as I thought,' said Ajarn Sonthaya. 'There is something in him that desperately needs to talk to us.' He murmured a few words in a language Chit did not understand, Sanskrit perhaps. Then he said, very softly, 'Lauren. Lauren. Lauren.'

Lauren moaned. But it was no sound she had ever heard him make. It was the flutelike whimper of a child's voice. The ajarn continued to drone on, occasionally making bizarre hand-gestures. The star sapphires that were his eyes glinted in the candlelight. Shadows deepened the furrows in his face and seemed to age him even as she watched.

Then she heard Lauren McCandless speaking . . . even though the painter's lips were not moving . . . 'It's the angel. He's come for me again. He's standing by the stern of the house-boat with his arm stretched out over the filthy water and his skin is pale blue maybe from the moonlight maybe from the glow of the neon across the way but it's like he has no blood running through his veins at all it's like he's dead . . .'

Chit looked at Lauren's face. His lips still weren't moving. But the lips of the ajarn quivered as though from a bitter cold wind. She realized that the words were not issuing from Lauren at all, but from somewhere in the vicinity of the shaman.

'Lauren,' she said softly, 'what else do you see?'

'The angel is leading me across the river . . . walking on the water . . . I guess that kind of makes sense since he's an angel.

Or maybe it's just that the water is so bloated from the filth of the city that it buoys you up. Then there's the girl there standing at the corner of Patpong 3 . . .'

And he went on and on with the walk down the alley up the stairs toward the bed and then a spurt by spurt description of the blood and always the angel there beside him, slurping the gore from the rent flesh, sipping the lacerations, licking the drenched palms . . . Chit looked at Lauren; still he lay unmoving; then at the ajarn's lips, quivering softly as another man's soul breathed through them. Pete had been taking notes assiduously, but now he was just jotting down the occasional word. Chit wondered how close these descriptions were to the case itself.

Pete said, 'What does all this mean? What is this angel? Is it some kind of multiple personality thing?'

'I don't think so,' Chit said.

'I've heard about such cases,' Pete said, 'where the murderer transfers the burden of his guilt onto some alter ego . . . you know, the Jekyll and Hyde thing . . .' He was talking too rapidly. Chit reached across Lauren's supine body and touched the police inspector's hand very gently. It was shaking.

'I really don't think so,' she said. 'It's not some complex psychological phenomenon. I know who this angel is. I've met him before.'

Beyond the door, the bamboo curtains rustled.

'I even know his name.'

There were soft footsteps outside. Was it the little servant boy with a fresh jug of ice tea? She didn't think so.

'What do you mean, you know his name? What name?' said Pete.

'I don't want to say it. He might think we were inviting him in.'

'Inviting?'

'Quiet. Quiet. Listen.'

The music of a Bangkok night: the temple bells tinking, the buzz of motorbikes, the distant thrum of a jackhammer, the crickets in the grass and the frogs in the stagnant canals; then suddenly, very close, the plangent howl of a wolf.

'Listen to what?' said Pete.

Suddenly, Lauren McCandless stirred.

'Hold him down!' said the ajarn in a rasping parody of his normal voice. 'You must hold him down . . . or else he's going to walk away . . . without his soul . . .' Then, in the voice of Lauren McCandless, 'Please . . . let me follow . . . I have to go with him . . . I have to see more . . . don't you understand, this is what I live for, this is what I always yearn to see, this is the place where love and death are one . . .'

Lauren moved again. He was struggling against invisible forces. Chit and Pete threw themselves down on top of him. He was inordinately powerful. He pushed Chit away and she flew backward across the room. Her head hit something hard, metallic – a Buddha image. She felt intense shame – irrational, she knew – at profaning the statue.

Again, the wolf's howl. Almost drowned in the chaos of city noises, but this time she was sure of it. She rubbed her head. Lauren was writhing. Ajarn Sonthaya rummaged in his tote bag once more and produced a ball of string. 'Quick,' he whispered in his own voice, 'use the *saisin* to hold him in . . .'

Pete grabbed the ball, tied one end to a leg of the shrine, threw the ball to Chit. Chit crawled over to the door and wound the white string around the handle, tossed it back to Pete, who tied one end to the ajarn's wheelchair and threaded it back to the shrine. Chit knew that the *saisin*, a sacred cord designed to keep evil spirits away from the space it encircled, would also prevent Lauren from escaping. The ajarn murmured more mantras as Lauren tried to break out of the circle. After a while he subsided, slumped back onto the floor. In the sudden silence, Chit heard the howling again. 'Don't you hear it at all?' she said.

'Hear what?' Pete said again.

'They can turn themselves into wild animals,' Chit said. 'That's how they blend into the night.'

'They?' said Pete.

'*Phii dip*,' said Ajarn Sonthaya. 'The walking dead. She's quite right, you know. I hear it too. It's quite near. For some reason it's formed some kind of attachment to our painter friend here . . . it feels a deep kinship for him. They are both, you know, as the Americans like to say, *alienated* . . . a difficult concept for us Thais to grasp, of course . . .'

'Look,' Lady Chit said at last. 'While the *saisin* is in place, he's not going to get up and walk away . . . right? Why don't you people just stay here? I'll go out and speak to the *phii dip.*'

'You're insane!' said Pete. 'I mean, growing up in America and all that, you're bound to be a little forward at times, but isn't it more sensible to leave this supernatural stuff to the experts?'

'But it's me he wants to talk to,' said Chit. 'You see, he's a friend of mine.'

But she did not feel terribly confident as she left the little room, bathed in the protective aura of the Lord Buddha, and entered the dusty corridor that led to the outer chamber with its Dantean murals.

7

PHANTOM PAIN

dissolve: angel

. . . but he has been trying to reach her for too too long. Now, in the sweltering night that sweats the sweet scent of jasmine, she has finally heard him. Perhaps she has been hearing him all along; but it is always hard to make humans listen.

Why is there still pain? he is thinking. There's not supposed to be any pain any more. Maybe it's phantom pain. I've heard that amputees feel pain in the arms and legs they don't have no more. Did Timmy Valentine ever feel phantom pain in his dick? Did he ever have a phantom erection? The boy vampire laughs out loud. No one will hear it, or if so they will perceive only the stridulating of crickets or the cry of a lovesick amphibian. *Chit!* he calls out. What will she hear? The mew of a cat, the howl of a wolf, or even the trumpeting of the elephants, hard at work lifting logs on the outskirts of the metropolis? Wolf, he decides. Wolf is better.

He has been hidden in the shadow of a jasmine bush. The shadow of wolf's fur blends into foliage. *Chit*, he whispers, *chit chit chit chit.*

At last, she comes to him.

'Don't come any closer,' she says. He knows she does not see him. She sees only a movement in the bushes. Perhaps there's an unwonted foulness in the air, but it might come from the stale sewage of a nearby canal, ill masked by the fragrance of jasmine. 'I'm wearing a very powerful Buddha image. Really old and powerful. You wouldn't want to get near it. It could hurt you.'

'Chit,' he says. 'You're just the way I remember you. You haven't changed none.'

'Show yourself to me.'

He condenses out of the humid air. He stands there, little different from the last time she saw him, except that he is no longer a clone of Timmy Valentine. His hair is the same dirty blond that it once was in Hangman's Holler, Kentucky, before he and his mother up and drove all the way to Hollywood and into the office of that agent woman, Gabriela Muñoz, the one who transformed him. But he knows that she will see in his eyes, in the crystalline candour of his skin, in the thin-lipped pallor of his smile, the things that make him both more and less than human.

'It *is* you,' says Premchitra softly. 'I knew it had to be. It was the only thing that made sense.'

'Hi,' says Angel Todd.

He reaches out a hand to her. He knows she will snatch her own hand back, wincing from the cold.

'Sorry,' she says. 'I didn't mean to—'

'Better than air-conditioning,' he says. And laughs again, that sound like the chittering of creatures of the night.

'Why did you come here?' she says. 'I kind of figured you'd want to stick around where you were.'

'I've become a wanderer,' he says. 'Maybe that ain't so surprising when you think about it. When I was a human I never felt I could go anywhere or do anything. I was chained to momma, and then to Stupendous Entertainment . . . I was even chained to my own flesh. At first all I could think of was to do all the things vampires are supposed to be able to do . . . turn themselves into wild animals . . . into a fine mist that can funnel through keyholes and under doorways . . . I did all that stuff. I wasn't too careful though. I left a couple of vampires around Hollywood. But they were mostly street people. Preying on each other, you know, never coming out of the shadows. Didn't think it would matter that much. And then I drifted. On the wind mostly. Tornado flew me across Kansas even. I was littler'n a spider. Didn't leave any vampires in those midwestern places, 'cause I learned better. Stopped at Hangman's Holler to see Becky, the onliest black girl in the seventh grade, the one who wanted to touch my thing once but I wouldn't let her because that was the bad thing, the one that only mommas were allowed to do. Jesus I was stupid. I came to her in the middle of the night in the barn where she and I, you know I can't really say made out, but I wanted to I guess. Yeah, she was there and someone was there with her. Dunno who he was. Some nigger. *Big* dude. I killed him easy though. She looked at me and her eyes went all blank. I took her in my arms and the cold inside me kind of burned into her, turned her blood to ice, and no, I couldn't get it up, I couldn't feel that way anymore, so I just drank her blood until there was nothing left, and then I did the careful thing, tore out their hearts and buried them a ways away, and I cut their heads off too, just being sure they wouldn't come back. I was good. Didn't make more vampires. But you know that was when I suddenly realized how much it hurt me, not being alive and not being dead.'

'But you can't feel pain,' said Lady Chit. 'That's the reason you gave up living. To stop feeling it.'

Angel says, 'There's pain in not feeling pain.'

He doesn't want to go on talking about that. He stands there. He can hear her blood, racing because her concern for him is tinged with fear. The hunger he feels is only part of his pain. It is always with him.

He tells her, 'After that the wind carried me many more places. The sea, too. I was a rat in an ocean liner, or hibernating in the hold of a 747. I wanted to get as far as I could from everyone I used to know, but I forgot, the world's kinda like a circle, you get far enough away you start coming back to the same place. The first time I stumbled on Lauren McCandless he smelled familiar. There was like a presence that clung to him. It was you, Lady Chit, and I knew I'd see you again and all the others, one by one, until, you know, we get back to Timmy Valentine.'

'You just can't stay away, huh.'

'Nah.'

The fear level's rising a little, he thinks. It's in the sweat that hangs in the air. That's what's weird about this city, smells never go away . . . too much moisture in the atmosphere or something . . . the smells just cling and cling and cling. Like the pain.

It's battering at his head now. 'Jesus, I'm hungry, hungry, hungry—'

She starts to back away. 'Remember, Angel,' she says, 'I'm your friend.'

'I don't have friends.'

The blood's racing now. 'I've got a powerful Buddha image. And there's a shaman sitting up there in the house. He'll bind up your soul and confine you to a bottle or something.'

'Soul?' says Angel Todd. 'What soul?'

And Angel begins to sing. The words are Timmy Valentine's, but the cadence is pure Angel; not rarefied, not ethereal, but raw and edged with a kind of lust . . . and with that country music catch in the voice, the sound of a breaking heart . . . not at all that unearthly purity that was Timmy Valentine. He knows that she's afraid. He knows she used to be his friend once, that she still cares for him. It only spices the terror.

> Don't matter if you hitch a ride,
> Don't matter if you pay;
> I'll be waiting at Vampire Junction
> To steal your soul away.

'What do you mean, steal my soul?' Chit says. 'How can you steal my soul, Angel Todd? You're just a little lost kid.'

'Yeah,' he says. 'I know that's what you see. But what you see's just the package, just the gift wrap. What's inside the box is gone.'

There's so much he cannot tell her. He's not the little lost kid he used to be. There was never this raging vacuum inside him before. Momma was empty like this, he thought. It was in her eyes. I guess that's how I must look to Chit. Empty. Maybe Momma was a kind of vampire too. Maybe she was the one who sucked my soul away, long before I traded places with Timmy Valentine.

He looks at her for a long time. She is spellbound by that emptiness she sees. His eyes are like wells that have run dry. He sings again.

> . . . to steal your soul away.

'You want me to steal your soul?'

'No. I want to help you find whatever it is you're looking for.'

'I'm not like Timmy Valentine. I'm a thousand times the vampire that he ever was. 'Cause I ain't had the edges knocked out of me by two thousand years of living among humans. I'm not all softened up the way he was by the time I knew him. I haven't had time to learn compassion. I haven't figured out how to have a conscience. I'm the real thing, just the hunger, the naked hunger. What am I looking for? Just blood, nothing but blood.'

'No,' says Lady Chit. 'You want a way out of the labyrinth.'

He can't rein himself in much longer. He can hear her pulse, her heartbeat, can hear the blood roar like a cataract. This is the blood that tastes sweetest, blood that has loved him. He knows that because of Becky. The blood of that thing that was screwing her in the barn, Jesus it was sour, like Momma's breath used to be. But Becky's blood . . . oh, it tingled in his frozen veins with the warmth of a phantom love. A way out, oh yes, he wants that too. But can he see what he wants, through the frenzy of his hunger? 'I can't stop,' he tells her. 'I can't.'

'My Buddha image—'

'You think I'm scared of a fucking piece of gold? I learned a thing or two from Timmy Valentine. Like how to become an unbeliever. Oh Jesus, Chit, I'm *hungry*!'

'All right,' says Chit. 'But only a few drops . . .' She tries to look away. But he knows she cannot.

He leaps upon her, half-back in his wolf-shape, half-human; she puts her arms around him. She shudders, but that shudder is also like a woman arching in erotic fury; she embraces him hard despite her terror, he can hear her heart beating and he wonders if she's thinking about PJ, half a world away, or if he has bewitched her utterly. His lips touch silk and the fabric tears and now he can feel the hot flesh recoil from his frigid tongue. He bites her just above the left areola. She moans. She doesn't back away immediately, but lets him draw out a smear or two of blood.

'Angel,' she says softly, 'stop.'

He doesn't want to stop. But in the end it is the Buddha image on its silver chain, glancing his cheek. It gouges the feelingless flesh, and then, suddenly, he smarts. He is startled. He steps back. Religious icons could not hurt him. He knew that. Timmy had told him. It was all in the mind. The symbols had lost their power over the millennia.

Or had they? He rubbed his cheek. Numb. Numb.

'It took Timmy Valentine a thousand years,' said Chit, 'to get over his fear of garlic and crosses and silver. What makes you think you can do it in a few months?'

And now she does look him firmly in the eye. The fresh blood is trickling down his throat. The scent of fear has dissipated. She has something he needs and the power to withhold it. She's not scared at all, any more, he thinks. She has taken the amulet from around her neck and is holding it aloft. It is not so much the figurine of gold that drives him back, but the faith it can command – not only from this woman, worldly and westernized as she is, but from all the denizens of this country steeped in ritual and superstition. *There is no magic!* he tells himself. *There is only the mind, infinitely malleable.* Timmy has told him this. And yet he is being pushed back as though by a wall of force, a wall of this woman's compassion. How can she dare to pity him, to love him even? He wants to obliterate this love so that he can be what he claims to be, this quintessence of hunger; why is it he cannot?

Confusion overwhelms him. He retreats. His human form begins to weaken. Monsoon-laden, the air begins to permeate his spectral flesh. I've got to hold my shape! I've got to! I need more blood! he thinks. But he is already being drawn up into the wind of night. He does not know where it will take him. He dissolves into the darkness, but to him it appears that it is the world that fades: the garden, the jasmine bushes, the teakwood-stilted house, and the beautiful woman with bare, blooded breasts.

dissolve: magician

Pete looked up when he heard the footsteps. 'She's coming back,' he said. 'Now what?'

The ajarn did not speak until Lady Chit was already in the room, so distraught she was only now remembering to remove her sandals. It took her some moments to regain the mask of serenity that one expected members of the aristocracy to wear at all times. Her silk blouse, Pete noted, had a spot of blood on it. He looked at the young woman for a while; she did not look at him; she had the look of a woman who has been raped and who is afraid she will be accused of having provoked the attack. Pete had seen that often enough. What had she seen? Who was this *phii dip* that she claimed was her friend? Perhaps, he thought, she knows who committed the murders; perhaps they're all in on it, the bored aristocrats and the wild expatriates; they're all just crazy enough, and between them they have enough power to do whatever they want.

Just then, the ajarn seemed to snap out of his rêverie. 'She has seen the face of the demon,' he said. 'She has touched him.'

'Ajarn Sonthaya—' Pete began.

'There's no time. The demon has left this house. Lady Chit was unable to . . . satisfy him. He's gone in search of more blood. Someone will die unless you—'

'Who will die?' Pete said.

'I can't tell. But this man can. His soul is drawn to the soulless demon. He can't help himself, he's a moth fluttering around a flame, and he is going to be crushed if I let him back inside that body . . .' He pointed to Lauren McCandless, lying quite still inside the sacred *saisin* circle. 'Do you want to prevent another death? Perhaps you can.'

'Another death?'

'McCandless's spirit wants to follow the *phii dip* towards that place which fascinates him so, the place where love and death are one. If I let him possess me again, I will again see what he sees.'

'And what am I to do?' Chit said. 'Sit helplessly by while you and Dirty Harry run off to save the universe?'

'Tend to Lauren's body,' said the spirit doctor. 'You've already given the creature a piece of yourself. You too are being drawn into his dark ensorcellment. It's too dangerous for you. Stay here. Get inside the *saisin*. This room will protect you.'

The ajarn lit a few more candles, then a bundle of joss-sticks, which he held in his folded palms until the incense had burned almost all the way to the stems; then he placed them in a little receptacle in front of the array of sacred statues. He took another pair of eyes from his tote bag. They were clear and colourless. He put his hands over his sockets and when he took them away the eyes had a cold glow, like a movie alien's. He hefted himself up into the wheelchair. It seemed to Pete that now the ajarn was no longer blind, for he steered his wheelchair confidently toward the door and started rolling into the corridor. Meanwhile, Lady Chit entered the sacred circle, seeming still to be somewhat in shock from whatever she had witnessed.

Pete followed the ajarn down the hall and through the chamber with its hellish visions. He lifted the wheelchair down the steps. 'This way!' the ajarn said urgently, pointing in the direction of the wall.

'There's no way through,' Pete said.

'Think I'm just a blind man, pointing aimlessly, don't you?' said Sonthaya. 'I tell you I'm seeing with the eyes of this painter's soul . . . I have the clarity of his artist's vision . . . and the madness of it . . . if you can't get me through this wall, help me find my way through this labyrinth of an estate . . . we've got to hurry.' Pete did not stop to think. One didn't argue with a shaman in the throes of a truthseeing trance.

The party was still going strong. The ajarn was able to wrest a drink from a passing servant without pausing. They reached the front lawn and raced down the driveway lined with rosebushes and stone lanterns. They had to call for a servant to unlock the front gate. Pete's Accord was parked in the *soi* outside. Soon they were rushing down the maze of tiny interconnecting alleys, with family compounds rubbing shoulders with high-rises and shanties, dodging taxis, pedicabs, and the odd waterbuffalo as they sped toward Sukhumvit, the main street, crammed with screaming traffic. 'It would help if you could tell me street names,' Pete said, exasperated and wishing he had come in a police car so he could have turned on his siren. Not that it would have done much good.

'I don't know the names. I just see things. In my mind. I see what the man's spirit sees, and that spirit isn't bound by streets.'

'Well, what do you see? Can I at least have a description?'

'Yes. There's a boy walking through the throng. He's not alive, not dead. He's an American boy, I think. He's running through the mass of people on the sidewalk, but now and then he's not a boy at all, he weaves in and out of the mass of people like a wild animal . . . but Lauren calls him the angel. What Lauren sees is a child, golden-haired and clear-eyed, drifting in a shaft of pale blue light; he's a beautiful thing, this angel of death, and each glimpse of death that Lauren catches is a presaging of his own death . . . the thing Lauren most longs for.'

They were passing the Erawan shrine now. The dancers were in full regalia; their pagoda-shaped gilt crowns bobbed up and down, coruscating in reflected neon; Pete did not take his foot off the accelerator as he took his hands off the steering wheel to pay homage to the god. He found himself turning left, heading toward the garish lights of Silom. Though it was night, his air-conditioning strained to cool the car to a barely tolerable level, and the sweat was still pouring into his eyes. The ajarn sat on the passenger seat in a full lotus position, and his crystal eyes, like every other reflective surface around them, were a kaleidoscope of brash fluorescence: shocking pinks, vivid turquoises, sickly greens. He knew now that they were going back to the Patpong district, where the prostitutes congregated; there was going to be another killing. How could that be, with the one suspect's body imprisoned in a circle of magic twine? He drove on. Now and then the ajarn gestured brusquely and Pete changed direction. If they were going to Patpong, they were taking an erratic course indeed. And what was this angel, this golden child? He saw no one. Except . . .

A dark bird swooped down over a flashing Coca-Cola sign, perched on the hood of the Accord . . . it unnerved him. It stared back at him, a sentient hood ornament, and its eyes, too, reflected the neon night. Was it a raven, a deathbird? Pete turned down Sathorn Road, inched his way past the Robot Building, silhouetted in the lurid sky like something out of a Japanese monster movie. Edged toward Suriwong, less tourist-infested, where the younger meat was peddled . . . patches of darkness on this avenue, sandwiched between swaths of brilliance . . . children of the night stood, unmoving in the pedestrian sea, waiting, waiting. How well he knew their stories.

The raven would not budge. Pete tried swerving, but he couldn't throw it off. He swerved again. Ajarn Sonthaya murmured, 'Please. Please. Go straight.'

The bird began to flap its wings. It cawed. Pete did not understand how he was able to hear its cry through the closed windows, with the air-conditioning wheezing. It was a shrill, disturbing cry, human almost. He turned on the radio, pushed the automatic station finder. Ten seconds of whining 'Country 'n' Eastern' . . . ten seconds of mindless disco . . . ten seconds of soap opera . . . ten seconds of funereal Siamese classical music . . . and then . . . a familiar song from the eighties . . .

> *Don't matter if you hitch a ride,*
> *Don't matter if you pay,*
> *I'll be waiting at Vampire Junction*
> *To suck your soul away . . .*

He jabbed at the buttons again, but nothing happened. The car resounded with the old Timmy Valentine song, but it wasn't the same as he remembered it from the New Wave era. It was still a child's voice, but laced with adolescent rebellion; the sweetness of its harmonies was transmogrified into a savage, percussive pounding and a howling guitar solo that resounded with Neo-Gothic despair. The music continued to crescendo although he turned the volume down to zero. He was losing control of his car.

A pickled guava vendor was wheeling his cart across the street—

He jammed down on the brakes. Nothing happened. He steered hard right. The guava vendor did not quicken. The Accord climbed up onto the median. Garbage flew. The raven's wings spread wide. They seemed to enshroud the entire windshield. How was that possible? Pete felt something crunch and hoped it was not human. The raven wrapped itself around all the windows. The song screamed in his ear. Underneath the chaos he could hear the ajarn mumbling some mantra.

Then the car crashed.

shadows

Inside the teak house, Lady Chit knelt in front of the images, protected by the *saisin*. The night seemed strangely calm. Lauren lay on the floor in what seemed to be a coma.

In Thailand children are taught from an early age how to seek out their inner stillness. But Chit had always been torn between being an obedient Asian girl and a rebellious American, and her parents, Anglicized by their British school education and their long stints in the diplomatic service, had done little to point her in one direction or another. She couldn't sit still; she fidgeted; she shifted her weight from one knee to the other; at last, reaching toward the sheaf of joss-sticks that rested on a silver-plated offering-dish, she lit three of them, folded her hands, and gazed on the face of a weatherbeaten, stucco Buddha image that had been salvaged from a ruined city by one of her ancestors.

She closed her eyes and saw . . .

What was it? Flap-flap. Flap-flap. The beating of giant wings.

. . . and thought of something she hadn't remembered in a long while . . . in her all-girl New England boarding school, age thirteen, acting in a school play, Oscar Wilde's *Salome* . . . a line she had to say, her little voice muffled by the cotton wool beard . . . *I hear the beating of great wings in the palace . . . I think it is the angel of death . . .*

. . . and quickly opened her eyes again. Just a memory, she told herself, weirdly vivid. Haven't thought about that play in a million years. The big robes they made me wear, the thick makeup, whiteface and gold . . . weird, weird, weird. That was when I first started listening to Timmy Valentine.

The memory faded as quickly as it had come. She could barely recall it now. She began her prayer once again. Lauren McCandless moaned.

And then, with her eyes wide open so she knew it was no illusion, she heard it once again. Perhaps it was only the wind. A monsoon downpour could be due at any time. Yes. She could hear the branches swaying beside the stagnant canal outside the walls of the estate.

. . . the beating of great wings . . .

Stillness. She closed her eyes once more. *Tranquillity*, she told herself. She imagined herself letting go, being swept up into the monsoon. She had not had an experience like that since the time she and PJ had made love in the forest outside Junction . . . could that have been only a year ago? She allowed the memory to soak into her . . . like the monsoon itself. She could hear the wind gusting now, bigger.

Then it came again, heavier and more threatening, this sound . . . she could almost see the bird, a black-winged creature with crystal eyes which echoed the lights of the city of night . . . and Pete's eyes . . . wide with fear and shock . . . and the phosphorescent features of the angel of death . . .

I have to stay here! she told herself. These visions are illusions . . . trying to pull me out of the safety zone.

There was a jolt. It was almost as though she were there: glass shattering, tyres squealing, metal ripping asunder.

8

MONSOON

magician

'All right,' said the shaman. 'We've arrived.'

They had rammed a wall – it looked like a travel agency. They were wedged between two sidewalk noodle stands. Pete, shaken, climbed out of the car. He wasn't too badly injured. He looked up at the sky. He could feel the weight of the impending rain.

'Quickly, now!' said the ajarn, still cross-legged on the passenger seat. 'Unfold my wheelchair! We haven't all the time in the world—'

'Ajarn . . . that bird or whatever it was . . .'

'A manifestation of *maya*, the state of illusion that will dog you and me until the day we finally reach nirvana. Get yourself together, man . . . we've demons to trap, spirits to appease.'

Still trembling a little, Pete assembled the old man's wheelchair and helped him into it. A police car pulled up and an officer leaped out. Quickly, Pete explained who he was and that he was hot on a trail and could not be interrupted, and asked the rookie cop to have the Accord towed. He turned back to see that Ajarn Sonthaya was speaking to one of the street vendors, who had a basket full of little bottles made of porcelain and ivory.

'What are you doing, Ajarn? Aren't we supposed to be in a hurry?'

'A hundred baht!' said Sonthaya to the vendor. 'You think I'm some kind of tourist? You know as well as I do that it's fake.'

'All right, maybe not two hundred years old,' said the vendor in Chinese-accented Thai. 'But still real ivory, la. Good price. OK, fifty.'

'Detective! Can you lend me fifty baht?'

'I don't understand . . . why are we shopping all of a sudden?'

'I need a little bottle. You know. It's for the demon.'

The ajarn stuffed the bottle into his tote bag. 'Bah,' he said, 'it's plastic. Good enough, though. Could have got it for less. Quick now, down that alley.'

The raven – if that was what it was – stood in the unpaved passageway, perched on a stone in a puddle. Pete pushed the wheelchair. It bounced over ruts as they turned a corner. They went further. This alley was lit only by the glow of bars and nightclubs a few streets over. The raven was slowly changing shape . . . growing tall . . . its feathers resolving into a black T-shirt and black baggy trousers . . . its scalp transforming into a baseball cap whose backward-facing legend read *Lakers* . . . and wisps of blond hair. The figure shimmered as it moved . . . its feet barely skimmed the ground and it was hard to stay behind him.

'What is it?' Pete whispered.

'I'm not sure. But follow him.'

And suddenly Pete could see there was something else there too. At times it appeared to be only the young boy's shadow; but now and then Pete could make out the outline of a man . . . surely it was only a trick of the constantly shifting lights . . . surely it was not Lauren McCandless?

'Surely not,' Ajarn Sonthaya said, reading his mind, it seemed. 'You are quite perceptive for a man who isn't gifted with psychic abilities. Or is that you simply have undiscovered talents?'

Pete pushed on. It would not do to show just how disturbing all this was to him.

They reached another main road. This street was well outside the tourist beat. A row of shanty houses leaned against the peeling stucco of a Chinese restaurant. The figure of the boy-angel was quite distinct now, but Lauren McCandless remained shadowy. At length, the boy came to a stop. He turned, acknowledged, it seemed, the presence of Pete and the shaman with a mock-heroic bow; then he pointed to Lauren, who stepped out of the shadow a little way, but still appeared to be little more than a blur, a movement in the branches of a mango tree that leaned across the fence of some tenement compound.

The ajarn urged Pete to push him forward a little more. They too rested beneath the mango branches now, and what Pete saw next made him feel queasily voyeuristic; it was a young woman, a prostitute, it seemed, leaning against an open doorway, casually rolling a condom over a banana with her teeth.

All at once, though the city screamed and buzzed and chittered all about them, it seemed that this was the only stranger in the alleyway, that all the urchins, vendors, beggars and even the stray dogs had been spirited away. She was a high-cheekboned girl, perhaps from the North, who compensated for her pale complexion with an outrageous black lipstick and deep purple eyeshadow. She had short, butchy hair and a silver stud in her eyebrow, like the punkettes Pete used to see in America.

When she saw she was not alone she whisked the banana into a nearby pile of trash, leaving the condom flopping in her mouth; and she laughed a little.

'You like my funny little trick, yes, farang man?'

She spoke to the shadow that was Lauren McCandless.

The wind sighed.

'For that you pay a little more,' she said. 'But look like rain coming soon, so we no bargain too long. Me tired.'

It was clear that the woman could see no one save the one person Pete could not see clearly . . . everyone else was invisible to her. We all live in different universes, he thought, but usually when they intersect we still fool ourselves into believing that our experiences are shared . . . but now, a thing like this, when you're standing right there and the woman looks right through you like you're a ghost . . . now that does make you wonder what's real and what's pure *maya*.

'You come to my special place?' says the girl. 'Oh yes. Of course, I invite you, I invite your friend too. No see friend. You making joke. Okay I invite your friend, Mr Shadow, Mr Nobody There, haha, you see, I laughing now. You funny man.'

'Why can't she see *us*?' Pete whispered to the shaman.

Sonthaya said, 'We are only the stuff of dream to her. The

unseen can be more real than the seen. You know that, and I
live with it every hour of my life.'

'And Lauren – a phantom – is real?'

'It's what she thinks she wants. Listen to me. I am a shaman
of no small ability, and even my wheelchair-bound infirmity is
sometimes just a cloak that disguises my inner nature. You've
seen me become possessed by the god Brahma, pronounce
oracles, make tap water holy, do all the things that a god can
do. Do not be amazed if you see more miracles tonight.'

They followed the prostitute, and as they did so it seemed to
Pete that the world itself was blurring around them. They
squeezed their way through alleys thronged with people; no
one saw them; it was almost as though they were walking right
through them. The storefronts broadcast their wares in a dozen
languages: *Pussy Palace, Motorcycle Man, Hermaphrodite Welcome.*
Neon swirled into neon. The air reeked of the coming rain.
There was lightning, and in the lightning chiaroscuro faces,
taunting, scornful, faces with pointed teeth and slitted eyes . . .
as if the infernal visions from the murals of Prince Prathna's
teak house had come alive and were leaking into the chaos of
the red light district.

Then there was a doorway without a door. The woman turned
and her smile seemed to encompass them all, visible and invisible . . . and she said, 'Come inside, now we make love,' and
even as she spoke came the downpour, water cascading from
the sky, men and women running to take cover; they entered
the building; Pete turned to see a jasmine garland drifting
down the flooded alley, flapping against the gutter.

Down a dingy corridor with naked light bulbs and a dozen
doorways with bead curtains; above their heads the clatter of
rain on galvanized iron; from behind the bead curtains the sighs
of purchased passion. The last room in the hallway, the woman
stood for a moment, half in, half out of the strings of milky-blue
beads. And then she went inside . . .

The boy and his shadow followed, and Pete Singhasri waited,
just behind the bead curtain, while the shaman prepared his
magic, muttering an incantation and making mystic hand-
gestures over the *faux* ivory perfume bottle . . .

dissolve: night creatures

The woman bends down to turn on a stereo. It is one of those novelty items, shaped like a big pink heart, and she pops in a cassette he immediately recognizes. It's *Vanitas*, and it's the first cut on side B, the one that begins:

> You're driving me insane, bitch,
> Cuz you never pop the clutch.
> I got holes in my hands, bitch,
> From loving you too much.

There's been talk of a harder edge, a new intensity in songs like these – some *Rolling Stone* critic even said something like, well, this has cars, and sex, and religion, and sadomasochism, all in one, and it kind of sums up the whole of the American condition in a single stanza of angry poetry, but actually no one much liked it. It wasn't the Timmy Valentine they knew. Angel isn't surprised to hear it now, though. He really can pick these girls. It doesn't matter who he picks, every blood-drenched road leads back to Timmy Valentine, does that make him Rome, does that make him the pope? Don't fucking make me laugh.

Lauren is a good servant. Even without a body he can still follow me, still be the bait for my victims. If I ever meet that mythic old count, I'll stake Lauren against Renfield any day.

Angel waits. He can sense the others who have followed him and Lauren. There is danger. The old man in the wheelchair . . . he sees things. He's not as blind as he acts. He has an in with the dark powers, and he's got plans for me. I can't fight him unless I keep my strength up. I have to have blood, more blood.

The prostitute speaks again. 'You want me take off everything? Or you like me wearing funny clothes?'

'No,' says the phantom Lauren McCandless. 'I want to see the real you. What's your name?'

'No name, I no give name, give name cost extra.'

'OK. So . . .'

'OK. But first, I hot, air not working now.'

She flings open the shutters of a window that overlooks the alley. Rain batters old wood. She flings aside her imitation

leather jacket (though its Naugahyde scent still clings to her
sweaty flesh) and she's not wearing a blouse or a bra, and on
one breast there is a tattoo of a bright red heart skewered with
a wooden stake; Lauren touches her breast with his spectral
hand and she shudders and says, 'Your hand cold, too cold,'
and she backs into the open window to let the scalding torrent
lash her skin; then, with practised languor, she begins to peel
down her tight imitation Calvins. He can smell all of her . . .
the bitter-sweet blood, tarted a little by a recent menstruation,
tingly from a touch of cocaine . . . she laughs at Lauren. All he
can think of is that blood. The smear of blood from Lady Chit's
breast has not assuaged him at all. Blood, he thinks, blood to
fill the chasm, blood to fuel my battle against the blind old man
. . . this woman was made for devouring . . . her breast already
bears a vampire's emblem . . . and, like all the others, she is
beautiful. If only she had loved him . . .

'You no have to use condom if you no want,' she says. 'I
don't care I live I die, no difference. They call Russian roulette,
I laugh.'

The smog-tinged rain mingles with the smell of sweat and
cheap perfume. She opens her arms out to the painter who
isn't really there and Angel moves in between them, a falling
shadow.

Lauren's ghostly hands grip the woman's arms and Angel's
dead arms grip her too. Lauren grazes her cheek with his insubstantial lips and the woman moans, 'Cold, cold, cold,' and backs
away again into the hot rain and Angel's lips, too, touch her,
his flesh made hard by death, his lips that cannot help slicing
into her skin because their softness is only an illusion that conceals metallic deadness, and already the blood is rushing to her
cheeks, blood that tastes of confusion and desire and yes,
already there is a little dread, although she is not a woman who
fears death, he senses, because she has always longed for death
. . . Angel can taste death in her blood.

'You're bleeding on me,' says the Lauren-soul. 'I don't want
to catch my death from—'

'I love, I kill,' says the girl.

Then Angel speaks: *No. I'm the one who loves and kills.*

The girl stops. 'Voice. You hear voice?' She stares at the

shadow that is Angel and she begins to know that he is there. 'You no who you say you are,' she says.

That's true.

What does she really see? He can only guess. To gaze on a vampire is to hold a mirror to one's innermost terrors. What does this woman fear? Does she see a ravening monster from a B movie, an ogre from a dysfunctional childhood, a wizened, withered version of herself, too decrepit to sell her body on the streets of some futuristic Bangkok? But she doesn't seem to be afraid of much. Perhaps, then, she sees Angel Todd's true shape . . . the clear-eyed child whose heart cannot beat. Perhaps she sees him as he reaches out to embrace her, as he bares his teeth and swoops between her breasts to rend flesh, to tear at the image of the staked heart . . . perhaps she sees his slender body swathed in a shroud of shadow, his ice-thin lips, his muss-blond hair . . . perhaps, perhaps. It does not matter to him. He sucks in her tainted blood. You can't poison what's already dead.

At that moment, the two men who have been tailing him burst through the bead curtain. The blind man has fire-opals in his eyes. He holds aloft a plastic perfume bottle. The other is the policeman Singhasri. He is holding a gun. Angel sees them only in the periphery of his vision because he is so intent on draining the woman's blood.

'Release the woman!' the shaman screams. 'Release the soul of the painter so I can return him to his body!'

> *I got holes in my hands, bitch,*
> *From loving you too much . . .*

Damn those Timmy Valentine songs! Is there no way I can ever escape from him? In a fury he grabs the stereo and smashes it against the woman's skull. The skull and the stereo fracture with a crack. Thunder answers. The woman doesn't scream or cry out; the blow has disabled her nervous system, Angel supposes, and perhaps she doesn't even know that she is dying. Her eyes have already gone dead. Angel turns his attention back to the tear in her body, widens it, lets the blood gush out over him as it mingles with the rain that reeks of jasmine and gasoline.

'Release her!' the shaman shrieks.

What power can an old man have? Angel says, 'You're just a snake oil salesman. Get the fuck out.'

But the old man doesn't go away. The police detective pushes the wheelchair closer. Lauren's shadow wavers, begins to lose its shape. 'I'll swallow the painter's soul if you come any closer,' Angel says. 'Then he'll never get back into his body and he'll fucking lay around like a zombie till kingdom come.'

'You don't want to devour his soul, Angel,' says the old man. His lips are not moving. His English is poor, Angel's Thai non-existent, but the world of shadows has but one language, and that language the language of night. 'You need him.'

'I only need blood!'

'You need so much more . . . that's why you cling to the shards of your human past.'

The old man moves inexorably closer. He brandishes the ridiculous perfume bottle and he's pulling something out of his tote bag . . . a strand of white string. And he's murmuring mysterious words.

'I ain't scared of this bullshit,' says Angel Todd. 'Timmy Valentine taught me not to be afraid of religious symbols. He told me the magic went away a long time ago.'

'That may be true,' says the old man, 'in America. No one believes in old things anymore there. But this is Thailand. You know it. You feel it in the air. It makes you stronger than you were over there.' And the ajarn moves still closer, his milky eyes glittering.

Angel Todd sucks out a few more mouthfuls of blood. He tosses the woman aside. She is in shock. She convulses against the floorboards but the clattering blends in with the pounding rain. The old man does have some kind of power. Angel knows he is in danger. Quickly he seizes the Lauren-soul by the hand. He thins the fabric of his human form until he can feel the very air rushing through himself . . . I am a mist, he tells himself, I am a shadow . . . he whirls, he scatters, he envelops the Lauren-soul, drags him toward the open window . . . the ajarn and his wheelchair come after him . . . they are at the window now, grappling as he makes himself more and more insubstantial . . . the magic rope slices through his attentuated flesh . . . he feels, not pain exactly, but a dull remembrance of pain . . . he panics.

He churns the air around him. Lauren's life-force flits inside the vortex like a Coke can in the wind. The girl is not dead yet, but she's writhing, jerking, haemorrhaging onto the floor. Bits of black plastic from the stereo litter the bed. The ajarn is making a noose out of the sacred rope . . . he's going to trap the vampire while he's a mist, he's going to draw the knot tighter and tighter . . . there's something suffocating about this room . . . and Angel twists away, whirlpools out of the window with the Lauren-soul in tow . . . reconstitutes himself in the alleyway, a small boy in soggy black clothes alone in the pelting rain . . . watched over by a man who isn't there . . .

He looks up. The shaman is in the window. He is still playing with his knotted cord, and the policeman is still standing behind him. Angel laughs at him.

Then the shaman begins to lurch out of the window . . .

Angel tenses.

Ajarn Sonthaya drifts out of his wheelchair. He is sitting in lotus position. He is levitating above the window sill. He's drawing on powers he can't control, Angel thinks. He's becoming possessed by one of those weird gods they worship around here . . . like the one that presides over the Erawan shrine.

He's going to crash to the sidewalk and smash his bones to powder. Why does he want to get me so much? Angel feels himself coiling up, ready to strike. The blood of the prostitute has only satisfied him for an instant despite its pungent bouquet of disease. I wouldn't mind swallowing a shaman. Maybe I'll be able to dream again.

The ajarn plummets.

Rain gushes from drainpipes, dances on corrugated rooftops, drowns out the screech of traffic.

Angel spins, gathering power. And leaps.

He has the old man in his arms. The old man looks at him with unseeing eyes and he stares back, and in the opals he sees fire, and he remembers . . . the fire that gave birth to him through death . . . the fire that burned down the city of illusions . . . fire . . . fire.

The fire shoots from the old man's eyes.

Grazes his cheek. Burns . . . *burns!* How can it burn him, who is incapable of feeling? Is it fear that crackles through his dead brain cells, his insensate nervous system? No. No fear. It must be rage. *Rage!* He is possessed by rage. He claws the spirit doctor, draws blood, drives himself to frenzy with its scent. Swoops again, fangs bared, rainfall sluicing down his throat.

Then Inspector Singhasri comes lunging through the front door, brandishing a pistol. He fires. A splotch of brilliance in the storm. The bullet punctures Angel's neck and flies out the other side. A sound like a train-whistle escapes the pierced trachea before the flesh regenerates; and Angel laughs again and again, a savage and despairing laugh, as the policeman empties two revolvers into him. Bone and skin and muscle reknit, regurgitate spent shells.

Angel turns and rakes the man's flesh. He catches the edge of his lip, rips the opening wider to reveal jaw and cheekbone, flings the flesh into a nearby pile of garbage. Rain lashes at the bursting blood. He pokes out the inspector's eyes and laps at the gore that spews from the sockets. Pete screams, tries to reload blind, flails with the pistols until Angel whisks them away and tosses them into the gutter. He feeds, momentarily forgetting the old man until once more he feels the touch of the *saisin*. It goads him more. He thrusts the inspector onto the pavement. He shrieks his anger in the language of the night. *Blood, blood, blood*, he cries out.

A pack of stray dogs, understanding his cue, leap from behind garbage cans, from further back in the labyrinth of alleyways, and start to tear the police inspector limb from limb. One mongrel dashes into the shadows with a hand in his mouth. Angel laughs again. Where is the shade of Lauren McCandless through all this? Flitting in the rain, inexorably drawn to the spectacle, not knowing the way back to his own body . . .

'Watch this, Lauren McCandless,' Angel says softly. 'You'll really have something to paint after tonight.' And he turns back to the old shaman, thinking, I'll just give him a quick snap of the neck and send him on his way, and I'll suck him dry as he's ebbing into unconsciousness.

He pounces again, and—

Tyre squeal in the rain! A white Porsche careens into the alley. A door flies open. 'Let him go!' shrieks a voice. It is Lady Chit. He smells her, is flooded with the same confusion he felt in the

garden of the estate. She yanks the silver chain from her neck
and runs toward him, lashing him with the Buddha image. It
gouges his cheek. Burning cold sears him. He releases the ajarn
for a split second only, but in that instant the shaman flings his
arms wide and throws himself upward into the torrent, calling
upon the god Brahma to possess him. And he begins to levitate
once more, and to glow with an eerie blue radiance, and his
voice deepens and his eyes once again seem to be on fire.

He folds his palms together and begins to utter a mantra in
a resounding voice, louder than the thunder, more potent than
the rain. And Lady Chit brings the Buddha image smashing
again and again into his face.

'What's he doing?' Angel shouts.

'He's enchanting the rain,' Lady Chit screams. 'He's making
the whole monsoon storm into holy water!'

And then it happens. Where the rain touches him, desolation
touches him. The slow blood in his veins turns glacial, shatters
like glass.

'You can't kill me,' he whispers. 'You're Buddhists . . .'

. . . and then he sees the perfume bottle in the shaman's
hand, shielded from the rain by a downturned palm, and he
knows what they want him to do . . . to melt back into mist, to
spiral back into the bottle like a genie in a Sinbad movie . . .
and the rain streams down and tears at his skin and digs into
his pores and pounds despair into him, and the ajarn turns to
him and smiles and whispers, *Angel, Angel, here is your sanctuary,
do not be afraid . . .*

He turns to Lady Chit. 'Don't you love me anymore? Ain't I
your friend?' he cries out.

And she says, 'Yes, I am your friend.' But still she flagellates
him with the silver and the icon that sears his flesh. He thinks
. . . *I was born in a fire, and now I'm gonna fucking die in a flood.*

The emptiness inside the perfume bottle calls out to him,
dark, seductive, feelingless. And he leaps.

And the shaman twists the cap back on the phial.

9

DEMON IN A BOTTLE

funeral

Police Inspector Pete Singhasri's funeral was a drab affair, but Lauren felt impelled to go to it. Even now he couldn't believe it was going on, in spite of the monks chanting up a storm in a pavilion next to the canal, in spite of the mourners, in spite of the golden casket in which his friend's remains lay, surrounded by flower wreaths and silver-framed photographs of the deceased in full regalia – police uniform, college gown receiving a degree from the king, another from his American alma mater.

One thing had changed, though, since the morning he had awoken in a teakwood house on Lady Chit's estate suffering from a curiously selective amnesia and an excruciating hangover. He had been sober for almost two weeks. He hadn't even had a joint, let alone a handful or two of his favourite pills.

That morning, someone from the police department had shown up to tell him that he was no longer under suspicion of being the serial killer of Patpong – there had been a killing in the night, and he had an airtight alibi – somehow Pete had been involved and had got killed. But somehow he didn't feel very relieved about that. After all, there were still the paintings. He was working on a painting now, the last one in the series. He had moved all his work to the old teak house. A *saisin* ran all the way around the stilts of the building, and for some reason Lady Chit never let him leave the premises without wrapping a strand of the white thread around one of his wrists; when he'd ask her about it, she would just say, 'Trust me.'

This was the painting:

The woman stood, leaning against an open window behind which a monsoon storm raged. She was naked. Over her heart was tattooed another heart, and through that heart a stake from whose pointed end depended three small drops of crimson. A leather jacket lay at her feet, and in front of her a cheap smashed ghettoblaster, and on the wall a poster advertising Timmy Valentine's new album, Vanitas – a poster that showed the boy singer nude beneath a sheet of canvas that was another painting by Lauren McCandless, the first of the dead yellow women. And . . . in the background . . . against the far wall . . . the shadow of a man who must have been standing just beyond the edge of the frame, a man whose silhouette many could identify as being himself, Lauren McCandless, present yet not present at the woman's killing . . . oh, and of course, the woman quite, quite drained of blood.

Half-finished, the painting rested on an easel in the main hall of the teak house. Flaming demons stared down at it from all sides. If you stood over the easel, hunched up, massaging the paint into the canvas, you could see, peering from the painting's edge, the eyes of the Lord Buddha, gazing down at the ravaged corpse in otherworldly compassion. A slide of the unfinished opus had already been couriered to Los Angeles, and an offer had already come in from the Corcoran in Washington – Lauren's first nibble from Top Drawer Establishment. Much was being made of its being the final painting in the series. Lauren wasn't sure how he knew that it was the last one, but he just did. When this was all over, he thought, I'm just going to clear out of this town. Maybe I'll move to fucking Timbuktu and paint camels in the sand.

Right now, though, he had to pay his respects. The pavilion was garishly lit; incense wafted out over the *klong* and into the air, which smelled clean after the rain had purged it of pollutants. He was soggy in his dark suit – Bangkok was not made for dark suits – and he was fidgeting as he attempted to sit, legs folded to one side in the polite *phab phieb* position, his palms together in an attitude of prayer. All around him on the matting, women in black sat, all coping with the excruciating position without shedding a drop of sweat. Some mouthed the words of the chanting along with the monks, nine of them, who sat on a dais with prayer fans held out over their faces, their mantras buzzsawing over the pavilion. A ragged temple boy crawled between the guests with glasses of ice water reddened with a bitter rose essence. Lauren took one and gulped it down and realized there was no convenient place to spit it out.

Someone tapped his shoulder.

'Hello. You, serial killer, you.'

He turned. A little old lady, no taller than the middle of his chest. She wore a lace black dress and too much makeup.

'I'm not a serial killer,' Lauren said.

'No, no, I know really. My son tell me many times you not a killer, you only *phii khao*.'

'No, I wasn't possessed either. I'm sorry.'

'My son he really like you, don't know why.'

'Are you Pete's mother?' he said at last. 'I'm . . . I'm really sorry.'

'Oh, no need. It's just bad karma.'

'You must have loved him very much.' Lauren racked his brains for the next cliché on the list, and wished earnestly that he had not decided to come to the funeral.

'Bad karma,' she repeated. 'The killer tear him in pieces, you know. Big piece intestine shove into his mouth, lot of blood go away. You think someone drink his blood?'

'I don't know. I wasn't there.'

'Pete talk about you a lot,' she said. 'You come back tomorrow?'

'Tomorrow?'

'Oh, you don't know Thai custom. Funeral last many days. He lie in golden casket for a while, then on last day we burn him. Oh, monks finish praying now. Come on, we eat.'

A feast had been laid out alfresco in a courtyard under a plastic awning tied to three poles and a pagoda. It was as elaborate a banquet as Pete's family could concoct. A few aged aunts and spinster cousins stood ladling out platefuls of rice, curry, spicy salads, and sinister soups full of the *Alien*-like limbs of strange sea creatures. Pete's mother steered him toward a huge platter of *foi tong*. 'I know you have to go,' she said, 'but have some dessert. White people like this.' Distractedly she began spooning the golden strands of egg-sugar-pudding onto a paper plate. It was all starkly bourgeois, and it made Lauren long for the pretentious chit-chat and plentiful marijuana of one of Lady Chit's soirées.

'I'm not hungry,' he said, desperately looking for a way out. 'Please. Let me go and pay my respects to . . . him . . . again.'

Why could he not shake himself of the notion that he had witnessed Pete's death? Why were there so many holes in his memories of the past few months, for that matter? There had been a blind shaman . . . he remembered that . . . a car chase through the rain . . . what else?

He made his way back to the pavilion and knelt before the golden casket that contains Pete's remains – and tried to remember. All he could see, when he tried to look past the shaman, the teak house, the girl in the street . . . were images of pelting rain . . . eroding the bedrock of remembrance, washing his trauma into the sea.

magician

Lady Chit went straight up to the ajarn's hospital room on the third floor of Sumitivej hospital. No one stopped her; the third floor suite was permanently on hold for members of her family, in exchange for a generous allowance from the dead prince's estate.

The ajarn was not in very good shape. That night had almost killed him; assuredly he would be dead if somehow, impelled by the force that linked her to Angel Todd, she had not broken free of the protection of the *hong phra* and blindly driven the Porsche to she knew not where.

Lady Chit sat at his bedside and waited for a while. He was swathed in bandages and connected via IVs and electrodes to all sorts of high-tech devices. She did not even realize he was conscious until he whispered her name at last.

'Oh,' she said, 'I've brought you some orchids. I got them at Jetujak, got up at the crack, took my mother's car and her driver . . . it's a shame you can't—'

'But I *can*,' said Ajarn Sonthaya. 'I see them through your eyes. Even though my vision is dimming and soon I will be as blind within as I am to the outside world.'

She smiled, and it seemed to her that he knew she was smiling. 'It's all because of those damned elephants,' she said at last. 'I knew I had miscounted them. I should have known better than to perform a *kae bon* ceremony without counting the elephants at least three times.'

'The gods can be pernickety at times,' the spirit doctor said, phis laughter turning into an alarming cough.

'Don't talk if you don't—'

'I'll be fine. But you know, one is given only so much power in one's lifetime, and I'm afraid that mine is ebbing fast. The levitation, for instance . . . intellectually one knows it can be done, and in the works of the great masters you're always reading tales of such things . . . but perhaps those were simply more spiritual times . . . or else it's simply that ancient gurus are as full of shit as contemporary ones . . . oh, don't laugh, I've read them all, Eddy, Hubbard, Joseph Smith . . . charlatans to the last . . . as, indeed, am I. Be a dear now and turn the spiggot to your left a touch . . . it's Demerol, my dear, and they do so love to withhold it from an old man who isn't much longer for this world, as though it would make a shred of difference if I became addicted.'

'A charlatan?' Chit said. 'But – I've seen you become wholly possessed by the god Brahma – and when you turned the entire monsoon shower into holy water and drove the vampire into the perfume bottle—'

'Misdirection, dear Chit, only natural in a conjurer.'

'But you *did* capture Angel.'

'We are all captives of *sansara*. The world is an illusion – not just this world but even the thousand hells and thousand heavens where dwell race upon race of demon and angel – all are illusion – your friend is imprisoned in illusion too – and the grandest illusion of all is life – for we are all less than the fragments of a dream that has not been dreamed.'

'You sound like a textbook.'

'Perhaps . . . would you mind . . . just a little more Demerol?'

She obliged; the old man smiled; an anxious nurse peered in for a moment, then departed. 'But Ajarn,' said Chit, 'you wanted to give me something, didn't you?'

'In the tote bag.'

She reached into the bag, which hung over one of the bed-posts. It was like exploring another planet. She felt soft things, slimy things, furry things, smooth things, jagged things. A pebble with the skin of a serpent. An orange encrusted with spikes. Loose gummi-cloves. 'This stuff makes me queasy,' she confessed.

'Me too,' said the ajarn. 'Concentrate a little harder. Think: little vial of perfume, fake ivory.'

She saw it in her mind and abruptly was able to fish it out.

'Is he really inside?' she said.

'Yes. Like *Mae Nak Phrakhanong*, the demoness imprisoned in a bottle and tossed into the *klong*, the one there's a temple to on Soi 71. You'll know when you can let him out. But you must keep him close to you at all times. We did not capture him in order to kill him, but to keep him safe, and the world safe, until he is free to find himself.'

'I'll wear him around my neck then,' she said, 'right next to the Buddha.'

'That is good. There are times when he can almost feel what you once felt for him . . . just like remembering a past incarnation, you see. Where will you go next?'

'I'm supposed to meet PJ and Timmy Valentine in Europe. They're kicking off the tour in London, I think . . . and ending in Bangkok, at the new Panyasai Stadium. Lauren will probably come with me; he and PJ have a lot of business to discuss. They're all going to be getting rich off all this bloodshed, I'm afraid. It's one of those male bonding things.' She talked too fast, trying to skirt the subject.

'Good. It's all coming together for him. Soon there will be a big reunion . . . and then Angel Todd will finally understand what he must become, and he will acquire the courage to complete his transformation.'

She cupped the perfume bottle in her hand. It was an ugly, cheap thing; undoubtedly she would have to make up some reason to wear it, some spiritual thing, perhaps, to please her superstitious mother. She squeezed it in her palm. A coldness emanated from it . . . it was though it were trying to drain away all the warmth in her body. Perhaps she would have it encased in gold. Gold is warm, she thought, like the sun. I'll go down to one of the gold shops at the Zen shopping mall and have a locket thing made . . . that'll appease mother, too, she told herself.

In the meantime . . .

'Is there anything you need, Ajarn, anything at all?'

'Well, yes. As I've told you, I've really done my last bit of magic – at least in this life. I need to find someone to pass on my gift to. Perhaps, in your wanderings – I know you fly around the world at the drop of a hat – you might find a suitable candidate? I'll be able to die in peace then.'

He didn't speak for a while, and Lady Chit sat down in the leather armchair beside the bed, fingering the phial and thinking back on the night of the storm. The sight of Pete Singhasri, puking out his intestines in the rain. The boy vampire shaking, curdling into mist and funnelling into the bottle. The old man floating above the wheelchair, legs crossed, eyes spurting flame. Then running up the stairs. Seeing the woman drained of blood. Trying to catch Lauren's soul as it flitted helplessly in and out of the prostitute's bedroom window. At last, trapping the pool of shadow in a loop of *saisin* . . . tying it up and tossing it into the tote bag . . . calling the ambulance and the police from her cellular phone . . . wiping the bloodstains from the white phone, from the white fur upholstery of the car.

She still couldn't remember it all. But she knew that Lauren's memory was in even worse shape than her own. She would not blame him if he were to block the trauma from his mind forever.

The wound in her breast ached.

brushstrokes

It was almost dawn. Lauren McCandless woke with a start, as though from a nightmare. But he could recollect nothing from it at all. He sat up on the futon they had laid out for him in the Buddha room of the teak house. He reached over and turned on the floor lamp. Outside, the mosquitoes and the crickets and the frogs were serenading in the drizzle. But there was another sound too. A kind of howling. It was close by. He'd have sworn it was a wolf, but they don't have wolves wandering around downtown Bangkok. Elephants maybe, but not wolves.

Lauren realized he was shivering. The *hong phra* was not air-conditioned. He decided to go into the outer chamber. Maybe I can even get a little work done, he thought. And staggered down the corridor.

A lone halogen floor lamp illuminated his painting. The woman was unnervingly beautiful in death. What with the pelting of rain outside, the rain in the window of the painting seemed almost . . . yes . . . it was in motion . . . a trick of the light perhaps, the roving shadow of his arm over the translucent highlights of his lines of rain . . . patter . . . patter . . . patter . . . I'm psyching myself into the nuthouse, he thought. Shit, it wouldn't be the first time.

Was she breathing?

Fuck no! She's supposed to be dead!

The howling came again.

He looked up at visions of hell. Across a lake of fire, demons rowed a canoe using screaming women as oars. Two men were impaled on bristly cactuses. A child was skewered on a kebab stick, about to be devoured by a slavering, three-headed monster. And the Buddha looked on, inscrutable and utterly serene.

Were those the kind of eyes that Ajarn Sonthaya used to have? How was it that the eyes had been ripped out of the shaman's sockets? For the ajarn was not blind in the conventional way; he had gaping holes where his eyes should be. Had he torn his eyes out himself – *one by one*, as in the Tom Lehrer song? Perhaps in exchange for knowledge, like the Norse God Odin? Lauren knew that he was skirting the very edge of his trauma. But he remembered no more.

He painted.

There was a knock.

'Come in,' he said distractedly.

It did not occur to him that there was any danger. The estate was surrounded by high walls, and there was a night watchman on every gate. Perhaps it was Lady Chit herself, fighting insomnia in the wake of that bloody evening. Or a servant, seeing the light come on, bringing coffee or a stiff drink. They were good about these things in this household, almost militantly offensive to the needs of their guests.

But it was Pete Singhasri.

'Mind if I come in?' Pete said.

The halogen lamp shone brightly on the painting, but the rest of the room was dim. Pete stood in the doorway's shadow, and what little Lauren could see of his dead friend made him not want to switch on any more lights. Pete wore a policeman's uniform, but it was inside out. He leaned in the doorway oozing rheum from a dozen wounds.

'Oh, you wondering maybe about my uniform,' Pete said. 'It's a Thai custom, you see. The dead wear their clothes inside out and back to front. It shows that we're dead. If we gatecrash dinner party, everybody notice and they can call exorcist right away.'

'You're dead, you're fucking *dead*. Go away.'

'You invite me, my friend. You can't make me go away.'

'What do you want?'

'I'm a vampire, Lauren, and it's all your fault.'

'My fault?' What *had* happened that night?

'You don't remember anything, do you? It's so easy for you. Just push the memory in the closet, slam door, flush key. I'm a good man, Lauren, don't deserve this.'

'No . . . of course not.'

'I just doing my job, man. Girls dying all over Patpong. Nobody care, just prostitutes. But *I* care. I'm a good cop, my friend. I know there was dark force at work behind all this . . . I know you didn't kill them . . . but I know the answer locked up inside you somehow . . . and now I know all the answers . . . and they going to cremate me in three days . . . oh, my friend, this is hell!'

I'm not on drugs, Lauren thought. I've been sober for days, haven't even had a drink. This is fucking actually happening.

'That's right,' said Pete, as though he could hear his very thoughts, 'it fucking is. Look around you. These paintings of hell are nothing compared to what I going through now. I don't deserve this. You got to do something!'

'What *can* I do?' Lauren said.

It was all too surreal. Maybe I did have a drink after all. Maybe someone slipped peyote into my Pepsi. I ought to be scared but somehow I'm not. It's like I've been through all this before somehow, I don't know how. Something in those holes in my memory. 'Since I invited you in, maybe I should offer you something?'

'Yeah. You give me blood.'

'But then I'll become a vampire too . . . won't I?' said Lauren.

'I don't know, Lauren. They burning me soon. I'm standing at beginning of such big journey, and I only have three nights left to live. Help me, my friend, help me—'

Lauren woke with a start.

He must have had another nightmare. But he couldn't remember anything at all. There was a pounding on the door—

Lauren woke with a start. He must have had a nightmare. Nightmares within nightmares and yet he couldn't remember anything at all. He woke with a start. He woke. He woke.

Now it really was dawn. The smog-purpled morning was streaming through the mosquito-netted windows. The breeze bore the promise of more rain. Lauren crawled out toward the inferno chamber, where his painting waited. Had he added a few more brushstrokes in the night? Were the lips of the woman more pouting, more sensual, were the lines of rain more liquid and coruscating than before? He didn't remember.

But the bloody footprints on the teak floor . . .

He went to the foyer, picked up the phone to call the main house where Lady Chit had her suite.

'Lauren! Come out to the pavilion, they're setting up a delicious breakfast bar right now.'

'Chit,' he said, 'Chit, when are they burning Pete's body?'

'I don't know,' she said. 'A few days, maybe?'

'Will they really burn it? Will we see the actual body going up in flames?'

'Why do you ask?' said Chit.

'I don't know,' Lauren said.

'I do,' Lady Chit said softly.

fire

Her white Porsche emerged from the alley into a muddy parking lot next to the canal. The temple was across the water, and the pavilion where Pete's body lay was already on fire. The flames could barely be seen against the massy crimson of the sunset. Lady Chit emerged from the car. The air was scalding. After a few moments, Lauren McCandless stepped out. He was slugging his third Black Label of the evening; his flirtation with sobriety had been brief after all.

The clouds had been gathering and another downpour would come soon. But surely the arsonist's purpose would be accomplished before the nightfall. After that, it would not matter.

'This is all I could arrange,' she said. 'You can't monkey with someone's cremation schedule, and we can't risk your friend getting out of his box again.'

It had been in the morning news: a man attacked by an unseen creature right in front of the Sogo shopping mall, in the middle of the night – seen by dozens of people who described it variously as a rabid dog, a tiger, even, in one case, a policeman, though the news commentator suggested that that might be due to the fact that *Maniac Cop III*, a B feature about a zombie policeman, had been playing on the monitor of a video store in the mall. It hadn't been broad daylight, but downtown Bangkok does not get dark at night – its colours only become brasher, more brilliant. The man was drained of blood.

A Japanese tourist with a camcorder had caught the whole thing in *vérité* style, but the blur on the videotape gave no clue as to the creature's identity.

'Look, it seems complicated, but this way no one loses face. I hired an American – some ex-pat junkie desperate for cash – to do the arson, he's not a Buddhist so he doesn't feel that it's blasphemous. The family will be making a huge donation to the temple that will more than cover any damages. And Pete won't stalk the night anymore.'

Lauren watched the fire. The pavilion was a cheap thing, just wood and plaster and gilt. They would build a new pavilion of marble. Between them and the flames, children dived naked into the brackish water. A dog howled, but Chit felt nothing supernatural about it. A wrinkled old Chinese guava vendor peddled past them, and Chit was about to wave him away; but Lauren was abstractedly buying a bagful of the sweet-sour fruit, dipping it in the pink-dyed sugar and shoving it in his mouth as smoke poured from the windows and a crowd began to gather in the courtyard by the water, monks and temple children and packs of the stray dogs that infest every temple compound.

The flames rose higher. Red-hot ashes spackled the canal.

'It's beautiful,' Lauren said, and Chit felt that his appreciation of the spectacle was more than painterly. Lauren was always drawn toward darkness; that was why he was so successful and why he needed to be constantly watched over. 'But . . . aren't you just a little concerned about breaking laws . . . about upsetting the temple? Aren't you going a little far just to avoid having the Singhasri family lose face . . . or your own, for that matter?'

Lady Chit laughed a little. 'I hardly expected that *you*, of all people, would come at me with this bourgeois protestant morality stuff,' she said. 'This isn't America, and this is how we're going to take care of this problem.'

'You've changed,' Lauren said. 'You weren't so, I don't know, *hard* before.'

'Maybe I'm becoming too much like my grandfather,' she said. As they watched, the roof of the pavilion collapsed and the sun disappeared beneath the horizon. Sparks danced in the neon dusk. *Hard?* she thought. Hard, me? Things aren't that simple, even in America, where everyone thinks you can send in the cavalry.

'Look!' Lauren shouted. 'The fire department's finally managed to show up . . . only twenty minutes, and rush hour down Sukhumvit at that . . .' It was true. One puny firetruck had turned up, and some of the monks were directing the onlookers to move further away.

Then, suddenly, it rained. She was glad the burning had been timed that way. There would not be much damage, and no one would be hurt, and it would all come right in the end . . . wouldn't it?

Maybe I'm becoming too much like my grandfather . . .

When had *that* started to happen? At the moment that her

grandfather's spirit, transformed into a ghastly monster by the black arts of a New Age sorceress, had finally been released back into the cycle of rebirth? Would Chit have so calmly and coldly figured out this stratagem to keep all the factions at bay? Would the old Lady Chit have nonchalantly picked up the phone, called up an uncle in the police department and a junkie at the Foreign Correspondents' Club . . . and arranged acts of arson, cover-up, and bribery? Prince Prathna would have, of course, before breakfast, not brooking more than a momentary distraction from his kippers and toast. Have I really become like that? she thought, as she backed away towards the Porsche to seek shelter from the storm.

Between her breasts, the demon in the bottle burned.

Part II

THE CAPTIVE ANGEL

Lips are for tellin'
Lips are for kissin'
Lips are for lovin'
But hearts are for dissin'

Hearts are for achin'
Hearts are for healin'
Hearts are for breakin'
But souls are for stealin'

Timmy Valentine

10

LADY CHIT'S DREAM

flying

Night over Asia: she was overcome by drowsiness yet could not sleep for a long time, even though there was no one in the first-class cabin with her. Lauren was supposed to have come with her, but after the conflagration at the temple he had gone into a deep depression; he hadn't even been able to work on the painting of the dead whore standing in the window in the rain.

Now and then a stewardess shuffled past her aisle seat, poured her another glass of that insipid airline Beaujolais; Lady Chit had one eye on the movie – it was *Schindler's List* – while in her earphones thrummed an easy listening adaptation of *Vampire Junction*. The cognitive dissonance did not inspire sleep. Nor did the dull ache in her breast, where the gash left by Angel Todd's bite had never entirely healed. It pained her now as she leaned back in the great leather seat and toyed with the controls of the stereo, switching from Pavarotti to k.d. lang to Kurt Cobain to Tori Amos and (by a sudden flick of the wrist) back to the familiar strains of Timmy Valentine.

It was disorienting to watch women being gassed in black and white while listening to the saccharine harmonies of Timmy's early music, the songs she'd loved as a teenager back in the New Wave days. Then she remembered that Timmy had once told her that he too had been gassed once, in Auschwitz, because they thought he was a gipsy . . . though he had not, of course, been killed, since he had not yet achieved mortality.

A pang in her breast; not dull like all the others, but sharp, urgent; she was reliving it, the fang penetrating the soft skin.

She touched herself through the silk of her blouse. It was throbbing, definitely throbbing, and with each throb a stab of pain. She reached in her purse for a Valium. Flying west, the nights are longer anyway, she thought, and now this.

As she groped in her purse, she came upon the perfume phial . . .

Why did I bring the damn thing with me anyway? she thought. Even though the ajarn had told her to wear it next to her skin, she had disobeyed him after the first couple of nights of sleeplessness . . . she had tossed and turned and heard at her window a sound like the beating of great wings. And she had turned to her dwindling supply of Halcion and Valium to get her through the night.

But she couldn't throw it out either. After all, it contained . . . could you really call it a soul, when a vampire has no soul? But it was some kind of essence, some part of what had once been Angel Todd.

She was looking at it again now. She was shaking though there was no turbulence and the sky outside the window was clear and cloudless and studded with stars. You could not see the original *faux* ivory; she had had it encased in silver down at the mall, and the ajarn had bound it tighter with a mantra of entrapment. It was warm to the touch. She could feel pressure against her palm . . . like a caterpillar in a jumping bean . . . like a baby kicking in the womb.

Then she heard the whisper in her mind:

Please don't put me away I need to feel you I need to touch your skin I need you I want you I need you to feel me

She put the phial down quickly.

It plunked into the airline Beaujolais, and the red wine fizzed a little.

I know, she thought, you 'nevairrr drink . . . wine.'

She fished it out and dried it off and popped one more Valium. This time it better damn well work, she thought. And it did.

Except that, stirring a little, an hour or so later, she felt an unwonted weight around her neck, a hunk of hot metal wedged against her breast, the stickiness from her once-more oozing stigma . . .

Then she fell . . . no, rather, she plummeted headlong into
sleep, a deeper, darker sleep than she had experienced in many
months . . . and, sleeping, she saw Angel Todd once again . . .
just as she had last seen him . . . on the threshold of undeath
. . . waiting.

dreaming

Listen to me. Listen. Listen.
Another time. Another soul.
You have to listen to me because you're the one who caged
me inside silver and imitation ivory. All that I am is in here until
you set me free. Bitch! You tricked me. I needed you and you
fucking tricked me. I came to you because I thought you'd
understand. In a way, you *do* understand. That's why you got
me here with you. I've touched the inside of you and your blood
is in me and I know that even though you're afraid of me there's
a part of you that loves me now with a love that's buried so
deep inside you it's like a dead body festering in a grave. That's
me. I'm your angel, your evil angel.
In this phial there's no time and no space. Everything that
ever happened to me is happening again, all at the same time.
I want you to see it with me. That's why I'm sending deep into
your dreams. So you'll see. So you'll believe. So you'll know
why you're going to set me free.
Look! Look! It's the moment of my becoming.
Look again! See me without seeing. Touch me without
touching.

vampire junction

You can say that life is a journey on a choo-choo train where
you can't choose where to get on or off. You can't pick first class
or baggage train or squatting in the tender with the coal dust
choking you. You can say that every life is a train trip. But most
lives don't pass through Vampire Junction.
Most lives, when they end, they go into a tunnel and they

never come out. The tunnels don't go nowhere and they don't end, they just, you know, they're just tunnels. But you know that me and some of my friends have been through the tunnel and came out the other side only we weren't the same no more. Think back. We were all caught up in the big dream together . . . you and me and Timmy and Brian and Petra and many of our friends . . . and then we were on the train . . . and one by one, you all got off . . . you went back to the real world. And finally there's only me, and Brian and Petra, and they're the ones that truly love me, and we're all like some kind of satanic version of Mary and Joseph and Jesus, you know. They want to nurture me. They're ready to throw away their humanness and go with me. It's a awesome feeling. They're hovering over me. They cocoon me from the darkness as we start trundling into that big old tunnel. They shelter me with their bodies and I don't have to look out of the window at the great black nothing that is all that the tunnel is.

And the tunnel goes on and on and on and I'm scared shitless at first even though this is what I chose to be, what I've always longed for. But it's not the way I imagined it, no way. I'm all thinking: This is it, I've ditched my life and I'm gonna start over as a vampire and it'll all be one long party . . . yeah, I saw *Lost Boys* and after I met Timmy Valentine I knew that wasn't all there was to being a vampire but I guess I still had this party feeling about going down into the darkness, but then it's like it goes on and on and on and time stands still and it ain't just the darkness and the loneliness but shit it's *boring* too, just moving on and on . . . and I'm starting to think . . . maybe there is no light . . . maybe there is no end to this. Maybe my death is just a plain-wrap death like any other death, a death that goes on forever.

Brian comforts me and Petra hugs me . . . but you know . . . I don't feel nothing. I can barely hear them talking. I hide myself inside them.

And then one day . . . can't really say *one day* 'cause there ain't no day here . . . I start to dig my way out. It's because of the hunger that started when I first began this journey . . . it started as a tingling feeling, like the prick of a painkiller injection . . . but now it's a huge and overwhelming thing that screams in my mind and doesn't let me think and all I want to do is make it go away but it gets bigger and bigger and finally it's as big as the blackness I'm travelling through . . . and I try to hold it in but at last it snaps and I don't know what I'm doing, I have to devour something, I don't know what, I feed and feed and feed and feed and then, suddenly, all at once, the train . . .

. . . has burst through the darkness and around me's all like, cornfields and shit . . . a sea of silver under the moonlit sky. And the hunger has popped . . . kind of like a zit . . . and I'm all peaceful again . . . all peaceful . . . and then I look around for Brian and Petra . . . and the train rattles as it curves along the bank of a gleaming river . . . I hear the train . . . I hear the crickets . . . I even hear the corn push up oh god so slowly through the packed dung and mud . . . but I don't hear Brian and Petra . . . until I understand that when they enveloped me with their love and protection it wasn't just *like* a cocoon, it was a cocoon . . . I ate my way out . . . by being born I had to devour . . . first the ones who loved me most and then myself . . . my own flesh . . . my own soul . . . I had to remake myself . . . in a new image . . . not life, but life's mirror . . . not death, but something deeper . . . oh God it scares me shitless because now I'm no one and I'm just this lost kid sitting on a train going to shit knows where and the train don't even have a train driver because the train is me, my life, my death, taking me to places no kid should ever see . . . oh Jesus I think I'm gonna cry and then guess what I fucking can't, I can't cry anymore and I can't even remember how the hot tears used to feel on my cheeks like, when my mother touched me under the sheets with her breath smelling of liquor like, when I couldn't get the song right and I thought they were going to kill me like, when I saw my brother lowered into the green earth like, when I begged Timmy Valentine to steal my soul away.

Don't even know if I'll ever get off this train . . . don't even know if I'll ever stand on something that ain't vibrating and clanging. We're whipping through station after station too fast to read their names. One time I think I see my mother standing in a churchyard but no, it's some other woman in a nightdress with one foot in, one out of a half-dug grave, and another time

I see couple other people I know they're really dead I mean like, people I sort of knew on the movie set when it was burning down.

The whistle and the brakes: screaming.

We stop.

I can smell my native earth.

It's Hangman's Holler.

love and death

I start walking and after I while I figure I don't have to walk. I kind of let go and the wind half drags me, half embraces me. The wind is even inside me because the stuff I'm made of ain't flesh exactly . . . it's the fabric of people's nightmares. People believe in me. That's why I'm real. Timmy told me that once. 'You'll be an archetype,' he said. Whatever the fuck that is. He's had two thousand years of book-learning and I'm just a dumb hick that happens to be the spitting image of him.

OK so I feel myself kind of half melting letting the wind and me take up the same space because I'm not totally *in* this space at all . . . and I drift. Hangman's Holler. Floating uphill. The grass is black in the moonlight and it's swimming in dew. I know where I'm going I guess. Past the church where Damien Peters used to preach before he got himself the fancy Bible-banging empire. Past Mr Flagstad's general store with its broken pane that ain't been fixed all of my life. Oh yeah. I'm not alive no more. Wooden houses with beat up pickups parked alongside lean-to mailboxes. Fences that trail off nowheres, weeds strutting up through broken concrete. I know this place so fucking well it would hurt if I could feel hurt.

The house on the hill: abandoned. Broken windows and the wind's blowing. We left that house when we drove out west and we never looked back and we never even locked it up 'cause there's nothing in it a body'd want to steal. Shit, it hasn't changed none, except for wasting away from not being tended to.

There's the hillock where we buried my twin brother Errol. Because only one of us could survive. 'The two of you'd have been the death of me,' my momma said to me once. And then we never spoke about it again.

I listen.

There's a rat running around the mattress of the old bed I used to lay in. There's cockroaches shuffling in the walls. I can hear them. I can hear Mr Flagstad grunting in his sleep. I can hear Mrs Flagstad snoring. There's a cat curling up in a trash can lid somewheres, a slick lick, tongue across fur.

That's when I understand that I can *really* hear now, hear for the first time. To be human is to be colour-blind to the billion hues of sound. Behind the crickets, behind the groping under cotton sheets, I hear the grass grow . . . a deep sighing that's the bass note of the big old thundering chord that's echoing in the wet wind . . . too deep for a human to grasp . . . and I know that if you can't hear the bass note, what's holding up the music? It's just noise. The music of mortals is just a mote of harmony struggling to stay alive in a humungous sea of discord. *They don't hear the music!* I'm telling myself. And that's the first discovery about what's changed for me.

Now I'm listening to the music for the first time.

And I understand a lot of shit I never understood before too. Like in Timmy's songs, sometimes there'd seem to be like, a missing piece, a hole in the texture . . . part of what *Rolling Stone* called a 'wayward eccentricity of structure'. But now I see that those are holes for hearing the echo of the universe . . . not just the grass growing and the whispering wind but even things that make no sound, like the planets hurtling through the empty spaces and the galaxies exploding a jillion light years away . . . if only you have ears to hear, you can know that every one of them songs has got like a piece of the life and death of the whole frigging universe in it. So now I know what Timmy's music was really about.

It ought to take my breath away but I don't breathe no more.

That's when I hear my name

You a angel

on the wind, coming from uphill somewheres . . . and I know whose voice it is, calling for me out of the human past. It's Becky Slade. She used to say that to me . . . *you a angel Angel* . . . the only black girl in my homeroom at Col Sinclair Junior

High . . . it's the same voice again maybe a little huskier maybe not and the only difference is I can hear it carried on the night wind and it's coming from further uphill, further than a human can hear. Maybe this is why the train has left me here, so I can start off at the same place where I started in my human life. Maybe I have to revisit my old life before I can start again. Or maybe it's just that the old place still clings to me . . . like the earth sticks to your skin when you're climbing out of a fresh-dug grave.

There's a barn where me and Becky used to go sometimes and that's where we went when she wanted to show me what she looks like when she's naked. And she wanted to see me too. That place where she showed me what a boy can do to a girl except that I'd already learned it from my mother . . .

You a angel!

She's there in that secret place and I ain't and I don't rightly know how I feel about that. No one was supposed to know about that place. The wind howls. I start to lope uphill and soon I'm more flying than walking because my body is shifting shape so it'll be more streamlined in the wind . . . what am I now? A bat, a raven? I don't know except that the wind picks me up and when I spread my arms I catch the moonlight, my feathers glisten, I tumble along the currents of the air.

angel

and yes, I'm black. I'm beautiful. I sweep. I soar. I screech and wheel across the silver moon

angel

hearing her tart voice, a raven, ravening. She's saying, *I use to come here with Angel you know the one he use to be called Angel but now he's Timmy Valentine. Ain't bullshitting you. At the Oscars. You watch them Oscars didn't you? but he wasn't just a movie star he was something special to me, the onliest boy that didn't call me nigger to my face. And we use to come here to this barn and he touched me, don't be getting jealous now, there wasn't much to it he was so ignorant about what to do, like a little child and all, sleep ever' single night in the same bed with his momma, I think she made him all twisted up inside wrapped him up inside of her fat flesh made it so he couldn't even you know, pop a boner, he shrivelled up inside when I tried to . . . he like a little snail coiling back up inside his shell, and I say to him, Are you afraid? Well when you bigger, when you not afraid no more, you come back and see Becky Slade and she jump your bones, baby. And you know what, I think he scared. Then I watch him on them Oscars and was almost like he wasn't the same person no more. He look right out at me from inside of the television set and I look into his eyes and I think, this ain't the same Angel Todd no more. I done lost him. He still a boy but not the boy I play with in the barn not the boy I said to him You a angel Angel.*

Then there's another voice. *Don't talk about that bullshit baby.*

Whose voice? I can't tell but it trips the rhythm of my flying and now I'm falling out of the sky like a stone, now suddenly I'm in a closed space, the smell of cowshit, dry grass, old wood, peeling paint, must have just funnelled in through the cracks in the walls, and I'm perched in the rafters of a big old barn and I see her from way up, see her eyes first, two polished smoky quartzes in that gloom.

Angel she says but not to me.

The boy that's with her, tall slender black glistening with his pants around his ankles, don't talk much, just touching her. Don't like the way he smells, don't like his musky sweat, 'cause I smell every hormone that's racing through his blood, know he's young and all he can think about is pounding that bitch till he comes, not paying her no mind at all except like a piece of meat.

And so I'm spreading my wings again, sending the straw flying from the roof beams, wavery raven shadow over their heads, but I reach a pool of shadow just beyond where they're sitting and I can't go no further. It's like battering against a force field. In a moment I understand why. It's the invitation thing. Gotta be invited. I should know that from all the fucking vampire movies I seen when I was alive.

But I gotta talk to her. She's gotta know that he's just using her up, she's nothing more than prey to him, all he wants is to suck her dry, just like, just like—

A vampire.

I flap and flap against the penumbra of hay. But she won't know it's me unless I—

Change. Transform. Flow outward, fill the shadow air with the image of what I used to be.

Angel!

And she's seen me, no she's seen an image kindled by her memories: me, twelve years old, torn jeans, muddy blond hair, big eyes; I'm standing at the edge of the force field and when she calls my name, the way she calls me with that faint promise of an invitation is enough to make the force field start to thaw and I can feel it soften and I'm swimming through like a bee through honey; and the boy looks up and sees no one because he has no image to fasten onto; but Becky looks at me and her brown eyes fill with longing and I know that I'm the onliest one she truly loved and that fills me with, I don't know, the ghost of a long-dead feeling; and she says to the boy, 'Look. He came back after all. Maybe I didn't lose him. Maybe Angel remember Becky Slade.'

'Let me come to you,' I say. Knowing the words are double-edged and they can never be free from deceit, because I don't have a soul no more, and I can't love.

'Come,' she says. And the barrier shatters and I'm standing right there. Becky on my right leaning against a pile of straw, the dude on my left, pulling up his boxers.

'Come and get me, motherfucker,' he says, and puts up his fists.

'Angel,' says Becky. For a moment I think I'm feeling what it was like to be a human being, to have my blood flushing my cheeks, my heart pounding, my dick getting all hard and then that feeling fades away and all I'm left with is that yawning hunger and I don't know what to do and I say, 'Becky, get away from me,' and she says, with kind of a half-smile in her voice, 'Why Angel, you become so high and mighty now that you rich? Did you think I was going to wait for you?' and I don't have an answer for her. I want to hold my memories but they are crumbling to dust. There's only the hunger. I don't even hear what she's saying.

The tall black dude slams his fists into my chest but I make myself hard, like eternity. His hands shatter. He screams. Blood sprays my face. It reddens the pallor of my cheeks and I can taste it on my lips and now the hunger's really driving me and I can't help myself no more, I just kind of surround him and swallow him up and spit him out, a desiccated sack of skin and bone, and all his blood just kind of sponges into me, not just through my fangs but nostrils, my eyes, even the pores of my skin . . . all at once dude, all at once, it's almost too much for me to take . . . my eyes redden. I look like a movie vampire now with the gore dribbling from the corners of my lips. And you know Becky just looks up and doesn't speak and it's like she's been waiting for this moment all her life. Doesn't she understand them memories mean nothing no more? What does she see when she looks at me? Timmy used to tell me that people see the things they're most afraid of. But she don't seem frightened.

She crosses over to me. She's naked and dark as the night. She hasn't grown much. Her breasts are shallow and her hips still narrow. There's only one naked bulb swaying over the piles of straw. She smells of her boyfriend's armpits. But beneath that smell there's the sweet odour of her baby blood. She tramples the dead boy's limp skin. It's like he never existed. She looks into my eyes and she says, 'I always knew you was an angel, Angel.'

'I'm not an angel, Becky. I'm . . . a monster.'

'Monsters don't be beautiful like you.'

'Ain't beautiful inside, Becky. Not any more. Something happened to me. You don't know how much I wanted to get away from my life . . . momma choking the life out of me in that sweaty bed . . . a life where everything was just pretend. I could hear Errol, my twin brother, calling to me every night out of the dead earth, and I wanted to be like Timmy Valentine because no one could hurt him and he was for ever. But it turned out he wanted to be me. So we became each other. Except . . . I guess it didn't work. Not all the way. Don't come near me, Becky, I'm a vampire.'

'Bullshit. You think you the only one who wants to get away. You think you the only one that get hisself shit on. It a thousand times worse for me. You got out of this fucking town. You got yourself money and fame. Becky Slade, she stay here. Nothing to look forward to in Hangman's Holler, Angel Todd, nothing but growing old and dying.'

And she's saying these words and damn it she's still so fucking young but her eyes are as old as Timmy Valentine's; and I know that I've come for her, that I am her hope and her redemption; and I know that her hope and her redemption are false.

But she takes one more step toward me. Jesus I can smell her blood. It smells of the grave. Already.

'Fuck me,' Becky Slade says. 'You always wanted to and then you thought about your momma and you couldn't get hard, don't think I didn't know, everyone at school talked about how you and Marjorie slept in the same bed and shit, don't you be thinking it a dark secret like inside a romance book. Now she's dead and you can.'

'But I'm dead too.'

'Then if you can't fuck me, do whatever it is you do. Kill me, I don't give a shit. Pop me with a straw and suck the grape juice out of me, 'cause I don't want to be Becky Slade no more.'

And we're both standing on the dead boy. I crush his skull with my heel and grind his bones into the floor planks, and the naked light bulb swings in a little circle, and she puts her arms around me and I see that to her I'm intense and burning cold and hard and full of passion but to me she is, I don't know, nothing more than the ghost of long-dead feelings and yes there is the blood that rushes through her roaring like whitewater like a cataract like the rapids in the hills behind the house where my mother took me into her sagging body and lowered my dead brother into the ground and swallowed pills like handfuls of M&Ms and all those memories are in the screaming of her blood because her blood is a thread that ties me to that past I've tried so hard to escape except that there is no escape because the past I hate so much has inside of it all the things I remember how to love. I didn't mind killing the other one, he didn't mean nothing to me, you know, but killing Becky Slade is what would have been making love for me if I was still alive. I guess I never got to make love, really. I only fucked. I mean, was fucked. Now I am making love for the first time. First a gentle pinprick in the fingertip, just a couple drops squeezed from the capillaries, silky on my tongue, then I'm probing a little further, biting into the arm, sending an icy pleasure shuddering through her, feeling the pulse quicken against my quivering teeth, then all the way up the arm, the two tiny holes on either side of the jugular, not quite piercing it because she doesn't want to die

right away, she wants to go on looking at me, drinking death
out of my eyes, and so I'm moving in and out of her, not in
some vulgar human way, dick in cunt, nothing so dirty, just
my lips and my tongue teasing the dark blood out of her, well
at first it's just teasing but then I start to suck harder and she
feels how urgently I need her and she thrusts hard against me
and I feel her dusky flesh against me and I feel the heartbeats
pounding and I reach through the flesh, invade the thousand-
branching web of vein and artery, I go inside of her, not just
the womb but all of her and at the centre of her there is the
heart and it shivers as I rip the ribcage open and part the lungs
and there it is, still pumping, but more weakly now because the
pleasure is too much for her . . . I bury my face inside her flesh
and the blood sluices from her, splashes my cheeks . . . I'm
snorting blood, blood is running in my ears, in the space
between my eyeballs and their sockets, pouring down my throat
. . . and for a moment I'm glimpsing, dimly, what it's like to be
loved.

But the glimpse is fading.

Too soon, she's dead, and again I'm left with nothing.

Another emptiness. Another yearning.

I don't know what to do now. I've heard that I can make
other vampires. But that gets complicated, don't it? I decide I'm
just gonna burn down the barn. So I do that, and I fly into the
night.

flying

Spiralling upward into the air now. It feels good, I think. Mostly
I hear the wind but underneath I can hear Hangman's Holler
sleeping. I see all the people living their dollhouse lives. Even
my own house seems like one of those HO scale model Appa-
lachian houses in Timmy Valentine's infinite train layout.

Look, there's the knoll where Errol's buried. There's a circlet
of little trees that Momma had planted there when we got our
first big cheque from Stupendous Entertainment. I remember I
used to put my ear to the earth and think I could hear him call
to me in his baby voice. The voice was echoey, you know, that

Poltergeist sound effect, someone in the studio showed me how they do that, run it through a digital box, human in, ghost out . . . it's wild.

Suddenly I want to do that again, so I plummet down out of the sky, bird of prey now, beak out, wings unfurled against the silvery moon . . . I'm *bad*, dude, I'm *down*, that's how they made me talk in Hollywood, *lose that Kentucky twang or we'll lose the market share* . . . Now I'm on the ground, morphing to human form just when my claws collide with grass and stone.

The grass is tall here. It's like it was sucking extra chemicals out of the soil, organic fertilizer I guess. I know Errol's body must have been consumed a long time ago but maybe there's something still here, some piece of him, hovering around the place Momma put him.

I put my ear to the earth.

And you know . . . I can hear so fucking much, the itty-bitty earthworms chomping the soil and shitting it back out as they burrow, the crickets rubbing their legs together . . . but I can't hear my brother.

What's wrong? There was always something. Yeah, my imagination, my right brain, something, calling to me. Maybe it's because I don't have an imagination no more. I'm an imagined thing myself. I'm only real because so many people have watched so many vampire movies and made me into a true thing. I can't imagine. I can't dream.

Or maybe . . . it's because life and death are linked together, flowing in and out of each other, a big old circle like PJ would say . . . and so the living can hear an echo of the dead, and the dead can whisper in the ears of the living . . . but what about me? I ain't alive and I ain't dead. I'm not part of the great cycle of infinity. I got through the cracks.

Yeah. It's all dawning on me now. Just how alone I am. Jesus is this what I bargained for prayed for exchanged souls with a vampire for? The hunger's still there. The boy I killed satisfied it for only a split second . . . Becky Slade a bit longer, because she was someone who used to feel for me when I was still alive. But now it's all come back. It will never go away. There used to be a whole rainbow of emotions and now there's only one.

Errol! My scream is the cry of a vulture. But there's no carrion to feed on. Feverishly I'm clawing up the soil because I want to know if there's even a little piece of my family I can cling to. But there isn't. I can't even trust my memory. I'm not even sure if Errol ever lived, or if it's just a thing I saw in a mirror once, a fucked-up reflection of myself.

The emotions have gone from colour to black-and-white.

No, it's worse than that. It's like the whole universe has become one humungous motherfucking video that I'm trapped in . . . some virtual reality thing . . . and everything I touch, taste, smell is hyper-vivid because it's all electronically pumped up and colour-jazzed and juiced up with mega-intensities but . . . but . . . I still don't *really* touch, taste, smell . . . no . . . I don't feel a fucking thing . . . nothing, nothing . . . only the hunger.

flying

The airplane was going through some kind of turbulence. Lady Chit stirred. A pang went through her chest and she saw that there was a small, dark, bloody stain where her bra had become plastered to the wound in her breast.

Please, came a still, small voice in the back of her head. *Please, please, release me.*

She ransacked her purse and finally managed to dig out one last dusty Valium. She swallowed it, and the rest of her wine, and once more tumbled down the well of nightmares . . .

And still it was night over Asia; flying westward, time stretches; a night can seem forever.

11

The Magic Flute

shadows

She was lying in wait for him all day long. She had camped out
for a whole night, been the first in line to buy tickets, and now
she was determined to see him.

Getting past the guards had been simple enough. She was a
slender girl, all in black. She had smiled at one of the guards,
disarmed him, spun daintily into the shadow of a *faux* Ionic
column.

She *had* to see him! It was the only thing that could validate
her life. The daydreams. The nightmares. Blood, blood, blood.
If he won't talk to me, won't tell me what I know he must tell
me, I think I'll just die.

Everything was ready. Everything she was going to do and
say she had rehearsed in front of the bathroom mirror, over and
over, until she had got it right.

And if I *really* get it right, she thought, I'll never have to look
in a mirror again . . . I'll never have to see myself . . . I'll never
cast another reflection, another shadow.

concert

What city was this now? Oh yes. Somewhere in Germany. Ham-
burg, Heidelberg, some kind of burg or berg or bourg . . .
couldn't fucking tell anymore. The song was in a new hard-
edged style, 'as though the harmonic subtleties of The Cure had
been cross-pollinated with Kurt Cobain's death rattle'. Not an

original observation, Timmy thought grimly, but a direct quote from some critic in the *LA Weekly*.

Didn't have much time to think. Shattering glass synth pads welled and wallowed around him. It had been PJ's idea to put in the long interlude section to give Timmy's throat time to recover between the two halves of the song, both orgies of shrieking. The words were inchoate; often as not he sang no lyrics at all or bawled out in stream-of-consciousness; this night in the first stanza he had suddenly found himself screeching in German:

> *Der Hölle Rache kocht in meinem Herzen*
> The rage of hell is cooking in my heart
> Death and despair!

and he knew them to be lyrics from a former life . . . hadn't he once been a boy soprano, and hadn't he performed in *The Magic Flute* right on this spot? *Thauberg*, he remembered. This place used to be the opera house. They must have levelled it to build this . . . monstrosity.

The crowd went crazy hearing him yelling in German and knowing the words so well – even the teenagers of the '90s knew *The Magic Flute*, harder to get away from culture in this place – laughing and applauding but never really hearing the meaning of those words . . . the flaming heart . . . the despair . . . *death*. There wasn't much of a crowd anyway. Not like in the old days. But what there was was decked out in full Neo-Gothic regalia. The hair. The androgynous black clothes. Stigmata were popular this year, and many of the crowd were proudly waving their hands and showing palms pierced with silver nails, just like on the cover of the CD single *Crucify Me Twice*.

The breakstrain segued into the final stanza. Timmy sang. He leaped over keyboards, danced in a strobing white-hot flame, belted out lyrics that had little meaning save to the fans themselves, who shrieked, wailed, slamdanced in the aisles, and finally gave an almighty shout when the black coffin lowered itself from the flies and swallowed him up whole and sent him spiralling into the trapdoor, down the chute, through the drapes and into the relative tranquillity of his subterranean dressing room.

He was able to breathe easy for only a few minutes. He could hear the thunder of stomping feet from upstairs. The closing bars of the song were still pounding away. He took a sip of the Diet Coke on the coffee table, sat back on the frayed couch, stared at the wall and the poster of himself, Schindlerian black-and-white, arms outstretched, one palm sporting the ever-popular silver nail, the black blood dripping onto the logo which read

TIMMY VALENTINE ## *VICTORY TOUR*

Quite a poster, he thought. Quite a concert. Maybe attendance wasn't all it could have been, but . . .

A hand reached out and touched his shoulder.

He started, turned, reached behind the couch, and grabbed two hands, pulled her up. 'Who are you? How did you get in?'

It was a girl. Teens. Long hair, dyed jet-black, face whitened, dark circles painted around the eyes; a silver nose ring and a silver bolt penetrating the skin above her right eyebrow. At least her hands didn't have holes in them. Just a tattooed nail wound in the centre of each palm. A fan, then. Not an obtrusive one like the many who had thrust themselves at him on his way to the theatre – one had even thrown herself on the cobblestones in front of his limousine, yes, they still had cobblestones in Thauberg, and they'd had to bus in the fans or there wouldn't have been anywhere to park in those touristy mediaeval streets – no, this one was a little different. For one thing, she had baked him a pie. She put the box down on the coffee table and opened it, and she smiled, sadly perhaps.

'I heard it was your birthday,' she said. 'I hope you like it.'

'It's not my birthday,' Timmy said. 'My birthday is whatever *Teen Beat* decides it is. But I don't think anyone's been saying it's my birthday. I think you're just using it as an excuse. Actually, I don't even have a birthday. I don't even have a life.'

'Why so bitter? Look . . .'

The pie was shaped like a coffin, and when you broke open the crust there was a marzipan Timmy Valentine inside, all dressed up in a black tuxedo, floating in a thick cherry sauce

. . . 'The blood,' said the girl. 'My name is Pamina. Like in *The Magic Flute.*'

'It's a nice pie. But—' He didn't want to tell her he just had no time, that he was dead tired and needed to sleep. Big stars don't need to sleep, after all. They have to be turned on all the time, for their fans to worship at any hour of the day. Perhaps she expected sex. If only she knew.

'Pamina Rothstein,' she said. 'Does that ring a bell? Surely the name *Rothstein* . . .' Timmy shook his head at first.

But she looked at him with purple eyes . . . gotta be contacts, Timmy thought . . . no eyes are really that colour, like deep, polished amethysts. Why did she suddenly look so familiar? There was a time when Timmy did not experience time at all, when everything that had ever happened to him was as freely retrievable as the ones and zeroes of a CD-ROM, but now there was too much past to cram into the brain of an adolescent boy. What fragment of his vampire past did those eyes bring back? There was something about this place . . . the spanking new auditorium rising from the husks of the opera house . . . this girl was the same way . . . something old in a shiny new package.

The intercom buzzed and it was PJ. 'Are you going to be OK, Timmy?' he was saying. 'I'm going to the airport to pick up Chit.'

'I'll make it to the hotel by myself somehow,' Timmy said. 'Hey, tell them to bring us, I don't know, champagne or something. Apparently it's my birthday.'

'You don't *have* a birthday,' said PJ. 'Don't tell me . . . a groupie.'

Timmy laughed and signed off.

'Perhaps this photograph will jog your memory,' Pamina said.

The picture had been slipped underneath the pastry. She pulled it out now. Timmy was already digging into the cherry gore and nibbling on his own candied head. He craved sugar . . . it was almost like the old thirst for blood. Perhaps, he thought, a vampire is just the dead version of a diabetic. He laughed again, to himself.

'You're not quite as bitter anymore,' she said. 'Your moods change suddenly, just like that. It's nice. The cherry sauce on your lips is like a bloodstain. It's becoming. I use cherries myself,

before I go out at night.' They were speaking German . . .
Timmy had begun to speak the language spontaneously as soon
as they had set foot in Frankfurt airport. 'Maybe now, looking at this photograph, your mood will change again.'

It was a picture of Timmy Valentine.

Frayed, sepia. Made up, the face ghostly, the lips dark; the
costume was vaguely Egyptian, the demeanour solemn. Standing next to him was a stately woman in a white robe. She was
heavily made up – stage makeup, obviously – again in the Egyptian style, with kohled eyes and an elaborately coiffed wig.
Timmy remembered—

Shall I lap it up? Like a cat?

The taste of sour, stale blood against a woman's pubes—

'It really *is* you, isn't it? I can tell by the way you're staring
at it. And that's my aunt, you know. Amelia Rothstein, the
well-known soprano. She gave her last performances ten years
ago . . . *Bluebeard's Castle*. Well, she had become a mezzo by
then. But you really knew her, didn't you? That photograph
was taken in 1947.'

'I—'

'Don't worry. You're practically family. And this is a family
secret. Aunt Amelia lives in a nursing home now, but when she
came to visit us in Goldbach last week, and she saw your poster
on the wall, she practically had a heart attack. But then, over
coffee and *käsetorte*, she trotted out this frayed old photograph,
and she said to me, "Give little Konrad my love." That was
your name in those days, wasn't it? Konrad Stolz.'

Timmy didn't answer her. The truth was that he could hardly
remember Amelia Rothstein. He was only able to dredge up a
few scattered images. Opera, yes . . . he'd sung here in Thauberg before . . . the little shepherd in *Tosca* . . . or was it the
child Yniold in Debussy's *Pélleas*? And there'd been that woman.
Shapeshifting. A little black cat that slithered beneath her skirts.
Amelia Rothstein: a young singer, curiously perverse. They had
loved each other. Yes. Insofar as love was possible between
members of different species.

'When I saw the picture I immediately knew what was going
on. There's so much I want to ask you . . . how do you manage
to make yourself disappear, especially whenever you become

too famous, too visible . . . how you go about creating a new identity for yourself . . . how you can keep your bank accounts and things like that going even when you have to become someone else before too many people start to notice that you never age . . .'

'I don't want to talk about these things,' Timmy said. 'It's all behind me now.'

'How can it be past? I've been doing a lot of research, Timmy. I think you've been on this earth a long time. And you have to help me. I really *have* to know the answers to these things. It's not just that I'm curious. I'm one too, don't you see? I'm a vampire.'

He took her hands in his. Beneath her skin, her blood pulsed like a human being's. There wasn't the glacial oozing of a vampire's blood. Her skin was soft and warm. He let go of her, felt her cheeks; beneath the filmy whiteface of her Neo-Gothic makeup, the flesh was flush and tingling to the touch. She was no vampire.

'You don't believe me, do you?' she said.

'I don't,' said Timmy Valentine. At that point, one of the theatre employees entered with a tray, a bottle of Bollinger, and two glasses; he popped the cork, poured the champagne, and disappeared discreetly. Timmy said, 'I've run into a lot of people who think they're vampires. They feel a special kinship with my lyrics. They collect all the Anne Rice and Nancy Collins books they can lay their hands on. There was a TV programme about them once. But you know, it's rarely true.'

'I notice that you said *rarely*.'

'I do have a little experience of these things.'

'So it's true after all. I knew it!'

'No, Pamina. You've come too late for me to help you at all. Go home.' He gulped down an entire glass of champagne. He was sweating. It wasn't easy to get used to sweat. She touched his cheek. He flinched a little. Took her hand in his, noted grimly that the tattooed stigma was just a decal after all; you could send away for a complete set by returning the little coupon inside the special edition of the CD. 'Even the stigmata,' he said, and peeled one of them away with a fingernail. She giggled. 'So why is it that you want to be a vampire so badly?'

'You know why!' she said. 'Please don't tease me about it. You are the only one who can possibly understand and I need so much to be understood.'

'Perhaps . . . once . . . a long time ago . . .'

'Bite me!'

'But I thought you said you already *were*—'

'Yes, but I have to be *sure* . . .'

'Sure? What do you mean, sure? There are no vampires. That's how we can tell that we're in the real world and not some fantasy or dream or inside the universe of one of my own songs – because there aren't any vampires, unicorns, ogres, creatures of the imagination.'

'But the real world isn't as hard-edged as we want it to be. And now and then, in the shadows at the fringes, in the loopholes of the laws of nature—'

'Fuck that. You're just quoting from what I said in my interview with *Stern* magazine. And you know I didn't really say those things. My publicist wrote them.'

'I don't think so. They are so you.'

And Timmy drank another glass of champagne. This time, when she touched him, he didn't exactly flinch. His cheek felt flesh. She kissed him. Her lips tasted of peppermint. His penis tingled a little; and that was strange, that the Mage and the Sybil had not completely shorn him of the roots of feeling that night, nineteen hundred years ago, when they had castrated him in a ritual of sex, blood and magic, infused their jaded immortality into his unused body so that they could be free to die. He wasn't sure whether to be glad that he could still feel something . . . or to be angry that he would never now be able to consummate that feeling.

'You're just how I knew you would be,' said Pamina, 'feelingless, like a stone. That's how I want to be loved.' She gnawed at the fingers of his left hand. *Ouch.* Her teeth were sharp. Maybe she'd had them filed. The ancient Mayans used to do that, he remembered, suddenly. He realized with a start that he was bleeding a little, and that the girl was lapping at the knuckle of his index finger . . . her tongue was teasing at the little wound . . . and now his penis was definitely stiffening. 'I can stop if you want me to,' Pamina said.

'I want you to,' said Timmy Valentine, but she didn't stop.

But when she paused to wash the blood down with champagne, he said to her, 'Why don't you take me to Amelia?' and finally, whooping with delight, she let go of his hand.

sybil

Amelia Rothstein sat in a wicker chair in the conservatory in a jungle of potted plants; an old man at a piano could be seen behind a sea of dangling orchids. It was stifling and humid, but beyond the glass walls was the cold and cobblestoned courtyard of the Goldbach Home for Retired Musicians. The old man played and Amelia was singing as Pamina entered and Timmy, who had told her they would come by taxi in order to avoid the PR feeding frenzy of a limousine arrival, came in behind her, switching off his flipfone and stashing it in his jacket pocket.

Aunt Amelia's voice had coarsened and acquired a nervous vibrato, but Pamina could see right away that Timmy Valentine recognized it. And not just from those recordings she made with Stephen Miles, either. Timmy knew the voice, had heard the voice perform this very piece, been one of Amelia's favourites: Schubert's *An die Musik*.

And if *one* thing from Pamina's fantasy could be true – if a boy could stand in the same room as her, unchanged from a fifty-year-old photograph – why couldn't all of it be true? Why couldn't she be a vampire after all? That blood had been sweet and intoxicating – wasn't it supposed to be like a full-bodied red wine? – and when she'd licked it from Timmy's finger it seemed so natural, so *true* – not at all like the time she had slashed Cousin Otto's black cat with a butcher knife and lapped up the spurting ooze and washed it down with stolen Schnapps.

At the part where the song speaks of how music kindles men's hearts and ennobles the world, Amelia broke off abruptly.

How old she seemed . . . a prim, grey-haired lady with granny glasses . . . and how strange he must look to her . . . still twelve years old, unchanged . . . a spectre from her haunted young womanhood. Pamina felt triumphant. She had brought

Tante Amelia's past back and was shoving it in her face. How must he feel?

'Konrad Stolz. But you *have* changed, *nicht wahr*?' Amelia said. 'The angel has come to earth.'

'Thank you,' he said. 'You don't know what that means to me, having someone who knew me from that other time see me now, and know that yes, I have come to earth; that I've become real.'

'It's true,' said Amelia. 'When last I saw you, you darted like a shadow, a mirror couldn't catch your reflection. But now you stand there in the grey light and yes, you are solid, quite, quite solid. It must pain you, to be so solid. For me it's different . . . getting old, drifting out of reality.'

Pamina stared at the two of them. This wasn't going the way she'd imagined at all. For days she had fantasized about it . . . edited and re-edited their conversation . . . imagined how delicious their dark secret must have been. There had been something between them, that was clear. Pamina thought it must be like that Dorian Gray story they had read in school once . . . that Amelia and Timmy had made a pact where the one would wither away and the other stay young forever. Maybe this confrontation would be the catalyst that would reverse the process. Maybe Timmy would age and crumble before her very eyes, and her aunt become a girl again. That would be wild! They could hang out at the Neo-Gothic clubs together. She could pierce Amelia's nipples. Pamina's immediate family was stolidly Teutonic, but she had always suspected Amelia of being capable of her kind of wildness.

'Tell her what I'm not,' Timmy said to Amelia, shattering Pamina's rêverie.

They looked into each other's eyes, the old woman and the boy, and Pamina knew she was being excluded. It was all so frustrating. After all the trouble she had taken to sneak backstage, flirt with the security guard, bake the pie. She stared at her tattooed stigmata and wouldn't look at her aunt even when she tottered toward her and gripped her shoulders with her palsied hands.

'It's too late,' said Tante Amelia, 'the magic's gone out of him.'

'But he used to—'

'Yes. Once he was a vampire. In my dressing room at the Opernhaus, he sat in my lap like a little black cat, and he drew blood from me . . . and a lot more than just blood. He drew sustenance, and I too was sustained because this creature of the night needed me so much. Oh, I loved him. But that was in another life, you understand. It was a time when there was still magic in the world.'

Pamina was seized by the kind of despair that only adolescents know. She did not weep. 'I had such a meaningful relationship with you,' she said to Timmy, 'only it was all me.' How could her aunt have experienced the real Timmy, the Timmy of her fantasies . . . *stolen* the very dreams that had kept her going through her desolate and alienated childhood?

Oh, the blood on her lips had tasted so sweet . . .

'I'll go now,' she said. The idea of suicide crossed her mind. She wondered whether it was just another juvenile fantasy, or whether she would indeed end up a pale corpse . . . nude in the snow with the blood-drops crystallizing on her lips . . . shrouded in black satin with her lips painted the colour of ripe strawberries . . . deader even than she already felt.

'No,' said Timmy Valentine, 'don't go . . .'

He looked at her with another kind of longing. It was not what she had expected. Timmy Valentine wasn't supposed to feel desire. He was supposed to be as colourless and cold as the melodies of his songs. He was supposed to soar above the raging world like a moonbeam, like a gust of mist. This was disturbing, profoundly disturbing.

He held out his hand to her. He smiled, a thin, vulnerable smile.

dissolve

PJ was waiting in the lobby when her taxi pulled up. 'I'm really, really sorry,' he started to say, but Chit shushed him and embraced him, and then allowed herself to be steered toward an overstuffed divan while PJ waved to a bellboy and pointed to her luggage.

'Sorry? Why sorry?' she said. 'Oh, God, what a flight, hardly a moment of sleep . . . bad dreams.'

'Sorry I couldn't go to the airport,' PJ said. 'Well . . . you see, there's something a little strange going on. I'm nervous.'

'Is Timmy all right?'

'Well, yes. He's upstairs. In the suite . . . you know they've given us the governor's suite, don't you, the one Himmler slept in once . . . three bedrooms . . . but I didn't want to go up there yet because . . . well, he's got a girl up there.'

'A girl . . . you mean, a sort of groupie? You mean *sex*? But I thought Timmy couldn't—'

'I know, I know . . . could be a breakthrough.'

Chit leaned into the brocaded cushions . . . the gold thread was prickly on her bare arms . . . and took a deep breath. The Valium had worked . . . or had it? Had she really spent that plane ride soaring above the Appalachians in the shape of a raven . . . ripping out a girl's heart . . . feasting on blood? The dreams had been so vivid they had almost seemed like her own memories. Even here, under the crystal chandeliers of the Fürstner-Regency, with the uniformed hotel personnel darting back and forth, part of her mind was still hovering over a dark hayloft on a moonlight night in Kentucky; she could even smell the hay, and the blood, and the rutting horses.

'Something happened to him tonight. He went insane. Started quoting bits of *The Magic Flute* in a rasping rap. Ice-T meets Kurt Cobain meets Amadeus? I didn't get it. The lighting guys were going out of their minds trying to improvise to match. What a mess! The audience went crazy, too, they loved it, loved him doing it in German, you know.'

'A lot of strange things have been happening back home, too—' But Chit couldn't begin to start telling him. It was just too bewildering. Instead, she asked a nearby waiter to bring her some of that caffeiney, creamy, nutmeggy *mélange* whose rich aroma filled the lobby. Perhaps the caffeine would cancel out the Valium.

'But anyway . . . you see . . . after the show he disappears for *hours*, in a taxi, no less . . . with this Neo-Gothic teenage girl . . . and then, just now, they came back and went straight upstairs. I'm wondering whether they're actually – well – doing it.'

'You are so tactful, PJ. And so protective.'

'Yeah. That coffee smells amazing.' He ordered a cup. Somewhere, a clock struck four.

'But the luggage – won't that—'

'Oh, there's more than one door into the suite. I suppose that I'm sort of dreading what I might discover.'

'Can't you . . . you know, close your eyes, make your mind blank, send your spirit double up into the bedroom?'

'You know I don't do that sort of thing anymore. Besides, voyeurism is against the shamans' union rules of ethical conduct.'

She laughed.

Then, suddenly, came a stabbing pain in her breast . . .

'Are you OK?' PJ sat down beside her on the divan, put his arms around her. It was good to surrender to this public intimacy after the months she had spent in Bangkok, where such displays are socially unacceptable. She closed her eyes and let his lips graze her forehead, her cheek, her earlobes; the musky scent of the forest always clung to him no matter how 'civilized' he became. She clung to him harder, but between them there was always the thing that hung around her neck, so cold that it had begun to numb the flesh about her heart.

shadows

The suite: brocade, tapestries, deep pile carpeting, plump upholstery, leather, mahogany, and a silver ice bucket with an unopened magnum of Moët Chandon, a bowl of ice, an ice pick.

Pamina sat on the bed; Timmy sat next to her; behind the closed door that led to the reception room, you could hear a porter piling up luggage. On the wall was a dark, varnished eighteenth-century painting of some kind; on the television an episode of I Love Lucy, dubbed in German.

'We want such different things,' he was telling her. 'You want all the things that I gave up. And I long for a thing in you that I still cannot have, even though I've made myself human, because of what happened to me two thousand years ago . . .'

'Can't you go back?' Pamina said. 'I've been listening to your music all my life. I can hear things in it that other people can't. It's like a kind of wind that blows through your songs, desolate and beautiful. An eternal winter wind.'

'Blow, blow, thou winter wind,' Timmy said softly.

Pamina realized that he wasn't just quoting Shakespeare . . . he was *remembering* it.

'At least tell me what it was like,' she said. 'Make the past come alive for me. Then I won't feel so lost.'

'Why are you lost?'

'I don't know.'

Perhaps I do know, Pamina thought, but I won't let myself think it.

Timmy said, 'I had an analyst once. She became almost like a mother to me. She took me back and back and back in time. It was like going into a big old house, but the house was inside my mind . . . then unlocking the doors, one after another . . .'

'Like in *Bluebeard's Castle*,' Pamina said, remembering that that had been one of her aunt's best-known roles after she had demoted herself to a mezzo. She'd seen Tante Amelia do that opera when she was only seven years old. There was this old, old Duke – her aunt played the beautiful Judit, his fourth wife – and this gloomy old castle. There were seven rooms that could not be unlocked. In the story, Judit keeps demanding the keys and the Duke keeps unlocking the rooms, one by one, until the last one, the one that contains Judit's own doom. The opera had given her nightmares. In fact, it may have been the first time she had started to think about blood.

If only she could remember more . . .

'But,' said Timmy Valentine, 'when you open the doors, they don't close again. At least, not all the way. And the gloomy old castle fills with light.'

'Not always.'

'Shall we play a game? Kind of like strip poker.'

'I'm wearing more items than you,' Pamina said, smiling, 'if you count all the piercings.'

'No, no,' said Timmy Valentine, 'we'll strip our souls.'

Pamina shuddered. 'I'd almost rather fuck.'

'The problem is,' said Timmy, 'I don't think I can. I haven't tried it. I know that I can still feel things down there sometimes, but . . . I don't know if . . .'

He was blushing! This two-thousand-year-old soul with the body of a fresh-minted boy was actually embarrassed . . . nervous about sex. And Pamina, who had known more men in her short years than she cared to remember, since the time that Herr Bergschneider, her English teacher, had cornered her in the classroom closet, found this curiously touching. She had come to him seeking someone invulnerable, the kind of person she most wanted to become. Instead, she had found something altogether human.

'You want to see if you can?' she said. 'Then, after that, we can play your soul-stripping game.'

'The last time a girl came onto me, I turned into a shark and bit her in two.'

'I won't let that happen. Because I'm not afraid of you.'

'How could you be afraid? The magic has gone away.'

She tossed aside her leather jacket. She rolled down her black jeans and slid out of her black T-shirt. He looked at her; she could tell he was trying to appear impassive, but there was still that trace of a flush on his cheeks. She placed his hands on her small breasts. He touched them gingerly. There was strength in his hands – she could well believe that he had once ripped people apart with them – but the touch of his hands was so light it could have been a breeze – or the wind that blew through one of his songs – the ones from ten years back – the songs before his vanishing.

She wondered whether he would see in her the same androgynous sensuality that so many had seen in her, had used in her; whether her bony hips, her left nipple pierced through with a jagged silver lightning bolt, her right tattooed to resemble a heart that bled a stream of purplish teardrops all the way down to her navel, through which there ran a white gold safety pin . . . whether all these things would make him slap her, call her slut, push her down on the bed, piss on her face, fuck her up the ass . . . her naked body seemed to incite that in all the men who had ever seen it, from Herr Bergschneider all the way down to Sascha Rabinowitz, the retarded boy from

the kosher butcher's shop at the end of Zuckerbrotgasse . . .
the first time she'd ever tasted human blood.

And Timmy Valentine had been in her thoughts even then
. . . that inhuman voice on the radio, echoing in the shuttered
shop, oozing over the glass-fronted counter with its slabs of cool
red meat . . . all the way through to the freezing little locker in
the back with its rack of lamb hanging from the hook where
they fucked for the first time . . . where he'd tripped and
slammed his cheek against the cleaver on the wall and she'd
tasted it, hot, spurting, making the whole room suddenly warm
. . . and the song on the radio was

> *Come into my coffin*
> *Don't wanna sleep alone*

and that's how she knew that she was born different from the
others . . . and when she started to hide from the light.

He wouldn't believe me if I told him, she thought.

She heard a toilet flush. Timmy had gone to the bathroom.
When the door opened, he was wearing only a plaster around
the knuckle she'd gnawed at. He stood in the swath of fluorescent bathroom light, paler than snow, his dark hair darker than
night, the traces of stage makeup making his eyes even clearer,
even brighter; for a long time his eyes transfixed her and prevented her gaze from wandering down the slender curve of his
throat, the concentrated smoothness of his torso, leanly
muscled, coiled, the flat, firm V of his hairless pubis, the tiny
penis swelling a little, the white scars of castration . . . and she
thought, me all stuck through with metal and ink and him with
nothing at all and yet I'm naked and he isn't . . . he's cloaked
in his past, his shadows, his ancient traumas. He's as beautiful
as the breath you take before you start singing, as the blank
page at the beginning of a book.

Does he think I'm beautiful too? Maybe he'll hit me. I know
I'm trembling and I'm starting to think about blood again.

'What do you think?' he said. 'Are you disappointed because
I'm only a real boy after all?'

'Oh, no,' she said. 'Never real, never completely real.'

She *was* afraid of him, after all. He came closer. Now they
stood just a handspan apart and she could smell him, a sweet

sweaty odour veiled by the scent of old makeup; but what had she expected, the putrescence of the grave?

'A little more blood, perhaps?' he said. And ripped off the plaster and squeezed out a single drop, glistening like a polished amethyst.

'I *will* be a vampire!' she whispered. 'I will, I will!' For she knew from countless movies and books that to become a vampire's consort you must not only be bitten but also partake of the vampire's blood.

And she knelt down, threw her arms around his waist, lapped at the single drop of blood, and felt through his fingertips the rhythmic pounding of his heart, felt his penis as it reared up to touch the corner of her lip, felt the shivering of his hips against her cheeks.

'The flute is broken,' he said. And giggled a little.

So he's nervous, she thought.

'I can mend it,' she said, running her tongue along the faded scar, 'I can make you whole again.'

He closed his eyes and sang dreamily to himself: '*Thou winter wind . . .*'

mirror

Of course, it was not good sex. He just stood there. He didn't really come or anything; at one point he let out a kind of whimper, and his stomach muscles convulsed, and his half-erect penis throbbed a little. Perhaps that was all you expected when you made love to a eunuch. And he had done little for her. He allowed her to rub herself up and down his leg, he tentatively fingered her vulva a little, he diffidently kissed her clitoris – a glancing sort of a kiss, quite dry – she could not really blame him. He had, after all, been dead for almost two thousand years, and before that, he had not really had much of a chance to study the art of love.

She had expected there to be more of the *frisson* of celebrity about their lovemaking, too, but that really had been absent. And now he was sleeping sweetly, his delicate features strobing in the television glow of an old *film noir* . . . one of those porcelain actresses emoting to a tempestuous symphonic music. Should she leave?

She watched him sleeping for a while, sitting beside him, head between her knees. Soon it would be dawn.

Should I leave?

Presently she became restless. She had never spent the night in such an opulent hotel, even when she went on tour with Tante Amelia, the last time her aunt ever performed in public. She wondered what they would think at the front desk when she slunk out into the street.

She looked in the bathroom, found a silk kimono that might have been Timmy's, threw it on, went back to the sofa, wondered if she should open the champagne . . . toyed with the icepick . . . and with the idea of stabbing the sleeping Timmy Valentine through the heart. Didn't he deserve it for abandoning her, for being so much less than the sum of all her dreams?

And then she heard a whisper in the gloom.

Pamina.

She thought that was what it was. But Timmy's lips had not moved, and no one else knew her name.

Pamina.

And she was seized by the thrill she had not known with Timmy . . . the same dark thrill she had dreamed of since before the lost memories of childhood . . . her pulse quickened. Where was the voice coming from?

Pamina.

Louder now, though still barely at the threshold of hearing. There was danger in the voice, and lust. The lust she recognized from past sexual encounters . . . the lust she felt herself when she sniffed blood in the air.

Pamina. Come to me. See me. Free me. You're the one who can do it, the one who understands.

But where are you calling from?

She tiptoed from the bedroom into the reception area. The only light was the glow of the city through the open curtains. One window was ajar, admitting a chill breeze. At first she thought, That's it then . . . a voice in the wind . . . not calling to me at all. Pedestrians outside the window. Someone coming home late from a party.

But no. *Pamina*. The voice was close. Fear pricked at the base of her neck. There were other doors leading into the main room. One led to the corridor outside . . . two others . . . one of them ajar . . . it was like an abridged version of *Bluebeard's Castle*.

Pamina.

She picked the door to the left. The bedroom was a mirror image of the one she had left Timmy sleeping in. The dread was stronger here. When the voice came it seemed to be inside her own head. On the bed, a man and a woman lay nude, in each other's arms, the woman Asian, the man of some indeterminate race; his long hair blanketed the two of them and blacked out the pudenda almost as though it had been arranged by art; on the dresser, beneath a mirror in a baroque gold frame, was an amulet on a silver chain.

The man and the woman did not stir. There was a magnum of champagne and a bucket here, too, but the bottle was empty. Here, too, the television was on, an old black-and-white American movie, dubbed. She tightened the kimono about her shoulders. The chill reminded her of the butcher's shop and the retarded boy. He had bled a great deal.

Touch it!

She slid over to the dresser. Touched the amulet. The cold! Like the meat cleaver that had sliced into Sascha's fist. Ice-cold. She gripped it hard, though. She wanted the cold to penetrate her veins. The voice kept calling her name. It was Timmy's yet not Timmy's voice. It was weak because it was encased in a silver coffin. But it called to her. To her!

I'm here, she said in her mind, knowing the voice would hear her without her having to speak.

But you have to invite me.

Invite you? Aren't you here with me already?

Invite me. Into your heart.

I—

Then she saw him in the mirror. The Timmy Valentine of her dreams. The translucent skin, the sunken eyes, even the sweet-sick stench of the charnel house. He too was naked. He was standing right behind her, but when she whipped around, he wasn't there. Only in the mirror.

'But you don't—' she said aloud.

*Cast reflections. That's true. What you see isn't me. They've shut
me away in a dark place. I'm not in your world at all. I'm only a
memory. I'm just in the looking-glass world. And it ain't a pretty
place. What you see in the mirror looks normal enough, but beyond the
edge of the mirror, what you can't see, Pamina, why that's hell.*

She looked at him more closely. Curiosity was overcoming
her fear.

Don't you really want to know what it's like, Pamina? To be me.

'But you seem to be Timmy Valentine . . . and Timmy's lying
in the other room, asleep . . .'

A bitter laugh. Peering closer at the reflection – it was difficult
to see him because he seemed to waver between reality and
spectral transparency – she could see now that he was not *quite*
Timmy Valentine. Under the shock of black hair there were
strands of blond. He was thinner, even more wraithlike, his
eyes even larger, more sunken . . . and when she glanced downward into the mirror she saw that *this* Valentine was no eunuch.
Who was this then? She wondered if, now that her encounter
with the real Timmy Valentine had been so ambiguous, her
imagination had conjured up a substitute, something closer to
her fantasies . . .

No, he said, seeming to read her mind. *The Timmy that's left
behind to live out the life of a normal boy, he's just a shell of what I
am. I'm the one who stole the magic from him. And it's the magic you
want, ain't it?*

And the boy raised up his arms and wiggled his fingers in an
eerie Lugosi imitation, and though his lips did not move she
could hear his voice in the cavern of her skull cry *Invite me into
your heart, Pamina, invite me. I can't come unless you call to me.*

I can show you the world behind the mirror.

*I can show you hell. And ecstasy. And passion. And death. Touch
the amulet again. Grip it tighter. I'm clearer now, ain't I? Tighter. Do
you want to put it on? Do you want to free me so I can make you part
of me? Do you want the two things you've never had, love and death,
both at the same time? All you have to do is—*

Another sound. She was startled. It was the woman moaning.
She dropped the amulet and the image of Timmy-that-
wasn't-Timmy wavered and was gone in a sparkling mist just
like on *Star Trek*.

Pamina backed away from the mirror. The woman moaned again and she could hear the sheets rustling. Pamina backed all the way out into the reception room and sat down on a black leather sofa. She had been sweating and the upholstery was chill and slippery.

None of this made sense. How could there be more than one Timmy Valentine? Was she insane after all? What did Tante Amelia know and how had she been so certain that the Timmy Valentine who had performed in the auditorium was no longer a vampire? She had to talk to Amelia.

What time was it? In the distance she could hear chimes. Six o'clock, perhaps? They woke up early at the nursing home. There was a phone on the coffee table and she dialled out.

'Frau Saenz?' That was the woman who was actually on duty in the morning. 'It's me, Pamina Rothstein. I was wondering whether . . . Tante Amelia was awake yet. I know that the guests don't usually receive calls this early, but . . .'

'I'm terribly sorry, but your aunt . . . heart failure . . . all very sudden . . . your aunt is dead, Fräulein.'

She replaced the receiver. Soon it would be dawn, and she did not know anyone here except for Timmy Valentine. Would they just look at her as though she was some kind of groupie? And her aunt . . . what would she do without her aunt? Tante Amelia, the only eccentric in her hidebound family, the only one who might possibly understand . . . I'm just thinking about myself! she realized. I'm thinking about how dreadful it will be for me when it's she who has gone, she who will never sing again . . .

On the coffee table, the amulet glinted against the ice bucket.

What was it doing there? Hadn't she dropped it on the dresser?

She reached for it, stopped herself at the last minute, afraid of what would happen if she—

Pamina.

No!

Would you like to see your Tante Amelia again?

Pamina reached for the amulet . . .

12

UNLOCKING THE DOORS

daylight

'PJ, it's the girl.' Lady Chit stood in the doorway. She didn't really see her so much as the amulet on the coffee table. The girl was hovering over it, about to reach for it. 'How did that get there?' she said, and swooped down to snatch it back.

'I didn't mean to—' the girl began. A Neo-Gothic, Chit thought. She's got the tattoos on her palms. They might be those stick-on things, though.

'Don't play with that thing, it's dangerous. It could do something terrible to you . . . oh, you wouldn't believe me.' She thrust the amulet in the pocket of her robe and she could feel its cold heat smouldering against her thigh. 'Let's order breakfast. Is Timmy awake?'

'You're not going to throw me out?' As though she were daring her to do it. A hard girl, Chit thought. Had she gone into their bedroom, tried to steal the amulet? But she did not think that amulet could be stolen . . . not unless it wanted to be.

'Of course not, why should we? My name is Premchitra. They call me Chit. I'm with PJ, Timmy's – tour manager, I suppose.'

'Pamina Rothstein. Let me call down for you,' said the girl. She picked up the phone and began ordering in German. As if she owned the place, Chit thought. Wait till PJ sees this! Timmy's getting more and more like a real boy every day.

'You don't look like you've had much sleep.'

'I haven't . . . oh, I've had such a night!' The girl seemed to go to pieces all at once. She began to weep bitterly. And Chit found herself, after an exhausting journey, after battling demons in Bangkok and nightmares on the plane, comforting this girl she hardly knew. The menfolk were no good for these things. She'd no doubt that Timmy and PJ would sleep until noon.

'PJ!' she said again, but her husband in the next room did not stir. She looked at the schedule hanging on the wall: Holland next, then England, then . . . heavens, Prague! . . . and then Bangkok. A lot of back and forth . . . about as chaotically organized as anything PJ ever did without her help. She saw that Damien Peters was supposed to be flying in to Amsterdam. The whole gang, one at a time . . . and every one a certified loony! She couldn't wait for Lauren to show up as well . . . he and Damien and PJ would soon be off on some spirit journey somewhere, no doubt, leaving the women to sit around in the real world. If the girl stayed, at least she'd have someone to go shopping with . . .

After breakfast arrived, the girl turned out to be something of a chatterbox. 'I'll tell you everything,' she said, 'about my life,' and there came a lengthy catalogue of the places she'd lived, the special relationship she had had with the old diva Amelia Rothstein, who had just died, apparently, poor thing – Chit remembered seeing her at the Met once when she was a teenage girl and snoozing through *Tosca*, only to be startled awake by the piercing high note at the end of *Vissi d'arte* – then the girl went on about how she'd got into the Neo-Gothic movement when she bought her first Timmy Valentine album, about her first visit to the tattoo artist, sneaking up to Munich on the train – but Chit had the feeling that she was skirting the thing she most wanted to talk about.

It was broad daylight now. The amulet seemed less powerful by day; now and then she could feel a kind of throbbing where it touched the satin that touched her skin. Had the amulet called out to the girl, too? Obviously the girl had some special relationship with vampires . . . perhaps she was one of those wannabe vampires, the ones who read all the books and saw all the movies and had their secret newsletters and computer bulletin boards. She was *not* a vampire, that much was clear. I've known too many real ones to be fooled by black leather and black lipstick, she thought. She wasn't quite a vampire groupie either, though.

She was about to ask her if she'd felt anything from the amulet . . . when Timmy came out of the bedroom. He had on a silk dressing-gown. His hair was tousled. He smiled sleepily and waved hello to the two of them.

'Hi, girls,' he said.

He came over to hug Chit; he didn't touch Pamina but merely looked at her wryly, wondering, perhaps, why she was still there. 'I thought I had only dreamed about you,' he said to her.

He had a plaster around one finger.

Chit stared at it. Could it be that . . . 'Cut myself shaving,' Timmy said.

'You don't shave,' Chit said.

'I lied. Actually, she bit me. She's quite the vampire.'

There was a dead silence. Trying to fill the space, Chit flicked on the television. There was a youthful Amelia Rothstein, singing away. There was a voiceover in German: '. . . *die berühmte Opernsängerin ist heute Morgen gestorben . . .*'

'Jesus,' said Timmy.

'She's dead,' the two women said at the same time.

'I knew her, you know,' Timmy said. 'In the old days. In my other existence.' He turned his attention to the newscast and started to translate for Chit. 'Listen. Instead of a memorial service, there's going to be a special performance of *Bluebeard's Castle* at – you know, what used to be the Opernhaus. That concrete monstrosity I performed in last night. Apparently it's all in her will. I've got to go.'

'Aren't you due to perform somewhere?'

'No, it's a travel day. If we send the trucks and equipment off today, I can get in tomorrow. It's only Holland, the Congresgebouw in the Hague. Takes an hour to fly there.'

'Tomorrow – you are leaving?' Pamina said. She seemed suddenly to be in a panic. 'You mustn't! I – I need something, someone—'

Chit said, 'Surely you're going home? Your parents are probably worried already. I don't suppose you've called them?'

'Fuck my parents,' said Pamina. 'Tante Amelia was the only old person who understood me anyway.'

'Suit yourself,' Timmy said, and disappeared back into his bedroom. From the other bedroom, they could hear PJ faintly snoring.

'All right,' Chit said. She gripped Pamina's hands in hers. 'Pamina, you must tell me—'

'You can call me Pami if you like. I don't let boys call me that. You can only call me that if you don't fuck me.'

'When I came in just now, you were about to touch something.' The amulet grew warmer. It was burning against her hip . . . sizzling! She could almost smell charring flesh . . . just an illusion, she told herself. 'I want you to tell me . . . if . . . you felt anything strange about it.'

'Let me tell you about the time my aunt took me to France,' Pamina said. 'We saw the cave paintings at Lascaux, you know. Very primitive, very violent. Bats everywhere . . . not that I really think bats have much to do with vampires . . .'

'Did you sense anything in the air . . . a kind of hollowness, something chill, maybe a breath of winter? Did you hear any voices?'

'The toast is getting so cold. Look, the butter is hard.'

She wasn't going to talk about it. Chit knew that her instinct was right about this girl. Or maybe it was just that everyone had a dark secret, one way or another; you can't escape dark secrets, they're a fact of life.

'What shall I wear to the opera tonight?' Timmy shouted from the next room. 'One of my Dracula tuxes?'

dissolve: opera

It was a sea of black this evening, and a veritable who's who of the music world. They had stonewalled Timmy's PR person, who called them to ask for an invitation for the visiting rock star – 'This is a serious affair, madam, not a circus-cum-photo-op for American teen idols!' – and in the end it was Pamina who arranged it. So she finally had to call her parents after all, and Timmy noted that it only took a moment's whining to get her own way.

But Chit and PJ and the rest of the entourage could not go.

Just as well, Timmy thought. They need time without me. And I need some more time alone with this strange girl who has thrust herself into my life.

They stood in the foyer of the auditorium. It was good to be surrounded by people who did not recognize him, or at least pretended not to; it was a welcome change from the previous night. Someone had lugged in some of the statuary that used to inhabit this lobby in the days when it was still an opera house. There was an elegant marble Mozart, and a weatherbeaten Wagner looking very out of sorts in a Roman toga. There was a bigger turnout for Amelia's death, Timmy noted, than there had been for his own concert. And a lot more jewellery too. Even, here and there, that most unpolitically correct of garments, the mink stole – though it invariably adorned some withered crone. In fact, he almost recognized some of them . . . wasn't that one Frau Pilz, the repetiteur? As for luminaries . . . there were quite a few. He thought he saw Montserrat Caballé waddling through the throng, and that elegant creature with the champagne glass had to be—

'Christa Ludwig,' Pamina said drily. 'Her recording of *Bluebeard* was the only one my aunt cared for. Actually, I think she learned the part off that recording, although I daresay she would never have admitted it.'

'I like Sylvia Sass, personally,' said Timmy, who had swiped a lengthy chord sequence – the 'lake of tears' section – from Bartok's opera and used it as an eerily shifting New Age sort of synth pad in his song *I thought I'd died and gone to Purgatory*. No one had noticed, of course.

'Bluebeard's very romantic, isn't he?' Pamina said. 'I mean, even though he makes Judit endure a living death at the end . . .'

'You wouldn't say that,' said Timmy, 'if you had known him.'

He sneakily enjoyed her double take for a moment, then turned away from her, tried to identify a few more celebrities among Amelia's mourners.

'You're putting me on, aren't you? *Bluebeard's Castle* is based on some fairy tale, it's in Grimm.'

'Shows you how little you know,' he said. 'The *real* Bluebeard used to fuck little kids to death. Did you know that? But I was different. I was already dead. He cut a hole in my side and shoved it in. Yeah. Just like Jesus Christ.'

'Is that what that song means, *Crucify Me Twice*?'

'My songs don't mean anything.'

'Yeah, but surely if something that dreadful happened to you, then your songs must hark back to it sometimes?'

He walked away. Human beings were always the same in the end. They just don't know anything, he thought. Comes from living like ants, no thousand-year memories, no ancient haunt-ings. Blank pages, all of them. And *I'm* getting that way too. If she hadn't said about the fairy tale, I wouldn't even have remembered . . . five hundred years ago . . . that awful thing that Carla Rubens dredged out of my memory and made me face . . . being human's like having great chunks of text wiped off the blackboard of your mind . . . it's like, I don't know, Alzheimer's or something . . . on a monumental scale . . . you lose a century at a time.

You slam the doors shut and throw away the keys.

amulet

'Vampires,' PJ said, 'dozens of them . . . just like old times. But we got them all. I think. Jesus, I hope.'

'Victims,' said Chit, 'dozens of them. But only one vampire. And now he's trapped and can't get out. But he talks to me in my sleep and I can't drive him out of my dreams.'

And so they both began telling each other about the horrors they had left behind in the two cities that are both called the City of Angels.

They were in a well-lit, crowded place, a little coffeebar at one end of a *Hypermarkt* in a little shopping centre; the former Opernhaus was only a minute or two away if you knew your alleys. They hadn't even allowed Timmy to bring bodyguards – but PJ could be reached by beeper if something weird were going to happen. It didn't seem as though it would. Bizarre though the Rothstein girl was, she seemed to be good for Timmy. This morning he had seemed almost domesticated – what a spectacle!

He couldn't help speculating about what might have happened between them. After all, PJ was a man, but he had also been a woman in a sense, for when he had gone on his vision quest as an adolescent a spirit had impelled him to go the way of the *ma'aipots*, the sacred man-woman of the Shoshone. Then, after he had defeated the witch-woman Simone Arleta in her attempt to bring about the end of the world, the power had left him . . . only occasionally did it possess him, and then it was only a shadow of what it once had been. He was sure that his memory of the years as a *ma'aipots* was what made him so able to satisfy Chit sexually; she had told him often enough that he almost always seemed to know what she wanted before she even thought it herself.

'. . . so I know how a woman feels, and how a man feels, but I can't imagine how *he* feels . . .' he was musing to himself, when Chit jabbed his arm playfully with a forkful of *Sacher Torte*.

'You only think about one thing,' she said.

'You're thinking about it too,' he said. 'You want to fuck me senseless.'

She laughed. 'Your barometer's off! I was thinking about something else . . . the amulet. I want to just flush it down the toilet.'

'Not a bad idea,' said PJ. 'What do you think would happen?'

'Vampires in the sewers?' Chit said in a Drew Barrymore-like tone. 'Oh, shit, PJ, why didn't the ajarn simply destroy Angel Todd and stake him in the heart and drown him in holy water so we could get on with our lives?'

'I've been thinking about that, Chit,' said PJ, 'and maybe it boils down to *balance*. Our dothead friends would call it karma, I guess, the precarious dance of cause and effect that keeps the universe in motion . . . but for us other kind of Injuns, it's all about circles . . . circles getting broken, circles having to be stitched back together again . . . you know?'

'Mysteries of the west,' Chit said, 'that's what I married you for.'

'Seriously, seriously . . .'

'What you're saying, PJ, is that none of this is an accident, right? The amulet, my flying here, me sitting here with you, Timmy sitting over there in the opera house – it's all part of

some predestination deal? That when Timmy and Angel
switched places, we only reached the midpoint of the story—'

'Yeah, they're like the two halves of a strand of DNA – mirror
images – spiralling round and round each other—'

'And every now and then they touch and where they touch
they can change places and take over each other's journey until
the next moment that the spiral comes around again and – Jesus,
it makes me dizzy!'

PJ laughed. 'Me too. Anyway, who cares?'

'Who cares?'

'Can we make love now?'

'I thought you were on Timmy duty.'

'Yes, but . . . listen . . . all around you . . . the sound of the
sidewalks being rolled up . . . we're in small-town Germany
now . . . no shopping after dark . . . we could do it right on the
cobblestones and no one would notice . . . maybe even . . .'

'Under that grotesque statue in the courtyard in front of the
hotel? The one that looks like Hitler in drag.'

'That happens to be Saint Catherine – very revered around
here.'

They got up. PJ threw a hefty banknote on the table, overtip-
ping outrageously – at the next table, a snoopy old woman in
a black dress tsk-tsked at his barbarian largesse – and, for good
measure, kissed Chit, noisily and wetly, right in front of the
woman's nose.

'Stop,' Chit said suddenly. She clutched at her bosom. 'It's
the amulet . . . I feel . . . I don't know.' What he saw in her
expression wasn't pain exactly, more like bemusement. 'You
know, I think Angel's jealous,' she said softly.

opera

Bluebeard is not a very long opera, but it can really drain you.
Much like a vampire does, thought Timmy Valentine ruefully.

The draining began before the opera even started, as impre-
sarios and superannuated divas vied to outdo each other in the
dull reminiscence department. If only they'd known the Amelia
he'd known . . . the wild woman who had clasped him to her

menstruating privates and made him lap up the old blood like
a kitten . . . Timmy smiled a little. Remembering. Silky thighs
against silky paws. Shrinking from boy to beast, compacting the
shadow-stuff of simulated flesh, purring against the hot skin,
forcing the furry head into the canal of dark red tissue that
contracted around him as if to propel him all the way into the
womb . . . there's something I can't do anymore, he thought.
One image triggered other images . . . keys unlocking doors
. . . running barefoot in the woods, his nose against the pungent
earth . . . plummeting naked out of the sky, the hooting
deathbird, the lunging bat . . . I have been all those things, he
thought. But now that I've gone from ectoplasm to protoplasm
. . . for a moment he wanted to whittle himself down into something small . . . a mouse perhaps . . . to skitter through the
forest of human feet with their odour of sweat and fungus . . .
maybe if I really concentrated, I could still do it . . . but that was all
wishful thinking.

They sat in the place reserved for Amelia's relatives . . . it
would have been the royal box before the renovations turned
it into a concrete alcove with a coffee vending machine. There
were not many relatives, though, and they avoided the familial
black sheep and her teen idol companion, even though she had
actually managed to put on a suitably sober black dress – one
of Chit's.

The opening words, muttered by an old man in a harlequin
costume who sat with folded arms before the midnight-blue
curtains, came in a menacing, mellifluous Hungarian:

> *Haj regö rejtem*
> *Hová, hová rejstem*
> *Hol volt, hol nem: kint-e vagy bent?*

'What's he saying?' Pamina whispered.

Timmy said, 'It's an ancient story, he's telling us, but who's
to say if it's about the world outside or the world within? . . .
Listen . . . *De nem abba halunk bele* . . . "inside, we do not die".'

'Don't tell me you learned Hungarian from Dracula himself,'
Pamina said.

'He spoke Romanian,' said Timmy.

And then remembered—

*A cobblestoned street, rats nesting in the open sewer, human heads
dangling in the wind, the air foul and rank, all the way uphill toward
the banquet-table of the king—*

Did that happen? he wondered. Or just another random
infopacket snatched from the chaos of my disintegrating memories? Did I ever know Vlad Tepes, the historical Dracula . . .
or do I just remember him from some history book, some chance
utterance?

'He was in a Turkish prison once.' He didn't know if that was
a memory or just something he had heard.

'You mean like in that movie with Brad Davis, let me see . . .
Midnight Express?'

'Not at all. This was in the Middle Ages. It was a lot worse.'

'You *met* him!'

'I can't remember.' Timmy was troubled now. He thought of
rats, running up and down a rusty grating, a leaking hole in a
dusty sky . . . now . . . a memory for sure . . . the scrape of the
rust against his hands . . . or were they paws? . . . pattering.
Pattering. 'Does it matter? *He* wasn't even a vampire. Just someone I met in a jailhouse five hundred years ago . . . You don't
want to worry about Dracula, silly. Listen to the opera.'

Now came the opening notes, cellos and basses creaking in
unison like the unoiled hinges of castle gates . . . a shrill twiddle
on clarinets announced the arrival of Duke Bluebeard and his
fourth wife, Judit, the woman whose need to know would
finally be her undoing.

What a fool Bluebeard was. You shouldn't give in to someone
just because she loves you and you desperately need to be loved.
You should slam the doors shut and throw away the keys.
Like humans do. But you're not a human . . . you're an
archetype . . .

The castle set: a sweeping staircase of black stone; the paint
on the flats still tacky; the set must have been in storage since
Amelia's triumphant ten-year-old performance, hastily dusted
off and repainted. The costumes were black and billowing; the
Bluebeard was the stooped and hollow-voiced Eduardo Briance,
noted for the role in the 1960s, and ancient even then. Perhaps
he had been a denizen of the same old musicians' home Amelia
had died in. There was passion in his performance, but almost

no volume; at times the orchestra engulfed him, at others he resorted to a kind of wheezy *Sprechgesang* instead of singing at all.

The Judit, on the other hand, was Patrizia Czaczek, one of Amelia's most promising protégées. She wasn't very subtle, but her voice could wake the dead; it sliced through the massive orchestral textures like a katana—

> *Hideg követ melegítem,*
> *A testemmel melegítem—*

'I will warm this ice-cold marble, warm it with my living flesh—' Timmy whispered . . . and he remembered countless encounters between himself, colder than ice or stone, and the human bodies bursting with the juice of life, drinking the echo of their living passions, and then he felt an unfamiliar wetness on his cheek, more swift than blood, more quick than dead.

The doors of Bluebeard's castle began to open, each one admitting a stream of blood-tinged light into the antechamber. The dungeon, with its racks and chains and iron maidens and flogging-posts . . . the treasure chamber, with its diamonds drenched in gore . . . the garden and its blood-dewed thorns. Horror was everywhere, and still Judit ploughed on, chainsawing her way into the duke's dark heart.

Then came the majestic fifth door, opening out over Bluebeard's empire . . . the hills, the meadows, the streams, the skies . . . flooding the stage with brilliance. Bartok's music thundered out in bright brass chords like the opening credits of a Biblical epic.

'So it's a happy ending after all,' Pamina whispered.

'I'm afraid not,' Timmy said.

> *Nyissad ki még a két ajtót . . .*
> Open the last two doors!

Again and again Patrizia Czaczek sang out those words, becoming ever more shrill and unbending. Passion seemed to rage in the aged Duke Bluebeard, as he staggered down the stair, reeling from the torrent of his lover's monomania. She swept after him, her black cloak skimming the balustrade in the stream of a wind machine. 'Open them! Open them!' she cried, and you could see that her need to get inside the old duke's heart was greater even than love, more powerful than death. It would consume before it could set free.

And Timmy, though he had seen the opera a dozen times before . . . once even in Budapest, on the eve of the Soviet invasion . . . he was drawn so deeply into the music, into the timeless archetypal drama, that he seemed to be on that stage with the two protagonists. Never mind the dead diva's relatives and acquaintances. Some were as absorbed as he, but most, as is the manner of many opera-goers, were only half involved, were fiddling with fur stoles, glancing surreptitiously at the exits . . . one was even whispering into a cellular phone, the very latest in philistine chic. Timmy was not even paying attention to Pamina, weeping noisily and even blowing her nose into the sleeve of Lady Chit's four-thousand-dollar dress. He felt himself dissociate from flesh, drift along the air currents, buoyed by the waves of sound. How strange it felt. He had always been able to float before . . . but now, it seemed, it took music to unlock the prison of his bone and blood. And it wasn't a total surrender to things invisible, not like the old times . . . he always felt the anchor of his body . . . always felt himself tugging against himself, the leaden ball at the end of the corporeal chain.

And yet . . . it seemed that he stood, unseen, between the two participants in the drama, that he was flitting back and forth between them on the tide of song. Bluebeard yielded up the sixth key. Timmy knew it would be the lake of tears. The stage darkened as the lit doors slammed shut; moonlight rippled over the flats. The staircase, painted plywood, seemed to acquire the coldness of marble, and the audience seemed more and more distant . . . their eyes like a thousand stars, the opera house itself like the great crystal sphere that once encircled the universe . . . in another place and time.

It was then that Timmy heard someone call his name.

Konrad . . .

The voice of a young woman.

A black cat ran across the stage, unnoticed save by him.

Timmy watched from the balcony. Another Timmy, attenuated in the music, stood in the shadow of the great blue drapes. Another Timmy stood in some half-remembered past. It was the third Timmy who heard the woman's voice. 'Amelia?' he whispered.

On the balcony, Pamina started from her rêverie. 'Timmy . . . do you see something? Do you hear something I don't hear?'

Bluebeard handed Judit the seventh and last key.

Behind the last door would be the three other wives . . . wives that the world thought dead but who still lived, entombed forever behind steel and stone . . . memories that could not die . . . and because she dared to probe into the places in a man's soul that are not for a woman to see, she too would enter the tomb . . . she too would become undead . . . that, Timmy knew, would be her fate.

One by one the women emerged and came down the marble steps. The woman of the morning, attired in the rosy dawn, fresh-cheeked . . . the woman at noon, her fiery hair piled high like the sun . . . and the third woman, the woman of the dusk . . .

> *Övé most már minden este,*
> *Övé barna búpalástja,*

'Hers,' the old man sang, 'is the sunset . . . hers the dark mantle of the grave . . .'

The woman who emerged at the top of the stairs was draped in a muslin shroud that concealed her body and most of her face . . . a wisp of white hair fringed the white cloth . . . her eyes were covered but you could see thin lips, a bloodless smile . . . you could smell the faint putrescence of the newly dead . . . and the perfume of embalming.

'Tante Amelia!' Pamina shrieked.

Timmy snapped back into himself. The spell was broken. The audience was trying to ignore Pamina's outburst, but one of the relatives was bearing down from the back of the box. 'The poor girl,' he was saying, 'she is quite griefstricken . . . she imagines something . . .'

'I'm not imagining a fucking thing!' Pamina shouted hysterically. 'That's my aunt down there . . . I swear it is! She's come back from the dead somehow . . . she's a vampire! Oh god, I knew she would come, I knew she would fetch me and take me to join her . . .'

Now eyes were turning on them, shushing noises were echoing through the theatre. He could hear other voices . . . 'Disgraceful! Such a shame! No sense of decorum whatsoever . . . the poor creature, out of her wits with grief, but you'd think she'd show a little breeding and not start screeching, I mean this is the opera, not some rock concert . . .'

'I'll take care of her,' Timmy said.

He helped Pamina up and began steering her toward the exit. She staggered, leaned against him like a drunken woman.

'But it's not over!' someone said 'Go and sit down at once, young lady. You're embarrassing us.' It was, Timmy realized, Pamina's mother. He ignored her and pulled Pamina out into the corridor. The opera continued to pour out of two television monitors on the landing; two uniformed ushers were watching fixedly. A third was speaking into an intercom.

Two paramedics rushed by with a stretcher.

'Is something wrong?' Timmy asked one of the ushers.

'Oh, it's one of the extras . . . she's had some kind of fainting spell . . . they found a substitute at the last minute . . .'

'Come on, Pami.'

'Don't call me—'

Timmy grabbed hold of her hand. 'No one will notice us. We'll blend into the shadows.' And they followed the stretcher bearers. Soon there were others too, a security guard of some kind, someone who looked like a journalist, all padding purposefully along the thick magenta carpeting and the walls of functional, naked concrete.

'How could she have become—' said Pamina.

'I used to drink her blood all the time. I never knew I had done that enough times to make her transform after her death . . . they say that if you continually drink a mortal's blood, it edges them closer and closer to the changing . . . but it was all so long ago . . . surely she must have got over it by now . . .'

'How can you say that, Timmy? How could any one get over you?'

Deeper now. Down into the bowels of the building. Down toward the very dressing room Timmy had used the previous night.

Flinging the door open—

She lay on the very couch where Timmy and Pamina had sat. She wore a silk dressing gown and nothing else. She seemed to have been watching for her cue on a television monitor on which the opera was still playing . . . and the music of Blue-beard's grief was pouring into the room from an overhead loud-speaker. She had been plump and homely, but now her skin shone with a pallid iridescence that reminded Timmy of—

'*Es gibt kein Blut!*' someone murmured. The paramedics began loading her onto the stretcher. No one noticed the two of them, the ex-vampire and the would-be vampire, just behind the door-way, watching.

'What do you mean, no blood?' It was one of the paramedics.

'No blood at all. She's been drained.'

They hustled the woman away. It was too late for her; she was clearly quite, quite dead. Timmy stood for a moment, watching the monitor. Bluebeard was telling Judit she was to enter the secret room and herself be locked away for ever . . . *És mindig is éjjel lest már* . . . from now on all will be darkness, darkness, darkness . . .

The woman of the twilight . . . it was Amelia Rothstein . . . spread her cloak wide to receive the new woman of the night . . .

'She's going to kill her!' Timmy gasped. 'Right there, in front of thousands of people . . .'

Judit rushed into the vampire's arms. Was enfolded in the sheer white shroud. Amelia Rothstein bared her fangs . . . bit down . . . red spurted from Patrizia Czaczek's neck, spattered the muslin, gushed out onto the plywood marble of the castle set . . . you could hear the audience gasp as one, awed by the high-tech of the gore effects no doubt, little knowing that Amelia's protégée had sung her last . . . and then the doorway closed, on cue, leaving Bluebeard alone in the dark.

The applause came.

'What are we going to do?' Pamina said.

'We have to stop this. It has to end,' Timmy said.

'You mean kill her? The stake through the heart and everything?'

'It's not really Amelia. It's only Amelia's earthly carcase, ani-mated by something else—'

'You know that isn't true. There *must* have been something in Amelia that yearned to be undead. There must be something of her still inside her . . . you should know. You were like her once. There was always a thread of you through life and unlife . . . and you know it.'

'Maybe so.' He knew he didn't sound very convincing. After all, he no longer had the ability to enchant men's souls, to conjure shapes from darkness. But now I'm only a real boy after all . . . reality sucks, he thought.

'Why should we kill her?' Pamina demanded.

'Because if we don't, it will all go on and on and on and—'

'As you have,' said Pamina Rothstein.

'Tell me where she's buried.'

'Don't *kill* her!'

'But we have to talk to her at least. Where is she buried? She has to go there before sunrise . . .'

13

NATIVE EARTH

vampire hunters

PJ was startled to hear his beeper go off, even more surprised to learn where Timmy was heading, and that he was going to have to go back to the hotel to collect a full complement of the tools of the vampire killer's trade.

It wasn't going to be easy.

They raided the suite refrigerator for a half dozen miniature Schnapps bottles, poured their contents down the toilet, then stopped off at the quaint little church on the corner of Eichendorfstrabe to refill them with holy water. Almost all the shops were already closed – this wasn't like Los Angeles, with its twenty-four-hour supermarkets – you couldn't just run down and pick up garlic, stakes, and crosses at any hour of the night.

'What are we going to do?' Chit said. PJ was driving the Valentinemobile, the long black limo they'd shipped over from the States in order to surround Timmy with a familiar environment.

'Look, over there . . . it looks like a Thai restaurant. Maybe . . .'

Indeed it was, tucked between a bookstore and a *Konditorei*. The world was becoming more and more like LA every day, PJ thought. Fancy finding a *Thai-Chinesisch* eatery in the heart of Bavaria! And it was the only establishment in the whole street that was still lit – garishly so – with a neon sign in *Miami Vice* pink and turquoise that screamed for attention amid the stone gables and cobbled paving.

'It's almost like a gateway to another universe,' Chit said. 'But they'll have garlic.'

They did indeed. It shouldn't have surprised PJ by now, but the proprietor of the store, a Thai-Chinese man by the name of Samak, not only recognized Lady Chit and PJ from their wedding photos, which had been on the cover of the upscale *Ploikaempetch* magazine, but hardly batted an eyelid when Chit explained that they needed some equipment for hunting down a *phiidip*.

'I've got a meat tenderizing mallet that you can use to hammer in the stakes,' Samak said, 'and we can probably come up with some shish kebab skewers, if you think they'll work . . .'

'What about crosses, crucifixes?' PJ said.

'I suppose I can lend you our Goddess of Mercy,' said Samak, 'since it is such an important occasion.'

Perched on a ledge above the cash register was the statue of *Jaomae Kuan In*, the Chinese goddess much beloved by restaurant owners. Samak folded his palms and whispered a brief prayer, then removed it and handed it to Chit, who reverently placed the goddess in her purse.

This is getting pretty fucking baroque, PJ thought. Exorcism goes multicultural. Native American uses Asian magic to defeat Transylvanian monster in the heart of Oktoberfest territory – Jesus. But what *about* that Native American business? PJ was no longer the *ma'aipots*, the sacred man-woman, slayer of demons. He knew he was more out of touch with his former self than at any other time in his life. A vision had changed him, and a vision had stolen that change away; now he no longer had visions. Hollywood has bleached my skin, he thought. Can I still fight vampires?

He felt Chit's hand against his cheek. 'Don't worry about it,' she said. 'If I can do it, anyone can.' She fingered the amulet around her neck.

He smiled a little. 'Thanks for the vote of confidence,' he said. And then, 'Do you think you should have left that thing behind?'

She said, 'It seems to have a mind of its own.'

resurrection

The stage door has slammed shut. She stands with the sheer white shroud-cloths billowing about her and the dying woman she cradles in her arms. The woman is barely struggling, barely breathing. But Amelia is not done with her. She is still unused to the insatiable hunger, still thinks, perhaps, that it can be slaked if one merely finds and drains enough victims, does not yet understand that the yearning is eternal. They stand together in the dark. Behind the door, the music of Bartók's opera is ebbing. The applause has begun. She knows that the curtain will rise again, that Patrizia Czaczek must appear to take many curtain calls. Perhaps Patrizia was even supposed to make some kind of *in memoriam* speech commemorating her deceased mentor . . . what an irony!

Amelia feels the irony acutely. But she feels no remorse, no compassion. Only the yearning animates her dead flesh, only the yearning. From the moment she awakened, clawed her way up through the goulash of worms and mulch that covered her coffin, she has been aware only of the yearning. She has made her way over to the opera house because it is a place she is familiar with, a place of former triumphs. She has run through the unlit streets, close to the cobblestones, keenly aware of the scent of blood – there! in a passing Volkswagen, an old man's blood, sluggish! there! from an open window, the whistling blood of newlyweds making love! And then here in the Opernhaus, thousands of mortals brimming with life force, maddening her . . . until she found the first victim in the bowels of the theatre, her eyes glued to the television set.

So simple to be invited in. So simple to saw into the jugular with her brand new razor fangs. But then came practical matters. Taking the woman's place in the scene was a good idea, but when the seventh door flew open and the scent of all that blood came bursting through all at once, she is unable to help herself. It was not only the blood of the singers on stage; it was the adrenalin-rich blood of the orchestral players as they concentrated on the conductor and their fiendishly complex parts, and most of all the blood in the audience, thousands of souls enslaved by the music's magic, their blood battering against

their bodies' imprisonment like surf against cliffs, like wind, like
rain. How could she not feed, amid this ocean of manna? And
having fed, what was she to do so as not to give herself away?

Patrizia! Patrizia! comes the roar of the crowd.

Amelia throws the door open for a second. She holds Patrizia
in her arms, moves her slender neck up and down and her body
in a brief curtsy. The applause is deafening. Then, as though
her victim were overcome with grief, she manipulates Patrizia
down the castle steps, makes her bow again. It is easy since the
vertebrae in the neck are already beginning to crack.

I should have thought this through, she thinks. What am I
going to do? The gore is coagulating on the costume, a starched
and many-layered symphony of black lace, *faux* pearls and brocade. If I drop Patrizia, she will crash to the floor and the noise
will attract attention.

Patrizia stirs. She is still not quite dead. Her movement brings
renewed applause. Doesn't anyone see what is really going on?
Their world is sheer illusion, she thinks . . . their reality just
the confluence of a million private hallucinations.

Patrizia moves again, as though acknowledging the applause.
How unlike the first woman, who just slipped into death without even blinking. I have to act quickly – get her out of here.
Like a puppeteer, Amelia supports the dying singer as she backs
up to the seventh door and closes it again.

Stage flats are stacked against one wall. She retreats through
the spaces between them. It is easy to carry the woman. It must
be true then that her kind have superhuman strength, for she
does not feel the weight at all. Indeed, she cannot feel her own
weight, and as she squeezes between the plywood and canvas
of the scenic paintings she realizes that there are times when
she is threading through spaces too narrow for her body to fit
through. She is only part flesh now, and part shadow, part
dusty air. She passes beyond the wings and out into the labyrinth of passageways that crisscross the hidden sections of the
onetime Opernhaus. Even the physical world seems to be in
flux, for there are times when she doesn't see the geometric
concrete slabs of the new building but the patterned velvet wall-
paper and rococo mouldings of the theatre where she first sang,
where she first encountered the cruel and beautiful child she

knew as Konrad Stolz . . . where she first fell in love with the
creature who, decades later, had returned to collect her soul.

There he is . . . isn't that him, darting from shadow to
shadow? Or is it a mere remembrance, impinging on a mind fast
unloosing itself from the jesses of flesh and time? The Timmy
Valentine who came to the nursing home has been but shadowy
echo of the creature who still lives in her memory. He should
not have chosen to become human! she thinks. All humans are
like that . . . vague reflections of the true things that do not
change . . . imperfect copies of the eternal. She exults in the
eternity that stretches ahead. She exults in its perpetual dark
and cold. If this is hell, she thinks, then hell has a transcendent
beauty that mortals cannot begin to imagine.

Far from the roaring crowd, in a dead-end corridor between
the staff women's lavatory and a janitor's closet, she finishes
feasting on Patrizia Czaczek. Then – because in her own way
she had loved her protégée, even though it had pained her to
hear her perform the stratospheric rôles she could no longer
sing, Fiordiligi, Arabella, Tosca – she carefully breaks Patrizia's
neck and, with a twisting motion, rips off her head.

'I'm so sorry, Patrizia,' she says softly, and then – even though
she has not thought about her father's religion since they
dragged him away, more than fifty years ago – she struggles to
remember the words of the *Kaddish*, and almost manages to get
to the end.

Methodically she dismembers the rest of the carcase. Tenderly
she wraps each piece in the copious material of Judit's costume.
She knows there is plenty of time, for she can hear every footfall,
every whisper, every breath that transpires in this whole place.
She stacks the gift-wrapped pieces of Patrizia Czaczek at the
end of the hallway, limbs criss-crossing over torso, head on top.
For the moment she is lazy, sated, like a plump cat curled up
on a sheepskin. Patrizia's blood has been hot and zesty, spiced
by the tension of the operatic role and the shock of sudden
death. She savours the memory of it. She has been thinking of
cats and now she realizes, with a start, that she has become
one, a purring shadow that stirs now, licks its haunches, hones
its claws against the carpeting.

She runs. She leaps. She hears them now, the opera-goers

leaving the auditorium, the shuffling feet, the murmured conversations: Did you see what I saw? It looked so real, so . . . intense . . . macabre, wasn't it, making the third wife up to look so much like Amelia Rothstein . . . ? Oh, I'm sure it wasn't intentional, I'm sure you were just seeing things . . . but the blood, the blood!

She scurries down the hall. They're coming: policemen, paramedics, journalists. They know something is wrong. The air has turned sour with the smell of fear. She hastens. The footsteps move from carpet-muffled to clanging against bare concrete. They must be following the trail of blood. They'll be here soon. She rounds a corner and suddenly she is among them: rain-slicked boots, stiletto heels, patent leather, the graveyard stench of dead animals and the quick scent of fear. She slips in between those legs, wriggles through, and then she shoots down the corridor toward the exit.

The lobby: the crowd is mourning, unaware that they have seen the very woman they mourn. Everywhere the racing blood. Everywhere the intoxicating scent. Maddening, maddening! She almost cannot hold her shape. But she must. Out. The long line of limousines and taxis stretches all the way down the narrow street.

She cannot see them, but she feels the sun and moon in her bones, knows how the wheel of time turns. She knows where she must go. The night air is brisk. Her paws pad over the cobblestones. She turns. Alley after alley. Dead, all dead, the brick, the stones, the pavement . . . now and then she senses the flickering life force of a cockroach as it skitters over a pipe . . . the twitch of a mouse's whiskers. A neon sign goes *dzzt-dzzt* as the bar it advertises closes down for the night. She heads for the outskirts of Thauberg, toward the country road that leads to her resting-place.

vampire hunters

About ten kilometres outside Thauberg proper lay the Friedensgärten Mortuary, a belligerently neo-classical building with Ionic columns, porticoes and statues of ancient gods. As the taxi pulled up, Pamina said, 'She should be somewhere in the basement . . . the actual interment isn't supposed to happen till tomorrow.'

If the taxi driver showed any curiosity at the two young people, in their evening finery, asking to be dropped off in front of a funeral home in the dead of night, he did not show it. Perhaps it was because he only spoke Turkish. He did seem a bit startled, however, when Timmy tipped him with a crisp hundred mark note and told him, in his own language, to forget what he had seen. He zipped away as fast as he could, leaving the two standing in front of the wrought-iron gates, gazing at the Hellenistic monstrosity at the end of the driveway of sculpted hedges.

'Turkish?' Pamina said softly.

'It's coming back to me,' Timmy said. 'Although it may have sounded rather archaic to him.'

A rat had been gnawing at the hostage's leg . . .

'What is coming back to you?'

'Memories.' Timmy did not want to think of it. It was different when Carla Rubens had been his guide through the labyrinth of two millennia past. Now he had only himself. He was beginning to understand now that there was one final darkness still to be faced . . . perhaps it was this that had caused him to become human. Maybe I can only comprehend this darkness as a human . . .

The dungeon . . .

'Tell me more about this place,' Timmy said. 'For one thing, do you think we'll be able to get in?'

'I don't know.' She gave the gate a push. It opened immediately. So far, so good. Not many graverobbers in the twentieth century, Timmy supposed. Security lax. 'This land used to be a Jewish cemetery, you know. Perhaps that's why Tante Amelia planned it this way. Or maybe it was just the most eccentric place she could think of for her funeral arrangements. It's very un-German,' Pamina said wistfully. It occurred to Timmy that Pamina was only now beginning to feel her grief.

'During the war, they knocked down all the headstones and put a factory on top. But that's gone too. Some American entrepreneur named Max Halperin bought it up and built this nondenominational funeral home. I think he wanted it to be a chain. Like your McDonald's.'

'An American! No wonder it's so overblown.'

They walked down the driveway. 'Are you sure she'll come back?' Pamina said.

'She has to. The native earth and all that. There's a lot of tradition at work. It takes a long time to get away from all that. And then, you know, there are all the dead people. You say they carted away all the headstones, but the dead are still down there somewhere. When you're dead yourself, you can hear them whispering. Alive, people think it's only the wind sighing through the grass. Or the leaves stirring. But if you're like Amelia is now, you will hear their voices sometimes. They cry out as the worms churn their flesh into fresh dirt. They have so few feelings. You envy them, really, because they're not driven by the terrible hunger.'

'I think I can hear something.'

'No you can't. I've tried. When you're human you have no senses.'

'Oh, you're exaggerating. I can see you, smell you, hear you. *Ja*, there's times when I think that vampires must feel more deeply, but—'

'Believe me. I know. Humans are blind. They are deaf. They are endlessly unaware of their surroundings.' Even as he said this Timmy was wondering why he had given it all up. At first it had been good not to know, not to feel. But now he was frustrated because he could not tell where Amelia was, how far away she was; because he could not smell the presence of death in the mortuary, could not know how many had already fallen to the undead diva. Was mortality worth it? There had been a downside, too, though, hadn't there, to his old existence? The bleakness. The thirst that could be quelled for a time but which never subsided altogether.

It was with such thoughts that he made his way down the driveway to the main building. Pamina followed him. They ascended five or six marble steps to reach the front portico. There was a bronze door – perhaps it was only a bronze veneer – that appeared to be a reproduction of the portal of some Italian cathedral – he was sure he had seen it before somewhere. The door swung open. Overhead, a television camera pivoted, pointed, flashed red.

'It seems that we're expected,' Timmy said.

Welcome, said a deep voice, just dripping with solace and solicitude, *to the gardens of peace.* Pamina jumped. The message repeated itself in German and French and Timmy realized it was just a tape recording. *We are open twenty-four hours a day for those who wish to commune with their loved ones.*

One by one, fluorescent overhead lights went on. They were in a circular hallway. In the centre was a kind of monument, a pyramidal collage of old headstones . . . with names and pieces of names that were redolently Semitic . . . *Sirota* . . . *Saperstein* . . . *Kaganowitsch* . . . *Levy* . . . *Goldberg* . . . it was the only thing here that was not self-consciously grandiose . . . it was, indeed, curiously moving. Pamina walked around the sculpture several times, reading off the names, and when she came to Jakob Rothstein, she said, 'Now there's someone I've heard of. I think that was Tante Amelia's grandfather.'

'I guess that's why she wanted to be taken care of in this strange place. It was the native earth, calling to her even while she was still human.'

'How odd. Tante Amelia was never very . . . well, you know, she was one of the *Halbjuden*, spent the war in hiding . . . afterwards, there were no survivors in that half of the family . . . only, of course, the Gentile half. I don't know very much about those other relatives. No one spoke of them.'

Their words echoed unnaturally . . . as though they were being picked up and fed through a signal processor . . . lending this small space the resonance of some mediaeval basilica.

Evenly spaced around the perimeter of the circular foyer were seven doorways. One was, Timmy knew, the way back out; the other six seemed to lead further into the labyrinth. 'We're going to have to try them all,' Pamina said.

'But why is there no one else here? There's got to be someone . . . a guard on the night shift, an undertaker working late.'

Music began to play. It was Vivaldi . . . one of those interchangeable slow movements that are said to evoke a sense of tranquillity and are therefore popular at funerals. Strings – you could not tell if they were real or sampled – swelled and ebbed.

The same voice that had greeted them earlier began to speak soothingly of eternity, of comfort, of the sleep of the ages. It all had a kind of robotic soullessness.

'Jesus,' Timmy said, 'I think I'm in Disneyland.'

'But somewhere here there are dead people. This is so fucking unnerving, it's making my nipple rings tingle.'

'Yes.'

'*Tante Amelia! Wo bist du?*' she shouted. Her voice reverberated. She tried one of the doors. They saw row upon row of stacked memorials . . . sort of like marble post office boxes, Timmy thought . . . and here and there a wreath.

'They must keep ashes there,' he said.

'Yes,' said Pamina, 'they do cremations, they do everything.'

He tried another door. This one opened out into a tangled garden. A statue of a winged boy overlooked a wilderness of flowers. Peering from the foliage were stone memorials, some with little statues of children. The moon looked down through a glass roof. Bells tinkled. A nursery rhyme played over and over, reminding Timmy once again of Disneyland . . . the *Small World* boat ride this time, the attraction adults most fear getting stuck in. How charming, he thought, a great place to bury your kids.

'From one Bluebeard's castle to another,' Timmy said. He laughed nervously. Pamina touched him and he started. 'Where *is* everyone?' he said.

'Let's try the other doors.'

The next door opened into a small room with vending machines: a full complement of Coke products, a coffee machine, and a machine that dispensed ham sandwiches. Suddenly, Timmy felt hungry, but all he had on him were hundred-mark notes.

The next door was a closet. When Timmy pulled open the door, the corpse of a security guard fell out.

He was nude, but you could tell he was a guard because his clothes had been neatly folded at his feet. A wallet lay on top of the pile of clothes – Timmy could not help noticing that the shoes had been spotlessly polished – and on the wallet was something that looked like a credit card – or one of those computer-generated hotel keys. The guard himself was soft and

bloodless. There were two round, purple punctures at the base
of his neck, which had been wrenched completely around and
snapped. His thighs were stained with piss and semen. He had,
perhaps, died happy.

Timmy looked at the body with a kind of professional detach-
ment, but he was soon interrupted by the sound of Pamina
retching. 'I'm sorry, I really am,' she kept saying. 'I just didn't
know dead people could be quite so . . . disgusting.'

'And you wanted to be a vampire,' Timmy said.

'It's not funny! Here we are in the middle of this death amuse-
ment park and all you can do is make fun of me!'

'I'm sorry,' Timmy said. He took her hand. She was shaking.
'Come on now, PJ and Chit will be here any minute. But we
have to find your aunt.'

'I'm all right now.' He could tell she was making a monumental effort to overcome her revulsion. 'I'm really going to be all
right. And yes, I still want to be a vampire.' She looked into his
eyes and for the first time he thought could catch a glimpse of
the desolation of eternity, and he thought, She knows something I don't know, she's *seen* something . . .

The next door was an elevator, and it only went one way . . .
down.

The two of them got in. There were apparently many levels
beneath the mausoleum, marked B1, B2, and so on, but you
needed to stick a card in a slot to make the elevator stop there
at the lowest one, which bore the legend *Labyrinthos*. 'Kind of
like the concierge level at the Sheraton,' Timmy said.

'That must be another one of those American jokes.'

'We'd better go up and get the card from the guard's wallet.
We were obviously meant to find that.'

'Is this going to be like the *real* labyrinth, I mean, in Greek
mythology, and we have to tie a thread to the door and keep
spooling it out so we don't get lost, and we're going to fight the
minotaur and all that stuff? Oh, I'm sorry; we Germans get a
more classical education . . . you're more American with your
Sheratons and Disneylands.'

Timmy laughed. 'I've forgotten more classics than you've ever
studied,' he said at last.

The levels flashed by and at last they reached bottom to the accompaniment of dirge-like elevator music. The doors opened and they stepped out into a limestone cavern. Timmy left the key card in the slot and hoped that PJ and Chit would realize where they were headed.

The only light came from the smears of phosphorescence that streaked the stalactites and stalagmites. It was cold and dank. Somewhere, machinery whirred. Surely this was where they kept the dead bodies. And surely this was the native earth to which Amelia Rothstein had to return. 'Scared?' Timmy said.

'So are you,' said Pamina.

It was true. The chill wasn't just from the refrigeration. There was something cold at the base of his neck . . . like an icicle. It had to be fear. He had smelled it often enough on his victims, in the old days.

'Come on,' he said hoarsely.

The floor was marked with arrows that seemed to lead through the maze of limestone columns. They passed a grotto bathed in purplish light. Here and there were steps, always descending . . . and the passageway itself seemed to incline downward as it turned and twisted. There was a niche with an altar to some horned god, the incense hanging in the heavy air. Now and then they seemed to have doubled back on themselves . . . for wasn't that the purple grotto once again? Or was it different? They descended. It was getting still colder now.

'It's like a meat locker,' Timmy said.

'Don't remind me,' said Pamina, and Timmy wondered what kind of trauma the image evoked for her; she shuddered and would not meet his gaze.

They descended. There was a faint medicinal whiff . . . perhaps formaldehyde . . . the perfume of embalming. Their breath clouded the already murky air. They descended. Were these caves a natural phenomenon, or had they been manufactured to appease the fancy of the American entrepreneur? But now the passageway seemed to widen, and recessed along the walls there were metal cabinets with corpse-sized drawers, as in a morgue. The odour grew stronger. There was also a sense of . . .

'Do you feel it?' said Timmy. 'We're becoming unmoored.'

'What do you mean?'

'The fabric of reality is loosening. Do you know what I mean?

There are places in the world where the tangible is tenuous. In my old house in Los Angeles, there was an attic like that. There were corridors and doorways that led straight from the real world into the territory of dreams. Not my dreams, you realize. Vampires, of course, don't dream. But they can cloak themselves in mortals' dreams; they can appear clothed in borrowed fantasies . . . that's what it was like.'

She held his hand tight and seemed to draw comfort from the things he told her, as though they were familiar to her from childhood. They turned a corner and now there was doorway after doorway and if you peered inside you could see dead people: lying on plinths, chained to lightning-rods à la Frankenstein, swimming in plexiglass tanks. The fear – he was sure it was fear now – was down to a faint throbbing in his spine. He had to overcome it. These things are nothing new, he told himself.

'How far to Amelia, I wonder,' he said. Too loudly. His voice echoed and reechoed. Speaking loudly makes you less afraid.

'Further. I can feel her.' And Timmy wondered anew that she could feel things he could not.

Lower. Lower. Creaky steps and cobwebs. Grey stone walls that dripped blood. Lower. The beating of leathern wings. A rickety bridge over an abyss of black fire. Lower.

'I'm afraid,' Pamina whispered.

Lower. The New Age music that had accompanied their journey churned, blurred, became jangled cacophony. And now from the chaos came song . . .

O thou beautiful Art . . .

'It's her,' Pamina said.

'It's Schubert,' he said. It was the same song she had sung in the greenhouse of the old musicians' home – Schubert's paean to music, the one redeeming Art that could quell the raging of men's souls and quiet the unquenchable longing of eternity. How well he knew that sentiment. He did not think he could have survived two thousand years without the gift of music.

The lake of flame. The rope bridge burning up behind them. Hurry, hurry!

The song called out to them, dispelled their fear. They stepped on to the cliff's edge as the bridge fell flaming into the void.

And now, suddenly, they were back in the Opernhaus – almost fifty years ago – in the little dressing room where Amelia used to sit. Every detail was the same: the gilt fading from the two winged *putti* that framed the mirror at the makeup table . . . the lumpy divan . . . the painting of St Cecilia on the wall, a tear on the saint's sleeve crudely patched with Sellotape. The music came from somewhere down the hall, the répétiteur's room where the singers went to thrash out their parts. Every detail, indeed, was as it had been, even the smell of dust, except . . .

On the sofa, the head of a grey-haired woman. Eyeless. A pearl choker around her withered neck had become entangled in a protruding vertebra. But not a drop of blood.

Under the painting, in a shaft of yellow light, the woman's torso, shrouded in black satin and mink. On the dresser, her severed hands, folded in a ghastly parody of the famous Dürer etching.

Pamina screamed.

The music stopped and the door swung open; and there was Amelia: no longer old, but ageless; no longer tired, but bright-eyed; wiping the last smear of blood from her lips with a lace handkerchief.

'Shush, Pami, shush,' Amelia said. 'I have become what you longed to become. Aren't you happy for me?'

'I suppose so,' Pamina said. But there was bitterness there. 'But I'm mad that it happened to you, not me.'

Amelia said, 'This was all predestined,' and she opened her arms wide to reveal the bloodstained paste and papier-mâché of her operatic costume, 'from the moment Konrad Stolz came to the Opernhaus to play the little shepherd boy in *Tosca*. You came to me in this room . . . which has been recreated for you from our conjoined memories . . . why else does it look, taste, smell so *true* to you? You gave me a gift that has no price, Konrad . . . you would perhaps prefer I call you Timmy, but you will always be Konrad Stolz to me . . . I was a lonely woman . . . as a child always living in hiding because of my father's . . . ancestry . . . always terrified I would be betrayed by those of my mother's friends who knew her secret . . . after the war, flaunting my father's surname as my stage name, I wanted to defy the past . . . but I was so lonely . . . and you . . . you

touched me. Oh, yes, you gave me a piquant sexual pleasure
that I was never able to repeat with any human being . . . the
coldness of your skin against my flaming skin, the icy fleck of
your tongue against my bloodstained labia . . . after you left the
Opernhaus I never had an orgasm again, did you know that?
Even though, *ja*, I had all those children with Herr Eckert. Oh
yes, Pamina, I know that you have had him too . . . but such
poor leavings you have had. Konrad . . . you know you regret
stepping away from your destiny. You know that you cannot
be human . . . how can you, with your manhood ripped from
you as a child . . . unable ever to find fulfilment? But now I can
repay you for the gift you made me fifty years ago . . . I can
give you back your immortality. All the others I killed, I broke
their necks, I ripped their bodies apart so that they could be
saved from the emptiness beyond, but you . . . you, Konrad,
will be my love, my angel, my divine consort. We will consume
one another for ever, and yet there will always be more to consume. Oh, Konradchen, Konradchen, come to me.'

Timmy looked into the vampire's eyes and saw that she was
drawing him with the same hypnotic gaze he had used himself
so many thousands of times through history. He felt himself
succumbing. It was so much easier to be the prey than the
hunter, so easy to tumble into the vortex of seduction, so easy
to lose the will to live . . . this is how they all must have felt,
he thought in wonderment. This yielding, this ecstasy in which
one relinquishes all the pain of life . . . it is like making love.
He barely noticed Pamina, glaring at him with longing and envy.
Amelia's eyes were keyholes through which shone light: white,
cold, ineffable.

'Don't you want it?' Amelia whispered.

'I don't know,' Timmy said softly . . . but he knew he was
failing to hold on . . . around them, reality was wavering once
more as the room and all its contents swam, melded into a
kaleidoscope of images from the time of his immortality . . . the
fire of exploding Pompeii . . . a witch woman burning at the
stake . . . fire in the Globe Theatre, an actor fleeing with his wig
aflame, a bear clawing at his chains in the bear-pit next door
. . . fire in the streets of Moscow, in the ovens of Oswięcim
. . . fire running down the wormhole passageways of a Turkish

prison, racing toward the cell of a Transylvanian hostage . . .

'You *do* know! You hate your flesh-bound mortal self! You are no Pinocchio. As a real boy, you're a failure . . . your music has lost its genius . . . you can't even have sex!'

'I—'

Suddenly Pamina pushed herself between the two of them. 'You're a coward, Timmy Valentine,' she shrieked. 'You're not the Timmy Valentine I dreamed about all those years I drank blood in secret . . . Tante Amelia, don't pay any attention to him. It's *me* you should have come for.'

She rushed into her aunt's arms. Timmy watched, still under Amelia's ensorcellment. The vampire stiffened. Timmy felt the spell weaken a little. Pamina was thrusting her neck against her aunt's lips, trying to force her mouth open with both hands. She pursed her lips, but he saw the telltale fleck of hunger in her eyes. Pamina's desire was a terrifying thing. Amelia could not hold Timmy in her power. The enchantment snapped as she flung Pamina away from her. He saw her fall to the floor . . . or was it the flaming flagstones of the temple of Isis in Pompeii? . . . and then Amelia turned her gaze on Timmy once again.

Come to me, she whispered. He felt the ancient seduction of the dark. He had whispered those words in a hundred languages and they had come to him . . . why should he not now be the hunted? He took a faltering step toward her. She opened her arms wide to receive him.

Come to me—

Come to me—

Love me—

Be one with me—

She smiled. Darkness encircled him: her cloak, the night, eternity. The only light was the glitter of her fangs—

Then a mighty peal, like timber crashing in the forest. Amelia's mouth closed. Oh, he thought, I'm dying, I'm dying for the third time and final time—

Light. A metal skewer burst through Amelia's bosom. Old blood oozed to the tip. Amelia was falling backwards and now, behind her, he could see that PJ twisting the makeshift stake through Amelia's heart.

'No!' Amelia screamed. 'Make them stop, Konradchen, make them stop . . .'

And there was Lady Chit. She was emptying the contents of a miniature liquor bottle on Amelia's face. The flesh was melting, charring as Amelia hit the ground.

Quickly, PJ stuffed the vampire's mouth with garlic. Then Chit took the statue of a Chinese goddess from her purse and placed it over the wound in Amelia's chest.

The porcelain goddess smiled. Blue light haloed her, and Timmy watched the light spread from the statue over the vampire's body, as she writhed. The light broke into a hundred jagged filaments and ate away the woman's skin . . . and her flesh . . . and her bones, which fell into a heap of fuming powder.

'Powerful stuff,' PJ said. 'That Thai restaurant must really rake it in.'

Chit put the statue back in her purse. A New Age soundtrack, cloyingly saccharine, began to tinkle away in the background.

'How did you find us?' Timmy said.

'Followed our noses,' said PJ. 'I'm glad you left the card in the slot in the elevator.'

'But . . .' What about the limestone caverns, the steep stone stairwells, the brimstone lake? It must all have been part of Amelia's spell of entrapment . . . a spiderweb with herself at its centre.

'I wanted to become a vampire again,' Timmy said. 'I actually wanted to . . .' And started to weep. Another new sensation.

And PJ, who had once been the boy vampire's mortal enemy, took him in his arms and consoled him, and wiped away his tears with a callused hand, and spoke to him softly, like a loving father. 'It's OK,' PJ said. 'You can't expect the past to just disappear. You can't expect to let it all go at once.'

Timmy sat down on what had been the divan. It was, he now saw, an armchair. The room they were in was a white-walled, antiseptic embalming room. A few other corpses lay on trestle tables, some covered with sheets, others not; the air reeked of formaldehyde. Lady Chit was now helping Pamina get up; there was a dark blue bruise on the girl's forehead, and her arms were scratched and bleeding.

'You killed her,' Pamina said. 'Why?'

Timmy could not answer her. He knew the stock answers: vampires are an abomination, vampires are evil, they'll spread across the world like a plague, like AIDS, it has to be contained, destroyed . . . but he also knew that between vampire and victim there is a kind of love. He wept for the death of that love, and for the irrevocable passing of a woman who had been his friend. He tried to reach out for Pamina, to share his mourning with her; but she rebuffed him.

'What's so special about you anyway? Why do they love *you* so much?' she said. 'That should have been *my* immortality. You stole my Tante Amelia from me.'

She whisked the blanket from the nearest corpse and sobbed inconsolably into it, and Timmy could not touch her aloneness; and after a while he let his two adult friends steer the two of them toward the elevator, up to the foyer with its reminder of the holocaust and its Bluebeard-like doors, and they drove back to the hotel in silence.

Part III

WHAT MUSIC
THEY MAKE

'Why this is hell,'
The poet said
He didn't say
Why *this is hell*

'Nor am I out,'
The poet said
But I am out
And can't go home

Timmy Valentine

14

PASSING IN THE NIGHT

night train

Something was coming in on the cellular fax. High-res, a jillion shades of grey . . . almost as good as a photograph. Amazing, those devices, fucking amazing. Especially now, hurtling at high speed northward through Germany, the fields and the phone poles reeling past in the moonlight. PJ had already arranged for plane tickets, but Timmy wanted to go by train even though it would only give them about three hours to get ready for the next concert. 'Indulge me, PJ,' he'd said. 'You know I miss my model trains . . .'

Once on board, Timmy took a Valium, went to his sleeping compartment, and was out like a light. Pamina was still with them: sullen, withdrawn, but refusing to go back to her parents. After moping all the way to Munich, she had finally popped a few pills and gone to bed herself. They had the whole car to themselves, a bodyguard at either end. For the first time, it seemed, since Chit had flown in from Thailand, they were able to sit quietly together, not talking, just watching the nightscape unfurl.

Then the cellular fax whirred to life. 'Don't bother to read it,' said Chit. 'It's probably my mother. She can't leave her fax machine alone . . .'

PJ glanced across a heap of luggage. Paper was extruding itself. In the moonlight he could tell that it wasn't words. 'It's a picture . . . it's . . . I think it's the newest Lauren McCandless!' he said. 'He must have been working like a demon.'

She is standing in the window lashed by rain. Over her heart is tattooed another heart . . . a cheap smashed ghettoblaster at her feet

. . . and on the wall a poster advertising Timmy Valentine's new album
Vanitas, *a poster that shows the boy nude beneath a sheet of canvas
that is another painting by Lauren McCandless . . . and in the background, a shadow of a man who stands just at the edge of frame, a
shadow some will come to identify as Lauren himself . . . part of yet
not part of the killing . . . and the woman completely drained of blood.*

'Funny to see it in black and white,' Chit said, as she tore
off the waxy sheet. 'Look . . . here comes another page . . .
handwritten.'

> Chit and PJ:
> Thought you'd enjoy this pitiful xerox. It's all done and
> now I want to hibernate for a million years. Great about
> the offer from the Corcoran. Just stash the money in my
> bank account, I'll pick it up one of these days. I'm gonna
> give up painting for a while. Well. I'll just get in the
> houseboat, turn on the motor, and go . . . somewhere. I hear
> Indonesia's nice . . . much, much more primitive. Maybe
> even Borneo. Shit, New Guinea. Didn't one of the
> Rockefeller boys get eaten by the natives there? Can you
> just see me among the cannibal savages? 'Mistah
> McCandless, he dead!' Great fucking deal. Those whom the
> gods touch are never quite the same. You know I'm mad,
> don't you? Maybe I was only faking before, now it's the real
> thing. Yippee-eye-ay! See you around, Love, Lauren McC.

'Wow,' PJ said.
'I hope he's OK,' said Chit. 'But you know, Angel possessed
him almost utterly. There were times when there was almost
no Lauren left inside that skull of his, only Angel Todd.'
'I don't know why you keep that amulet then. You ought to
throw it away, flush it down the toilet, drop it out the fucking
window.'
'I just can't. He possesses me too, sometimes; he needs to go
somewhere, sometimes I think I'm just a train and he's the
passenger, paid the fare, got to make sure that I don't crash.'
'But is it a gravy train? Or are we hurtling toward the old
Cassandra Crossing?' He was trying to make her laugh, but she

obviously hadn't seen that old movie. So he went on, 'You know, don't you, that we've almost seen the last of Timmy Valentine . . . that he's made an agreement with Giler at Stupendous that he'll mysteriously disappear in a puff of smoke in his opening concert in Bangkok?'

'What for?'

'God, who knows? The sales figures . . . the thing in the *Weekly World News* . . . who knows?'

'Timmy doesn't *need* to disappear every couple of decades anymore. He has nothing to hide. He *will* grow old. He *will*—'

'I know. But this time the disappearing act isn't about protecting Timmy Valentine; it's about money, plain old money.'

'What's Timmy going to do?'

'Who knows? Maybe he'll even become Angel Todd.'

'Don't joke about it . . .'

'I'm not . . .'

'Shh.'

It was time for them to make love again, so that is what they did; but after a few moments PJ began to wonder why what had once seemed so miraculous had suddenly become so perfunctory. They put their clothes back on and sat down at the window, staring at the small town station platform where they had come to a stop. He decided it must be the amulet. The amulet had come between them. It was as though their love were an electric current and the amulet was somehow siphoning it away. 'I know what you're thinking,' Chit said. 'But it won't last forever. The fear will go away.'

'The strange thing is, at Junction, when we fought Simone Arleta and all her demonic forces, we all had our own magic powers . . . I had the vision . . . Timmy had the forces of shadow . . . today, we battled vampires too, but we had become just ordinary people.'

'We had magic things – the statue, the holy water.'

'Yes, but they were just things. The magic didn't come from inside ourselves. Lauren McCandless has painted his last painting, so the inspiration has left him too. Your ajarn has died. There's no magic anymore. Not even in making love,' he added bitterly.

'Then,' said Lady Chit, 'we'll have to find it again.'

'But where?'

'Where did you find magic last time?'

'Out there somewhere. Alone. The wilderness. There's no wilderness here.'

'I wouldn't say that if I were you,' Chit said, and PJ knew that she was right. Nature was tame compared with the wilderness of the heart. But he wasn't sure he had the courage to go back into that wasteland. He wasn't an adolescent anymore, after all. Successful gallery owners don't run around half-naked following their bliss in the forest. Well, maybe they did, but only in some safe, supervised, Sedona-like setting, with their *Iron Johns* in their briefcases. Have I hugged my Inner Child today? he wondered wryly. Jesus, I've turned into a fucking yuppie. Worse – what are they called – a zippie – the old Zen-inspired professional pagan. How could a six-figure income spoil a man's soul in only a year or two? It must be worse for Timmy – he has seven figures. Or more, he reflected, considering what he must have put by over the last nineteen hundred and fifteen years.

'PJ?' Chit said softly.

'Yes?'

'We can try again, if you want.'

She smiled at him and was so beautiful in the moonlight, so clear-eyed, so mournful even though her lips spelled joy, that he could not help weeping.

They made love again, but even as he climaxed PJ was staring at the moon and agonizing over how to recapture his vision.

shadows

There had been no monsters in the nightmare. It was a dream of emptiness, total, all-devouring emptiness – the *vanitas* of Timmy Valentine's last album. The void. The abyss. The great nothing. The most frightening thing in the world.

She woke up screaming and alone.

Pamina had a private sleeping compartment in the car, between Timmy's and the one shared by PJ and Premchitra. She didn't switch on the bedside lamp; moonlight flooded the cramped space. On the bunk above hers, luggage rattled. A sudden tunnel: the instant blackness put her in mind of her nightmare; she almost screamed again.

But before she could, there came the whisper:

Pamina, Pamina.

The voice that was Timmy Valentine yet not Timmy Valentine. It was happening all over again. As though the descent into hell at that awful mortuary hadn't been bad enough . . . watching them turn Tante Amelia into a handful of dust . . . knowing they'd all betrayed her, denied her the one thing she knew she wanted, the thing that had finally been in her grasp.

Pamina.

Why had the voice returned to torment her?

They emerged into moonlight once more. There was a river; across it, a prospect of squat industrial buildings pouring smoke into the night. The train moved with a dreamlike smoothness. Maybe I'm not even awake yet, she thought, maybe I've only woken up inside my nightmare . . .

Pamina, I'm still here, still waiting for you.

I don't trust you, she said in her mind. Everyone else has lied to me.

Have I lied? I said I would show you hell. And passion. And ecstasy. And death. You saw all those things tonight.

But not the way they were supposed to be! It should have been *my* passion, *my* death, *my* resurrection, *my* ecstasy, and instead there was all this unfinished business between Tante Amelia and Timmy Valentine that happened thirty years before I was even born, and they had all those secrets they shared and *she* was the one who got the ecstasy and the death and—

Just a foretaste, Pami. You didn't take the amulet yet, did you?

I couldn't. Lady Chit grabbed it from me. And now she's wearing it.

Why don't you go and get it?

But I'll wake her up—

You won't. She's dreaming. Did you know that when you dream, you're paralysed?

But what about PJ?

Oh, he's off somewhere. Trying to find his lost childhood or some-thing. Come on, Pamina, you gotta do this soon or it'll be too late . . .

I ain't gonna be here forever . . . if no one comes for me I'll have to go.

Go where?

You don't want to know.

Pamina sat up, carefully pulled on the pink kimono she had borrowed from Lady Chit, and pulled open the door of the sleeping compartment. There was no one in the corridor. Well, no, there *was* a bodyguard, but he was sleeping sitting up on the floor, leaning against the toilet door, lit cigarette in hand. The train swerved; she propped herself against an open window sill, sucking in the fresh chill wind. After a moment, she gingerly pushed down the handle of Chit and PJ's compartment door. The voice was right; PJ was nowhere to be seen, and Chit was fast asleep; she had not even bothered to convert the seat into a bed, and the side table was still up.

There was a fax on the table – it was kind of like a painting, but it might have been a photograph – it was a dead oriental woman leaning against a window, with the rain pouring down into a filthy room – with a Timmy Valentine poster on the wall.

There was also an open Louis Vuitton purse, a hand mirror, an open bottle of nail polish remover . . . the smell of pear drops mingled with a faint whiff of Calvin Klein's Obsession . . . she couldn't stop herself rummaging in the purse a little . . . even though she disdained high fashion, she couldn't help noting how Chit had all the right brand names for just the right image . . . pricy, but sassy . . . nice, but naughty.

Chit lay curled up on the three-seater in her day clothes, and yes, the amulet was round her neck, and her eyes were darting back and forth beneath her lids in the manner of those who dream.

Pamina!

She picked up the hand mirror and the boy looked back at her, taunting . . . haunting . . . and oozing an animal sexuality . . . she could almost smell him in the fumes that swirled about his face and seemed to funnel out through the mirror's surface . . . was he really leaking out into the real world, or was it some kind of holography?

I'm here, she told him in her mind.

Take me into your heart, Pamina. Everyone else has fucked with you, but I'm going to give it to you straight. I'll never betray you. I'll give you the darkness that you've always wanted. I'll give you the gift of blood, I'll—

Chit stirred. Opened her eyes for a moment, moaned: 'No, no, let me finish the dream . . .'

Pamina dropped the mirror. The train hit a curve and the mirror clattered to the floor and smashed. A shard of the mirror sliced at her calf. She bent down to pick it out, and then she saw that the angel was still staring at her from all the broken pieces . . . solemn . . . tiny . . . twentyfold . . . and the moon in every fracture too, twenty small moons and twenty smiling angels. She recoiled. Chit moaned again.

I wonder what she's dreaming about, Pamina thought.

flying

Hey, Chit Chit Chit—

I'm inside of you again and you're seeing the world I see and there I am again you see flying flying on raven wings through the cold Kentucky mountain night yeah, my wings are the night wind. Smell, touch, taste the clean keen bloody air. Oh, you can feel it with me, you can follow my flight with your eyes flitting beneath closed lids, flitting in the dark cave of your skull. Oh Chit Chit Chit hear the night-birds chittering. Children of the night. Chitter chatter chitter chatter.

It's still a day or two after my changing and I can see I got to leave my earthly home behind because all the people I used to love here, well, I done killed them all, I guess, ain't nothing pulling me down into Hangman's Holler no more. I come to the place where I was born and I found this ain't my native earth after all, so I guess like I don't have to lie in it day after day waiting for the sun to set, I can find my native earth somewhere else . . . and so I go . . . westward . . . following I guess just behind that sunset that I can't look at no more.

I figure Hollywood is next. It's the running-away-kid capital of the world, and it's the place where I started to lose my Angel self and get drawn into a new personality. The night is fine here, all noise and neon, and the buzz of the advertising signs keeps you alert all the time, it's a *dzzt-dzzt* pulse like a hungry mosquito and it almost drowns out the zing of liquid fire as it races through a million bloodstreams, but no, you can always hear the blood scream out to you, tickling the hunger in the pit of your stomach, if only it was just your stomach that growled for blood and not your soul, I blend in easily, I find the homeless taste the worst, they don't take care of themselves; I never drink enough to kill.

You want to see me kill someone? After a while I have to because the moment of dying is where the blood becomes sweetest and most bitter. I know I've come to Hollywood because I still have to be around the people who loved me. For a long while though there's no one. Until one day I see the Valentinemobile come down Santa Monica Boulevard, and I think, Timmy's out cruising the night, and I think, I want to tell you I'm still out there, we've changed places but we still can't get away from each other totally, you know what I mean.

It's three or four in the morning and I'm almost ready to doss down in the dumpster I've been using for a coffin. But he pulls up to a stoplight and there's I think Rudy driving, but Rudy doesn't see me. Timmy's in the back seat and he's watching television or something. Santa Monica's deserted. The homeless kids have all gone home with their johns. The street signs are going off one by one. There ain't a more desolate place than Hollywood in the middle of the night.

I think, I'll go up to the car, just say hi, Timmy, it's me, I'm a vampire now – as if you didn't know – hope you're having a cool life, things ain't so bad for me, it's a living, ha, ha. So I swoop down onto the hood . . . I'm the black raven with spread wings . . . I cry *Timmy, Timmy,* in the language of darkness . . . but you know, he can't hear me.

I call his name and he sits there, absorbed in that fucking television and when I fly around to the back of the car and peer over his shoulder I see that it's just a Michael Jackson music video . . . and I beat my wings against the bullet-proof glass and he looks at me for a moment and I can see his mind ticking away behind those great big eyes, and he's thinking 'Is that . . . maybe . . . could that be . . .' then, 'nah.'

He's become deaf to the music of the night.

OK, I tell myself, we'll go our separate ways. He'll go home to that palace in the Hollywood Hills and go to sleep and dream . . . he can dream now and I can't dream no more . . . and maybe I'll come to him then . . . I'll beat my wings against his window pane and call out to him in a soft sweet voice so he'll invite me in . . .

Oh God, do I want to kill my maker?

Shit.

I stalk the night. Hollywood, Sunset, Vine, Cahuenga, the Strip, Santa Monica, I know them all in a few weeks' time, and still I don't kill no one. Those corpses in Hangman's Holler were different somehow . . . they were people who betrayed me, that's why it was OK I guess, to kill them . . . I don't have nothing against these people in the streets. I just feed enough to get me through the night. Sometimes they piss me off, like the ones who want me to suck their dick. They get more than they bargain for. When that thing gets hard it's brimful of blood, like one of momma's tits. Left a few fags wounded for life over there in West Hollywood somewheres. But I didn't kill them. Not that I'd never love a guy. Sometimes I think that momma and Becky ruined me for girls and that's why I can only drink their blood now even though I know I make them hot, make their little pussies water, 'cause I'm fucking beautiful and I always will be. I love Timmy you know. He made me. But that's totally spiritual. He gave me half his soul and I gave him half of mine.

That's why I can't fucking stay away and so I start to shadow him again. He's friends with people I used to hang out with, especially PJ, who's changed now since he came back from Thailand, and Chit, who shows up maybe once a month and just sits around being all serene and perfect-looking. I start to wander over the hill into the Valley and that's when I see that PJ's opening up that gallery.

I can get into the gallery without being invited . . . well there's this big old sign outside that says 'welcome' . . . it's a blanket invitation . . . is that cheating? I can get in when it's closed, I can be a mouse and slither under the door, I can even funnel in through the keyhole although I don't have that trick down yet.

PJ works late. I hear him mutter things like, 'This fucking opening, I have to get something *really* different, I can't just try to get by on some Native American culture thing, everyone's doing that . . .'

I wish *I* could paint.

Here's my fantasy: I show up one evening with a couple dozen canvases that I painted and they're these big abstracts with like hidden erotic meanings and they're totally done in blood.

The blood of the street people . . .

OK so I watch PJ in the shadows and he never sees me because he used to have the power to sense where things like me are hidden but now his power has been taken away from him or maybe he used it all up in that mini-Armageddon they had over in Junction, Idaho.

Well sometimes I think he kind of knows I'm there like when he pricks up his ears and looks around and I have to swirl down lower into shadow. Maybe he hasn't totally lost all his magic yet. Or it's still inside of him like me inside this fucking amulet, banging to get out.

And I'm all thinking, maybe I can find a way to get him the unusual thing he needs to make his gallery opening as wild and crazy as he wants it to be . . . maybe I can find someone who will do those canvases in blood . . . maybe maybe maybe . . .

Are you still listening, Chit Chit Chit Chit?

I need to find PJ some brilliant, crazy, genius kind of artist who can . . . you know what I'm going to tell you, don't you? You know that I followed you all the way to Bangkok . . . and you led me to Lauren McCandless . . .

Chit Chit Chit

Know how easy it is to hitch a ride on a 747? You can be one of the pets in the hold. Between Bangkok and LA there's a lot of exotic animal trading going on. You can be like a black jaguar or a tapir or . . . I know. Contraband. Or you can be a mouse in a lady's purse. You can scurry into those big pockets in front of the seats . . . the ones in first class are real leather and real roomy. You can even be a raven in the tailwind.

I ride with you all the time. I love the way you smell. You

never notice. I never bite you though. Not until . . . you know. I don't want to bite my friends, not if I don't have to.

One day . . . *big* art show at the Dusit Thani hotel . . . you lead me to Lauren McCandless. But I'm getting ahead of myself ain't I. I'm still in LA here, and tormented because I'm all alone. The night is mine and I can't share it. And Timmy can't or maybe won't see me.

I keep trying. He used to appear to *me* in mirrors, in reflections, speaking to me from the half-world where Simone imprisoned him . . . but I don't know how to do that. All I know is stand in the shadows . . . stay out of the light . . . steer clear of churches and holy places . . . I don't know how seriously to take that because Timmy's used crucifixes in his act, and they haven't hurt him, but when *I* see one it makes me nervous. Maybe I'll get over it. I hope, I hope.

Sometimes I perch on the sill at Timmy's mansion and I listen to him. He has a big studio with computers and keyboards and digitizers and samplers all linked together with MIDI and late at night he's often in there alone, and the sounds that come out of there ain't the 'Timmy Valentine Sound' but something much more scary. Like there'll be these clanking, roaring electronic rumbling sounds and then above them the screech of a dying animal . . . explosions, bombs, gunfire, buildings tumbling to the ground, all blended in with the whimper of a child . . . and he feeds the sounds through all these distorting echo machines so it's big and totally THX-Dolby-surround-sound-terrifying. And he doesn't know I'm there . . . my wing wrapped around the intake of the air-conditioning unit . . . about to dissolve and funnel in through the hair-crack-open window . . . but too frightened to come in, not knowing if I'm still invited, not knowing the rules, if I'll like vaporize if I break them. Shit.

Why doesn't he see me? Don't he know, I can hear each drop of sweat that slides down his smooth cheek, I can hear each gasp of wind that his lips suck in, each corpuscle as it swims through the great red rivulets that sustain his life, Jesus I can zero in, hear his heartbeat, feel his natural rhythm . . . and he just about stares through me. Could it be I'm not substantial enough yet? That the dead flesh is still hardening? Or is it just

that he's become so fucking human he can't even taste my deadness in the air?

I call to him: *Timmy! Timmy!* I think he only hears the caw of
a raven, or he thinks it's just one of those electronic music
machines acting up . . . yeah . . . the hum of an ungrounded
wire. When he plays, he's completely coiled up inside himself.
That hasn't changed. The song remains the same but he don't
hear it the same.

One time I even sit by the window and watch him soaking
in the jacuzzi tub. I think about the time I was staying at the
hotel, waiting for the Timmy Valentine look-alike contest, and
I saw him reflected in the water when the bubbles died away.
Maybe I can get him to see me. He sits in the white marble and
the passionfruit-scented bubble bath and he stares into the water
like it's gonna hypnotize him, and I'm concentrating on his
name real hard, but no . . . after a while he gets up from the
tub and takes a shit.

I don't shit no more. Don't even remember what it feels like.
Never have to go. You drink blood, it soaks right into you like
you're a coffee filter, it feeds your soul, you use it all up, nothing
wasted. It's weird to watch my mirror image doing all the things
I can't do. Why can't I just leave?

And why can't he see me? Others see me. I think they do. I
don't know for sure. I can't see myself anymore, remember, not
even in a puddle of water lit by the full moon. No reflection,
no shadow.

I guess I feel a new kind of despair.

I don't want to be alone, and Timmy's the only one I know
who's been there . . . who's inside of me, knows me.

Don't get me wrong. I love the night. I love to fly. I love to
be the shadow no one sees. But there's a part of me that's inside
Timmy Valentine now. And I miss it sometimes I guess. Finally
I realize there's only one way I'm going to get Timmy to know
I'm here. I have to show my power. I have to kill again. I have
to infect someone else. I have to *force* my presence on his self-
absorbed consciousness. I have to become more vampire. So I
start again . . . not in anger, not lashing out, but calmly. Timmy
told me once that if you can feel compassion, that's the beginning of the end for a vampire, time to see a shrink, check into

a vampire support group . . . *took me fourteen hundred years to feel it*, he told me, *and now it's made me into you*. I'm slowly starting to understand. These people are like flies. You swat them. You crush them. But you go on forever.

The first time it's some homeless dude, he's sitting on a bench at a bus stop, but three buses have gone by and I can see he ain't waiting for a bus, probably doesn't have the money and doesn't have nowhere to go. I sit down next to him. It gets cold in Southern California at night because it's all desert really, they keep it green artificially. He's freezing even though he has about six jackets on. I think he's sick. He doesn't ask me for money. Just stares straight ahead, shaking.

Finally he says, 'You new here?'

'Yeah.'

'Could get you somewhere to sleep cheap. For a couple of bucks.'

'Don't have no money.'

'Doesn't matter. Just talk to me for a while.'

Black woman in a fur coat comes out of Popeye's, turns up her nose at us. A couple of people browsing at the Cahuenga newsstand. This late at night they mostly come to stand around reading the porn. I don't have nothing to talk about so we just sit there. His lips move now and then.

After a long while he says, 'Thanks for talking to me.'

And I'm all, 'Wasn't talking.'

'You can kill me now, Angel,' he says.

'How'd you know my name?'

'Been waiting here for you for twenty years. Before you die an angel comes.' And I realize he wasn't really calling me by name, he just thinks I'm the angel of death; but does he know that it's only the hunger that's made me sit down beside him, not God, not destiny? 'I was an altar boy. I know what angels look like. They look like altar boys.'

'How do you know I'm who I am?'

'Trick question.'

'No, seriously.'

'Because you're sitting right next to me. A human being wouldn't do that. No human being has sat on this bench beside me in all these years.'

'Why not?'

He laughs. 'Let's play twenty questions before I die,' he says. 'It's because I stink. I'm a bum who's gonna beg for dough. There's booze on my breath and vermin in my clothes. I got lice and fleas. I got sores. I drool. I puke. I'm a multiple personality. You came to the right place, Angel.'

His face is striped with yellow, pink and blue from the neon marquee of the El Capitan on one side of Hollywood and the Chinese on the other. No one is on the street. A convertible cruises by and a forlorn unshaven man peers out; he sees us, we're not what he's looking for, speeds up; right then and there I sink my teeth into the old man's neck.

'Thank you,' he whispers.

His skin is paper-thin and his blood is thin too, like diluted orange juice. It is only lukewarm. He was dying anyway, I guess. His face and neck are covered with brown patches. I don't know yet that this is called sarcoma, don't know yet that the watery flavour is the taste of AIDS. Blood is blood even though this blood is only half alive. I have to suck hard to get it in me. I gorge myself and finally I feel the tingling and know that my eyes are reddening and I'm blotting up his life force. It's really almost an accident that I totally drain him. Most people . . . a pint or so gives you an awesome jolt. But this dude . . . six, seven pints, before I knew it I'd sucked my way to his heart and more, made his heart cave in on itself like a McDonald's cup crumples up when you keep on sucking after it's all gone.

I don't like the way AIDS tastes because it takes so much more to give me satisfaction. The only good thing about it is that I'm immune. Can't kill me twice. The flesh I'm wearing is the night that has like sculpted itself into the image what used to be Angel.

But I like the old man's death. Death is the only thing that does it for me. It only does it for a moment but that moment is so fucking intense I know I'm gonna come back to it again and again and I'm gonna get addicted and I'm gonna have to kill because I have to feel that moment again and again.

I don't close his eyes for him. That way they'll think he's awake . . . the cops won't throw him out . . . it's illegal to nap on a public bench, but you ain't napping when your eyes are

wide open . . . they won't even know he's dead until morning
. . . the sun will come up and burn him to a cinder.

But then I get to thinking . . . I don't have to be alone.

I can make more of us.

Timmy will *have* to notice.

memory: 1611

Ariel, chick, farewell . . .

Whitehall, artificial light, stage machines, the night made
bright by a thousand candles, the aging actor weighed down
with robes, and gold thread, and tinsel, and tassels, and amu-
lets, and rings, and chains of silver, and an orb set with a
polished onyx . . . the boy, not weighed down at all, for only
his waist-length hair, and the branches of a potted ficus, serve
to conceal those parts which may not with propriety be shown
to the ladies at court.

The flickering tallow weaves about his person such a luminous, sheer fabric . . . one ought not call it baseless, that would
be to filch the master's words . . . he seems as much enrobed
in light as the old man in damask, wool, ermine, leather, silk
(but that silk must be returned to the merchant of Venice by
dawn or there will be a forfeit of a half groat). Ariel steps out
from behind the tree. The play has gone well and soon will
come the epilogue.

Prospero has said goodbye to the world of magic. Prospero
is Master Will himself tonight, and he has spoken the words
with a peculiar poignancy:

Leave not a rack behind.

The boy who has been one of the children of the Blackfriars
Theatre when he was first noticed by Heminges, an actor in the
King's Men, who has been inducted into Mr Shakespeare's acting company, who has remained mysteriously young for three
summers . . . *age cannot wither her!* the apprentices say of him
when he struts about backstage in the leafy apparel of Titania
or the dusky face paint of Cleopatra's Charmian . . . he knows
it will soon be time for him to go too. Before they suspect the

truth. And before they lay the deaths on him, for the past three years have been blighted with inconstruable tragedies: Lady Catherine Darling, a favourite lady-in-waiting of the queen and ardent lover of the stage, perishing from loss of blood despite the physician's unorthodox decision to use no leeches; Willie Hughes, another of the children ex-Blackfriars, and the boy's chief rival, perhaps, in the affections of the court; some stable-hands in the households of the Wriothesleys and Somersets.

All, were one to pursue the truth, linked only through having once been in a place, alone, with the pale boy of the dark tresses and the eyes that, like lodestones, impel the looker toward Polaris. Sometimes a drawing room, sometimes an alley; Lady Catherine was seated at a virginal, struggling with a Byrd that would not sing to her; the boy would sing, however, or Byrd, or Tallis, or Dowland, and her favourite air fast became her funeral march. It was a lovely funeral; the king came.

The king has come this evening too. But it is not the poet that he watches with those ratlike little eyes; it is the boy. The boy looks away.

Stage hands with giant fans stir up the wind. The boy reaches up to catch the golden harness, flies upward into the ether, his hair strategically draped about his hips; with his free hand he waves to the throng, all silks and brocades and brightly-coloured doublets. Then, as he nears the balcony, he lets go, seems, to the audience, to defy the earth's pull, somersaults in the empty air and dissolves into the shadowy eaves . . . *into air, into thin air* . . .

Applause for another miracle of illusion.

He is still up there, of course; but he has become one with the smoky evanescence of wax, with the tendrils of tobacco fumes (for the court is agog with the new-discovered vices of the western Indies), and from above them he can see them all, bepowdered, bewigged, bewildered; Prospero stands alone for the epilogue, thumping his staff on the boards like a master of the choristers, then like a slave craving his own masters' indulgence; and indulgence comes in the languid handclaps of the king, the squeals of delight of the ladies, the surly smile of Buckingham, the king's friend, catamite, some say.

And later, the poet kneels at the king's feet, and the rest of the company with them, and the king is pleased to grant the company five pounds in old silver, undebased, Elizabethan silver. The pound has been scruples lighter since 1604. And as a special token of favour, the king gives Shakespeare a choice of rings from his second-best bauble tray.

And then he asks, 'But the boy, Master William, where is that excellent boy? We would see if his tresses be his own.' The king's English is still intermixed with the accent of the north, though England and Scotland have been one for eight years.

Heminges looks nervously at the wings; the boy is suddenly there. He has shot down from the rafters in the shape of a bat, transformed too fast for any to notice; he too kneels, keeping his eyes downcast.

'Come closer; we would study that visage, for time soon spoils a youth's smooth features. Silver is too soon tarnished, and alabaster cracked.'

And he looks down at a fold of the king's doublet, which, though it is cloth of gold, is frayed. He smells a rank desire inside that doublet. The king toys with the hair, twines it in a callused finger.

'Wilt not look us in the eye, bairn? Do we affright so much? Thinkst thou that we would smite those delicate cheeks, when, troth, 'tis thy puir monarch who lies smitten? What do they call thee?'

'Ned, Your Grace.'

'Why Ned, here's gold.' He takes another ring from the tray – 'Aye, there's a carbuncle of a manly size,' and slips on the boy's finger. He gasps; for the boy's hands are colder than the metal. 'He sucks the warmth from me,' says the king.

'Then,' says the Duke of Buckingham, 'Your Grace must needs receive warmth in return.'

The king's friends laugh. But the king looks dark, and says, 'Take care, Buckingham. I have made buggery a hanging offense, for I will not have loose morals in my kingdom, now that our scriptures have been properly Englished.'

'And the commonfolk have finally found out what sins they have been committing,' says Buckingham, 'even without benefit of Latin and Greek.' More laughter, some real, some merely polite.

'Hast thou sinned, Ned?' says the king. And that same gnarled finger is descending down the boy's neck now, glancing the left collarbone, tracing its way downward toward the nipple. The fingertip moves southward, stopping to count each rib. The more the finger lingers, the more the boy feels anger. But the blood does not come rushing to heat his cheeks; what blood there is in him is dead blood. 'God's death, but thou'rt cold. I would see thee naked, yet—' tugging at the hair, 'would I not dis-tress thee,' laughing, 'for thou art bonny.'

And the moving finger writes, scratching words on marmoreal skin, in a spidery scrawl, *Ned Ned Ned Ned* and *Wilt thou to bed?*

And the boy says, 'But Your Grace – by your own decree—'

'There are no laws,' says Buckingham, 'for them which make laws; though we shall answer to God in due course.'

'In due course,' says King James Sixth and First. 'Shall we compare carbuncles? I shall not have it said I gave thee too rich a jewel.' And his hand has penetrated the thicket of hair and reached down to caress the place beneath. 'What, no carbuncles at all?' he says. 'Comely yet incapable. Thou sad wee thing.' And the king laughs.

'I pray you, do not belittle me, Your Grace,' says the boy.

'Belittle, quotha!' says the king. 'Well, go thy way. But first thou shalt kiss my hand, that's little enough to ask.'

The king stretches out his hand; forces it to the boy's lips. Ned looks at the king's face for the first time. Cannot these humans look at him without seeing some fantasy of lust? Do they not understand that what they want from him he cannot give, has never been able to give, has had that gift forever stolen from him in the fiery death that swallowed up Pompeii? For fifteen hundred years he has fed, and killed, and turned men's lusts against them, and deemed himself completely evil, and content to be evil. But he has finally learnt that there is no evil; there is only that which is pitiable; he learnt it from a man most men would regard as the most evil man of all time, Gilles de Rais, Bluebeard, the child-killer.

That is why I pity the king, he thinks. Look at him. He desires; he does not love. I am a bauble to him. He cannot know that the bauble is death. And as he and the king gaze at each other he knows his shape is shifting, for men see in him not only what they most lust for but what they most fear. I must look away or I will betray myself. He tears his glance away, but as the king's hand pries apart his lips, instinct takes hold of him.

He bites.

The king guffaws at this. 'Thou'rt unmanned in more ways than one,' he cries, 'thou strugglest like a vixen.' And at that the court bursts into uproarious laughter and applause, as though the king has uttered the wittiest of euphuisms, and even Master William has a little smile, no a big smile (more lines than hath the new map with the augmentation of the Indies) and so, unwatched, the boy feeds, feeds, feeds, feeds on blood that is no bluer than any man's . . .

The king does not even see. He basks in the tumult of sycophancy.

Tonight the boy will have to disappear. He has tarried too long among these people . . . it maddens him, for here, in the company of those who have brought about in the world a very renascence of poetry and song, he has found men who did not think him an abomination. Like Kit Marlowe. (Though there were those found Kit abomination enough.) Kit is dead now, and soon these will be dead too, and the rebirth of poesy will be re-death. The boy feeds. He will need strength. The blood of kings does have a kind of potency. Tonight he will flee.

Tonight: away from Whitehall, away from London . . . perhaps even across the sea . . . he will take passage to the New World . . . or to Cathay . . . or to the frozen uninhabitable north . . . the world's mortality weighs down his mind . . . it will all dissolve . . . *into air, into thin air* . . . all but himself, who is already air.

morning

Pain – a wedge of pain that burned against her left breast like a branding iron.

Chit woke up suddenly. The train had snarled to a halt. She heard voices: *Paßkontrolle*. She reached for her purse and her passport. 'PJ—'

He wasn't there.

Instead, there was Pamina Rothstein, a shattered mirror on the floor, and a hand over the amulet, about to—

'I'm sorry, I—' Pamina began.

'Don't worry. I understand. I really do.' But Chit firmly pried Pamina's fingers loose from the silver. 'Let's do the passport thing and order breakfast . . .'

Dawn was breaking. The terrain outside the window: flat, green, canals, the old windmill here and there; picture-perfect.

'Where's PJ?' Chit said. 'Have you seen him?'

'No.'

'You've been here all night?'

'You know it.'

'Did you see Angel?'

'Who is Angel?'

'Long story. Angel Todd was—'

'Angel *Todd*! I read about him in one of those trashy magazines, how some people say Timmy isn't really Timmy at all, but this boy from Kentucky? *Doch*, but I didn't believe it. I mean, the name alone, it's some kind of joke? Maybe a German wrote the article. Because you know, Angel Todd – *Todesengel* – *Engel des Todes* – "angel of death" – only a German speaker would get the pun. Then, that night in the hotel suite—'

There was a rap on the window. '*Aufmachen! Polizei!*' in an exaggerated, rasping war movie storm trooper sort of a voice. They both looked. First it was a shock of black hair dangling from the upper lefthand corner of the window, blowing in the wind, and then . . . PJ's face, upside down, then his chest, then more of him . . . 'Oh, my God,' Chit said, 'he's hanging on by his *feet*!'

Quickly Pamina opened the window and PJ wriggled through.

'*And* you're naked,' Chit said. 'There are children present!'

PJ grabbed a blanket and wrapped it around himself poncho style; with his hair loose, he looked like a Cheyenne buck in a John Ford western – not least because his half-Caucasian features made him appear to be only playing Indian. In fact, Chit decided, he looked kind of like Sal Mineo in *Cheyenne Autumn*.

'You're smiling at something, darling, share the joke.'

'Sal Mineo.'

They both burst out laughing, leaving the German Neo-Gothic teen completely mystified.

'PJ . . . you've been sitting on the roof of the train all night in the nude. Can I ask why?' Chit said.

'I've been seeking a vision,' he said. 'You're so right, the wilderness is in the heart.'

'What did you see?' Pamina asked.

'Patience! A vision quest takes longer than one night, even in these accelerated times. Where's Timmy?'

'Still asleep I should think. Dawn, you know. What a vampire,' Chit said, laughing again. 'Do you have your passport?'

It was at that moment that Pamina, exhausted, more or less keeled over on her seat.

'There's your vampire,' PJ said, 'or your vampire-in-waiting.'

'Only she can't get anyone to bite her,' Chit said.

Timmy, yawning, slid open the compartment door. 'I've had,' he said softly, 'the weirdest dream . . .'

15

CONTRARIWISE

news of the world

From the Dutch newspaper *Het Parool*:

VOLCANO ERUPTS IN WEST IRIAN

Orbiting satellites have recorded the eruption of a large volcano in the most impenetrable part of West Irian, the Indonesian half of the island of New Guinea. The extent of the damage is unknown, though ashes have been detected in the atmosphere as far away as Australia and Malaysia. There are no roads in the region, which is a densely forested mountainous area inhabited by aboriginal peoples, many of which have never had contact with each other, let alone outside civilization. Seismic activity has also registered on the dials of seismologists in Tokyo and at the earthquake centre in Pasadena, near Los Angeles, and there is every indication that this is one of the most spectacular eruptions of this century. Four vulcanologists, each claiming to have been the first to notice the volcanic activity, have christened the volcano with four different names: 'Nemesis', 'Mt Doom' (after Tolkien!), 'Vesuvio Secundo', and 'Bert'. None has volunteered to go to West Irian in person, however; all four cite the danger as well as fear of being captured and eaten by headhunters . . .

'What are you doing now, PJ?' Chit asked him over breakfast at the Savoy; Timmy and Pamina were already down at the Albert Hall.

For the London concerts, there was to be a full symphony orchestra in addition to all the MIDI gear. But Stupendous and David Giler had been too niggardly to hire the London Symphony or one of the other top-notch bands in town; instead, audiences were to be treated to the downtown debut of the

Tooting Bec Philharmonic, an orchestra from the suburbs, full
of little old ladies fiddling on the side.

'I'm reading the paper,' PJ said.

'But it's in Dutch.'

'I've been trying to puzzle it out since we left the Hague. A
lot of it's pretty easy to figure out . . . look, a new volcano has
erupted in New Guinea . . . and there's a review of Timmy's
concert.'

'What does it say?'

'Hmm . . . "Neo-Gothic wunderkind seems short on *wunder*
these days, and we're wondering how much longer his supernatural *kindheid* is going to last . . . what kind of hormones is
he on? . . . voice shows the first signs of strain in the upper
registers . . . boring laser effects left over from the eighties . . ."
Doesn't sound very flattering.'

Ticket sales, PJ reflected, were doing better than expected in
London; perhaps the *Zeitgeist* here was more attuned to the
Neo-Gothic sensibility; perhaps people needed a spectacle to
distract from the ever-present scandals of the royal family. They
had taken, as expected, a bath in Germany and Holland; but
that was part of the Giler game plan; as soon as Timmy did his
big disappearing act in Asia, sales would skyrocket and there'd
even be room for a posthumous *Timmy Valentine – the Secret
Recordings*, the ultimate Neo-Gothic laundry list.

'More kippers?' said Chit, spooning some out for him from
the silver platter they were served in.

'More nightmares?' he asked her, knowing she would still
refuse to throw away the amulet. 'You're looking . . . dare I say
it . . . anaemic.'

'I'm *fine*!' said Lady Chit furiously. 'Why don't you go off and
run with the wolves again, or whatever it is you do all night
long?'

'I have to do that. I have to find my vision again. So we can
fight the vampires . . .'

Sullenly, Chit munched on a rasher of bacon. Around them,
men in dark suits sipped coffee and studiously ignored the quar-
relling couple. But presently they became aware of a big man
not in a dark suit, looming over their table. A white suit, actually, not unreminiscent of Colonel Sanders, the chicken king.

'You're both looking mighty glum,' said the ex-Reverend Damien Peters. 'But as you can see, Our Gang is rapidly a-reconstituting itself . . . and things will be a whole lot better now that Spanky has arrived in London.'

'Damien!' Chit said, delighted.

But PJ, though he wanted to be happy to see his old enemy and friend, was preoccupied and merely stared into his kippers.

'My God,' said Damien. 'That bad.'

'I'm really sorry about PJ,' Chit said, 'but he's sort of in the middle of a vision quest . . .'

'In the heart of London?'

'That's what *I* thought. But it's true. He is gathering power.'

'I see,' said the preacher turned actor. 'Then it's true; we're in for another apocalyptic, Bible-thumping war with the fate of the universe at stake. I'm getting too old for this shit. Do they have 900 numbers in London?'

'I heard what happened the last time you had girls up to your hotel room, Damien.'

'Oh that! We *burned* all them vampirellas. I understand you had to deep-six a passel of them yourself, over there in Bangkok.'

'True enough. And another in Germany. Holland, however, was clean, and maybe we're through for the rest of the tour; the one in Germany was unfinished business from fifty years ago.'

'It ain't over till the fat lady sings.'

'Well, she sang all right. But we're still running scared; I get bad dreams, PJ streaks through deserted tube stations in the middle of the night, we've acquired a groupie who wants to be a vampire but can't get anyone to bite her, and Timmy's show is losing Stupendous a million a day.'

'Oh, fuck Stupendous; Giler's trying to prevent a Japanese buyout by faking big losses.'

PJ watched their banter; on one level he was amused and wished he could join in; but he was waiting for nightfall. So, doubtless, was the reverend; he probably couldn't wait to hit the strip joints.

He thought about the night.

The train through Germany . . . he had flung off his clothes, climbed up to the roof of the sleeping car, assumed the lotus position, let his hair thrash in the wind, let the cold pound at him . . . tried to bring back the time he'd gone into the wilderness as a boy and come back a *ma'aipots*. The moon had come to him in the shape of a beautiful woman. She had handed him a sheaf of corn and told him, you will be both a woman and a man, and through this you will become the most powerful person among all living Shoshone. And it was true. From that time on, whenever he entered the trance-state of the sacred man-woman, he could send his soul into the wind, could see with the eyes of the hawk and the badger, could feel the presence of all the denizens of the spirit world. But years later, when the great war in heaven had been fought to a temporary truce (it can only end in a truce, for the war in heaven must go until the end of time) the moon-woman had taken back her gift.

The moon hung full over the rushing train. But she did not transform into the pale-skinned woman bearing sheaves of grain. PJ cried out to her in his mind: *Come back to me, my gift, I beg of you* . . . and at the same time he was thinking, I don't deserve it this time because there's no cosmic battle for possession of the world, this time I want my gift for selfish reasons . . . because I want to pull back my friend from the brink of darkness . . . because I don't want the woman I love to tumble into the abyss . . . because I don't want to feel powerless against the evil spirits that are coming back into my life. But what do a few human beings matter? That's why the moon doesn't speak to me . . . why the wind whips my bare flesh but carries no message.

PJ had despaired that night, though on the surface he tried to appear cheerful. He did not want the people he loved to know how much he was suffering. They had never had his vision and could never know how impotent he felt now that it was gone.

The second night, walking barefoot on the shingle at Scheveningen, four a.m., slipping through the barricade and running to the end of the pier, alone, the moon beginning to wane but still almost all there, he thought he heard the woman's voice:

You're going the wrong way.

And that was all the vision the whole night vouchsafed him.

Perhaps, he thought, tonight . . .

'I'll skip the concert tonight,' said Damien. 'I'll just show up in time for breakfast . . . give Timmy a little surprise.'

'Heavens,' said Lady Chit, 'I hope you packed your condoms.'

'The Lord looks out for me,' Damien said, laughing.

dissolve

The orchestral introduction to *Crucify Me Twice* is a new addition and I wasn't even around for the full rehearsal because the schedule sucked and Stupendous won't pay overtime for the orchestra but never mind, they're not that bad even if they *are* from Tooting Bec. And anyways, Kenny Ojima, the orchestrator, did a great job, it's like he can read my fucking mind. Listen to those rolling string harmonies and the way he's sugared them with little glockenspiel cascades.

But now I gotta sing.

Timmy Valentine appeared centre stage in a puff of silvery smoke. Applause, of course. More people than he expected, and a *big* contingent of Neo-Gothics, all in the front rows, presumably they answered the ad, they were all paid for, so they would stand to sit up close to the hot lights and the cameras and the foggers that released a steady stream of gasoline-scented mist into the throng . . . break up the glare of the inkies . . . they really know how to pick 'em, central casting couldn't have done better . . . they held up their palms with holes you could knock a golf ball through, not fake either, 'cause they broke the stream of light into little shafts that danced over the swirls of mist.

Gotta sing.

Chit was the only one of his friends there tonight. She was watching from one of the balconies, the one where the MIDI-controlled lighting command centre had been rigged up. Otherwise these people were all strangers. He started to sing and . . .

Jesus they're singing along with me and . . .

How weird to be back here again, the first time I've been here since I became human. Don't lose your concentration, just sing, just leap out there to the front, never mind the spotlight, it'll

find you by itself, autopilot is fine but hug the line the arc of
the song whether right or wrong just dance prance trance glance
lance stance stamp the plank like a drum in a mantra move
move move. Autopilot now. The song is a pattern you weave
in the air don't matter as long as you know it's there.

Oh God these old Victorian stones I came to a concert once
with Bram Stoker, the symphony of a thousand; he wept and I
fed. Oh God these streets I drifted along them once, knew them
all, Dr Jack who ripped up women's insides, Dr Jekyll who lived
inside a book; urchins and whores; further back, jigsaw pieces
of memory keep floating up from the void like: the long winter
where we danced on the rock-hard Thames and, the plague
when all the blood was thin and unsustaining, and, and, the
great fire, and, the rats, and, and, Kit Marlowe ripping the
leeches from his chest.

dissolve: vision seeker

Pamina wandered through Piccadilly Circus, wondering
whether there were any vampires among the living who
crammed the video arcades and clustered around the window of
Tower Records and sat in the passageways of the underground,
strumming and begging . . . what would it be like if these
chattering, polyglot multitudes were cattle, dumbly waiting for
their time to bleed, to feed their masters?

dissolve: vision seeker

Night takes forever to come in the summer this far north; PJ
paced the lobby of the Savoy for a couple of hours. Still it did
not get dark. Finally he went up to his room. A balcony overlooked the park; people still jammed the street. Hardly a barren
wilderness where he could commune with the spirit world. But
the moon had risen and already was peering down between the
ruddy brick and gingerbread moulding of Victorian row-houses;
and he called out to her, Speak to me, speak to me, and still, it
seemed, she would not listen.

The rooftops, he thought, there are no people on the rooftops
. . . the rooftops will be my wilderness.

He undid his ponytail; put on a headband – not entirely
appropriate since it showed the Japanese flag and the legend
'kamikaze' – and began to remove his clothes, knotting a loin-
cloth over his privates – the English, he knew, could be quite
fussy about indecent exposure – called on his dead grandfather
in the Shoshone tongue, then sang a song he had learned from
a Cheyenne mystic who had visited the reservation:

> Taeva nama-eyoni
> Tze-ihutzittu nama-eyoni
> At night I am holy
> When I go my way alone I am holy

He stood on the ledge now, balancing on the wrought-iron
railing. If I lose my footing I'll die, he thought. He looked down.
Thought about smashing his skull and ending it all. But then a
feeling of lightness came over him, and he knew he must not
think of falling, not think of being in danger . . . he must run
up the wall of the hotel like a spider, clinging to the old stone
with his palms and soles, moving so quickly that inertia had no
meaning . . . most of all he must stop thinking like a human
being, always frail, always afraid. A good day to die and all
that! he thought. And sprang upward, into the moonlight, trust-
ing the spirits to catch him and hold him fast against the pull
of the earth.

memory: 1593

'Oh Ned, I am slain,' Kit cries to him in an upper room of the
tavern in Deptford. 'Look at me, I bleed from the guts, it is
fatal.'

And the boy who has called himself Ned Bryant comes to him
from the shadows where he has been hiding, mouselike, since
the brawl over the reckoning began.

He knows that the poet is right. The wound is the kind that
kills by a slow inexorable haemorrhaging; nothing can reverse
the course of death now. How could the man have been so

careless? Did he not know how many enemies he had? Did he not know that half those who professed themselves his friends had sold his misdemeanours to the eyes and ears of justice?

A doctor with a tray of leeches is huffing up the stairs, preceded by the mistress of the place, one Eleanor Bull. 'What a terrible thing,' the innkeeper is saying, 'he is the greatest poet of our times, for all that he's an atheist and a sodomite.'

'Mayhap not the greatest, after all,' the doctor says. 'For I was even this afternoon at the theatre, where I saw *Romeo and Juliet*.'

'Oh, that old sack of bombast.'

'I warrant not; 'tis a *Romeo* new penned by that Shakespeare . . .'

'Ah, the poet of *Titus Andronicus*. This *Romeo*, I take it would be far more violent; the pig's blood gushing in torrents on the boards; mutilations, rapes, stabbings; faith, my son Peter did importune me to be taken to see *Titus*, but I would not have my children exposed to such modern extremities, for they are yet tender.'

'This, sir, was not bloody at all; bawdy more like—'

Kit Marlowe groans. 'Boy,' says the doctor, 'help me with my leeches, or thy master dies.' The leeches wriggle in a glass jar, and the doctor pulls one out with a pair of sugar-tongs.'

'Sir,' says Ned, 'he dies anyway.'

'Begone,' Marlowe whispers harshly. 'If I must be bled, let the boy do it. Boy, suck the blood from my wound, as thou art wont to do.'

The doctor and the innkeeper look at each other, wondering, perhaps, what strange perversities have passed between the man and the child; but then they shrug, go downstairs.

'The constabulary must know of it,' Ned hears the woman saying. 'And I shall have to find a priest.'

And then it is that the boy kneels by Kit's bedside. Blood is seeping from the poet's belly. The boy bends, laps up the blood with swift flicks of the tongue, as a frog plucks flies from the air. As he feeds, the playwright's features soften in a kind of ecstasy. The blood is potent, as it always is when a man lies on his deathbed, still young, unplagued by illness. 'My Ganymede,' says Kit, 'my Hylas, my Patroclus.'

'Those are all Grecian catamites, are they not? I have not been your catamite, only your extractor of gore.'

'Greek, aye . . . nay, rather Ganymede was Trojan. Oh, if you could have but been in my plays! You would have made a fine Zenocrate; as Helen of Troy you would have had no equal. But I know you cannot go abroad by day.' Yet Ned knows Marlowe's verses well; he has many of them by heart. A few years past, following the scent of untainted blood through narrow streets wretched with rats and plague-ridden corpses, he saw the flicker of a candle in an upper room, and heard a voice mumbling to itself, heard the squish of a quill being sharpened, the scratch of pen on paper, and the voice was saying, pausing between each little phrase to set it down:

> Sometime a lovely boy in Dian's shape
> With hair that gilds the water as it glides,
> Crownets of pearl about his naked arms,
> And in his sportful hands an olive-tree,
> To hide those parts which men delight to see,
> Shall bathe him in a spring . . .

There was such music in that muttering and scratching, music that assuaged the horror of the death-strewn street, that the boy could not help but fly toward the sound; and presently found himself tapping at the sill, crying in a small piteous voice, that the window should be unlatched; and Master Marlowe lighting another candle the better to see what had flown into the upper room, saying, 'Surely thou art no angel. It would be a hard thing for me to believe in thee, seeing I believe not in God.'

'Hardly an angel,' said the boy, 'yet sooth, not human neither.'

'An evil spirit then. That is more to my liking; for though I can no longer find it in me to acknowledge a higher good, evil is another matter altogether; why then welcome, evil spirit. What seekst thou here?'

'What were those words that danced about mine ears, and dragged me hither through the streets of death?'

'My words dance well – for thou hast caught their rhythm. Hast a knack for singing, I'll warrant. That was a play, boy! Hast never seen a play, sirrah?'

'Nay. I dare not stir forth by day.'

'I knew it! An evil spirit indeed, why, thou hobgoblin, thou imp, thou puck! Not stir forth by day! We shall put on a play by night for thee, at court, with a thousand candles for the sun.'

'Can you not merely speak the play to me, without actors, without a stage? It was words that drew me here, not spectacle.'

'Oh, you are a flattering evil spirit.'

But then, pulling a sheaf of paper from a chest . . . the ink was not dry on some of it . . . he did begin to read his *Edward II* to the boy. The boy listened without a sound. He did not even breathe; perhaps that unnerved the poet, but he did not seem so; he was caught up in the perfervid vigour of his lines, in the tragedy of love so hopeless that a king would lose his queen, his kingdom, and finally his life. The boy said not a word till almost the end, when the assassin Lightborn slew the king by thrusting a red-hot poker into his arse; and then he cried, 'No more, I pray you.'

'So! The evil spirit hath a delicate stomach, it seems.'

'I have seen too much of such things.'

'Thou goest to the gallows of a Sunday, dost thou, to watch the felons being hanged, drawn and quartered . . .'

'Nay. I mean that I have seen too many men, women, and children impaled through the fundament with stakes, spears, spikes, even red-hot pokers . . . I once had a friend, you see, who loved impaling.'

'But this is the sixteenth century! Such atrocities belong to some barbarous forgotten time.'

'Indeed. But *I* have not forgotten. It was a hundred and thirty years ago . . .'

Thus it was that the boy, whom Kit christened Ned, began telling the poet stories of the dark past. He did not know if Kit Marlowe believed the tales; but many a dash of colour in Kit's plays owed something to the boy's storytelling. And the boy returned to the upper room frequently, for the poet's blood was clean, and he never drank enough to harm his host; for how could he kill the source of so much music?

But now, Ned thinks, the man dies anyway.

This time he sucks the very life from him. And thinks, This

one should come back from the dead; the world should not lose
one such as him, though it call him an atheist and a sodomite.
And so he does not desecrate the body, but leaves it lying as
though asleep, bloodless and pale; and then, shrinking to a
mouse again, he dives into a hole and flees through the labyrinth
of tunnels that spirals through the house.

The sadness that wells up is still new to him; he has only
been able to feel it for a century. It reeks of a human childhood
he has not thought on for a thousand years or more. He feels
this sadness now as he burrows through beam and plaster. It
animates the blood and makes him a little less dead.

And in the night, his grief driving him to an overpowering
hunger, he kills again and again; in another tavern, foaming at
the mouth like a rabid mastiff, he bites a pregnant woman
through the belly and gorges on her unborn child, spitting out
the caul into a tankard of ale; snapping a drunken seaman's
neck and quaffing from the upturned neck-stump as if it were
a wineskin; and then at last, overcome, he finds a resting place,
which as it happens is in a sewer next to the river.

The next night he goes to Mistress Bull's boarding house once
more. The body is still lying where it was left, for there has
been no inquest yet. The mistress and an agent of the queen's,
one Walsingham, are deep in talk downstairs, next to the fire.
The body lies untended, in the dark, but for one who sees with
the eyes of night, the room is awash with cold dead light. A
cross hangs above the bed; it pains the boy only a little; time
has conquered his superstitions; but still, he does not like to
look at it. Another, he sees now, has been placed above the
poet's heart: a silver cross, encrusted with amethysts; a costly
thing, surely.

'Kind Kit, you must awake now.' The boy touches the corpse
with a finger; yes, yes, he can sense the inhumanly slow pulse
that is the heartbeat of the undead; but Marlowe does not open
his eyes. 'You must awake, and come with me; I cannot answer
for you; they say you are an atheist; perhaps they will mutilate
you; then I will have given you undeath for naught.'

It must be that damned cross above his heart, he thinks, and
he grasps it and flings it to the floor; it burns him for only a
moment, and then the skin grows back over the cruciform

brand. Then Marlowe's eyes open. And he says, very softly, 'It seemed to me that the whole world weighed upon my breast. But that is gone now.'

'Come,' says Ned Bryant.

'Come? What am I now? What is this thou hast made me?'

'What you have written is immortal; why not then you yourself? Listen, Kit, thou and I are kin now . . . I do not take liberties with my betters, but now I shall thee and thou thee, for thou art no longer Master Kit, and great teacher, and by a score of years my senior. In this new life thou art many centuries my junior, and it is I who must teach. How to transform into creatures of the night. How to thin the body into mist – *O soul, be changed to little water-drops* – how to feast on the blood of the living. And most of all, how to feed on the blood of the living, as I have done since before Rome fell. Oh Kit,' says Ned, 'I have done this for the sake of thy poetry, and for myself, because of my terrible aloneness. I have been a child for fifteen hundred years, but my thoughts are not a child's thoughts. I could recite lost verses of Catullus to thee, and poems of Sappho that were burned with the library at Alexandria; I can repeat all of Dante, even the cantos he discarded. I can speak to thee of Pythagoras' metampsychosis, of Aristotle, of Copernicus, of Mohammed, of St Augustine, for I have lived through fifteen centuries of philosophy.'

'But what of love, my little Ganymede?'

'Oh, but there is that in the universe of night which surpasseth love; there is the contemplation of eternity; there is the coldness that breaks the mortal heart, but which for us does make the night burn brighter than the sun; these things are deeper than love, more powerful than death.'

Kit Marlowe grips the boy's hands, pulls himself up from the sleep of the dead. He is not glad, the boy thinks. He is still afraid; mortality still clings to him. 'What of the soul?' he says. 'I am not a believer in souls. Death should be an ending. This likes me not, to die then have to wander once more in the world.'

'Why trouble with the soul?' says Ned. 'If thou didst have a soul, and hadst thou died an ordinary death, would not that soul be even cooking in the everlasting furnace?'

'Why this *is* hell,' says Marlowe, 'for it is not the *vanitas* I yearn for. Free me, Ned, free me, I implore thee.'

How can I free him? Ned thinks. And how can he resist what I have to offer him? Is it not what all men most desire? Did not Faustus sell his soul to the devil for less than I have offered? Ned cannot understand at first that he is being refused. In fifteen hundred years, he has become secure in his seductive powers. No one can deny him. Is he not more lovely than any angel? So many have told him this, and come to him, and let him drink up their life. A savage anger rises in him. He seizes the silver cross, heedless that it chars his fists, and pounds it into Kit's chest, snapping bone and cartilage to penetrate his very heart; the poet does not cry out at all, but only, as he closes his eyes for the last time, whispers, 'I thank thee, gentle Ned.'

The boy casts the cross aside. The wounds in his palms are already healing. 'I have been here long enough,' he says. He must away. A long dark sleep of a hundred years will mitigate his sorrow. He has yearned for renascence and found himself stillborn. He almost weeps.

He leaps from the open window, and in mid-leap takes wing, and leathern-winged swoops down the foetid alley, toward the river, away from London.

profane love

Damien Peters had spent the evening pub-crawling, then hitting the strip joints one after another, after getting lost somewhere around Berwick Street. No one recognized him; a year after *Vampire Junction – The Motion Picture*, he was nobody again; the hair weave helped, too. The little strip shows with their inept dancers shimmying their pasty flesh appealed to his provincial sense of decadence. Watching fat women wiggle was one of the things his daddy used to beat him for, although he had seen his daddy with plenty of fat women; for a third-rate country and western singer he got around quite a bit; Damien had learned many show-biz aspects of being a televangelist from watching his father work the bitches at the county fair. Watching these British creatures made him feel kind of funny inside, and *safe*, like he was back home and a boy again, even though the audience in the tiny smoke-filled room consisted mostly of Germans and Japanese.

There was a black woman on, with a fake American accent, and she tossed out her panties and sighed, 'I think I see a old man masturbating in the northeastern corner, there,' and the man turned beet-red and rushed out of the theatre. Damien had to laugh.

So, around three or four, he found himself walking aimlessly and drunkenly about. He wanted to find a woman for the hotel room, but the streets were empty. Until he heard a voice call to him, 'Mr Peters! Mr Peters!'

And there, standing next to one of those red British pillar-box mail things, was a young girl in full Neo-Gothic regalia, lit first green, then amber, by the faint glow of a traffic signal. She wore black; her hair, nails, lips were black as well, and her face pale as the moon; and at one corner of her mouth was a smear of lipstick, smudged to look like a bloodstain. She held up her hands to the light, and Damien could see the tattooed stigmata. The black leather bodice had a belly opening wide enough to see the tattooed wound in the side; this girl had gone the whole hog.

She said, 'I recognized you from the Timmy Valentine movie.'

He said, 'You're a cute one.' He hoped she was not underage, but then again if she was, why was she out so late at night? 'Valentine fan, I suppose.'

'*Ja*, I came from Germany for the big concert. But I couldn't get tickets.

'I came for the concert too,' said Damien, 'but when I got here I changed my mind; I've seen many Timmy Valentine concerts.'

The girl's eyes went wide. This is gonna be a pushover, Damien thought. Candy from a baby. Throw in the baby too. He was salivating at the prospect. A Timmy Valentine groupie type of girl would surely do *anything*. What a pity there was so little of the night left.

'My name is Pam,' she said. 'Shall I call you Damien?'

'I'm a sinful man,' he began, but she descended upon him and silenced him with her lips – with a mushy hint of tongue – she had no perfume. She smelled of a good strong soap, the way some children smell. 'I do hope you're of age!' he said. Lord have mercy! Who was hustling whom around here?

'Oh, I'm old,' she said, '*very* old.'

Even better, thought Damien. This is one of the ones who actually thinks she's a vampire. She'll be dazzled when I tell her I can actually—'

'Mr Peters, do you think you could—'

'Why, honey,' he said, 'I sure could. Timmy Valentine's a close personal friend of mine, and I do believe I could get him to agree to see you.'

'Oh . . . I'd do *anything*.'

'Well, why don't you come on down to the Savoy, and I'll see what I can do. You'll have to wait till morning, though. But I have a room—'

'Oh, Damien, you are *naughty*.'

vision-seekers

And after the concert, Timmy and Chit sat in Timmy's suite, watching CNN International. The news was all bad. Recessions here, civil wars there . . . and that volcano in West Irian . . . still only photographed from way up in the air.

'I hate volcanoes,' Timmy said softly.

'Yes,' Chit said, 'you were created during an eruption, weren't you?'

'Yeah,' he said. ' "The Last Days of Pompeii" is my middle name.'

They laughed. And then there was an extra tidbit of news:

Authorities are beginning to worry that controversial painter Lauren McCandless, last seen reassembling his houseboat in Java, may actually be lost in the pristine wilderness of New Guinea, with no one able to reach him because of the chaos of the volcano. The painter, best known for his portrayals of the victims of a Bangkok serial killer, was, for a while, a suspect in that celebrated case. Traumatized by his ordeal, he vowed to follow his bliss no matter where it leads him.

> 'I'll take the houseboat upriver. But maybe Thailand isn't
> wild enough, isn't remote enough. Maybe I need somewhere
> else . . . I need the ultimate frontier of civilization . . .
> the place where human nature itself breaks down . . . the
> boundary between manhood and godhead . . .'

'My God,' Timmy said. 'We should do something.'

'What *can* we do?' Chit said. 'You remember that fax, where
he said, "Mistah McCandless, he dead," and we all thought it
was so funny?'

'Poor Lauren,' said Timmy Valentine.

dissolve

Slower . . . slower . . . mustn't act as if I've been in this hotel
before, or he'll know I'm playing him like a violin.

Pamina let the former televangelist walk on ahead, get into
the lift, push the button himself even though she had the idea
that he was probably staying on the same floor as everyone else
in the Valentine party.

She followed two steps behind him down the plush corridor.

Damien talked the whole time, slurring, obviously drunk.
Told her he could set up a meeting with Timmy in the morning.
What a delicious irony, she thought, that he thinks he's manipu-
lating me when he has no idea I've been on the prowl, trying
to find just the right victim.

In the room, she became impatient suddenly. She didn't want
to deal with the champagne and the ice bucket, even though
Damien was already hacking at the ice with a silver pick. She
didn't want to order caviar from room service. 'Shall I take my
clothes off now?' she asked him. She wanted to get it over with
so she could pursue her own agenda . . . acting out her fantasies
. . . maybe even going all the way.

Hungrily, he stared at her. 'How old did you say you were?'

'Older than time.' She did her most ominous smile, wondering whether he found it sexy or merely ingenuous.

She doffed the leather jacket, peeled down the leggings,
folded them neatly on the armoire. Peered into the mirror for a

moment, saw the angel, silent, sneering a little; heard him whisper, *Go for it, Pamina. It can only make you stronger.*

'Don't be so goddamn eager,' Damien said, 'or I'll come in my fucking underwear. Go slow, angel; I ain't getting any younger.'

'You pick up a lot of women,' said Pamina. 'Ever pick up a vampire?' Toying with him, but from the look in his eyes she almost thought he was going to say that he had. 'You don't mind bleeding a little?' She glanced at the mirror again, but the Timmy-Angel of her fantasies wasn't there anymore.

'Hadn't thought about it, but the idea does kind of excite me. Shit, Pam, I'm a venal man, I never could take all that religious bullshit, it was just a living to me . . .' He unbuttoned his pants, removed his tie, and sat down on the bed, waiting to be entertained. This was obviously a man who expected service. What a pig, she thought. 'Jesus, your nipples are pierced,' he said like a fool. 'Did it hurt?'

'Not much,' she said.

Having decided that she was going, by hook or by crook, to be a vampire, even if it meant faking it until such time as some real vampire would take pity on her and make it all come true, she began to wonder whether this was the right person to experiment on. Even Sascha Rabinowitz, who had had no brain, had been comely in a strange sort of way. And Herr Bergschneider had been sexy indeed compared to this lump. Still, he was probably not very strong. Maybe even had a weak heart; that would save her a lot of trouble.

She had been hunting for the right person all night. At first he had seemed perfect, with his predatory look, his eagerness to use the Timmy Valentine trump card on an impressionable fan, his pompous manner and funny way of talking . . . but now that he was lying there on the bed, heaving gelatinously and leering, she was beginning to wonder if she should have picked someone a little more . . . attractive.

She felt a twinge of guilt, but then she thought of the butcher's boy's blood dripping from his cheek and she felt all hot inside and so she pounced on Damien, still only half undressed, and suddenly she was gnawing at his chest, biting at the hairy belly, and he was laughing because she was tickling him but abruptly he stopped laughing when she chewed off his left nipple and

spat it out and started to tongue the hole where the blood was
spurting out and he was shaking her and screaming, 'Bitch,
bitch, bitch, I'm gonna make you pay for this—' but the taste of
the blood was so exhilarating it seemed to lend her superhuman
strength and she held onto him, he couldn't shake her off,
couldn't reach for the bedside phone, couldn't scream after a
while because she bit off another chunk of his chest and now
he was in such terrible pain that he could only whimper and
stare unbelieving at the nipple which flecked the bedspread and
spattered its design of primroses with gore . . . the blood was
just spewing now, it didn't look real it was so bright . . . Pamina
lapped it all up, she squeezed his tit to make the blood spurt
higher . . . and all the time she was thinking, this'll show you,
Tante Amelia, Timmy, all you people who tried to tell me I
wasn't for real . . . and spat out another wad of flesh and
slathered the sluicing blood all over her own small breasts,
plunged her fist into the wound like a dildo . . . Damien twisted
away . . . he was rummaging in the bedside drawer . . . pulled
out a sterling crucifix . . . 'Got you, bitch!' he shrieked, and held
it aloft . . . she thought, well, at least I'm going to feel some kind
of *frisson* now but no, there was no effect at all, and she realized
that in some ways what she was was *better* than a real vampire
because she was immune to the crosses and the silver and the
garlic . . . she grabbed the crucifix from his hand and jabbed it
into his left eye. Pus and rheum squirted out. She backed away,
found the ice pick, cracked open the skull and began to feed on the
hot fluids . . . like a field mouse sucking a stolen egg . . . Damien
convulsed . . . flung his arms about like a crazed marionette . . .
then, all at once, crumpled onto the bed.

She smothered him with hungry kisses, and with each kiss
drew more blood from him. You had to be quick, she could see,
because it started coagulating almost the instant it hit the air.
How long had it taken Timmy Valentine to master the art of
controlling the blood flow? Or did true vampires simply know
these things by instinct from the moment of their first waking
to darkness?

She drank and drank. How many pints did a human hold,
six, eight? She drank. Chewed the muscle tissue and spat out
the residue as though she were sucking the juice from an

orange. The chest and arms and legs were best; the belly's blood was tainted with sour odours, but had a certain piquancy. At length she was bloated. Her eyes did not redden, her cheeks did not flush or her complexion glow with the stolen life-force.

But I've still done what Timmy did, what Tante Amelia did before they killed her, she thought. They can't presume to judge me. If no one will make me a vampire, I'll fucking well make myself one. I don't need any of them. They're just like my parents, always knowing what's best for me, trying to do all my thinking for me. I have to drink blood. I don't care about the consequences . . .

She wiped her mouth on the bedspread and went to look for Timmy Valentine.

moonlight

Running across the rooftops. Naked. The moist wind rubbing against his skin. Running. Leaping from gable to gable. Running. Above the tiny streetways of the city, running. Here a gutter, there a gas duct, over there a row of gargoyles, weathered, sightless.

The moon was waning.

If the moon spirit doesn't speak tonight, she will not speak to me at all this time! She will have abandoned me forever . . . I'll be an orphan in the white man's world . . . I'll be blind.

He ran. Tiles stabbed at his feet. He crouched down, lumbered over the roofing like one of the four-footed brothers; sprang over eaves; up, up, up; spiderlike, up masonry, up stone; up, up.

Where now? Stones stung his feet and hands. Tines of brightly coloured light . . . a stained glass window. An ancient chapel, illumined from within; sideways he crawled along the bumpy glass, watching his skin change colour as he glided, cerulean, vermilion, viridian, obsidian.

I cannot become one with the forest, one with the earth; but what is timber, what is brick, if not the children of tree and soil? This is still the forest; yes, even this stone edifice, even this translucent wheel of colour that is the window that overlooks

the altar; this is still wilderness. And most of all it because men's
hearts are still inside that wilderness; before this tiny interlude
of civilization dawned, there was a million years of wilderness,
and the wilderness is in everything we think and do; it is what
we are. He thought these thoughts as he climbed . . . what was
this place, Westminster Abbey? It was too dark, he moved on
pure instinct, and always it was upward, into the cold; foothold
after foothold he found, now stepping on a piece of shingle,
now on the neck of a gargoyle, now the wing of an angel; he
climbed.

He climbed.

And now a place to rest, open on all sides to the night wind,
yet enclosed; cold metal touched his flesh; a belfry. Eyes stared
down. A bat even, he thought. Sad, huge eyes, Timmy-eyes;
but Timmy no longer had the power to turn himself into a
bat; the bat was a bat, nothing sentient, just a brother of the
night. The bat blinked once, twice; he turned away from it to
gaze on the moon. If I look into the moon long enough I'll
hypnotize myself and maybe that'll cause me to slide into a
trance so that the spirit can come to me, he thought, aware even
as he thought it that he was trying too hard to contrive the
vision, when he should just empty his mind completely, let the
vision come of its own accord, if it wanted to come.

The moon swam through turrets of cloud.

He sang his song to the moon, sang it loud, knowing the
wind would carry his words to the corners of the world. The
moon hid herself behind the clouds. He closed his eyes, sang
to the moon of his imagination. And even in his thoughts, the
moon concealed herself. And when he opened his eyes again,
there was the bat, hanging upside down, with eyes that seemed
so human, that seemed almost to speak . . .

Am I not then to receive the magic of the *ma'aipots*, to become
the sacred man-woman? How can I defeat the vampires again
without magic? he thought. Despair flooded him. He thought
of leaping from the belfry. He wondered whether he would
crack his head on the pavement or whether he would drown in
the river. There seemed to be no point in going on. This was a
wilderness with no way out.

Then, at the very periphery of hearing, he heard a high-pitched whistling . . . it was *so* high it did not seem that a human could possibly hear it . . . and he looked again and found himself gazing into the eyes of the bat . . . and words seemed to condense out of the ultrasonic whine . . . calling him by a Shoshone name, the name his shaman grandfather had once given him in secret, the true name that no human had ever been allowed to hear, not even his beloved wife . . .

Little brother, he said to the bat, are *you* the totem animal that has come to be my spirit guide out of the wilderness of the heart?

And the bat replied, *Contrariwise* . . .

memory: 1593

And, on leathery wings, swift as the wind, he swoops, swerves, sweeps along the narrow streets, thinking only that he must get out of London, bury the ugly memories and his identity, find another name, another time . . . he must enter the dark forest and renew himself so that he can emerge, healed, ready to feed once more . . .

Beyond the river . . . over the cathedral . . . past the palace . . . into the wood . . . swooping . . . down low. He drops to the ground and his wings disintegrate . . . he has become a rodent now, sniffing through the damp grass, each blade silvered by the moon.

He moves into a clearing. There are toadstools. There are human voices. He cannot help himself. He can hear the music of their blood, and his hunger rises a little. The hunger he can control; the grief will not go away. In human shape again, he rests in the shade of an ashtree at the edge of the clearing. The ash does not sting him even though it has been said that, of the stake that must be driven through a vampire's heart, ash-wood is best, for it partakes of the most ancient of magics; it is an ashtree after all which supports the world, so said the rune-readers of the north. He leans against the trunk and watches.

Three humans come into the clearing. Their faces are eerie in the chiaroscuro of moonlight and forest. They are laughing. One is a raven-haired woman, dark, serious and soft-spoken, one a young man with a slight beard and an extravagant ruff, the other a younger man, a boy even, whose doublet is festooned with pearls. Ned has seen the young man somewhere before: now he recognizes him; it is the Earl of Southampton, Harry Wriothesly, who has occasionally visited Marlowe in his garret.

'Sooth, a fairy ring,' says the young man. 'Will, come see.'

'Dare we enter it, Harry,' says the woman, 'with the moon so bright, and the hour of midnight fast approaching?'

'What, fear you hobgoblins, witches, pixies, pucks?' the young man says, and skips over a line of toadstools; he bows and beckons his two friends.

Ned sees that at the centre of the clearing the toadstools form a circle. Solemnly, the three mortals enter the circle. They stand equidistant and link hands so that it seems that the magic circle circumscribes a triangle. And Ned moves closer, intrigued by the curious ritual of their interconnecting; for it seems to him that one loves the other who loves a third who loves the first yet none is loved by whom he loves the most; the boy has seen this from the way their glances dart, one to the other, the other to the third, and so on round and round in a roundelay that will not play its final chord, will not resolve. It is a game to them, yet the stakes are human hearts.

'I pray you, no more sonnets,' says the fair-haired boy, 'I am for plays: tears and laughter, revenge and retribution.'

'Let us do a play now,' the dark lady says, laughing. 'A play for Will, and these toadstools shall be our groundlings.'

'Groundlings! Toadstools should have more taste,' says Will. 'But truth to speak, 'tis an excellent open space for a play – look, yonder brake shall be your tiring house, this fairy circle the apron of our stage, and the moon hath all the light we need.'

'All the world's a stage for you, Will,' says the boy. And kisses him on the lips, daring him to go further; and the lady covers her laughter with a coy clasped hand; and Ned sees in Will Shakespeare's eyes confusion and inner torment. 'Why, what's the matter?' says Harry. 'Inside this fairy ring, we are invisible; it is May; nothing is as it seems; nor night, nor day; nor love, nor death; nor man, nor woman.'

'Harry, Harry, thou speakst in riddles.'

'No riddles, Will, but visions!' He plucks a velvet sack from his sleeve, waves it past the others' noses, and cries, 'Fresh nutmeg . . . the fruit of this, chewed thoroughly and long, induceth the condition called "midsummer night's dream" – the mad enhancement of the senses – monsters, fairies, creatures of light and darkness dancing in the air – whorls, patterned patens of bright gold—'

The dark lady shrieks with laughter, takes the first bite. ''Tis bitter.' And after a moment: 'But now 'tis sweet.' And laughs again. Her breasts are but slender; she too is young, Ned thinks.

'I am not one for drugged delusions,' says the poet. 'My brain is fevered enough.' His two companions laugh. 'But I would see you act, Harry.'

'You see that often enough,' says Wriothesly, 'when I'm with my mother the Countess.'

'But how would you act,' says the dark lady, 'an you were on a stage, and gowned and gartered as a queen?'

'I'll show you, if it like you. Lend me your dress. But you, lady of shadows, must play a man, for I would not have you naked in the wood.'

'More nutmeg first!' she says.

And then the two skip over the fairy ring and into the shadows, leaving Will alone in the moonlight. Closer, Ned thinks, I must come closer. Mist has begun to swirl up from the ground, and Ned attenuates himself and joins that mist, and floats above the poet's head, and smells his very breath, a cold clean breath quite unlike Kit Marlowe's, that was always clogged with cloves and wine. The poet is mumbling to himself . . .

> *I know a bank where the wild thyme blows,*
> *Where oxlips and the nodding violet grows*
> *Quite overcanopied with luscious woodbine . . .'*

Music again, thinks the boy, music surpassing even Marlowe's. How can I leave this place? he thinks. How can I retreat into the shadow?

And from the shadow come the dark lady and the boy. They are dressed in each other's clothes. The lady has become a dandy, beruffed, bepearled, and her hand resting on a jewelled pommel; the boy, corseted and enrobed in lace and satin, has become more girlish than ever. And the effects of the drug have made them even giddier. They laugh and point at one another and tell each other what they see: 'A jackanapes!' 'An ass-head!' and Will Shakespeare observes, inscribes their antics in the ledger of his mind, and says nothing at all.

They posture, they orate, they yell out random passages of bombast; and now and then, the poet smiles; and finally, exhausted, they fall into a heap in the middle of the fairy ring; and Will kneels down and looks from one to the other, and softly he says, 'Thou master-mistress of my passion,' but Ned, the funnelling mist, cannot tell to whom he addresses those words, though he engulf the three of them within his vaporous arms.

And Harry says, 'Tell us what play you are writing now.'

And Shakespeare says, 'I cannot tell thee much. It is in an elfin clearing such as this. A fairy king and his dark consort are battling to possess a boy, an . . .' he thinks for a moment, '*Indian boy.*'

'To possess him carnally?' says Harry. 'Why, that rivals Master Marlowe.' And he and the girl giggle softly.

A field mouse darts through the circle. Startled, the lady sits up; the nutmeg has made her easily affrighted. For a moment Ned loses control of his shape. But like quicksilver he pours himself back into the air.

'Behold – some personage – a beautiful boy – condensing out of the mist,' says Will. 'Tarry, thou wanton boy! Gods, but he was comely! If only he had played my Juliet, and not that snotty-nosed Alfred Walmsley, panting like a pregnant sow. Boy, come back!' And tries to pull young Ned back out of thin air.

'So, nutmeg after all!' says the lady.

'Nay,' says Will, 'I *saw* him. It was a thin, pale boy, seeming almost one with the mist and moonlight, not quite substantial.'

'It was only a puck,' says Harry.

Will sits awhile in thought. 'If peradventure such creatures of the night could be conjured up on a stage,' he says at last, 'there would be magic indeed.'

'How?' says the lady. 'They cannot come abroad by day.'

'Indeed,' says Harry, 'they do fear the dawn; the sun doth send them screaming back to Hell.'

'But if,' says Will, 'the night becomes as day . . .'

'Yes!' says Wriothesly. 'Thousands upon thousands of candles
. . . the great hall of one of our castles . . . a dais set up, courtiers
and royals in their most gilded vestments . . . I have heard they
plan such a spectacle at Blackfriars . . . with the children of
some chapel choir. A merry prospect indeed, unscrubbed young
quiristers flouncing about in petticoats by candlelight.'

'Yes . . . in such a place, in such a time, a thing of darkness
could recite my words . . . and how such words would sing,
an the tongue that sing them be not normal, but itself of air
excorporate; for poetry is air, though it err not; it is the air
the ear is heir to. Nay, "ear" is too much; I must retool the
conceit.'

I cannot sleep yet, thinks the vampire who has called himself
Ned Bryant. I must to this new theatre that performs by night.
I must bedazzle with my singing until they make me one of
them. I must attract the notice of this poet until he gives me
words to speak. I cannot depart this time till I be the thing
of darkness he acknowledge his; I must become that immortal
tongue.

In the pageant of blood that has played through his unlife for
fifteen hundred years, there has been too much horror. He has
apprehended so much evil that he has finally come to know
there is no final evil. It is this that has mitigated his superstitions,
so that he no longer recoils from the cross, or the sacred host,
or the holy blood of Christ. I must have blood to sustain me in
this half-existence, he thinks, but there are other things I need
too; even a monster can know beauty, and yearns to utter
honeyed words, and sing in languages other than the voice of
night.

I shall to London . . .

vision-seeker

. . . and hung, high above London, his knees hooked over a
bar of iron, eye to eye with a creature of the night, and gazed
into the bat's eyes until at last he saw the worlds within, the
hells, the heavens, and the many earths . . . and still he cried

out, 'What is the message you have brought me? What am I to
do?'

And the bat said again, *'Contrariwise . . .'*

vision-seeker

When Timmy flung open the door to his hotel suite, she was
sitting in front of the television sobbing her eyes out. And he
saw the rim of blood around her lips, and the blood that was
drying on her arms, saw traces of blood through the ripped
black fabric of her clothes, and he suspected the worst. But it
was even worse.

'Who?' he said, thinking to himself, some bum, some busker
in a tube station.

'Damien Peters,' said Pamina.

'You killed Damien Peters?'

'And drank his blood. All of it, I think. I couldn't squeeze out
any more.'

'Jesus fucking Christ,' Timmy said. And slowly sat down at
the edge of the sofa; he didn't want to get too close to her. 'You
killed him?'

'Well? Didn't you kill my Tante Amelia?'

'She was dead already!'

'You won't tell, will you?'

'Won't tell?' Timmy said. God, irony piled on irony; the wannabe vampire pleading for sympathy from the ex-vampire. 'He
was our friend.'

'Didn't act very friendly. He practically raped me in the street.
And he was taking your name in vain, telling me he could
arrange a meeting with you just so he could fuck me.'

Timmy sighed. It was true that, once he had lost religion,
Damien Peters had become a man without a direction, seeking
refuge in libido, discovering suddenly that he had no need to
hold his lust in check, that there were those who actually
approved of his philandering. There had been, Timmy suspected, a part of Damien that had longed for death ever since
God had deserted him.

What could he do, though? Go to the police? Have Pamina

arrested, arraigned, declared unfit to stand trial because of her deepening psychosis? And how to explain this girl's peculiar madness?

'You've got worse,' he said, 'since you joined us. Maybe it's my own fault, letting you taste my own blood, letting you think there's all this glamour in being undead.'

'I've seen you in mirrors,' she said, 'only it's not you, it's a you with *sex* written all over you, a stronger you, a you that doesn't turn his back on the truth . . .'

'Not me, Angel,' he said slowly. 'You've seen Angel Todd.'

'Chit mentioned him too.'

'Angel has been captured and confined. But his thoughts are so powerful, it seems – or *your* vampiric self-delusion so strong – that he has been able to break through to you.'

'I've seen him. He was there when I killed Damien. I don't know how I feel about that. When I was ripping him apart there was so much elation, I almost burst with joy . . . and now . . . I feel a terrible sadness . . . I want to kill myself because of the shame of it . . . but there's another little part of me that's saying, *Kill again, kill to forget the pain of the last kill, kill and go on killing, because a killer is all you are.* What am I, Timmy? Oh, Jesus Christus, you must help me.' And she sobbed again, and again Timmy made no move toward her. She scared him shitless. He hated what she had become, but who was he to cast blame? How many people had he killed over the last two millennia? He could not even remember. Yet the weight of all those dead had had a numbing effect on him. Perhaps that was why he was being relatively calm about it all.

'Pamina,' he said, 'we're bad for you, you must leave us, go back to your parents; see a shrink, even.'

'A shrink! So that he can reduce this, the grandest of all passions, to some childish neurosis? What's he going to do, put me on Prozac?'

'I think this has gone beyond Prozac.'

'Fuck you.'

'Pami—'

'You've betrayed me in every way. I put my trust in you. I thought you of all people would understand me, save me. But you've rejected everything I long for. You killed the one person

in my life who *did* understand. And now you want to stop me
from becoming what I know I am. You're no Angel, Timmy
Valentine; you're a pale shadow of Angel Todd, a little boy
forever on the verge of pimples, with no passions and no balls.
You've lost it all.'

Timmy listened, did not react. There was some truth in it.
They both knew it. But Timmy did not want to face it yet.
Instead, he took out his wallet and slowly counted out twenty
hundred-pound notes. 'You'll need this to get home,' he said.

She stared at the proffered money for a moment; then, sobbing, took it and fled.

contrariwise

Over breakfast, Lady Chit had been listening to Timmy tell her
about Pamina, who had already taken a flight to Munich. 'I
haven't checked in on Damien,' he said. 'I don't quite know
how to . . .'

'We'll be in Moscow by nightfall,' Lady Chit said. 'Are we
going to just . . . leave him?'

'How should I know?' Timmy cried. It was then that they saw
PJ coming toward them.

PJ was dressed in his best Armani; he was all cleaned up,
shaved, his hair in a neat ponytail. But he was walking backwards. Very skilfully: he seemed to know exactly where he was
going, threading his way through the breakfast tables as though
he had eyes in the back of his head.

'My God, he's had a vision,' Timmy said.

It had to be true. Peculiar though he looked, Chit could see
that he had a familiar glow to him; it was the very aura that had
first drawn her to him. He walked backward all the way to their
table, and then he said, 'Goodbye.'

'Are you all right?' said Timmy.

'No,' said PJ.

'Did you have a vision?' said Chit.

'No,' said PJ.

Chit laughed. 'Oh, what am I to do? He's become a contrary.'
Timmy said, 'Oh, you mean where they have to do the

opposite of everything they mean? I think I've seen that in a movie or something.'

'Yes,' Chit said, 'I'm afraid it's one of those really strange Indian customs . . . it's a vow that he takes to do everything backwards . . . until, I guess, the great goal is achieved, the victory over the enemy or whatever. It's a very sacred and powerful vow . . . it's like becoming a holy man-woman, kind of, but different . . . mostly this is for victory in war . . . it makes them completely berserk in battle.'

'And we *are* on the brink of a war, aren't we,' Timmy said.

'No,' said PJ.

Sirens were sounding outside. Chit saw a team of paramedics with a stretcher trotting through the lobby just past the entrance to the breakfast room. The maid must have found the body of Damien Peters. How terrible to die that way, she thought. And that little girl must have been possessed to be able to tear him apart. The same little girl I've been so sorry for, the girl I comforted. It was just as well she had not seen her this morning; it might have given her a nervous breakdown.

'I guess you'd better have some breakfast,' Chit said. 'Looks like you've had a really rough night.'

'You're welcome,' he said. He sat down beside them and carefully started cutting a slice of toast with the flat end of his knife. As she watched her husband painstakingly spreading the marmalade on his toast *before* his butter, Chit realized with a chill that, crazy as it looked, the magic was coming back, after all.

16

BURIAL OF THE RATS

memory: 1593: 1600

'I shall to London,' he has told himself, but he does not . . . he plunges further into the forest of the soul, seeking to purge the memory of Kit's death, and only finds himself afflicted by memories more horrifying still: Bluebeard writhing over a child's decapitated head; dining alfresco with Vlad Tepes amid a forest of impaled citizens; burnings, floggings, flayings, human sacrifices . . . when he emerges, he finds he has made a wrong turn in the labyrinth of space and time . . . it is Rome, where he finds Caravaggio, is painted as the angel of darkness in *The Martyrdom of St Matthew*, endures the odious affection of a cardinal and a painter's twisted passion . . . then, fleeing *that* suffocating milieu, he re-enters the dark forest and comes once more to England . . . and Shakespeare.

But there are no more midsummer night's dreams for Will, who has lost his son Hamnet and turned to tragedy.

But an evening comes, in another inn, in another inner room, burning a different candle, a different poet scratching with a different pen, murmuring poetry even more sublime than the words which first caused the boy to tarry in this time; and the boy who calls himself Ned finds himself materializing from the shadows; and this time he weeps a little, almost like a human child.

'Who art thou?' says Will. 'Oh. I remember. I glimpsed thee once, in a clearing in a forest, hovering over a fairy ring. Nigh on seven years ago it was. No one saw thee but I, clear-sighted because I did not partake of the drug that blurred my lovers' eyes.'

'Oh Will, shall I be thy son? Even though I can only come to thee by night?' says the boy. 'I know thy son is dead.'

'What, art thou a changeling? Have the fairies brought thee, and him barely cold beneath the earth? Get thee gone.'

Then the boy recites, from memory, the words he heard in that fairy ring seven years ago:

I know a bank where the wild thyme blows . . .

Even without notes, there is music. The words surge in an unceasing stream of sound, for Ned never breathes from line to line; he has not breathed in fifteen hundred years. It is an utterance untainted by sublunary corruption; of poesy it is the very quintessence. The poet can only gape at such a rendition, word-perfect after seven years, and of an absolute beauty.

'Oh Will,' he cries, 'shall I not now be that creature of the night who will sing thy words in an immortal tongue? Shall I not, shall I not?'

And Will remembers his conceit about the theatre where night is day, and says, 'Aye, but thou shalt.'

news of the world

From *The Morning Star*:

Televangelist murdered in London hotel

Damien Peters, the former American televangelist who achieved world-wide notoriety when he renounced his faith and took on the rôle of an evil priest in the trash cinema epic *Valentine – The Motion Picture*, was brutally ripped to pieces in his hotel room in London yesterday. The identity, motive and modus operandi of the assailant are unknown. The preacher had arrived in London the previous night to join the entourage of superannuated child rock star Timmy Valentine, who is trying to revive his flagging ratings with a world tour described by our in-house music critic as 'decidedly lacklustre'. The body was discovered by the maid. The rock star, en route to Moscow for his final European stop – the remainder of his tour will be in Asia, where his popularity is somewhat higher than here in the jaded west – could not be reached for comment.

From *Scandal International*:

Vampire's curse stalks Neo-Gothic rock star

Timmy Valentine seems to be living out some ancient curse as his tour sweeps across the world bringing mayhem and death in its wake. And we're not just talking about the usual violence that besets the appearances of the twelve-year-old gore-loving new age punk goth-rave cyberdeathrock puke popper. Timmy's had his share of that, with Neo-Gothics driving nails through their palms right in the middle of his concerts, and strange hairdo-sporting punks branding each other with hot irons right outside the auditorium. But there seems to be death of another kind. In Germany last week, the corpses were piled high at a performance of an opera in Thauberg – which Timmy Valentine attended. In fact, he pulled a lot of strings to be there, says Hans Übermacht, guest list supervisor for the opera which was in fact also a memorial service for Amelia Rothstein, a singer Timmy is known to have visited in her nursing home *the day before she perished of a heart attack*! In London, things fared no better when a prominent ex-televangelist was savagely *ripped to shreds* in his hotel room where he had arrived *specifically to meet up with Timmy Valentine*!

Scandal International has learned from Joshua Levy, the world's leading 'Valentinologist', that similar inexplicable scenes of senseless violence were also in evidence at a rock concert in Boca Blanca, Florida, in 1982 . . . after which Timmy Valentine disappeared for ten years.

Wait a minute! This kid's only twelve years old?

None of this seems to add up.

For Levy, the answer is simple. 'Timmy Valentine,' he says, 'is an apocalyptic manifestation of the collective unconscious which appears in the world at times of special horror, crisis or endangerment. He is the dark side to the equivalent sightings of the Virgin Mary, Angels, Jesus, and Elvis, which appear to bring solace and comfort to those blessed with the visions. But it's basically the same phenomenon.' Levy has written a book, *Valentine Unbound*, which purports to present evidence of Timmy Valentine manifestations throughout history – from a Nazi concentration camp to the Roman Empire, from the Ming Dynasty to the London of Jack the Ripper.

'Nonsense,' says world-famous horror writer Douglas Clegg, author of such masterworks as *Breeder*. 'It's plain as day, the kid's a vampire.'

flying

In Russia, Timmy Valentine was *hot*.

Teens mobbed the ticket-scalping kiosks in the squares. The T-shirts, posters, CD singles, coffee mugs, and tour jackets sold like hot cakes . . . the *fake* T-shirts and posters sold even better, and you could barely tell them apart except for the odd spelling error . . . Timmy Valantine, for example. Pirated cassettes everywhere, too. But Timmy didn't care. The magic really was returning. God, he sang, he sang.

In a packed auditorium where the whole audience seemed to breathe along with him . . . and that was a whole new experience . . . in the old days, he had not breathed at all, of course . . . and at the first concerts he had breathed alone. But no. They watched. They were dead silent when he floated the soft high notes. He found a new technique for hitting those notes now that he had to breathe; he sucked in a great mouthful of air and socked those high notes right from the diaphragm, head on, so they seemed to come tearing from his lungs, like it was killing him to sing, like he was losing a piece of his soul with every soulful phrase, and there was this new cracking in his voice, this new strain, that drove the heartbreak home. They roared at the end of each song, and in the long instrumental interludes they danced with a freedom from decorum he had not seen in centuries. They knew all the lyrics; even when they hushed themselves he could see them mouthing the words, and wondered whether they understood how much they spoke of outrage, despair, and desolation; or whether they were just shiny new words in a shiny new language from a shiny new world just beyond the horizon.

He signed autographs from midnight until four in the morning; then he strolled through the square – a circle of bodyguards keeping the mob at bay – with his two friends, Chit and PJ, close by. The Russians found them an odd couple, but more people knew what a *contrary* was than Timmy expected. People seemed to read voraciously and to know a great deal about such subjects as the Native American culture – indeed, during the age of communism, the genocide of the Indians had been universally taught to schoolchildren as a prime example of the evil inherent in a capitalist society. Still, having the fastidious Asian girl and the Shoshone brave who always walked backward in his immediate circle certainly made Timmy Valentine seem eccentricity personified.

They stopped for a moment; PJ sidled up to Timmy with a cellular phone; he handed it to him and said, 'It's not for you,' by which Timmy understood that it was.

It had a phony British accent, and Timmy knew at once that Hollywood was calling. 'Please hold for Mr Giler.'

'Timmy, the figures for Moscow are uncomfortably high.' Giler hadn't called since they left the US, except to cut the budget. 'What's wrong?'

'Don't know, boss . . . for some unfathomable reason, they seem to love me.'

'Those killings . . . you have anything to do with them? It's in the fucking *Enquirer*, you know. I couldn't have *paid* for better publicity.'

'Don't look at me, David; I thought you'd already written off my contract.'

'Perhaps I've been over-hasty.'

Timmy laughed. 'No, you haven't. You're so right. I do need to disappear. If this tour accidentally makes you a few million, I'm still only a flavour of the month. Axing me's fine, I'm cool with it.' The moon was waning and the air, though clear, was chill.

'Well, I was thinking more of you staying out there on the Europe/Asia circuit, perhaps a few exploitation movies . . . maybe, a year or two down the road, a comeback . . .'

'I've already come back . . . from the dead.'

'There you go, believing your own hype again!'

Timmy looked around and noticed that he was walking right into the lobby of his hotel, a stark grey building refurbished for the tourist upsurge. 'Listen, you really don't need to get me back.'

'Well, listen, someone from Mosfilm is going to give you a tour tomorrow. You'll love it – biggest studio in the fucking world, even if their equipment's from the stone age – they could really use a big but about-to-be-washed-up name like you on some thriller—'

'OK, OK, I'll talk to them.'

'Great. Well, I'm off to a breakfast meeting with the Big Three.'

Timmy didn't stop to wonder who the Big Three were this week. He merely handed the phone back to some lackey and went on up to the suite.

contrariwise

'It's like an *Alice Through the Looking-glass*,' he told Chit in one of the moments that he came down out of his contrary state. 'You remember the scene where Alice is walking, and walking, and walking, and she never seems to be able to get to the beautiful place she's been looking for, and finally she realizes that she has to walk in the wrong direction . . . and then right away she finds herself exactly where she wanted to go.'

'I remember,' said Chit. They had spent the morning trying to find toilet paper – 'sandpaper,' the Americans called the kind they had in the hotel – to no avail, until a kindly tourist from Milwaukee sold them a roll for five bucks ('I always carry extra.'). Now they were in the room, killing time; tonight there was going to be an even bigger concert – oversold by 10%, according to Andrei, the booking agent. Timmy had gone off with two mirror-shaded, grey-suited gentlemen from the Russian film industry.

'But can you feel where people are . . . can you feel the presence of supernatural powers, like you used to be able to?' asked Chit.

'It's different. Now, if I look *away* from things, it's like I can suddenly come face to face with them . . .'

'What about Pamina? What's happened to Pamina?'

PJ closed his eyes. Imagined himself back up there, hanging in the belfry, with the wind roaring about him. Imagined the little lost girl at the hotel in Thauberg . . . imagined the ravaged corpse of Damien Peters . . . then imagined himself turning around, stepping away, leaving them far behind . . . fleeing into the cool dark forest.

Suddenly, in a clearing, in the moonlight, a mouth leered wide, dripped blood from glistening fangs and—

'She really is lost,' he said.

'But did she go home to her parents, is she getting some kind of help?'

'I can't see that clearly,' he said, and already as he tried to fasten onto the image it was dancing away on a moonbeam, dissolving in the shivering of the leaves. He started to follow, remembered in time, backed away in the opposite direction . . . felt an icy hand clasping his shoulder, whipped around, heard only a silvery giggle, then the flutter of wings, then the sigh of the night wind. 'There's a bunch of other stuff in the vision that I can't really understand . . . for example . . . an . . .' he squeezed his eyes harder, tying to make it out . . . 'an elephant?'

'Oh, my God,' Chit said. 'A wooden elephant, right? Slipping from my purse, onto the hot concrete—'

'Breaking in two,' PJ said, seeing that for the first time.

'Shit. It was the *kae bon* ceremony at the Brahma shrine . . . my mother called me on the cellular right in the middle of it . . . I could have *sworn* I mislaid an elephant somewhere. But I thought that, with all those disastrous Lauren McCandless encounters, with Pete Singhasri getting so *horribly* killed – well, I thought we had all atoned for that wayward elephant. If I miscounted them at all.'

'But what could it have to do with Pamina Rothstein?'

dissolve

The two mirror-shaded grey-suited men might as well have been identical twins, and the fact that they were named Aleksei and Alexander didn't help. But Timmy had promised to give them a chance to show their stuff, and their tour of the Russian film facilities was actually pretty impressive.

'Is largest film studio in the world,' Aleksei said, waving expansively at the almost deserted lot, which did seem to go on and on, 'in its heyday, produced prodigious propaganda films, huge historical epics, very big, very big. But now, alas, just sitting around rotting away.'

They were trekking through the back lot in a sort of golf cart-like contraption. Aleksei pointed out the sights. Several mediaeval castles, variously dilapidated, stood in the distance. There was a Victorian street, a New York street, a Persian bazaar, a cathedral, a bit of the San Francisco wharf, even a Cheyenne village.

'But what exactly do you want me to do?' Timmy was asking them. He knew he was supposed to be impressed by all this, but there had to be a catch to it somewhere.

'Well,' said Alexander, 'we are setting up below the line deals for movies. Basically your American $200,000 buys a ten million dollar looking movie, OK? And you are attaching yourself, so big pre-sales. We have six vampire scripts in development, you take your pick. Also a true history of Vlad the Impaler from his captivity in Turkey to his death and accession of his brother Radu, very nice script that we picked up in Romania.'

They drove through warehouses loaded with lights, lenses, dollies, cranes, battered cameras – Mitchells, Timmy thought in amazement, why, they filmed with those in the Stone Age – chaotic prop rooms and rooms piled high with scenery flats, while the two Alexes regaled him stereophonically. There didn't seem to be many people around, though, until they rode past an enormous reproduction of the palace of Versailles; the Bastille, and the façade of an enormous cathedral, could be seen in the distance. In front of that façade, a team seemed to be filming some kind of period piece, for the characters were dressed like something out of *Les Miz*. 'What's that?' Timmy said, pointing.

'Oh,' said Aleksei, 'big new Roger Corman movie . . . *Bram Stoker's Burial of the Rats*.'

'God, that's Adrienne Barbeau, isn't it?' said Timmy, as one of the great scream queens of the American cinema rode by on a horse.

'*Very* big movie,' said Alexander. 'Millions of rubles.'

In the commissary, they ran into Beverly Gray, a diminutive powerhouse of a woman who appeared to be running the show. She recognized Timmy and asked if he might sign something for her daughter. 'Oh, Hilary will be thrilled,' she said. 'I see they're trying to rope you in, too; are they giving you money, or trying to get it from you?'

'I'm really not sure,' he said, wrinkling his nose up at the proffered borscht. 'You don't seem to be enjoying this that much.'

'Well . . . let's just say that I'd rather be analysing the effects of the great vowel shift on early Norman literature. Not that it's not an amusing film – Bram Stoker on a grand tour of France, getting abducted by lesbian highwaywomen – well, we've had to tone that down, the script came in a little too wild even for us – learning important lessons in feminism from scantily-clad Amazon women – not to mention getting the germ of the idea for *Dracula* from a young Romanian ex-sex-slave—'

'Astonishing,' said Timmy. 'But you know, that's not how it happened at all . . .'

memory: 1888

The centuries swirl by. The darkness gathers and whirlpools about his senses. He spins, he drowns, he is spat out. The space is the same but time has passed; he does not know how much time as yet; but there is a great deal that has not changed. A staleness in the air. Rats scurrying along the sewers, though the streets are no longer cobbled. People shuffling past in great-coats, their hands in their pockets, their eyes downcast. The city more crowded now; and all night long, the thrum of mechanical engines that live on the lives of the young; for vampires have become great steel devices that smother the air with smoke. The same moon shines down, but grey brick has replaced beam and plaster. There are the same alleys, and the same river under whose bridges sleep the armies of half-feral children; and cities that were distant from one another have become conjoined by streets and row houses and monumental buildings that mimic the long-dead Roman Empire. All these images are careening through his mind as he suddenly comes to, in the midst of a crowd, jostling, calling out, selling wares, pushing and shoving through the alley; it is a summer night, unseasonably warm. Up and down the street, leaning against walls, standing under lampposts, there are girls with their petticoats hitched up. They call out to him: 'Sir, would you like a taste of my cunny?' and 'Only a shilling for an hour's dalliance,' and other such things, and some as young as seven or eight, he suspects. And in the shadows, just beyond the periphery of most people's vision, gentlemen in frock coats, mutton chops and top hats are thrusting away in the darkness, now and then casting furtive glances at the passersby, who pretend to see nothing.

Too many people at once. Too much blood. He must feed, but by now he has become too heavily afflicted with the curse of compassion to feed entirely at random. But the smell is maddening him and he knows that he must duck, or he will give in to temptation. So many kinds of blood, too, all at once . . . the odour of absinthe-tainted blood, the acrid scent of fresh menses, the blood of a man in the sewer, coughing up his lungs as he lies dying of consumption. The blood, the blood . . . he turns a corner.

A side alley, even narrower than the first. There's no one. He darts into a pool of shadow and collides with something . . . a man's boot. Startled, he collapses into a rat, sniffs the foetid odour of old socks, is about to dash off, when he suddenly catches a whiff of fresh blood. Staring upward, he sees what the man is doing. One of the young prostitutes is pressed against the wall. Her petticoats are lifted high above her waist. The man has cupped her mouth with his right hand, while with his left he is carefully slicing away her vulva with a razor blade. Little squeals are all that escape from her muffled lips. The man tosses aside the wrinkled nether lips. Blood is gushing out now, and the boy feels the hunger rise up, an implacable thing that his horror cannot stifle. The man becomes more playful. The blade slides upward, widening the slit; in the moonlight the blood is black as tar. The boy sees the man's eyes; they glint; they study the struggling woman as a doctor might study a scientific specimen; there is in those eyes a calm, cold reason, far distant from this spectacle of gore. It is a madman. The boy knows his kind well – has he not been one of Bluebeard's victims? – and he knows that nothing can save this innocent, this little whore.

The blade plunges, jerks up; a piece of kidney has been impaled. The girl has lost consciousness. She is slumped against the brick wall with a puddle of urine at her feet. The man removes his hand from her mouth, pops the kidney in his own, idly munches it, then spits out the residue. The softest of strangulated cries escapes her throat before he slits it open. His hands are drenched in blood. He is tall; his skin has a pallid bluish tinge, perhaps because of the moon; he seems almost to be one of the boy's own kind, except that when the boy listens he can hear the breathing, the bloodrush, the curdled slosh of body fluids that proclaims this is a human being. The man thinks for a while; perhaps he is wondering whether to slice the girl up further. In the distance, there is a noise like a foghorn. Perhaps suddenly afraid of discovery, the madman lets go so that the girl suddenly crumples to the ground.

As he walks away, the man does not see the rat that clambers along the woman's leg, that greedily licks the mutilated privates before running up to the neck with its spurting arterial blood. The rat drinks, drinks, becomes so intoxicated with the blood, laced as it is with the spice of violence, that he can no longer hold his rat shape and swells to the size of a boy again, a boy caught in a necrophilic embrace with a dying prostitute whose eyes, staring, disbelieving, pleading, are slowly losing their light.

'I'm sorry,' the boy says. 'You would have died anyway. Now at least your death is not utterly in vain. Or is it?'

He wipes the blood from his lips on the girl's matted, flaxen hair. 'I wish I had known your name,' he says. 'What you and I . . . did together . . . it is, in a sense, a relationship. I would it had not been so anonymous.'

Should he follow the madman? Would the killer lead him to more sources of blood, assuaging his growing guilt at having to kill?

'I can't even tell you my own name,' the boy says. 'I've come to this era so recently, I haven't had time to find a name . . .'

But the girl has died. Footsteps in the alley. What will they think of this boy, lips dribbling blood, his arms wrapped around this mutilated woman? Panicking, he shrinks himself down to rat size once again. Men and women are pouring into the alley now. He scampers through a forest of legs. He hears what they are saying. 'Ripper's got another one.' 'Cor, look at her. Cut to ribbons.' 'Not much blood though.' 'One of Mrs Sitwell's girls?' The feeding frenzy is more sordid even than his own. He is repelled by this new time. He darts in and out of the moving boots, shoes, and dirty feet, out of the alley, heedless of where he is going, once almost getting impaled by the heel of a lady's pump; finds himself leaping onto the steps of a hansom.

He jumps onto the seat. An opera cloak has been thrown over him. He smells a wilting carnation and a scented pomade. Peers through the folds of the cloak: black velvet, satin lining, shiny, new. Once again he cannot hold his shape, and the young boy slowly begins to form out of the shadows; but the blinds are tight shut, and there is only a slit of moonlight that reveals to him a pair of large, somewhat sheeplike eyes. The cab turns a corner. The horses whinny, as they are wont to do in the presence of supernatural beings. The boy loses his balance, and his face comes into the light; and the hansom's passenger sees him for the first time.'

'Company!' he says. 'And I never even heard you breathe.'

Another rut, and he tumbles forward; he is almost in the gentleman's arms. The moonlight plays over his silvery skin and the man, holding him at arm's length, gazes at him with more than curiosity . . . with something akin to lust. I am naked, the boy realizes suddenly, and pulls the opera cloak about his shoulders.

'My God,' says the passenger. 'What a find. Did Bosie send you?'

The boy does not answer.

'What's your name, boy? Dear me, your lips are drenched in blood; I do so hate a mess. No name, then, I see. You are, I take it, an anonymous gift from Lord Alfred Douglas. But he hasn't bothered to have you cleaned. Well, you *must* have a name. I shall call you . . .' He squints at the boy, and toys with the carnation in his lapel. 'Sebastian,' he says at last. 'All beautiful youths should be called Sebastian. For St Sebastian is the patron saint of beautiful youths.'

'I remember him,' the boy says. 'Caesar had him shot up with arrows. There wasn't much blood, though.'

'You sound almost as if you witnessed it.'

'I've witnessed many things, Mr—'

'Call me Oscar.' The man peeks through the blinds, shouts something at the driver; and the cab abruptly changes direction. 'You don't *sound* like a telegraph boy,' he says to the boy who has now been named Sebastian. 'This *is* one of Bosie's frightful little pranks, isn't it?'

Sebastian does not respond. How the world has changed, he is thinking. How crowded it is. Even in the dead of night, people are about. Here and there the light that leaks through the blinds is almost like daylight. He does remember daylight, he thinks.

'The Emperor Diocletian and the martyrdom of St Sebastian,' Oscar says. 'Next you'll be telling me you saw Jack the Ripper.'

'I did, sir,' says the boy.

'I take it then that you are at least . . . fifteen hundred years old, if I know my hagiography.'

'Eighteen, sir,' says the boy, 'hundred, I mean.'

'An extravagant claim! It is worthy of my own outrageous wits. Dine with me tonight, and you shall tell me more.'

The hansom pulls up to a building with a façade of caryatids, topped with a frieze copied, the boy seems to recall, from the Parthenon in Athens. Still draped only in the opera cloak, the boy steps down. Oscar rings a bell; a portly gentleman in evening dress opens the portal only a hair's breadth before slamming it abruptly. A side door opens, and the imposing gentleman is there once more.

'Mr Wilde,' he says, 'you really mustn't ring at the front if you're planning one of your . . . special dinners.'

'Yes, yes,' says Oscar, 'have you any clothes for the boy?'

'One of your previous . . . guests may have left a few vestments behind,' says the gentleman, who is clearly quite flustered at having to deal with his client at this particular hour.

He ushers the two of them down a corridor . . . the boy hears the sounds of clinking wineglasses and the clatter of silver on porcelain, but he sees nothing . . . and presently they are in a private room with a mahogany dining table. The only seating is a capacious divan. The gentleman rummages in a closet and produces some ragged garments – mostly from the uniforms of telegraph boys, who seem to have been Oscar's private guests in this establishment. Coyly, the boy changes behind a marble pilaster, and when he emerges he is the very image of a child of the streets.

'Food and wine,' Oscar says to the gentleman, 'you know the

sort of thing I like.' And to the boy, 'Have you ever had turtle soup?'

'I'm not hungry, Oscar.'

'Oh, nonsense. You're all always hungry. Plenty of time for dalliance after we've eaten. Did Bosie pay you? It would be just like him not to have.'

'I'm not really . . . what you think I am.'

'I can see that. You materialize inside my cab, the loveliest creature I've ever laid eyes on . . . the skin with the texture of satin and the colour of ivory, the mouth like . . . oh, God, I shall soon start to talk about branches of coral in the twilight of the sea, the vermilion that is found in the mines of Moab, and so on . . . but I'm quoting *Salome*, how terribly vain. You are entrancing, young man, but you don't have that rough, unlettered quality that I've come to find so delightful in your sort; in fact, you seem to know rather a lot. And those ripe red lips of yours; the blood which I thought must be your own, from some injury doubtless sustained in the rough and tumble of street life . . . why, I suddenly perceive that you are not wounded at all, and that that wine-red juice must perforce be another's; you must have drunk that blood from some victim . . . dare one surmise, a human victim? . . . I find myself not unconcerned for my own safety – if one may stoop to litotes – and I am beginning to think you are a different kind of creature of the night altogether.'

'Yet,' says Sebastian, 'you do not flee.'

'Flee? but this is delicious . . . I would never flee from you. I play with fire for a living. May I kiss you?'

Alas, the boy thinks, it all boils down, after all, to some sordid assignation. He thinks I am one of the wildflowers that bloom in the sewers of London . . . a more exotic one than most, but still to be plucked, collected, ravished, then locked up in the dusty closet of remembrances.

Yet there is something fascinating about this man. Most of all it is the fact that he seems to show no fear at all. Usually one can always smell fear in the air; there was fear even with others in olden times who loved him: Caravaggio, Marlowe, Gilles de Rais, the Emperor Hadrian; their love was made piquant by the fear of someone supernatural.

This is an age, the boy is coming to realize, when the super-natural is being explained away. There are great machines here, and the machines do not have souls. Faith is fading from the world.

The boy has not said that he may, but Oscar puts his arms around the boy's narrow shoulders. First he wipes his mouth with a silken pocket-handkerchief. He brushes his lips against the boy's bloody lips. He tastes the blood of the murdered whore. The boy feels tweed against his dead skin.

Oscar Wilde recoils. 'Cold, cold,' he exclaims, 'freezing cold!'

'The cold of the grave,' says Sebastian, 'which the blood of a living being warms for only the briefest moment. I am a vampire.'

'In that case, I don't suppose you'll be wanting any of this mulled wine?' Oscar quaffs an entire glassful.

The imposing gentleman has been hovering somewhere the entire time, attempting to look inconspicuous. Now he responds nervously to a knock on the door, tiptoes back to the two guests, and taps Oscar on the shoulder. 'There's someone here to see you,' he says.

'But you know I'm not to be interrupted—'

'Oh,' says the gentleman, 'this is one of your friends.'

'Very well.'

A door opens and another man enters the private chamber. He is removing his cloak. He has a somewhat sickly complexion, and is dressed entirely in black. He appears mournful, obsessed. He is clutching a playbill in his hand on which the words *Henry Irving* appear in large print. 'I've just come from *The Tempest*,' he says. 'Henry was superb.'

And I too have come from *The Tempest*, thinks the boy. And Will, too, was superb, though that Prospero has, in the seconds since I entered and departed the forest of dreams and delusions, become worm fodder, perhaps centuries ago. Thin air, thin air.

'Ah, Stoker,' says Oscar Wilde, 'I've found you a real vampire.'

flying

You've sent the girl away but you still have the amulet and I can still possess you in your dreams Chit Chit Chit Chit and make you see all that I've seen and make you live through every minute of my undeath . . .

I've made more of us and finally Timmy's starting to understand I need him to notice me I need him to come to me we need to do something because we're both still fucked up this hasn't solved a fucking thing

Chit Chit Chit!

I'm looking for other ways to reach him. That's when I start flying back and forth to Thailand, following your scent along the trade winds as they blow over the Pacific Ocean. Nights I stalk you. You don't see me, in the garden watching you, in the jasmine bushes, in the pavilion above the pond, watching the frogs on the lotus pads, beneath the pollution and the stars. Nights you go out, too . . . social functions, dinners, charity balls, every time you're in a different dress, Jesus you never repeat yourself, I don't know how you do it. I follow you, sometimes I'm even inside one of your Mercedes, I'm a gecko curled up on the plush floor next to your stiletto heels, once I'm even a mosquito, but it's uncomfortable because of the dryness of the air-conditioning and they're always spraying repellent so there's always like a trace of it in the air so it doesn't feel too good.

I think about how I'm gonna suck your blood.

That'll get noticed.

But I don't know, I'm still sorting out this weird connection between love and death, I still don't understand what made me kill Becky Slade. I start to think maybe I shouldn't kill you, I should just make things so you'll see me, touch me, and through you I'll reach Timmy.

One night there's this big art show at the Dusit Thani and you're talking to this crazy American and he tells you how he's living on a houseboat nearby, it's docked near the Oriental, and you take a taxi out to the river with him and I'm there with you, I'm sitting between you and neither of you knows it because all I am is a mist. The mist is a cool trick.

His blood is an amphetamine cocktail. I know how that smells. My mother's breath had the same odour.

We reach the river. He hops across to the boat, helps you over. Inside, bright lights are trained on an empty canvas.

He rambles on. 'Chit, Chit,' he says, 'I don't know why I came crawling out of the jungle. Jungle's more like where I really belong. I hate this place, hate the constraints of your million-tiered class system and the bullshit of the party scene. I want to find something *real* to paint.'

'You'll find something,' you say, though maybe you're being polite and wondering why you and PJ are investing in this wasted has-been. 'Give it time.'

He laughs. 'All art is about sex and death. But I've never experienced both at the same time, have I? I've never dared step off the precipice. Never been able to stomach plunging into the abyss. I'm not even a real draft-dodger for God's sake. I'm a fucking phony.'

And later, when you've gone home, I come to Lauren McCandless tossing and turning on his woven reed mat under the mosquito netting inside the houseboat and I whisper in his ear: 'So you want to experience sex and death at the same time?'

And he murmurs, 'Yes, yes,' and so I wave my hand over his eyes and they open and he sees me and he says, 'Angel, a fucking angel.'

And all I have to say is, 'Come.'

news of the world

From the *Bangkok Times*:

Eccentric American painter feared dead

Lauren McCandless, the ex-patriate American painter who has been living in Bangkok for a number of years and who was for a while a suspect in the notorious Patpong murders of last year, has been missing for some time and is now feared dead. Last month he disassembled the houseboat which had become a landmark on the Chao Phya River, took it to Indonesia, and reassembled it, with the help of natives, in West Irian – one of the wildest and most remote regions in the world – announcing that he was planning to journey toward the 'heart of darkness'. He faxed a dramatic written statement to the *Bangkok Times*, full of other quotes from Joseph Conrad, and made his way upriver toward the centre of the island popularly known as New Guinea. When a volcanic eruption shook the island last week, all communication ended, fueling speculation that he may have perished in the cataclysm. With the immense success of his macabre *Dead Yellow Women* series of neo-realist portraits of slain prostitutes, Mr McCandless has become a multi-millionaire, but he may never be able to spend those millions; and since he has no next of kin, no known relatives at all, in fact, and no will, there is some question as to who, if anyone, *will* spend them . . .

music

Came another Moscow night. A bigger crowd, even. He was mobbed as he left the auditorium, and a fan made off with one of his shoes. It was midnight; he even managed to catch the screening of some dailies of *Burial of the Rats*, and he told the director that he thought it might become a cult classic, if he could maintain the delicate balance between camp, comedy and culture. And again he could not help remembering the real Bram Stoker's face . . . the utter absorption with which he listened to young Sebastian's narrations of some of the most terrifying episodes of human history . . . when Oscar, and the guests at other dinner parties to come, saw him more as a diversion, a teller of tall tales . . . yes. Memories were flooding back. And this was strange, because since becoming human he had been forgetting huge segments of his past. It was another sign that the magic was returning, and that events were rushing headlong toward some new rendezvous with the myths that men call destiny.

The next stop on the tour was to be Bangkok.

17

SONG OF THE NIGHT

vision-seeker

It had not been hard to book herself a flight to Bangkok. Dealing with her parents had been a little more difficult. They did not, of course, realize that she had murdered someone. But it was plain to them – as it would have been to anyone, perhaps – that their girl was profoundly disturbed; and the minute she stepped off the plane to Munich she had been shipped off to a sanitarium for observation.

But the psychiatric hospital was by no means a prison, and on their first visit to the ward Pamina's parents had been so appalled by the sight of schizophrenics, catatonics and psychotics that they had taken their daughter straight home. Once there, Pamina manipulated them to perfection. She doffed her black leather and put on a floral print dress, combed her hair into a semblance of decorum, and spoke longingly and lovingly of God. After stealing the appropriate credit cards, getting her passport out of the drawer in her father's study, and telephoning a few travel agents, she talked her parents into attending mass. It was during the elevation of the host that they noticed her absence, but they assumed that she had merely gone off to one of the confessionals or side chapels in the Cäcilienkirche.

By the end of the service, she was already in a cab, on her way to the airport. She was not entirely sure what would happen in Bangkok, although she did know she would arrive in time for Timmy Valentine's three-day stint there. She supposed she would somehow find Timmy's entourage, attract Timmy's attention once again, and then . . . what then? Assassinate him? He deserved to die for what he had made her do. Or perhaps she would merely sabotage his concert somehow. Or gun down the audience with a semi-automatic, like they do in America, she thought grimly. Yes. Go out with a bang. Turn the weapon on myself. Fiery apocalypse. 'Cool,' she told herself in English.

The voice in her head would tell her what to do.

I have to trust the voice, she thought.

The flight – it was the cheapest one she could get – turned out to be a chartered 747 whose entire passenger list, apart from herself, consisted of middle-aged businessmen on one of those sex tours. They eyed the young woman with alarm; but as soon as the beer began flowing, they seemed to forget her existence. Instead of a pleasant family film or thriller, the video in the economy class cabin turned out to be a grim documentary about safe sex, complete with a reminder that two dozen free condoms would be distributed in each guest's welcome packet on their arrival at the appropriately named Sexy Hotel.

She slept.

When she awoke, they were showing another video guide, this time about the night spots of Pattaya, the once-pleasant beach resort that had been turned upside by the rampant sex industry. She trekked up the aisle, through clouds of cigarette smoke, to the lavatory. I must look terrible, she thought. Have to at least freshen up a little.

He was waiting for her in the mirror.

Held out his arms to her. Almost, it seemed, those arms were about to burst through the watery surface of the mirror and embrace her. '*Grüß dich*, Angel,' she said to him. His name still seemed weird to her. Angel Todd. *Engel des Todes*. Reality reduced to a series of pat metaphors.

'Hi yourself,' he said in that melodious voice. His eyes held a bluish radiance that was no reflection of the flat fluorescent lighting of the toilet. 'So you found out I'm not Timmy Valentine. That's good. I'm fucking sick of haunting you under that wuss's name. I'm me, and I'm immortal, and I belong to the night, and you belong to me, you always have, ever since you started to dream about me . . .'

'But it was Timmy's last album that got me started . . . you know, the soundtrack from the movie . . .'

'Sung by me!' said Angel Todd. 'And the *hugest* fucking hit that dreamboy ever had. And now that he's me and I'm him, he flops. What a loser.'

Pamina reached out to touch the image in the mirror. For a second she thought she could feel the glass soften. There was a sexual tension in the toilet. And claustrophobia. The odour of the grave was closing in on her. 'I love you,' she cried, and pummelled at the mirror surface with her fists, only to see Angel fracturing, melting into quicksilver liquidity . . . 'I'm going to free you, I promise, I promise.'

dissolve: the night air

It was one of the few places Timmy had not been. The night air, hot and humid, assailed him as soon as he stepped out of the glacial air-conditioning of the terminal lobby. One of Chit's family limousines pulled up, and they were whisked away, once more cocooned inside an unnaturally frigid environment. He had been in contact with the infamous air of Bangkok – polluted, sultry, overpowering – for only a few moments. And now – along with a police escort, sirens blaring, lights flashing – they were turning into a highway that arced up over the huge metropolis, simultaneously archaic and futuristic, that was Bangkok, the *other* City of Angels.

This time, thank God, they did not see the inside of another hotel; Lady Chit had plenty of room. When Timmy saw the teak house, rising on stilts from a sea of jasmine, with two maids in traditional dress bowing low on either side of the entrance which was topped with a gilt-edged serpentine frieze, he said, 'Perhaps there is something to this ancient oriental wisdom thing after all.' And laughed aloud for the first time in days.

Chit said, 'This house has a lot of . . . rather weird karma attached to it . . . maybe you'd rather stay in one of the main buildings . . .'

'No, no. It's great.' Timmy watched as an army of uniformed staff members carried each piece of MIDI equipment carefully up the steps, pausing only to remove their shoes before they crossed the threshold. 'I'll be able to make as much noise as I want all night long. It's about time I wrote some new songs.

Even though I'm not long for this world, as you all know.'

'Hello,' PJ said abruptly, and started back toward the main house.

'Jesus, it must drive you crazy,' Timmy said to Chit. 'The sacred man-woman was bad enough, but this contrary shit—'

'It's a very serious thing,' Chit said. 'It's really helping him to see more clearly.'

'But does he see a way out of all our dilemmas yet?'

'I don't know, I don't know.'

Timmy didn't really hear her. Music was pounding in his head: headstrong, dissonant music unlike any he had ever conceived before. The music seemed to grow out of the sounds he heard around him: the crickets, the frogs, the traffic, the pile drivers, the whispers of the servants, the ripple of an artificial waterfall. 'In spite of it all,' he said, 'I've become kind of attached to reality. It'll be a shame to go back into the world of shadow again . . .'

'This time,' Chit said, 'you won't really be going back.' They mounted the steps, and Timmy, carefully following Chit's example, removed his shoes at the outer veranda of the house. The threshold was very high; he noticed that she avoided treading on it; it must be some ancient ritual, he thought.

'In the past,' Chit said, and they entered an antechamber where the musical instruments were being set up, and Timmy saw that it was covered with murals that depicted the torments of some Buddhist hell, no less horrific than those of Catholicism, 'you would pop up in some time and place and, before anyone had time to really notice you, you'd vanish . . . really like some kind of vision or manifestation . . . it really was magic. This time it's more the David Copperfield kind of magic, isn't it? It's a grand illusion that Giler and Stupendous have set up, but afterwards, you won't have vanished at all . . . you'll still be right there, in the cubbyhole, under the sheet, in the secret compartment . . . you'll be right there, except you'll be invisible. Sleight of hand . . . not magic.'

Timmy said, 'Unless Giler gets more than he bargained for.'

'Come on,' Chit said, 'when you've finished unpacking, I want to take you to a very special place.'

'And PJ?'
'He'll come by not coming.'

ashes

The Porsche threaded through the twisty labyrinth of narrow *sois*, and they suddenly found themselves pulling into a temple compound. Pagodas, next to the canal, were silhouetted against the neon glare of the skyline. Chit parked; Timmy got out. 'Don't be afraid,' she said to him. And that was strange, that she should be reassuring him, when he had spent the last two thousand years consorting with dead things; but he was in her country now. 'Come on. This is just a little family temple, one that my grandfather used to endow regularly. Perhaps it's done him some good, donating all this money; maybe it's gone some way toward reversing all the evil things he did in his life; I don't know.'

'We're going to pay our respects to Prince Prathna's ashes?' Timmy said.

'Actually,' Chit said, 'that was only part of what I wanted to do tonight. I also wanted you to meet someone. Although I'm not sure he'll be here.'

They crossed the cemetery. The gravestones were tall, and many were festooned with garlands and crêpe paper hangings; some had photographs of the deceased, and others had banners inscribed in Chinese. The air was thick with jasmine and incense. Further on, there was less Chinese, and the tombstones had a sober, more grandiose look to them, with inscriptions in Thai and English. The city lights gave the night air a perpetual brightness; Timmy was taking advantage of the light to peer at the various writings and try to puzzle them out.

'Are you OK?' Chit asked Timmy. The way the boy was gazing at everything, wide-eyed, perhaps he was making mental notes for some future song. He didn't act like someone who was planning to vanish into thin air in less than twenty-four hours.

'It's odd, this is the least mournful cemetery I've ever seen.'

'Well, when you believe in reincarnation, you don't get that upset about dying . . . it's just a rite of passage . . . a new doorway to a new stage of your journey.'

'Who have we come to meet?'

'I think we're almost there.' They reached the family pavilion. Unlike some of the gaudier structures in the compound, this was a quiet, wooden structure, tasteful and serene. The timbers were teak, the roof ceramic tile, and the entire structure open to the elements. Large rainwater jars stood along the entrance. 'There, look.'

Seated on a straw mat in the pavilion, surrounded by white candles, sat Ajarn Sonthaya. His palms were folded in an attitude of prayer, and Chit could see that a sacred white cord was stretched all the way around him, from pillar to pillar of the pavilion. Two coils of mosquito repellent burned in aluminum bowls on either side of him.

'Ah, Chit,' said the ajarn. Uncanny how the blind man could recognize her just from her footsteps. 'You're probably surprised to see me still kicking around. And you've brought a friend.'

'Yes, Ajarn.' And to Timmy, 'We have to kneel now. Just do what I do.'

She sat down in the *phabphieb* position, folded her palms, and made obeisance before the aged shaman. Timmy followed her lead. He has a natural grace, she thought, even though he's never performed these motions before.

'You've taken care of the amulet?' said the spirit doctor.

'Yes. Even though . . . it's caused me terrible pain.'

'I know, child. The creature inside it has done everything in its power to suck the life force from you. But you have been strong. And the wound in your breast?'

'It throbs, ajarn.'

'And your friend is the infamous Timmy Valentine.' She wondered if Timmy could understand Thai; he knew so many languages, had lived in so many lands. But though he was studying them both he did not seem to know what they were saying. 'Timmy Valentine,' said Ajarn Sonthaya, 'the proximate cause of all the trouble you have been going through. And much of the joy, too . . . since it was because of him that you met the man you have come to love.'

'Hi, Ajarn,' Timmy said.

The shaman then spoke to Timmy in his halting English. 'Timmy,' he said, 'every journey must end, extinction, cessation of all being, words of the Lord Buddha, maybe I tell you you understand. Desire is cause of suffering. Give up desire. Give up, give up.'

'I've already given up immortality,' Timmy said, 'but it's not enough, is it? I wanted to become a real boy, but maybe that's not really possible . . . maybe it's just two thousand years too late. And what did I do to Angel? He yearned for death, but was it the right death to yearn for?'

'You approaching wisdom now, my child.'

'Ajarn,' Chit said, 'you told me that I should wander the world to find someone to whom you could pass on your gift. Do you think that—'

'I don't know, child,' said the ajarn in Thai. 'But since you've brought him here, that must be part of the plan.'

He turned and gazed into Timmy's eyes. Timmy stared back. It seemed to Chit that something was going on between them. It was as though Timmy's eyes were a bottomless chasm, and the shaman's eyes were sending forth a flood of light, and the light was descending into the inky depths and would never get out again . . . falling through the event horizon of a black hole.

Timmy's features showed no emotion. Whatever was transpiring between the two of them continued for perhaps fifteen minutes . . . and then, abruptly, Timmy broke away. And began to weep uncontrollably. He shrieked, he banged his fists against the floorboards until they bled, he tore out hanks of his own hair. She had never seen him like that before. She did not dare comfort him, so terrible was his grief and rage.

She did not notice for a long while that Ajarn Sonthaya had stopped breathing. In fact – she touched his wrist – he was stone cold. The *saisin* dropped from his clenched fingers. The circle was broken. It seemed to Chit that perhaps he had been dead all this while . . .

'I was inside him when he—' Timmy cried out. 'I actually felt his *death*!'

Timmy wept while Chit rummaged in her purse for her phone so that she could call the authorities. It would probably take them some time to get there, what with the traffic; most people did not know all the short cuts and the back *sois* – you had to be born and bred in Sukhumvit to comprehend the maze. It was not as terrible for Chit to see the ajarn go; it seemed to her that even in that hospital room at Samitivej he had been half in, half out of the spirit world. And she had not actually experienced his death, as Timmy had. She wondered how it must be for him, who had eluded death for so long, to finally feel death and still remain alive.

In time, Timmy's weeping subsided. A breeze stirred the stagnant waters of the nearby canal. The night-creatures chirped, stridulated, croaked out their mating calls.

'There's a plan,' Timmy said. 'You're wrong, Chit. Apparently my disappearance is going to be more than sleight of hand after all.'

And at that moment Chit felt such a stabbing pain in the wound in her breast that she thought she was being bitten afresh by Angel's fangs. 'Oh,' she cried out, and clutched her chest, and the amulet swung back and forth in the dark air, leaving a faint trail of silvery light.

'Are you OK?' said Timmy. He put his arms around her.

'Yes. Yes.' They heard a siren in the distance. 'They're here now. Let's slip away.'

daylight

On the stage of the Panyasai Stadium was a gigantic reproduction of Lauren McCandless's last painting, the most terrifying of them all . . . the dead whore in the rain. At the climax of the concert, the picture would seem to materialize out of the darkness behind Timmy. As his biggest hit song, *Crucify Me Twice*, reached its searing, discordant climax, the dead woman would seem to come to life, go through an elaborate morphing sequence, and finally pull Timmy Valentine into the picture . . . into the McCandless Timmy Valentine poster that McCandless had self-referentially painted into the background of his masterwork. All done with mirrors, of course. And smoke.

PJ, who had descended from his spirit-induced contrary state in order to supervise the effect, was watching the effects team from a seat on the far edge of the stadium. The heat poured down; his cellular phone was slick with sweat and kept slipping out of his hand. 'That leftmost mirror,' he was saying, 'you're going to have to tilt it a tad more . . . left, no, back to the right now . . . otherwise the people on this side of the picture aren't gonna get a seamless illusion.'

The image of the woman moved . . . morphed . . . peeled away her skin to reveal the Valentine beneath . . . transformed into a snow leopard (it was a barefaced steal from a Michael Jackson video, but what the hell, nothing but the best for Timmy Valentine) . . . then into a whirlwind, into Judy Garland from *The Wizard of Oz*, and faster and faster and faster in a kind of homage to Jittlov's *Wizard of Speed and Time*, and finally back into the corpse of the prostitute, growing in stature until it became a sort of Asian zombie version of *The 50-Foot Woman*, and finally seemed to emerge from the McCandless canvas and reach her arms out into the crowd . . .

PJ had to admit that the effect was almost more magical than the real magic he had lived through.

'How does it look?' It was Levon Jihanian, the techno-shaman behind all the effects, a compact little Armenian guy who, rumour had it, was about to be named exalted grand pooh-bah of Stupendous's entire optical effects division. 'I wanted to put in more sex, but I got worried about the censorship board so I substituted more gore.'

'Impressive.'

'You like the morphing?'

'Well, it's derivative, but nicely done.'

'Maybe I should have included a Native American motif? So you won't breathe down my neck?'

'You might not have got it right, and there is such a thing as being *too* politically correct.'

'Cool! Well, let me get back to it. It's amazing, huh! And the whole thing is driven by one little Power PC. Had a heck of a time getting it to talk to the Amiga that was in charge of the actual morph algorithm but . . .' He went on in this vein for a while, discoursing learnedly on handshaking, gigabytes, and baud rates, but PJ finally just put a finger to his lips.

'Don't talk too much! You're spoiling the magic for me.'

'Huh? Oh yeah. I guess.'

'Can I see it again, Levon?'

He could indeed. Jihanian waved at someone in black and it happened all over again: the painting materializing out of the darkness coming to life changing form reaching out seizing the empty air and reeling it in (halfway through the reel the empty air changed into Timmy Valentine, presumably since the real Valentine would have ducked down a trapdoor while the smoke billowed around him, and would then be replaced by a computer simulacrum) and even with the sunlight streaming down and the mirrors not quite firmly in place it was impressive, damned impressive. PJ whistled.

'It's all MIDI-driven,' Levon said. 'That means that if the music is stretched out or sped up in the heat of the performance, the morphing will still be on the beat . . . it's tied to specific triggers in the sequence.'

'Whatever that means,' said PJ.

'Doesn't matter what it means, let's just say it's cool,' said Levon. He dashed down toward the control booth, two steps at a time down the aisle.

As soon as he left, PJ began to feel the contrary stirring in him. It was tickling feeling at first . . . rubbing his eyes . . . seeing double. The world was spinning and suddenly he began to feel the cold . . . biting, bitter, blizzard cold, like those mountain winters back in Idaho . . . *It's 107°!* he was thinking, but he still couldn't shake off the cold because it was inside him . . . and he could hear the beating of great wings . . . *the wings of the angel of death* . . . bat wings . . . I'm hanging upside down again in the belfry off the edge of the world . . . he hugged himself, looked around for a blanket or an overcoat, saw nothing except a folded tarp that had been covering some of the seats, yanked it up, wrapped it round and round himself as though he were spinning a cocoon, knew that he was sweating but still felt cold, cold, cold, cold, cold . . . because the sun was an illusion and the cold was truth . . . there was something nearby . . . something dark and thirsty and so terribly alone that it needed to suck all the warmth and love and light out of the world just so that it could have some fleeting surcease of its hunger . . . and that something was nearby. It was not even a spirit, for even an evil spirit knows its place in the universe and plays by the rules of the Great Mystery . . . it was human and not human.

What was it?

death

'I'll just take a quick wizz,' said Levon to his friends, and disappeared down the spiral staircase that led down to the toilets in the Panyasai Stadium. These were the VIP toilets, with marble floors and actually seats in the stalls, and toilet paper that you didn't have to put a nickel in a vending machine for (and that only gave you three sheets anyway, as he had discovered to his chagrin down at the Central department store). What a relief. I'd hate to find myself squatting in the public bathrooms out there, he thought.

A wrinkled old woman was polishing the fixtures in the urinals. Having women scrubbing in a men's room had really weirded him out the first time he'd taken a leak here, but now he was used to it. He tipped her ten baht so she wouldn't stare at him while he pissed.

It was a strange urinal, filled with ice and mothballs for some reason; he didn't quite finish, but felt an urge to get away from there. He reached up to flush. Something in the handle caught his eye . . . a reflected face . . . *Timmy Valentine*? I've been working too hard, he thought . . . and then the face of Timmy Valentine suddenly morphed into the face of a teenage girl with death-rock black hair and black lipstick, your average Valmaniac.

I've *really* been working too hard.

'Mister,' said the girl. A slight German accent. Obviously she wasn't here to Ajax the toilet bowls.

'This is the men's room,' he said.

'I'm sorry, I followed you down here . . . you have a light?'

He turned. She was a slight thing. She was a Neo-Gothic all right. She had the tattooed stigmata in her palms, and she was dressed head to toe in dominatrix black, laced up so tight that what little cleavage she had was just oozing. What the hell, Levon thought, and pulled out a lighter while he zipped up with his other hand. She was smoking one of those filterless Thai cigarettes. 'Aren't you a little young to be—' he began.

'I'll be in the grave long before cancer can catch up with me,' she said, and blew the smoke in his face.

The girl was attractive. He felt a momentary attack of lust, then reflected that she was, after all, just another groupie; there'd be plenty more after the show; he could line them all up and take his pick.

She gripped his shoulders. She had sharp fingernails. He had a weakness for girls with sharp fingernails. 'That hurts,' he said, but he smiled.

'Please,' said the girl, 'I really want to meet Timmy Valentine . . . I stowed away in a plane from Munich just so I could meet him here . . . he's my God. I don't know what I'd do if I couldn't see him, I'd probably kill myself.'

'Well,' he said, 'I do work on his show.'

'Oh, you're so close to him . . . there are probably times when you could almost rub up against him and . . .' The girl was rubbing up against Levon now. Horny little vixen! he thought. Maybe she was a little young, but she'd clearly been round the block. 'You like what I'm doing?' said the girl. 'Sometimes I almost feel that I *am* Timmy, I mean, I want to drink blood.'

'That's just an act, you know.'

'But I am reading in all the magazines that Timmy is thousands and thousands of years old—'

He found himself caught in a sort of hug, although she was squirming too much for him to get much of a purchase on her. She was thrusting against his loins and really getting him excited. As she squeezed harder against his body he saw that the cleaning lady was staring at them, leaning against her mop, not looking at all inscrutable. He scrounged around in his pocket for a tip, and produced a hundred-baht bill. He waved it at her; she snatched it from her hand and vanished, and then he lost his balance and half fell, half stumbled to find himself face to face with the side of the urinal. The girl was fumbling with his zipper. 'I'll do anything if you let me meet Timmy . . . anything at all,' she was saying. She had his jeans down his ankles, and was already working the tip of his penis with her tongue and raking at his thighs with those spiky nails.

'I think I can arrange it,' he found himself saying. The pain was exquisite. This girl really knew her stuff. He moaned. He kept banging his head against the urinal. If only he could lure her off to the hotel for an hour. This toilet sex's strictly for fags, he thought. He was about to ask her to hold on a second when she bit off one of his testicles.

He screamed. She raked even harder at his thighs . . . cutting into them . . . making deep gouges that filled up with blood . . . and she began to suck. He screamed his throat raw. Tried to throw her off him, but she had him wedged in tight between two urinals. She just pushed him down. He saw his testicle bobbing up and down in a pool of piss and mothballs. He could feel her tongue ramming into his ravaged scrotum. He was in shock now. He couldn't even scream anymore. He wanted to faint from the pain. She kept sucking more blood out of him. Suddenly he blurted out, 'You can't kill me, who's gonna run the effects, the concert's gonna fucking be ruined . . .'

He was on the verge of passing out. She looked up at him. Blood was on her mouth, her teeth, her cheeks. 'Don't worry about that,' she said sweetly. 'We'll make sure that you don't miss the concert.'

He was rapidly sinking into oblivion. *We?* he thought. *Who's we?*

Then the girl's face began to morph.

The hair shrinking back. The nose becoming sharper. The eyes widening. The cheekbones rising. The skin becoming more pale, more luminescent . . . Jesus, he thought, she's turning into Timmy Valentine, my work's leaking into reality, making me go mad . . .

'Timmy,' he gasped.

'I hate it when they call me Timmy,' said the creature with the face of Timmy Valentine. And pounced.

dissolve

Chit cried out. The wound in her breast. It was throbbing now, each throb sending a burst of pain through her whole being. Oh, God, she thought, I can't bear this, I'm going to die . . .

dissolve

PJ suddenly knew that his wife was in mortal danger. Shaking, he dialed the number on his cellular. He was completely possessed by the contrary spirit now. 'Goodbye,' he said to her.

'PJ? PJ?' she said.

Goodbye means *hello*, he thought, in the speech of contraries. But when you speak as a contrary, what comes out, even though it's the opposite of what you mean, can be the truth . . .

He pushed the off button. The sun was blazing over the Panyasai Stadium. I have to turn away from her, he thought. The cold and hungry thing is coming closer and closer. It wants me because I know it's there. It'll kill Chit to get to me. Better if I turn my back on her . . . better if I act as if I hate her . . . do the contrary thing. It'll kill *me* to get to Timmy Valentine. And it'll kill Timmy Valentine because, above all, it longs to kill itself . . .

memory: 1888

'I can tell you,' says the boy, 'so many things. You can believe or not believe; that is your own decision. But if you should choose to believe, then I will tell you, in images so clear that you will see them for yourself, in voices that imitate so well the accents and mannerisms of the dead that you will no longer think them dead . . . who do you want me to tell you about? The poets and painters of past times, Shakespeare, Tasso, Caravaggio? Emperors and kings, lovers and madmen? I've known so many of them . . .'

'For God's sake, Wilde,' says Bram Stoker, 'this boy is sensational. We have to show him off at some great society func-

tion. Why, tomorrow, there's a tea-party at the Duke of
Clarence's . . .'

'No daylight,' Oscar says. 'Surely in your copious researches
you must have learnt *that* at least!'

'Give him another glass of wine, then. Perhaps he'll become
even more loquacious.'

'Won't work,' says Oscar, laughing. 'But if you'll prick your
thumb and mix a few drops of blood into the posset . . .'

'I see,' says Stoker. 'By the pricking of my thumbs, and all
that.'

With a tie-pin, he jabs his thumb. The blood beads up; he
moistens Sebastian's lip with it. The boy feels a flicker of
warmth; then once more he settles into eternal cold.

'Whom should I speak of?' he asks the two of them.

night

Pamina stared into the mirror. What had happened? The dance
of pursuit and death was over. The prey lay dead on the bathroom floor. She was bent over the corpse with blood on her
lips, with the sweet taste on her tongue, and yet . . . something
else had happened.

At the very moment of climax . . . when she penetrated the
man and the juice began spurting from him . . . someone else
had been there. Inside her. Clamouring to get out. Wanting to
mould her body to his body.

She thought abut the other times she had killed. Had the
same thing happened then? Was killing *not* the orgasmic fulfilment she thought she had experienced? In that hotel room in
England . . . that arrogant old preacher . . . the seduction, the
attack, and then . . . had she blanked out and let this other
thing take over? She wasn't sure now.

Pamina . . .

The voice. The angel. Soothing her. The only one who never
lied to her. She could hear him again, she could see him forming
slowly in the mirror.

Don't be afraid, said the angel. *Every time we hunt together, you
bring me closer to the world of men.*

'But I've been *killing* people!' she said. 'This isn't like Sascha in the butcher shop, not even like catching a mouse and biting off its head . . . you've made me steal people's souls . . .'

You didn't kill anyone. I killed. You're only an instrument. Anyway you should be glad it was me. I'm a real vampire, not a fake like you. So he'll be able to come back and finish doing the special effects for the concert.

'What about Damien Peters?'

Oh, he won't be back. You ripped him into shreds.

'I thought you said you—'

I killed. You ripped, *you little goremongering sadist! You belong in a loony bin. But they'll never lock you away. Once I'm free, we're going to be together for all eternity.*

'Yeah, but now I'm scared. I think maybe Timmy was right and I *should* check myself into the sanitarium.'

You're going to turn back now? Pamina, Pamina, don't you love me?

'Of course I do, but . . .'

Then get the fucking amulet, bitch!

'The amulet. Yes. The amulet.'

night

When Lady Chit arrived at the stadium, the sun was setting. She found her way to the special VIP box, which was already filling with the cream of Bangkok society. I could buy a small Caribbean island by pawning their Rolexes, she thought. An awning shielded the special guests from the elements and from the gaze of the less fortunate, squeezed in so tightly that they probably constituted a fire hazard.

The place *was* packed, even with tickets at a thousand baht a pop. Every row, every aisle, even, jammed with fans. A lot of Neo-Gothics here, though they were a less rowdy bunch than had greeted them in Europe. This concert was obviously the event of the year. If only they knew, Chit thought, that Timmy plans to disappear for good tonight . . . but then she also knew that Giler was talking about maybe not for good . . . maybe

trotting him out again, a year or so down the line . . . and
Timmy was saying no, gone is gone.

PJ was backstage somewhere. He had been impossible to talk
to all day. If there was a purpose behind his latest fit of mystical
possession, she could not fathom it. She reclined in her special
chair – brought over from home – and tried to chat with some
of the guests. There were *khunyings*, each one more ostentatious
than the last, in brightly coloured silks, glittering with jewellery;
there were a few critics among them – she spotted Robert Halli-
day of the *Bangkok Post*, and celebrated Thai pop singers, each
thronged by admirers. Then there were the more culturally
snobby crowd, who were all clustered around Bruce Gaston, an
expatriate American – much like Lauren McCandless – who had
become the leading exponent of Thai classical music. There were
a few politicians, looking a little out of place, but stalwartly
attempting to cultivate hipness in time for the next general elec-
tion. There were such media figures as Vitawat, the David
Letterman of Thailand, laughing and mugging for the television
cameras. What a spectacle! And Timmy wasn't even due to come
out for at least an hour.

The first warm-up band was a local group. Almost identical
young men, very pretty, very slick, all dressed in brash bright
colours . . . a sort of pop music version of the *Power Rangers*.
They sang and danced their hearts out, and were dutifully
applauded through a set of cutesy, synth-semi-techno numbers,
like something you might see on MTV during the off-peak
hours. Their final number even included a laser battle with ani-
mated computer chips that mutated into Godzilla-like monsters
and trampled the set in rubber suits. The kids liked that too,
but they were really waiting for Timmy.

Then there was another warm-up band . . . which seemed
almost interchangeable with the previous one. Even Chit, who
should have known better, was starting to get impatient, but
she knew that Timmy would only come at the moment when
the crowd's excitement reached orgasmic proportions.

'Bullshit, utter bullshit,' Gaston was saying into his ice-cold
Singha beer. 'The same harmonies, the same melodies, even
the same synthesizer patches, for god's sake! Bring on the real
thing!'

At that moment, PJ came skulking into the back of the VIP box. 'Chit, Chit,' he said, and he was in such a hurry that he actually elbowed one of the *khunyings* out of the way, 'I've gotta talk to you.'

Her breast began to throb.

'What's wrong?'

'Something really big is going down tonight. You know. One of those great big moments when the tension in the real world is so screwed up that anything can happen?'

'Is Timmy OK?'

'Yeah. He's in his dressing room. Jihanian is late, but I'm sure he'll turn up. He's always going off for a quickie. But Chit, Chit . . .'

He had a strange, wild look about him. He had let down his hair and it was billowing about his shoulders even though there was barely any wind. Every inch the savage. God, I love him so much, she thought. But there are so many parts of him I can't hope to touch. Thank God I'm not like the woman in that opera, always wanting to unlock his doors . . . I know better than that.

'Chit,' said PJ, 'this big thing is raging all around me like a tornado and pretty soon I think it's gonna suck me away . . . out of Kansas, out of reality, whatever . . . do you understand? The real world is like a tiny piece of dry earth reclaimed from the sea, and all around it there's all this horror, and all this mystery, all this transcendence . . . and now and then there's moments when the tension in the real world gets wound up so tight that the dike starts springing leaks and you know, all that other stuff comes bursting through and . . . it's about to happen now. I know it. In a moment the contrary spirit's gonna grab hold of me and I won't be making *any* sense and I just want you to know, now, for ever, if I can't tell you later, how I love you.'

'PJ—' But something was happening to him. A manic quality was coming over his features. A vein in his neck was pulsing. 'PJ, couldn't you at least tell me—'

'Hello,' he said, and walked away, backwards, not missing a single step, as if he had eyes in the back of his head.

The pain again. She didn't dare cry out; it simply would not do in this kind of company. She took a stiff shot of whatever they were serving – it looked like champagne – and crammed a couple of Ibuprofen down her throat. Then, looking out over the stage, she thought she saw that effects guy PJ had been talking about. He was shambling about back there in the control booth. Look, he was tripping over a mess of patch cables. Obviously he'd been having a little too much fun in between acts here.

Jihanian settled into his control chair . . . he was a tiny figure down there . . . even his console seemed to dwarf him. God, she thought, that man has a lot of power. He touched a lever or something; she couldn't make it out.

The lights were dimming now, the last of the warm-up acts was bowing and being borne into the wings on wires, waving and blowing kisses to the audience. Applause rippled across the audience, died down. Tension was mounting. They were really waiting now, they wanted Timmy, nothing but Timmy.

A series of quiet chords stole in. Strings, beefed up with celestial New Age-sounding pads. Pretty music, slow and solemn. There was semi-darkness – the city still glowed faintly all around them. There were few stars; Bangkok by night is a smoggy city. The traffic rumbled. You could make out the braying of car horns, the tuk-tuk of the pedicabs, the buzz of unmuffled motorbikes . . . even, at the periphery of hearing, the trumpeting of an elephant. Yet all these sounds seemed part of the music. Above the chords now came the cadence of Bela Lugosi's voice . . . *listen to them . . . children of the night . . . what music they make*. The voice had been sampled from the old movie and then played back recursively over itself until it was sounded more like the murmur of the surf than a human voice . . . and yet one knew that it was Dracula, that it held menace.

A single shaft of light shot through the gloom.

Timmy Valentine stood in the lone spotlight. Isolated, mournful, yet charged with a sombre joy. The whisper of the crowd rose to a murmur then a roar then a crashing thundering chant of *Timmy, Timmy, Timmy*. But beneath it all were still those long-held chords and the sussurant whisper of the thousand Lugosis. The sullied idol still possessed his otherworldly beauty. His hair, long and unruly in the '80s, was now short except for

one long lock that lashed across his blue-white brow. His eyes
needed no makeup; they were wide, jewel-like, strangely vulnerable. He wore black, but the pallor of his skin showed
through the torn, unbuttoned shirt and the slashed jeans. A
diamond in his left ear . . . even from this far away, it caught
that light and glittered.

Timmy smiled.

And even that smile drew a new wave of applause.

The band – invisible – seeing anyone else on the stage would
have detracted from Timmy's splendid aloneness – began to
play the opening riff of *Vampire Junction*.

And Timmy sang.

18

INTO THIN AIR

night

The song seems almost trite by today's standards, PJ thought. The lyrics had almost a country-and-western quality to them, and the harmonies were militantly saccharine. But then again the early '80s weren't all that memorable musically, were they? and *Vampire Junction* was surely a product of its time. But the kid's singing his guts out and somehow that makes it beautiful.

I can tell though, he's straining where he wouldn't have had to strain before . . . those long long musical phrases that used to just come belting out without a pause for breath . . . now he has to work on it, has to conserve air, control his diaphragm, do all the things that real-live singers spend their whole lives fussing about. But he does it well, damn it! PJ thought, as he watched the proceedings from a booth on a tower connected to the catwalks that overhung the stage and the sides of the stadium.

Things were going smoothly . . . but there was a presence out there. He could almost smell it. The odour of death. At first he thought it must be Pamina . . . he knew that Pamina had made it to Bangkok on her own, he had sensed her presence as soon as the contrary spirit had seized his mind . . . but Pamina wasn't this dead thing that seemed to be moving somewhere in the shadows . . . somewhere backstage, perhaps . . . if he closed his eyes he could feel every soul that was present, like candleflames, dancing, flickering . . . but there was another candle, a black candle whose flame was a plume of ice. Out there. Who was it? Hadn't all the undead been taken care of

already? Surely Pamina hadn't . . . but she's not a *real* vampire,
he thought. She can't create other vampires.

Who could it be?

But the music was going so well . . .

A long orchestral interlude now. Timmy leaped and the spot
leaped with him. He darted. The spot followed. He danced his
vampire dance, smooth and silken and serene over the storm
of synth and cymbal . . . he stroked the crowd with his whole
being and the crowd purred back . . . then came the reprise of
the melody with its unsettling lyrics:

> *Don't matter if you hitch a ride*
> *Don't matter if you pay*
> *I'll be waiting at Vampire Junction*
> *To suck your soul away . . .*

The invisible band crescendoed, then faded, and with it
Timmy too, dissolving into Jihanian's techno-mist. The next
song was another big number from Timmy's first career . . .
Come Into My Coffin. People like me and Chit grew up hearing
those songs, he thought, and look where we are now, and look
where Timmy is . . .

The undead thing was on the move.

The air: unnaturally chill. He knew the temperature was still
in the eighties. It was his contrary-sense, picking up all the
latent opposites around him. Where was it coming from? He
couldn't zero in on it. He had to look away. What was as far
away from death as he could imagine? Love. He looked over
the arena, trying to pinpoint Chit.

There she was.

Talking to one of the glitterati, sipping a glass of champagne.
Nothing out of place, except—

There . . . in the audience . . . Pamina Rothstein. Shoving
through the crowd, climbing over seats, inexorably moving
toward the VIP section . . . elbowing two teenagers out the way,
clambering now, clinging to the railing—

Have to get to her—

PJ eased out of the platform. Made his way along the catwalk.
Giddy, giddy. A new song was beginning. Not a Timmy Valentine song. Another of the pretty-boy Thai groups was doing

a number while Timmy changed clothes. He couldn't hurry or he'd fall. Clutched the railing. A few more paces, then down the pole with its slippery footholds and all the time thinking backwards, backwards . . . stop thinking stop thinking just let go, fall, fall, fall—

Tumbled onto the carpeted aisle between rows of frantic fans. A vendor wheeling a cart of Thai ice coffee . . . American kids, lumbering over their Thai friends, staring, pointing . . . two boys dancing broke PJ's fall. Pamina hurrying up the steps toward the glow from the skyline, temples, skyscrapers. Follow. Follow . . . no, losing her. Backwards, backwards. Go the other way, duck into an exit, steep steps leading to a passageway that ran all the way around the stadium, iron railings, steel floor, feet on metal, tramp, tramp, and there she was. Walked right into him.

'Pamina—'

'Can't stop. Got something to do.'

'Have you killed someone?'

'Can't stop.'

'Where are you going?'

'To Angel.'

'Is Angel controlling you? Is Angel inside you?'

Shaking her, trying to make her stay put. She twisted, she struggled, shit, she was strong. He was strong too, with the berserker strength of the contrary spirit, but so was she . . . driven . . . and the dead eyes. Like she was already halfway in the grave. And as he shook her something in her seemed to change . . . her features narrowed . . . her eyes widened . . . her hair spiked up . . . 'Angel!' PJ cried. 'But you're trapped . . . inside the amulet, you're trapped . . .'

'Not for ever.' The face wavered . . . became Pamina once more.

'You can't have Chit!' he screamed.

'She's in the way. She's a goner anyway, don't you know that, she fed the angel blood from her own breast, she's his now, she wears his mark over her heart and you can't do anything with your stupid native ass-backward magic so just leave her to me . . .'

'No! Not Chit!'

'Get the fuck out of my way.'

She shoved him hard against the steel walls and started to run. She knew where the amulet was. She was making a beeline for it. It was reeling her in like a fish. Couldn't stop her, she was too singleminded, too strong. Backward. He started walking in the opposite direction.

Backward. Backward.

Tripped and started tumbling down steps, endless steps, and no one saw him because they'd all risen to their feet and were leaping up and down and screaming *Timmy Timmy Timmy* and shoving back and forth in an impromptu slamdance as Timmy came out on stage to the wailing lead guitar lick that introduced *Crucify Me Twice* and you could hear the pounding pounding pounding of nails into human flesh and bone that substituted for the bass drum in the opening of the song and then—

He didn't know how, but he had managed to walk blindly backward all the way to Chit. He grasped her arm and pulled her out of her seat.

'We've gotta go,' he said. 'Come on, quick.'

vanitas

She obeyed right away. When PJ *knew* things he was always right. 'Where are we going?' she said.

'I don't know, just come.'

Bruce Gaston was just saying, 'That Lauren McCandless, I knew him in Pasadena, he really thought he was the cat's ass, what a pretentious piece of shit—'

PJ steered her up the aisle to the exit. 'Pamina's here,' he whispered. 'She's after the amulet.'

Chit hurried. She knew she was in mortal danger. And yet . . . there was a sense of lightheadedness, almost of abandon. As they reached the exit – she ignored the strange stares of her rich acquaintances – she realized why. It was the pain in her breast. It had suddenly gone away.

'PJ, something wonderful has happened—'

'Come on. Hurry.'

He pulled her by the hand. She could see he was possessed

by whatever spirit had come to him in his vision in London, because he did not even look where he was gone. They dodged a woman hawking coconut milk, a kid who was mischievously taking a leak over the railing into the parking lot, and at length she found herself perched on the catwalk that spanned the arena . . . a long narrow ribbon of a metal bridge that ran all the way around, hugging the top rows . . . that was where the street kids and the gatecrashers were all perched, a hundred pairs of legs dangling through gaps in the steel . . . their gaze trained on the boy in the pool of light . . . clutching the railing they squeezed their way sidelong toward the stage area where there was a spiral stair that led down into the wings and the control consoles and even further, down to an underground network of dressing rooms and staff lounges.

She followed PJ. She didn't look down. A flock of pigeons rushed right through them. She could hear the strains of *Crucify Me Twice*, but up here the song blended with the music of the Bangkok night – the screaming motorcycles throbbed against the whining feedback of the lead guitar, the night creatures buzzed along with the crystal textures of the synthesizers . . . she ran.

And suddenly there were a thousand Lady Chits. Up and down, on ramp after ramp, looking down, around, wild-eyed. She let out a cry of startlement. A thousand PJs as well, dark-maned, ferocious. 'We must be inside Levon's big mirror contraption,' PJ said. 'They're all on rotors. He controls them from the console. They're part of what generates the mega-morphing scene later in the song.'

She saw it now. There were about a hundred mirrors, each about ten feet tall: some cylindrical, some concave, some flat . . . they were all moving in different directions . . . it was almost as though they were on the surface of an insect's compound eye . . . thousands of reflective facets all differently angled, all in motion, fluid. They were at the very top of the wall of mirrors, where the catwalk ended in a ramp that zigzagged down the ranks of mirrors all the way to the stage floor. A thick barrier of scrim and smoke concealed the array of mirrors from the goings-on upstage, but she could see that when the climax came the scrim could be hoisted instantly into the flies.

'We're *inside* the illusion.' She stopped. Breathed heavily. 'Think we can fool Pamina?'

'I don't know.'

She could see her face a thousandfold . . . now clear, now blurry, now shifting into something else . . . a wolf . . . a skull . . . the face of Timmy Valentine. 'Look,' PJ said, 'there's Levon. He must be making some adjustments.'

She could see Jihanian now. He was moving up the zigzag ramp. Quite silently. No footsteps. 'There's something wrong with him,' she said. 'People don't move that way . . .'

She remembered how strange he'd seemed even from way across the arena. Shambling. Unsteady. He wasn't that way now. He moved abruptly . . . liquidly . . . like a blob of mercury . . . he'd be here, then he'd be a blur, then he'd be there . . .

'Jesus Christ,' said PJ. 'It's my contrary spirit. It tricked me. Damn that trickster to hell. Oh, God, oh, God—'

Never had PJ sounded so full of despair. 'What do you mean? What are you talking about?' Chit said.

'It made me think I was leading you away from Pamina – when – Jesus – I was leading you *to* another vampire – a fucking *real* vampire—'

And then Levon was right beside them.

Just like that.

A dark, little guy. As short as Chit herself. He was standing right next to her. Not breathing. She stepped back. His face was not in any of the mirrors. Only her own. She saw her terror, and terror fed on terror until she could not even scream.

Softly she said, 'PJ – save me – fight him—'

Jihanian said, 'I'm sorry. I'm really *hungry*. I'm not used to this, I don't really know how to do it right, forgive me—'

The wound in her breast began to throb.

'I don't know,' said the vampire, 'I don't understand, this morning I was just one oversexed computer nerd, really into my inner world, seeing demons behind every bush you know, and then suddenly my brain's all fried and every circuit is fucked up, you know, and there's all these connections I never knew existed – but I'm so *hungry* I can't even stop to think about it because the hunger is *driving me crazy*—'

PJ made no move to prevent what was going to happen. Why

doesn't he stop Levon, why doesn't he jab a stake right through
his heart? Why does he just stand there?

'PJ—' Chit said softly. Is he going to let me *die*?

PJ said: 'Pamina told me it's too late to save you . . . because
you've already nursed the angel with blood from your own
breast . . . you've given him life . . . and because of that there's
no hope for you, and after death you too are going to
become . . .' He began to weep. He looked defeated, lost. 'The
contrary spirit is showing me that the only way to save you is
a dangerous and desperate way . . . that I have to step away
. . . turn my back on you . . .'

'Oh God,' she screamed, 'I don't love you, I hate your visions
and your spirits, how can you believe it when they tell you you
have to let me die?' How could I have said that? It was appalling.
There was a gulf between them after all . . . race, social class,
culture, something . . . 'You're just a fucking savage, PJ . . .'

PJ stepped away. His eyes showed no trace of the love that
had kept them warm and dry in the great rain that had swept
over Junction to douse the fires of the aborted apocalypse. But as
he turned, she thought she saw their stony hardness soften . . .

She watched him in the mirrors. Weeping like a child. She
hated him then, and more than that, she was seething with jeal-
ousy because he heard his spirits and not her, he did what *they*
commanded him, they possessed him utterly, and her love was
not worth a flying fuck to him, and now there was this strange
little man who was putting his wintry hands about her neck, her
cheeks, her arms, each touch driving an icicle into her soul, and
she looked into his eyes that held vain desolation, and she heard
his silent plea and she answered, silently, despairingly, *Yes, yes,
I do invite you, I will share the emptiness with you, because now I hate
the man I love*, and felt the first kiss on the wrist, the comfortless
bitter kiss, and slowly, slowly, slowly, her blood ran cold . . .

vanitas

Gotta remember to breathe, Timmy thought, from the gut, don't
let the music get away from you, catch those high notes like
you're netting wild butterflies, catch them, let them go . . .

climax is coming soon. The song will end, everything will end.

The climax is coming. I hear the rustle behind me as the mirrors start to shift into place. As soon as I hit the big high shrieking note at the end of the song I have to hold my hands up high leap through a burning hoop of flame that's just a holographic projection and when I reach the other side I'll be inside a box that will drop down through a trapdoor and the other me will take over, the me that's only a computer-generated image, that me is the one who will do the big disappearing act and by that time I will already be gone . . .

Don't worry about the leap. They got mattresses everywhere. The smoke machines are working overtime to make sure that there are clouds all over the stage, to hide the mattresses . . .

It's coming now! Rock-steady. Steady. You only get one chance. Your whole life has been careering toward this moment, fast-forward, ever since you elected to be human. No regrets now. Hit it!

Timmy opened his arms wide. He could hear the gasps. Only a few at first because they were too stunned at what they were seeing for it to register. He wished he could see it. He had always rehearsed facing the imaginary audience, never looking back at the spectacle, petrified of losing his place and pacing. But he knew that the monstrous reproduction of Lauren McCandless's painting had just swum into view behind him. The scattered cries of amazement swelled to a sea of applause. The dead woman was as high as a ten-storey building and now she began to stir . . . as if waking to the night of undeath for the first time.

And to transform . . .

Here comes the ring of fire! Condensing out of the thin air, a roaring flame, miracle of projection and sound synthesis, even Timmy began to imagine its searing heat. He coiled himself up, ready to spring. I'm a panther . . . slicing through the fiery air of the jungle night . . . jump, jump!

At that moment everything started to go wrong.

The crowd was screaming. *But I didn't do it yet!* he was thinking. But they were all pointing past him. Clambering up out of their seats. Shouting. Shocked.

Timmy turned. But before he could appreciate the illusion—
A woman catapulted out of the wall of mirrors, shot skyward like a rocket, then came plummeting down . . . Timmy glanced up, glanced down, saw her crash down onto the mattress . . . Oh God is she OK? he thought but didn't dare stop singing because the song possessed his voice and would not let him stop . . . he spun, did a little kneeling thing so he could see who it was . . . it was Lady Chit . . . the audience couldn't have known, it was all so fast . . . the band takes up the melody now, the mirrors start to move again, the illusion must continue . . . is she dead? he thinks. The audience has no idea, thinks it's all magic, all effects . . . and then . . .

Two more figures . . . in the catwalk above the stage . . . wrestling . . . and now they both come tumbling down . . . they hit the mattresses, a resounding crunch, but they barely seem to notice, they're so busy trying to kill each other . . . PJ gripped something in his hand, something sharp and shiny . . . it's a piece of broken mirror, Timmy thought, and as he watched, PJ plunged the shard into Levon's chest.

Levon rolled away screaming, pounding the stage floor with his fists in time to the crack of the song's percussion . . . he was convulsing now, and PJ strode over to where he lay and forced the mirror splinter in deeper, twisted the glittering spike so that the blood spritzed up and PJ's arms were soaked, his face was dripping blood, and still he wouldn't let go but drove the glass in harder, harder, and Jesus, Timmy thought, his eyes are like pieces of that mirror, glasslike, dead . . . he pulled something from his pocket . . . holy water Timmy guessed . . . shoved the phial into the vampire's mouth . . . the way Levon screamed, no human could sound that way, it's as if the very earth cried out in anguish . . . Levon tried to stand up, the blood still spurting from his gashed chest . . . then he started to catch fire. Inside. It was the holy water working on his entrails, causing him to sizzle from within. He was breathing fire. He ripped out his own tongue and flung it away from him and it zipped across the stage like a ball of fire and now his scream sounded even stranger, like the whine of an Arctic wind . . . and the fire was still pouring from his throat. His eyes exploded. The sockets were windows into inferno. He turned against himself, trying to put himself out, bashing himself against the floorboards, the massive speakers . . . consumed himself.

The audience roared their approval. Neo-Gothics were leaping up and down in their seats, rushing the stage, slamdancing in the aisles. Their enthusiasm was unquenchable. They were stampeding the front row, trying to hop onto the proscenium while security officers looked nervous and started to take out their clubs.

PJ watched Levon burn to a crisp . . . then he ran over to where Chit lay, still concealed from most of the audience by a steady stream of artificial fog. Timmy continued to dance. He danced around the burning hoop, somersaulted through it, improvising wildly, delaying the final notes of the song . . . so that the mirror-driven illusions behind him, keyed to their MIDI triggers, would not launch too soon into the big climax . . . but he didn't know how long he could keep that up.

PJ was holding Chit in his arms. She must be dead, Timmy thought. He could feel the grief building up inside but he dared not give in to it. He had to finish the song somehow. He gave the secret SOS signal to the offstage band, which segued, not skipping a beat, into a reprise of the instrumental interlude. String pads soared. Lush waves of sound swept over the audience, and it calmed them a little, for above the restless ostinato rhythms the chords were slow, serene, soothingly static . . . a strange cross-breeding of speed metal and New Age.

Timmy danced.

Inched closer and closer to where PJ was, Chit cradled in his arms, both of them submerged in mist. He could see now that PJ was trying to remove an amulet from around Chit's throat. Chit's spectacular evening gown was ripped, and Timmy could see that on her left breast, above her heart, was a gaping wound bordered with white scars, an old wound that had never closed. PJ was struggling with the clasp of the amulet . . . an ugly shapeless silver thing . . . but it wouldn't give . . .

Then there was someone else on the stage with them.

It was Pamina. Fully Neo-Gothic now, she wore only a few shreds of black leather over her scrawny body. She was drenched in blood from head to toe. She got into step with him. She had studied all his moves, knew almost by rote what he was going to do next even though he was improvising the dance movements, desperately filling time. He waved to the band to go into the interlude once again. Longest breakstrain in a pop song, he thought, it's gonna be in the fucking Guinness Book of Records.

'Always wanted to be your dance partner, Timmy,' Pamina whispered. 'But I can't stay. I have business.'

'Pamina,' he whispered, 'you're terribly sick . . . some awful trauma, some twisted gene, I don't know what it is . . . *you're not a vampire!* Get out while you can . . . can't you see that you're going to get destroyed?'

'I have seen the angel,' she said, 'and the angel is Death.'

They danced. He tried to move away from PJ as he fumbled with the necklace, but Pamina circled ever closer . . . and he had to follow her. The crowd whooped with delight at this unadvertised companion who mimicked every move to perfection, like a feminine mirror.

PJ said, 'You can't have the amulet . . . can't take it from her . . .' He got the clasp free. He yanked the necklace but it wouldn't come loose. Chit's dead hand gripped the chain so tight he could not pull it off. He tried to pry the fingers apart. They wouldn't give. 'Chit, Chit . . . oh God, Chit, help me,' he moaned. But the dead hand wouldn't budge. 'Why did you have to say those awful thing to me?' he cried. 'Don't you know that I couldn't choose what I did, that there's only one precarious way for me to save you and that is to let you go? Chit . . .'

Pamina danced.

Timmy followed, and now it was the star who was mimicking the young girl's gestures, following her as she made her way closer and closer to PJ and Chit.

Pamina reached out her hand and—

'No!' PJ screamed, and—

Chit's dead arm thrust itself out of the smoke! It held the amulet aloft! The silver caught the light and shone bright in the churning fog. Gasps from the crowd now. None of this had been in the pre-release publicity or the programme books or the buzz or the rumours that had been flying weeks in advance. PJ backed away. He stared at his wife's body. Timmy saw an awesome longing in his eyes, and also recognition . . . resignation.

The amulet was meant for Pamina, always had been meant for Pamina . . . and Chit's death had been ordained from the moment she heard Angel's voice, calling to her and her alone in the garden of her estate, in the chamber of painted hells.

Timmy knew that to the audience it must seem like something out of Arthurian legend, a lady's hand bearing a mystical gift rising forth out of a mist-girt lake . . . and Pamina took the amulet and danced downstage, perilously close to where members of the audience were once more trying to scramble onto the proscenium . . . Timmy stood still. PJ, still kneeling, watched.

Pamina swallowed the amulet.

For a moment, nothing happened. Timmy caught his breath. So did the entire audience. The tension ratcheted up one last notch. Then—

Pamina Rothstein began to moult. Her skin liquefied and streamed down steaming red flesh. Her eyes squeezed free of their sockets and began slowly to slither down her melting face. Her muscles writhed, tied themselves in knots, and started to contract, making her bones pop and rattle. Her lungs bloated and expelled clouds of blood-tinged vapour. Her sternum cracked open to reveal a fibrillating heart. Her head rotated as it shed skin, blood, hair, teeth and finally bone.

And all this while, Pamina Rothstein danced.

The dance was neither horrific nor grotesque. Rather, the convulsions of flesh, the clattering of bones, the sizzling of blood, the twisting of muscle, all combined into an eerie music that kept time with the song's austere melismas. It was a beautiful thing, this dance, beautiful in its melancholy; Timmy recognized in its precision the imprint of a cunning mind, more convoluted than a human's.

As the interlude dragged on for a fourth and fifth time, the thing that had been Pamina Rothstein began to put itself back together. Bones flew together. A skull pushed its way out of pulsating brain tissue. The audience cheered each piece of reconstructed flesh. Skin began to form. Organs coalesced, muscles oozed out of new bones. The skin was paler than the girl's, and the hair a dirty blond, though it showed traces of having once been dyed black. The eyes were wide and deep and starry, like flawless cabochons. The chest was firm, flat, hairless. The arms flung themselves out, entering without a pause into the rhythm of the dance. It was a boy. You knew that only because he was naked, for his body had the languid androgyny that Timmy himself possessed. He was not a eunuch though. In fact, the way he leapt, the way his hips thrust out, the way he pursed his lips and seemed to flip off the audience with every wave of his arms, all flaunted a core of sexuality that Timmy's performances had never shown.

Angel Todd was back.

'Dance with me, Timmy,' Angel said.

The audience cried out with delight. *Two* Timmy Valentines! How could they not see how different the two of them were . . . the one human, the other inhuman? But of course they can't see, Timmy thought. Blind, fucking blind.

He danced with his own reflection.

'Timmy, Timmy,' said Angel, 'this sucks. Some witch doctor put me away, and I had to kill everyone I cared about to get back.'

'Are you gonna kill me too, now?'

'Don't know. Haven't read that far ahead in the script. Shut up and dance.'

They danced again. Changed places. Embraced, almost kissed; Angel was like Narcissus, virtually masturbating at the spectacle of his own beauty, while Timmy, mirroring his gestures, danced aloof, cold, with geometric precision.

'You hate it, don't you?' Timmy said. 'Being dead, I mean.'

'And you can't deal with being alive.'

'Is it love you miss?'

'Fuck love. Never had it, don't need it now.'

'If you hold out long enough, compassion comes. And love too. I know. It happened to me. In eternity all things are possible.'

'Don't got not time for that. Come on, Timmy, let's go now.'

'Where are we going?'

'One day at a time, bro.'

'Is Chit going to become a vampire?'

'Ask too many fucking questions. Dance. Jesus look, they love us, we should go on the road, maybe cut an album.'

'Fuck you.'

They danced. And this time Timmy didn't do the SOS gesture, and the music launched into the final stanza of *Crucify Me Twice*. This was the big one, the part with all the effects. The ten-storey-tall dead woman – the animated Lauren McCandless painting – began to morph. Each change was greeting by a collective yell of pleasure from the crowd. Here came the leopard. Now the whirlwind. Now Dorothy. Now the great lion of Narnia. Shout! Shout! Shout! One multiple orgasm shared by ten thousand people.

'Watch!' Angel said. 'Lot of energy in this crowd. We can feed on it. We can make things *happen* around here!'

The giantess's arms reached for them, making mystic passes in the air, as tesseracts of Tessla light lasered out of her outstretched hands. One hand was to Timmy's right, the other to Angel's left, and they were engulfed in coils of blue lightning. Through a cataract of cadent light, he could see PJ enfold Chit in his arms and lift her up, as tenderly as a lovelorn Hollywood monster, kissing her frozen lips again and again.

'PJ—' Timmy cried out. 'You have to come too—'

'I'm coming!' PJ said, and began to walk away, carrying his woman, receding into shadow.

The world was a whirlwind and Timmy and Angel were its centre. The hands of illusion, weaving a cat's cradle of light, soon enveloped them completely. Timmy could hear the roaring crowd, but it was distant, like the whisper of surf when you cruise along the Pacific Coast Highway with the windows rolled up and the stereo blaring. Unfinished business, Timmy thought, that's what me and Angel have to deal with.

'I'm going away now,' Angel said.

'Where to?'

'Find me.'

'Just tell me. I want to get this over with as much as you do.'

Finger to his lips. 'Do you dare, Timmy, do you dare dare dare? 'Cause you're only a little boy now. You can't turn into the wind, or a raven, or a ravening wolf. You can't funnel into keyholes. You can't possess a mad young girl from a million miles away and drive her over the brink of madness and then eat up her soul and put her body into the blender and rearrange every fucking molecule of her and end with *me*; that's a trick not even you learned in your two thousand years. See, I got mysteries of the east. Picked up a few things you missed. I can do everything you can't do no more. And more.'

'But you can't go out in the daylight.'

'Can too!'

'Prove it.'

'OK, so I'm still saddled with a couple of goddamned super-stitions. But my dick works.'

'Let's finish this.'

'We can't. You still want to save your friends, don't you? The brave little Indian, stuck inside a vision where up is down. And the girl. She's dead – *un*dead – unless you finish things my way. And don't you want to know what happened to Lauren McCandless? So long, Timmy. Next time we meet, I'll have figured the whole thing out.'

And there was light—

God so much light light exploding all around them boring into his brain closing his eyes didn't help the light just pushed right through didn't matter how hard he squeezed the light the light the light—

Darkness.

Under the stage. The trapdoor. The compartment.

The audience was over the edge now. He could hear it all overhead. Trampling the stage, smashing the speakers. He could hear harsh voices barking through PA systems. Gunshots. A riot, a fucking riot.

He could see a little more now. It was murky in here, and stiflingly humid. No lights. But there was someone. Two people. Someone living, someone dead. 'PJ?' he whispered.

'I killed her,' PJ said.

'PJ – you know that's not what happened—'

'I had to let her die! But how can I ever explain it to her – how can I ever look at her when she wakes up tomorrow night and she's a vampire? – I've got to do the stake in the heart thing, and it hurts, it hurts—'

'No. PJ. Don't do it. There is a way out. Angel wants me to do it. Maybe . . . I can make Chit . . . the *price* of doing what Angel wants.'

'What price? He can't bring her back from the dead!' PJ said, and began to weep. Timmy dared not comfort him, for he himself did not believe. In two thousand years, he had known only one kind of resurrection.

And yet, he thought . . . *I'm* human.

How did we do that?

memory: 1889

One of the Duke of Clarence's very special soirées: midnight, a room hastily and discreetly rented at one of the lesser-known establishments, then claret, caviar, and conversation of a decidedly un-royal nature.

There is opium, hemp, and the newly fashionable cocaïne as well. And there are no taboos. The duke's propensities are not only tolerated; they are positively lauded. Others with even darker secrets have come calling – Charles Algernon Swinburne, a funny little Old Etonian poet, who cannot start the evening without a liberal dose of the birch; a detective named Holmes, much addicted to the white powder; Oscar Wilde and Lord Alfred Douglas, who were the first to introduce the boy to this inner circle. And there are, of course, the telegraph-boys, though have surely not come to deliver telegrams as they recline, in shocking *déshabillé*, on the overstuffed fauteuils and divans of this drawing room, to which admittance can be gained only by a secret knock – the 'fate' motif from Beethoven's Fifth Symphony.

Which is even now pounding on the door once more.

The boy looks up. It is Mr Stoker, who, though he does not appear to possess the Uranian proclivities of most of the inner circle, is endlessly fascinated by them, perhaps obsessively so. Or is it that he puts up with it all, just so that he can hear another historical fable from Sebastian's lips?

'Ah,' he says, 'I'm late.'

The chalice is passed around. A ritual pricking of the thumb with a hatpin, a few more drops of blood added . . . something faintly blasphemous about it all . . . and finally one of the telegraph-boys proffers the cup. It is, as it were, a bribe; he is singing for his supper.

'A lovely name, Sebastian Melmoth,' Wilde is saying to an unidentified guest. 'I would give it to myself if I could. Perhaps, one day, I shall.'

Sebastian drinks.

The warmth seeps into cold veins. His eyes redden.

'What's he going to tell us about today?' asks the duke. 'Not Jack the Ripper again, I hope; we're all quite tired of him.'

'Sebastian . . .' says one of the boys, rouged and powdered, with a lilac in his hair. 'There's some what say his Grace was the real Jack the Ripper. You saw him. Is it true?'

The boy looks into the bemused face of his royal host. He is not sure whether the man he saw almost ten years ago is this man; it was all so quick, and he was still disoriented from having been flung through the void of time . . . it could have been. What does it matter? he thinks. It's an old story, and will probably not be remembered past the turn of the century.

'Bluebeard,' says Clarence. 'I loved your encounter with that French madman. When you told us how he had actually cut a hole in your abdomen and penetrated it with his masculine member, I almost lost control of my own!'

'Heavens,' says Dr Watson.

'Not to mention the deliciously irreverent Christian symbolism of it all, the wound in the side and all that,' says Bosie.

'Oh, you are obvious sometimes,' says Wilde, and kisses him abstractedly. To Stoker, he says, 'Bram, I do believe it's your turn to question our supernatural guest.'

Sebastian smiles. Bram Stoker is writing a novel about a vampire, and has frequently asked the boy for those little details that add so much verisimilitude to a literary work. It is just as well, for Sebastian has been reading some of Bram's other works, and he does find them a trifle listless. 'I am at your disposal, Mr Stoker,' he says, 'now that I have drained the last drop of the blood your lordships have been so kind as to offer me.' He smiles; they are mesmerized; he knows that they all, in one way or another, desire him: whether it is his physical beauty, his otherworldliness, or his immortality they are after, it is always, in the end, a kind of lust.

'Well,' says Stoker, easing himself into a chaise longue next to the ottoman on which Sebastian has perched himself and lighting a cigar, 'you have told us about many of the most depraved personages of history . . . and even of the present, as witness your little encounter with Jack the Ripper . . . of Gilles de Rais, of Cardinal del Monte, of Moctezuma; of grand inquisitors and witches, of persecutors of Christians, of human monsters great and small . . . yet none of those, it seems, was ever a vampire. Are you being a little self-serving perhaps, in your portrayal of the villains of history as far more evil than your innocent self, who are by your very nature a creature of Satan and necessarily pure evil?'

'I don't think about those things, sir,' Sebastian says. 'I merely see, and having seen, relate.'

'But surely there must have been *one* villain in history who was also a vampire. Or are you all, as you yourself, poor victims of circumstance, unable to prevent what destiny has made you?'

'That's hard to answer. I've come to believe that evil itself is man-made, and illusion.'

'That's all very profound, Sebastian,' says Stoker. 'But I, as one who writes for a living, must also think of the exigencies of the marketplace . . . and there, I think, a vampire who is not evil simply will not sell.'

Sebastian smiles sadly.

'I've studied many of the villains you've described in my search for a sort of prototype of evil for my novel,' Stoker explains. 'And I think I've found someone *truly* monstrous – a man who used to sit around eating dinner while surrounded by thousands of his dying victims, men, women and children.'

'It sounds very human.'

'Tell me, Sebastian. In your journey through the shadows of history,' says Stoker, 'did you ever come across one Vlad Dracula, a prince of Wallachia, sometimes known as the Impaler?'

Sebastian closes his eyes. The pageant of horrors past plays through his mind. He remembers: rats. The dungeon walls. Narrow, moist, malodorous . . . the oubliette of the Sultan of Turkey.

A rat was gnawing at the hostage's leg . . .

Dark. Dark. Dark.

I long to lie down in my native earth.

A child is singing in the dark . . .

It is a boy in chains. The rat runs up the cold metal. The boy does not even bother to shoo him away. He is lost in his song, a song about a vanquished homeland.

He has dark, haunting eyes; in the gloomy they are the only thing that shine; his teardrops glisten.

'Dracula,' says Sebastian . . . 'Ah, Dracula . . .'

Part IV

VANITAS

Don't ask me how to find it
Don't ask me when or where
Can't show you Vampire Junction
'Cause you're already there

Timmy Valentine

19

RADU THE HANDSOME

dissolve: darkness

So where are we, PJ?
   I don't know.

news of the world

From *Scandal International*:

ROCK STAR VANISHES – AGAIN!

Just when you thought Timmy Valentine was all washed
up, here comes another sensational disappearing act. You
remember the Florida incident, ten years ago, at Boca
Blanca, with the exploding old woman in the wheelchair?
And the pre-teen rock idol vanished without a trace for a
decade, only to appear, *completely unchanged*, at a Timmy
Valentine look-alike concert at Universal Studios? And the
mighty powers at Stupendous Studios all taking his resurrection at face value?
   It gets better.
   Two nights ago, at a spectacular concert in Bangkok's
brand-new Panyasai Stadium – the latest architectural
showpiece in a city where futuristic skyscrapers tower over
ancient temples and palaces – Timmy Valentine was, to say
the least, *smokin'*. The effects for his final number, created
at a cost of over two million dollars, proved a little too much
even for the caped wonder, who was sucked into a vortex
of mirrors and hasn't been seen since. The wizard behind
this morphing spectacle, Levon Jihanian, was found dead
onstage with a dagger-shaped shard of mirror glass staked
through his heart, though no one can figure out exactly
how or when it happened. Some others are reported miss-

ing too, notably Lady Premchitra, a young Thai aristocrat
and close friend of Valentine's and her husband, Native
American art gallery owner PJ Gallagher.

The weenie-bopper wonder's career *had* been flagging a
little, according to number crunchers at Stupendous. There
is some speculation that the star's disappearance – so
uncannily echoing his previous vanishing – may have been
orchestrated by Stupendous in order to cash in its Timmy
Valentine chips all at once, but David Giler, the quixotic,
reclusive genius behind the company's rise to the top, could
not be reached for comment.

Where will Valentine turn up next? Jason Nicolosi, a
scientist at the Los Angeles Institute of Cryogenic Studies,
has a theory. 'I think that Stupendous has put Valentine
on ice,' he told *Scandal International* when we interviewed
him at a Pizza Hut in Baja California. 'If they slowed down
his bodily functions and cooled him down to the temperature of liquid nitrogen, they might be able to keep him in
a kind of stasis for about ten years during which time he
would not appear to age. They'll probably trot him out
again in 2005. Would you believe it?'

We asked Nicolosi if there was any proof that his theory
would work. 'Here at the centre, we've done it on rats. I
think Valentine's a fool for agreeing to it, though. Ought
to be a law.'

night

Where are we going, PJ?

I don't know.

Then how do you know we're going the right way?

Because it's the wrong way.

It's that contrary sense of yours again, isn't it? All right. I
know that we're heading south. It's the night train to Penang.
After Malaysia, you say we're going south some more. So short
of falling off the edge of the earth, that leads us to Indonesia
. . . New Guinea maybe. Is that where we're going? Toward
that new volcano? Do you feel a source of power there, a place
where there's such a maelstrom of energy and emotion that it
is possible to slip through the cracks in the cosmos? Is that it?

I don't know, Timmy.

There was a time when I could have felt those sources of

energy. But now I can't. I have to rely on you because you're more in touch with these things. But I do know one thing. I was born in fire. Maybe I'll die in fire. Is it Angel who is calling out to you? Is he speaking to you in the clatter of the wheels on the traintrack? In the wind that rushes through the coconut trees that whip past our window in the night? I listen and listen and to me the wind is the wind. That's all. But you can hear the spirits.

I think I can.

I think I can I think I can – there, PJ, I've made you smile. It's so hot in here! The further you get from Bangkok, the more you seem to enter some primaeval past . . . the forests of the night. Maybe there are tigers in those hills. It's so dark out there. I'm pressing my nose to the glass and still I can't see much. I know *you* can see though. You can even talk to the animals. Any tigers?

I don't think so. But there's a raven.

I see it! There! The break between two hills, the crescent moon, the dark bird crossing the sliver of light.

I think Angel is in the raven.

The harbinger of death. Well, that would be nice and mythic, wouldn't it? Yeah . . . how's Chit?

I'll just check the coffin.

OK, I'll get the light. You haul it down from the luggage rack. Here. I'll help you with the lid. There she is. Oh, god, she is beautiful. It's just like she was still alive. Except for the wound in her breast. That wound will never close up, will it? Not even in death. It can't heal. But for that wound, she's perfect.

She smells good, too. It's Semsara, isn't it? She bought some when we went shopping at Central yesterday. Oh, god, was it just yesterday? Oh, Jesus, she's still soft. Touch her cheek. There's a give in it, like living flesh. Has she turned? Is she going to wake to the terrible darkness tonight? Did we bring a stake to drive into her heart, PJ? Could you do it? Could I? Quick. Close it again. Quick, quick, before she – what's that? A little statuette – the Chinese goddess of mercy? You say she wielded it that day in the mortuary in Germany, the day the two of you neutralized Amelia Rothstein? What's it in the coffin for?

In case she awakens. And the seals on the coffin – silver. And the heavy odour of Samsara – it's because I've stuffed her mouth with bulbs of garlic. Just in case. If she *does* become a vampire—

But she hasn't woken up. She's not a vampire.

But she's not dead either. She's even less than undead. She's in a kind of limbo . . . her soul is at a crossroads. If we don't get to Angel in time . . . she'll turn . . . one way or the other. Come on. Help me shut the coffin. This is upsetting me.

OK.

Timmy—

Yeah.

Nothing.

OK. I've shut the coffin and now I'm fastening the silver clasps. You really thought of everything.

There's a coffin dealer by the temple that Chit's family have endowed. I picked it up yesterday.

Beforehand?

I'm a contrary.

You knew this was going to happen.

I didn't want it to, but . . . I guess so. It feels terrible that I let her die, that she said awful things to me and then got wrapped up in that vampire's embrace and fell dead at your feet and I never told her I loved her and when she died she was angry at me, she hated me. Timmy, you don't hate me, do you?

Why should I?

The place I'm taking you to . . . it may be . . .

Death.

Are you scared?

Yes.

Do you want to turn back?

No, PJ. Death is old hat to me. I died the first time in that big old eruption of 79 A.D. I tried to die in the fire at Junction but didn't quite die, not until the second fire there, the fire of illusion; I died and came back as a mortal. Now . . . well . . . third time's the charm, I guess. I hope it's for good, this time.

You want to die?

PJ, PJ, I've been dying for two thousand years. Put me out of my misery already! Good. I made you laugh again. You know, it occurs to me that I've had three great adventures in the twen-

tieth century, and they've been sort of religious experiences. I
mean, in the first adventure, with me and Carla Rubens and
Stephen Miles, it was all about the holy trinity, and about
redemption, and all those Judaeo-Christian sorts of things; and
then the next time round it was more of a pagan thing, deities
and spirits all taking sides in a massive confrontation of male
and female principles . . . and now I'm having a sort of Buddhist
adventure, aren't I? I mean . . . reality being illusion. Relin-
quishing one's desire for the material. And the ultimate goal
being the utter extinction of the self. This time it all seems very
final.

No.

[Which in contrary talk means yes (which means I don't know.
{Do you?}).] I'm thinking parenthetically you see. Oh! Made you
laugh again. Cool. Totally.

It's weird how you can leap back and forth between the oldest
man in the universe and a twelve-year-old kid.

Look out of the window! The sea. I think it's the sea. It whispers. The raven's still there. It's following us. Listen! They're
coming up the aisle now, I guess we're getting to the border.
It's almost dawn. What are we going to say about the coffin?

Leave it to me. A contrary has many tricks up his sleeve.

OK.

Do you love me, Timmy?

How can I say? I used to be love. I used to be death. Now,
I'm just a little boy. But I can remember things sometimes. Do
you want me to tell you a story? Kill the time?

—He's *murdering* the time!

A quote from Lewis Carroll. The Reverend, that is. He came
to the Duke's one time, you know. But he was never comfortable. Had a thing for naked little girls, but couldn't admit it to
himself. Could have fucked them easily enough. Whitechapel
was full of little ones, and they were only sixpence a pop. Hated
the big ones, you see. Maybe *he* was Jack the Ripper. Am I
digressing? I was going to tell you more about Dracula.

memory: 1445

. . . there is blood where the cuffs have chafed him. The scent, of course, arouses the hunger . . . but the boy vampire, still a rat, does not yet drink; he is listening to the prisoner's lament. The language is the tongue of Rome, the dialect of the Dacians; strange how little it has changed since the last time the boy spoke Latin, a thousand years ago.

> I long to lie down in my native earth,
> In the soil that holds my mother's blood,
> I long to sleep in the ancient hills
> Where I watched the stars with my father.

When was the last time he heard that song? Was it from some towheaded young centurion as he stood watch by the tent of the Emperor Diocletian? The boy vampire's heart aches. He has no native earth. And suddenly, in that cramped cell in the oubliette of the Ottoman sultan, he finds himself, too, singing the ancient song; without thinking, he has slipped out of the rodent's shape and into his human form.

The other boy hears, then, perhaps, makes out the silhouette of the vampire in the gloom. But he does not seem surprised. He only calls out, 'Radu, Radu. You always were a better singer than I.'

Having left the prisoner's lips, the name now wraps itself around the vampire; he must answer to it, for he is, as always, the mirror to the human world. And it is the invitation that he still feels he must have before he can impinge on this boy's life. 'But,' he says, 'you sing it with so much more sadness.'

'Have you come to mock me?'

'No. I don't even know you. I don't even know where this place is.'

'You're not Radu the Handsome, my much-too-pretty brother, come down from your master's private boy-brothel to make fun of me?'

'I can be whoever you want me to be,' says Radu, 'but you have to tell me more.'

'I see. Let me touch you.' The boy feels a callused hand upon his cheek. The fingers probe his ears, his hair, his nose. They do not shrink from the chill undeadness of his flesh. 'No,' says the chained boy at last, 'you're not my brother. But the resemblance is uncanny.'

'You can tell even in the dark?'

'I've been down here for months. I'm not supposed to be in a dungeon, you understand. I am a prince, a royal hostage. They stuck me down here because I'm stubborn. This town is called Gelibolu. It's on a strip of land that juts out into the sea, so you can hear the waves both left and right, before and behind, if you listen carefully enough.'

Radu hears the water lapping the sand and the stones, and a wind from the Aegean, and a contrary wind from the Dardanelles; he hears the cry of seagulls. He does not think a human being can hear these things, not from behind the three-foot walls of this imprisonment. Perhaps, he thinks, it's the rush of the boy's own blood and the ringing of his ears, which he imagines to be the sounds of nature.

'*Buna seara*. My name is Vlad,' the boy says. 'I'm fourteen. If you want, you can call me by my nickname, Dracula.'

'Little dragon.' A fierce name for one so young.

'You speak Romanian well. Are you from Wallachia?'

'I don't think so,' says Radu, for he is not sure where that is. 'But I've heard your language spoken, and it's not that different from one I used to speak.'

'I think you *are* from Wallachia. I think you're a creature from the dawn time of my country. They say that we were all once spirits, children of the night. Perhaps you knew our land as Dacia.'

'Perhaps.'

It is true that the boy remembers almost nothing of the time before his changing, let alone his real childhood, his parents, his capture, his enslavement to the service of the Cumaean Sibyl. It may be true. Perhaps they are even of the same blood. After all, the family resemblance . . . even over fourteen centuries . . . did the prisoner not mistake him for his own brother?

Water drips constantly. Each drop is a world. He can hear the countless creatures in it, screaming for blood.

'Are you sure . . . I'm not imagining you? Sometimes, Radu,

I feel feverish, and then my brain's on fire and I see, oh, so many awful things; I have visions; I harrow hell. My brother Radu's weak; he does anything they want; that's why I'm in the oubliette, and he's lying on perfumed sheets, being buggered by some Ottoman aristocrat. I prefer the dark. I love the dark, really. I don't even mind the visions. Hell can be beautiful. Will you be my friend? I need someone to talk to sometimes. Oh, I talk to the spirits. But you seem real somehow.'

'I am real. But I'm a spirit, too.'

'If you really are a spirit, then you can go through walls, and you can flit unseen among the living.'

'I can.'

Dracula's eyes are fixed upon some other country. That is why the present darkness does not oppress him. Is he mad? the vampire thinks, for he has just left another madman, Gilles de Rais, in France, burning at the stake. 'I can't leave this place. They won't even let me out to shit. I crawl out to the furthest extent of my chain . . . they've left a pile of hay for me to wipe my ass on . . . you see how it is. Couldn't you do something for me? Fly through the palace and tell me how it really is with my brother? I imagine the worst, I call him a weakling, and yet I fear for him.'

'Yes,' says the boy vampire. 'If you like, I'll do that.'

And the one who calls himself Radu slips away into the shadow.

He has escaped from a dungeon in one place and time only to emerge in another dungeon in another world and time. But where the dungeon of Bluebeard was devoted to one man's madness, this place is more banal, its torments less singular. He slips easily beneath the crack of the iron door; he is no more than a drafty wind, a breath, a sigh. The corridor stinks of blood and excrement. There are men and women chained to the walls, thin, mutilated creatures, their eyes void of emotion. The blood stirs the boy's appetite, but he cannot stomach this much horror. As wind, he wraps himself around the dying, taking from one a vaporous taste of blood, from another a coagulating drop; he is just one of a million vermin that infest the oubliette; leeches, rats, mites, fleas, mosquitoes, ticks, each one of them a being like himself, a bloodsucker; the difference, he thinks, is of

degree, only degree. Water runs down the walls . . . foul, part
salt, part sewer water.

The air becomes less murky. The prison has many levels, and
Dracula was in the lowest, lower than the sea-bed. Now the
odour of sweat and piss and pus is mixed with attar of roses
and essence of civet cat, the rarest of perfumes. He is running
along the upper stratum of the dungeon, and above his head
are grilles through which wafts a more delicate air. He mingles
with the air; he floats; he rises; and as he siphons upward
through the vent, it is as though he has entered another world.

He swirls; fills out his human form again. He is standing in
a courtyard; the floor is a mosaic, a complex pattern, like a
Persian carpet, only done in porcelain. He can hear the sea.
Moonlight illumines a white minaret that rears up above the
domed roofs of a palace. From somewhere comes music: the
silky sawing of a *rebab*, the dizzying plucked pyrotechnics of an
'ud. They are joined by a human voice. It is the voice of a child,
a voice that reminds him so much of himself, before his changing, that he wishes he remembered how to weep.

It is the song that Dracula sang in his prison cell:

I long to lie down in my native earth . . .

But the voice is not Dracula's rough-hewn voice, poised at
the edge of manhood; it is a sweet, high treble, floating pure
above the complex cross-rhythms of lute, drum and fiddle; and
when he listens again Radu can hear that there is an audience
. . . he hears the hiatus of a hundred held breaths. As always,
when the boy hears music, he follows.

Across the courtyard of the glinting tiles. Beneath taut arches,
along a Grecian colonnade, through a second atrium with fountains, broken statuary and caged nightingales; into a grand
megaron built in the Hellenistic style, except that the murals on
the walls depict no lovely dancing kouroi, no nymphs, no gods
and goddesses, but are instead intricate, abstract patterns.

In the centre of this grand hall, there is a boy; it is the one
who has been singing. Surrounding him, reclining on rich rugs,
are courtiers, viziers, soldiers; on a grand cushion rests a prince,
and at his feet sit four nude children, two boys and two girls,
their swan-feathered wings strapped to their backs with golden
harnesses, facing the four directions like the four beasts that

surrounded the throne of God. It is strange to go from the sub-
dued hues of the night to this brash spectacle. Veiled women
sit in the sidelines. There is food everywhere: figs, mutton, and
a pastry made of paper-thin dough, eggs, chicken and powdered
sugar; kebabs soaking in lemon juice; sweet, minty tea. Why
are they eating in the middle of the night? Is it some festival?

The boy vampire, standing in the shadow just outside the
door, moves nearer to the music, and as he does he changes
shape once more. Some see a black cat, others a spotted dog;
some see a crow with bright obsidian eyes. He slips in a amongst
the musicians, squatting on the lap of a man so absorbed in the
rhythms of his drum playing that he does not notice the vampire
at all. And Radu watches the singer.

It is, he is sure, the other Radu, Dracula's brother. Not for
nothing is he called the Handsome. He is as pale as the moonlight, and he wears his black hair long, tied in a knot. He has
been dressed in the court's best finery: a jacket of red silk, a kilt
of cloth-of-gold, a boy-sized scimitar with a handle studded with
rubies. He does resemble the vampire a little; perhaps it is not
surprising that, in the dark, his brother misnamed the vampire;
but the name has stuck now, and that means – names being
carriers of magic – that the boy vampire now partakes in part
of his namesake's identity.

The boy has finished singing. He bows. There is applause.

Then the prince on the cushion speaks: 'Radu,' he says, 'don't
you know any happier songs?'

'No, Prince Mehmet,' says the singer. 'Where I come from,
there aren't any happy songs; nobody's happy there.'

Thoughtfully, Prince Mehmet twirls the end of his moustache
with a sharp-nailed index finger. 'No one at all?'

'How,' says Radu, 'can there be joy in Wallachia, when my
brother and I are hostages in Gelibolu?'

'But it's Ramadan!' says Mehmet. 'We're supposed to be feasting, not whining over lost patrimonies. Don't I treat you well?'

'Better than my brother,' says Radu.

'You're insolent,' Mehmet says, 'and the insolence makes you
even more beautiful; that's why I put up with it. But I'm growing
weary of this foolery. I've got a harem with a thousand plump,
doe-eyed women with smooth, quivering bellies, and a

thousand delicious boys with slender hips and tight, round arses, and God knows how many eunuchs; but I'm held captive to the caprice of a barbarian hostage. But it's good to hold out for more; shows you're not just another little tart.'

Mehmet claps his hands. A dancer enters the circle, leaps about, wiggles her belly, all with a great sword balanced on her head. She is youthful, unpractised; halfway through the dance, the prince holds up his hand, summons the dancer, who prostrates herself before him. He picks up the sword, gazes at it curiously, then, picking an orange from a silver platter at his feet, brings the sword slashing down. The orange is barely dented. The court bursts out laughing; then Prince Mehmet calls to one of his guards, a burly Negro, and takes the scimitar from his sword-belt. He demonstrates its sharpness by splitting the orange with one blow; then he places the sword on the belly dancer's head. He motions for the music to start up again.

She dances. There is terror in her eyes. With every jeté, the crowd gasps. She sweeps across the floor. She gains confidence. She waves her arms and clangs her finger cymbals. The audience ululates in appreciation, and some of the men throw gold, which she catches in mid-leap. She bends back, leans forward, trips, does not even have time to scream as the scimitar slits her throat and makes her head snap. You can hear the crack of bone. And now her head lolls down her back, held on by a single vertebra.

Blood sluices onto the tapestries. Prince Mehmet guffaws with delight while some of his courtiers mutter darkly about profaning the sacred month of Ramadan. Yet most of them laugh with the prince. Is it that they dare not show their feelings of revulsion? The scimitar clatters against a stack of silver goblets.

Only Radu, the singer, recoils. He runs over to the corpse. Blood is still spurting everywhere; the wings of the mock-Cherubim are soaked, but none of them react; they continue to sit, frozen by fright or apathy. The boy vampire is too hungry now; the jugular blood fairly sizzles with the body heat of sudden death; he is still catlike as he moves in and begins to feed. The body of the woman is still twitching. Her heart has not stopped beating.

Radu is shaking the woman. He cannot bring her back to life, of course. He begins to sob. He sees the cat lapping up the dancer's blood. 'Stop that . . . stop that . . .' he whispers. He tries to shoo it away, but the vampire's thirst must needs be slaked. The cat hisses, yowls, scratches at the prince's hand. Prince Radu looks into the cat's eyes. Suddenly it is as if he has seen something else . . . yes, the boy vampire thinks, the line between our two selves has been blurred . . . because Dracula called me Radu. He sees my true shape. *You know me*, the boy vampire thinks; and he fancies he hears, in his mind, the prince say *Yes, I do*.

Radu caresses the shiny sable fur. The cat purrs; he is sated and content. And the houri breathes her last. Radu weeps; and the vampire feels with him, though he does not weep, of course, being a vampire.

'Such a delicate sensibility,' says Prince Mehmet. 'I've had enough waiting. I'm going to take you right now. This weeping only gets me more and more aroused.'

He rises from his cushion. Pulls the Wallachian prince up roughly from the dancers corpse. Puts his arms around him, tries to thrust his tongue into his mouth. 'No,' says Radu softly. But his resistance is crumbling; the vampire can see that.

'No more expensive gifts, Radu,' says Mehmet. 'If you don't do what I want, I'm just going to have you impaled.'

'Your Highness!' a grizzled vizier protests. 'He is a hostage, and he's under the protection of your father the king; you know he can't be killed unless Vlad breaks the treaty—'

'Perhaps you'd care to be boiled in oil?' says the prince. 'Oh, I see.' The vizier backs away, prostrating himself all the way out of the chamber. 'Now, Radu, listen to me. I swear to you by the beard of the Prophet that by sunrise you're going to have a hard, pointed object thrust up your arse. *What* object is entirely up to you.' And with those words, he drags the young prince from the chamber, leaving the court in an uproar.

dissolve

What's in the coffin?
   My dead wife. We are taking her to be buried in West Irian.
   Carry on.
   I told you, Timmy, I had a few contrary tricks up my sleeve.

In this case, I simply told the truth. Contrariwise, they dis-
believed me.

Where do we go next?

Jakarta. Then Bali. Then, perhaps by boat to New Guinea, to
the edge of civilization; and after that, I simply don't know; the
vision is too vague.

Do you think we'll see Lauren McCandless?

We're going to see *everyone*, Timmy.

news of the world

From *Curious Times*:

Weird Rock Formations Resemble Corpse Painting

A bizarre aerial photograph of New Guinea has tongues wag-
ging and scandalsheets tattling all over the world. It was taken
by an ordinary weather satellite and this computer-enhanced
– otherwise unretouched – image was generated at the
Altongaga Observatory after a visiting astronomer joked that
what he thought was a smudge on the photograph resembled
one of the paintings of Lauren McCandless, macabre neo-
realist painter of serial killer victims, who recently disappeared into the forests of New Guinea.

Hold the image about two inches from your nose and focus
on it. Then slowly move the page away from your face. You
ought to be able to see it, though a survey of the staff in our
office shows that one in five can't do so.

Experts can't agree on *which* McCandless painting it is, but
this phenomenon – called by geologist Dr Spencer Jones a
'serendipitous occlusion of mica particles, molten quartz and
feldspar, and massive sulphur deposits thrown up by the volcanic activity in the area, resulting in the appearance of transi-
tory images on the surfaces of the mountains,' – is certainly
attracting attention. 'Definitely McCandless,' art historian
and consultant at the Los Angeles Museum of Contemporary
Art Irena Periera pointed out on CNN. 'The subtle admixture
of brimstone and ash, the sensual texturizations of flesh tones,
the pagan intensity of the subject's expression, the searing
stippling effect of the smoky quartz deposits and the crystalline arc of the ridges of quartz that highlight the dead woman's
obsidian irises . . . pure McCandless. Even though it's a
smidgin oversized for our gallery . . .'

'All this from a *smudge*?' was the title of the *Entertainment
Tonight* segment. We tend to agree . . .

dawn

A tiny village on a barren shore. The motorboat, a shuttle from the cargo ship that was on its way to Australia, unloaded a coffin and two visitors. A white man stood on the beach; it seemed that he had been on the lookout for them. He motioned to two black men sitting under the shade of a coconut tree, and they carried the coffin into a bungalow; he turned to Timmy Valentine and PJ Gallagher.

'It's amazing to see you at last,' he said. 'I got your wire.' And then: 'I feel that I ought to kneel.' And he did so, prostrating himself at Timmy's feet and knocking his forehead against the sand.

'Timmy,' said PJ, 'this is Joshua Levy, the world's leading "Valentinologist" – you remember, on the late late show one day, he was the one who had catalogued all your sightings, who had the big Jungian theory about why you manifest yourself in the world.'

'Words fail me,' said Levy, as Timmy bemusedly raised him up to his lanky six three stature and gazed up into his knotty brow and clear blue eyes. 'I'm finally face to face with God.'

Timmy said, 'Think you got the wrong guy, dude.'

'No,' said Levy. 'It's not what you think. I'm prepared to accept that you, personally, are just some spoiled young superstar who's trying to escape his poor little rich kid life. But what you represent, Timmy—'

PJ said, 'Thanks, at any rate, for offering us your hospitality.'

'More than hospitality. I'm so glad that my theories have proved correct . . . that you are going to end this particular epoch in the Valentine phenomenon by metaphorically sailing off the edge of the civilized world . . . I had a hunch it would be New Guinea; I've been waiting here for you ever since the look-alike contest . . . the TV show I did . . . when you did that spectacular transformation scene right there on television, and nobody noticed that it was more than just special effects, that it was *real* magic . . . they always call me, those *Enquirer*-type magazines, for some crackpot bullshit about you, but you and I know, don't we, Timmy?'

'I suppose we do.'

Timmy smelled air: it seemed somehow electrically charged
. . . ozone, perhaps? Or was it that, beyond this beach, there
lay the most impenetrable of all forests, the crazy quilt of eight
hundred languages, eight hundred kingdoms and eight hundred cultures that was New Guinea? He heard PJ and Levy
talking: about how they'd corresponded, on and off, since the
time of that television special; about Levy's belief that all the
Timmy Valentines of history were manifestations of the collective unconscious, warnings to the world in times of darkness;
how Levy's telegram had been awaiting them at the hotel in
Jakarta, which was how PJ finally realized that he must be on
the right track.

It doesn't matter, Timmy thought, how true or untrue their
wild theories are. It only matters that my own story is reaching
its climax. I, who for two thousand years have never really had
a native earth to lie in, may soon awaken from my millennial
nightmare and find myself . . . home.

'I'll come with you part way,' Levy said. 'I'll see you to the
foothills of the Pegunungan Maoke mountains. After that,
you're on your own. Tomorrow, we'll drive down to Jayapura
for supplies.'

And that night, in a shanty shack that served as a bar for
the village locals – a few Indonesians, some Melanesian copra
farmers, and a pith-helmeted, eccentric expatriate German who
had been there since the time of the Dutch – Timmy did what
he found himself doing more and more: told stories.

And found the past more vivid and more haunting than ever
before.

memory: 1445

The moon is full; in another courtyard, far from the one ringed
with marble and minarets, Radu the vampire finds Radu the
Handsome close to death. A spike has been thrust into his anus,
and he has been strung up next to a fig-tree. His thin, pale flesh
is bound so tight with ropes that flies are buzzing around its
lacerations. But he is not entirely dead, for the stake has been
inserted with such cunning as to rupture few vital organs; it has

not penetrated the boy's heart; it will take him days, perhaps, to die.

Radu the vampire has crept out from the dungeon once again at Dracula's bidding. Again, he is a black cat, invisible against the lush foliage of this inner courtyard. Again, he drawn to the sound of singing, for in his agony the boy still sings of his lost homeland. It is a hot and windy night; the very air tastes almost as salt as human blood.

A lone guard keeps watch, but he has fallen asleep beneath the fig-tree. The cat comes closer. The pavement is rough, the flagstones broken, not like the elegant tiled courtyard outside the feasting chamber; weeds thrust in mad profusion through the rock. As always he hears the sea; it affords a shimmering accompaniment to the boy's lament. To hear the song is painful; more painful yet to know how meaningless his suffering is.

Radu looks down from his impalement. 'I see you,' he says, 'I know who you really are.'

Thus it is that the vampire knows that the boy does not fear him. I take the shape of what men fear most, he thinks; if he fears nothing, he will see me as I really am. 'Who am I?' he asks the boy.

'You are myself,' says Radu. 'My mirror. You are the secret part of me; you are what I most yearn to be.'

The pain must be unbearable. He cries out – feebly, for the stake in his innards has sapped almost all his strength – then loses consciousness.

'No!' cries the boy vampire who shares Radu's name. 'You don't want to be my mirror . . . you don't want to share the darkness with me . . .' and he thinks of Bluebeard, who also claimed to see himself mirrored in the boy vampire (he had yet another name then, did he not? What was it? Ah yes . . . *Jeannot*) and who wanted nothing more than to become just like him. Am I the dark mirror to *all* men? he muses, and the thought fills him with surpassing melancholy. He wonders whether there will ever come a time when he would willingly trade places with some lost human soul.

For a long time he gazes at Radu beneath the moonlight. The boy's pale features are mottled by the shadows of the fig branches. The blood still courses, he thinks, the heart still thumps a little. The blood has hardened where the spike has ravaged his rectum; it glistens on the wood like a dark sap. 'Radu, Radu,' the boy says, 'what have you lived for?' And howls his anger to the churning sea.

He thinks of attacking Prince Mehmet in his sleep. Where can this prince be found in this palatial compound? Surely by his scent . . .

He has become the wind. He spirals up from the flagstones. He embraces the boy. His essence seeps into the boy's pores, into his nostrils, mingles with the breath of dying. There . . . there is the princeling's odour . . . a musky man's smell liberally doused with attar of roses . . . there, there, still clinging to the bruised flesh . . . there . . . he wraps his tenuous substance round the arms, the narrow chest, the eyes that gaze on emptiness, the lips that taste salt wind and salt tears . . . tenderly he draws the blood from wounds, from sores, from oozing lacerations . . . he loves the boy to death, the way the west wind once loved the youth. Hylas in the old myth he once heard at his mother's knee . . .

My mother, thinks the vampire.

He has not thought about his mortal life for fourteen centuries.

The wind squeezes the boy tight and stops his heart. The heat of his hunger sublimates the blood and sends it frothing up through every aperture so that a gaseous blood spurts from the lips, nostrils, eyeballs, sweat pores of the boy; and the vampire wind sucks it all in, is sated, and, growing heavy with appeasement, condenses, resolves once more into the shape of a human child.

With the smell of Mehmet firmly imprinted in his memory.

'No,' he cries once more. 'You don't want to be like me. There will be no more suffering for you.' And saying so, he rips the boy's heart from his chest and flings it over the parapet into the sea.

He is a bloodhound now. The scent is stronger, fiercer. He can tell that the sultan's heir was in the courtyard earlier tonight. Gloating, perhaps, jeering at Radu's torments. Anger drives him as he follows the odour. Through the palace kitchens where the dregs of the evening's banquet are now being hastily devoured

by the servants, for dawn will come soon, and with the dawn
the observance of the Ramadan fast until the hour of nightfall.
Through endless corridors, all decorated with writings, designs,
and abstract motifs – for these people are not fond of graven
images – through empty hallways, over vast carpets with intricate patterns, and the smell grows ever more powerful now as
he ascends a spiral stair that girds a white, phallic tower capped
with a golden dome.

At last he enters the prince's bedroom.

The bed is huge and strewn with rose-petals. A sheer white
canopy hangs over it from posts of solid gold. Marmoreal moonlight shines from a white balcony. Mehmet reclines on a silken
cushion, studying a scroll by the light of an oil lamp. There
are others on the bed too. There is a sleeping woman with
mountainous breasts, who tosses and turns. There is a little boy
with gilded eyelids and painted lips. There is a eunuch at the
foot of the bed, who has fallen asleep over his lute.

The boy who has drunk Radu's blood says, softly, 'Mehmet.'

Mehmet sees no reflection in the shiny lantern, and so looks
up. 'Radu . . .' he says softly. 'You *did* come back from the
grave.' Radu can smell the terror on him, but the prince is striv-
ing to mask his fear, as a well-trained prince should. 'You told
me you were going to come back and take revenge . . .'

Radu does not speak.

'But you're not even bleeding,' says Mehmet. 'I watched you
scream as that rod was rammed into you. And I wept inside,
don't you know that? I spoke in jest when I threatened you,
truly I did. But a prince cannot jest. The words that fall from
my lips must always be true. Have you come back only to
reproach me, then, before you return to paradise, and the celestial maidens, and all the pleasures you denied me?'

'No,' says Radu. 'I came to kill.'

But this is the strange thing about it: he does not want to kill
this man. He does not want to kill at all. For he remembers poor
crazed Gilles de Rais, desperately trying to prove himself evil
enough so that he could be worthy of receiving the keys to
the kingdom of the night. It is since his confrontation with the
madman who calls himself Bluebeard that he has begun to question the nature of good and evil – the existence of absolutes –

of God. He does not believe there will a harrowing of hell, or a paradise with doe-eyed houris. He believes only in the present.

The prince says, 'Well, that is fair enough. I killed you, Radu; you've returned as an avenging spirit; I suppose it is only reasonable that you should kill me. Yes, I'm cruel. If I had lived to be sultan, no doubt I'd have been a hideous despot. But you see, in my own way, I am just; and Radu, I did love you, for you were beautiful, and when you sang, I wanted to forget the Ottoman empire, the war between our peoples, the hatred that brought your father to Constantinople in chains, and left you and your brother hostages. Radu, it was your singing that I loved the most. I have whores and catamites aplenty to keep my member sturdy and erect. But none of them sang with such pathos, such purity . . .'

And with those words Radu knows what he must say. He sits down beside the prince. The child, the eunuch, and the woman have not stirred; it is as if an enchantment has taken hold of them.

Mehmet caresses the vampire, flinches at the iciness of his pale shoulder. 'If I kiss you,' he says, 'my tongue will turn into an icicle and break off.' His fear is still there, still palpable; but he has managed a little joke.

'Then do not kiss me,' Radu says. 'I am not flesh and blood as you know it, Mehmet; I cannot yield to your embrace, however passionate, feigned or unfeigned. But I can still sing.'

'Sing, Radu,' says the heir to the Turkish throne. 'Ease my suffering.' He reaches over to the eunuch and takes his lyre. It is a Macedonian boy, towheaded, probably not willingly castrated. Radu remembers his own disfigurement. Again it troubles him that so many images from before his changing have begun to surface. The prince shoves the eunuch off his bed with one foot; the musician crumples to the carpet and curls up again. Mehmet hands the boy vampire the harp. 'Sing, Radu,' he says, 'of lost hearths and vanished homes. I want to be sad. I didn't ask to be a prince, you know. I didn't ask to be cruel. I'm sorry I killed you, Radu, so terribly sorry. Sing, Radu, sing.'

'On one condition,' says Radu.

'Anything,' says the prince.

'You must free Dracula.'

'Why? He's always hated you, envied your beauty, called you a sissified masculine strumptet; why, you yourself told me you did not mind if I threw away the key.' And so Radu is made privy, for the first time, to the sibling rivalry between the brothers. 'If I release him, especially with him knowing it is at your behest, he'll think it was in payment for giving in to my . . . craven lusts.'

Radu thinks of the chained boy in the dungeon. He's right, he thinks, he'll probably hate me for it, and he'll never believe that the prince has never violated me. Maybe it's better if I don't ask for his freedom.

And yet . . . Radu remembers how, in spite of all he said, the boy was concerned for him, begged him to find out how he was, worried about him incessantly. He cannot leave him there to rot with the rats and the excrement.

'Free Dracula,' he says again, 'and then I'll sing.'

20

MISTAH MCCANDLESS, HE DEAD

angel

Finally, after a journey of intense torment, Lauren had come
face to face once more with the Angel of Death.

The angel stood at the shore of a lake of fire. Beside him was
a host of the dead; and there were many faces that he recognized. There was the shaman who had once englobed the angel
in an amulet. There stood the whores of Patpong, some dis-
membered, some mutilated, yet each in her way still beautiful,
for Lauren had made from each one's dying a fierce, im-
passioned work of art. There, too, stood the dead that Lauren
had heard about from stories that were told about Timmy Valentine: the murdered children of Tiffauges, the slaughtered
Aztecs of Tenochtitlán, the victims of the Holocaust . . . they
stood there in their shadowy multitudes, on the shore, all the
way out into the lake, and the lake spewed forth fire and brimstone, and exhaled great sulphurous clouds, and was as deep
as hell.

'Lauren,' said the Angel, 'we meet again.'

'But I'm not on the drugs anymore,' Lauren said. 'I threw
them all overboard.'

'This is reality, Lauren.'

'Reality?'

'Yeah.'

'What is reality, Angel? Can you tell me? I mean, you're an
angel, aren't you? Tell me.'

'*Vanitas*,' said the angel.

twilight

The nearest town: a dull and sleepy place. Shanties, shacks, and a few colonial mansions, most dilapidated, half crumbling into the island's all-consuming vegetation. A street full of merchants, Indian and Chinese mostly; a *pasar malam*, a street market just beginning to set up as the sun went down; the night air redolent with the smell of peanut sauce. A Christian church and a mosque stood side by side in a little plaza.

Through it all moved Joshua Levy's Landrover, with the coffin in the back, the two Melanesians on either side; Levy driving, PJ drifting in and out of his contrary trance, and Timmy observing the sights, sounds, smells of this town on the border of madness.

Here and there they stopped. Levy jumped out and bargained for provisions. '*Mahal, mahal*,' he said in Indonesian, shaking his head, refusing to count out more banknotes from the stack of thousand-rupiah notes in his pocket. '*Berapa itu?*'

Then, to his servants in Pidgin, '*Yu kisim dispela*,' making them haul more supplies onto the Landrover.

'Quite a linguist,' Timmy said to PJ.

'I'm not impressed,' said PJ, meaning that he was.

Timmy pushed on further into the crowded market. The smells! Sweat, flowers, fruit, dogshit, *saté* sizzling on charcoal, unmuffled cars. Then, glancing down a long alleyway bordered on either side by canvas stalls. Timmy saw something he knew could not be there.

'PJ, PJ,' he said, pointing. 'Do you see that?'

'No,' said PJ. But Timmy could tell he meant yes.

At the end of the alleyway, there was a great blue mist, and beyond that mist the outlines of a house. Timmy's house in Encino . . . the one with the great wrought iron gates, the gargoyles, the circular driveway, the marble pool, the attic where he had built the model railroad to end all model railroads, and poured out his life to Carla, the Jungian analyst.

Timmy said, 'It's begun. Our retreat from the here and now. We're seeing the edge of reality, the place where dreams collide.'

He began walking toward the house. PJ followed, although it seemed that he was walking away at the same time. Behind them, the Landrover moved slowly, squeezing through the throng, the coffin going bumpety-bump in the back. The mass of people seemed to thin out, grow translucent, almost; realities were shifting. He remembered the sensation from Pompeii. The very earth was bursting from its chrysalid confinement. Death and rebirth were happening here, where a new portal had opened into the bowels of the world.

In no time at all, it seemed, they had reached the gate. There in the front was the statue of Konrad Stolz, lifted from one of Timmy's old gravesites. There was the house, a wacky amalgam of architectural styles from Frank Lloyd Wright to urban hacienda.

Darkness fell swiftly: the lights and sound of the *pasar malam* were obliterated by curtain of blackness; and then, just as suddenly, the moon came on like a spotlight, and a shaft of light ran down the side of the house, through the driveway, over the face of the statue, onto the face of Timmy Valentine.

The gates creaked open.

'I guess it's OK to . . .' Timmy began.

But PJ was already forging ahead. And behind them, the others followed. The air was abruptly chill and windy, like a Hallowe'en night in Hollywood. They trooped across the front lawn, a weird procession indeed, with the coffin held on the shoulders of the Melanesians, with PJ walking backward, with Joshua Levy squinting at everything and pausing now and then to shake his head and take notes . . . and . . . was that music in the distance? . . . wasn't it a grotesque version of *Frère Jacques*, all played on double basses? What was that from . . . Mahler's First Symphony, wasn't it? . . . the movement that's supposed to represent the funeral of the hunter, with all the animals bearing the dead human's coffin . . . joyful yet macabre. How do I even know that? Timmy thought. And then he remembered Stephen Miles . . . the old conductor . . . the madman . . . the pyromaniac. Wasn't he dead?

The music sped up, transmuted into a bitter parody of Viennese café music . . . that was in the Mahler too.

The front door swung open and they stepped inside.

'Master Timothy,' said Rudy Lydick, elegantly tuxedoed, coming down the sweeping staircase and bowing.

'But . . .' said Timmy.

'I'm dead? Alas, Master Timothy, I am. I'm only a ghost, kept alive in the cauldron of your memories. But not, I fear, much longer . . .'

A woman stepped into the foyer. Middle-aged, still firm, her hair a mess; trying to brush out the tangles before anyone could catch them—

'Carla,' said Timmy.

'Hi.' She held out her arms and they embraced. Oh, she was dead all right; his living flesh passed right through her arms.

'Oh, Carla, I've missed you . . . there've been so many times when I needed someone to explain me to myself, and . . .'

'Hush, Timmy. You don't have to say anything. Oh, my, you're a real boy now! You could be my son. I've missed you too, Timmy, as much as a heap of earth and offal can miss anything. That was a great adventure that we had.'

The music welled up, climaxed; then came applause. And then, behind Carla, there was Stephen Miles . . . an old man but still spry, immaculately dressed to conduct a symphony orchestra, his baton still in his hand.

'A great adventure. Indeed.'

'We became separated somehow,' Timmy said. 'The house in Junction was burning down . . . we rode the dark train into the forest of the mind . . . and then what? The witch captured me . . . you were killed . . .'

'Yes. But the journey soon will end.'

'These final moments,' said Carla, 'have been given to us, so we can travel the last few miles together, because of what we once were to one another.'

'Let us rejoice,' said Stephen Miles.

vision-seeker

'Do you see it?' Timmy asked him in the alley, pointing at the blue mist in the distance.

'No,' said PJ, meaning yes.

He saw a house. A house on the side of a mountain, looming over the street that had the only stop sign in Junction, Idaho

. . . the house they called *the spook house*. And he started running
toward it . . . backward, always backward, because time itself
was spiralling backward faster than light . . . he was a kid again,
a dirty boy, half red, half white, and his two dirty white boy
friends, and they were biking up toward the spook house and
sneaking inside and . . .

In the bushes, peering at the house, PJ turned to Terry and
David. They looked back at him. Alike as peas, people always
said, but no, you always tell by the pattern of their freckles . . .
Terry's cheeks had the heel of Italy, David's the blob of France.
Then PJ suddenly realized something. 'Dudes,' he said, 'you're
both dead. I killed you, Terry.'

'And Terry killed me,' said David.

'Then why are we here?' said Terry.

The house: a withered woman suckling an animal at her
breasts . . . but is it milk? or blood?

The animal leaps from the woman's arms . . . and it's Timmy
. . . but before the twins can run screaming away PJ stops them
. . . and Timmy, softly, says, 'Forgive me.'

'How can I?' PJ screams. 'I can't even forgive myself.'

dissolve: attic

Now where?

Up to the attic, Timmy. Take my hand.

But Carla—

Yes, I know. You're afraid. But you'll get used to fear; one
day fear will be your friend.

memory: 1445

Radu is sitting at Mehmet's feet, in a grand throne room in the
palace at Gelibolu.

They bring in Dracula. He has been bathed and anointed with
perfumes; he has been dressed in a becoming tunic – saffron-
coloured and embroidered with little topazes – and wears a
jewelled turban. Dracula's face resembles his brother Radu's

closely, but where Radu's eyes held sweetness, his are bitter; where his lips smiled, Dracula's are twisted in perpetual scorn.

Mehmet says, 'My wayward little dragon, you are free – thanks to your brother's earnest supplication, and his pledge that you will behave with proper civility toward my father and myself, your captors.'

Dracula rushes at the vampire who calls himself Radu. 'Cata-mite!' he screams. 'Whore! When I become King of Wallachia, I'm going to ram a spike up your all-too-eager arsehole. At least I've learnt one good thing from you people – how to make a man really suffer.'

Radu looks at Prince Mehmet; the prince looks back.

'If only you knew,' says the one who now calls himself Radu, the son of the Dragon. 'But you never will.' For the first Radu is already dead, his flesh consumed by carrion crows, his bones cremated and tossed into the Adriatic Sea.

junction

Do you recognize this place?

Yes . . . it's the train layout that we used to tell the story of my life! There it goes . . . the HO tracks, tunnelling beneath sofas, rounding the legs of an old Victrola, climbing a mountain made from a stack of books. And here are some of the buildings I put up . . . the Coliseum . . . the cave of the Sibyl . . . the Opernhaus in Thauberg . . . even your office in New York, Carla. But there's new stuff, too. I don't remember making that building . . . oh, it's the Lennon Auditorium in Universal City, isn't it? Where Angel won the look-alike competition. And look . . . there's the train station in Junction, Idaho. Look at that waiting room . . . the weathering's been so carefully done . . . must have taken an eternity. And those two trees . . . oh! Look! Transylvania. Ruined castles. Tiny figures of mediaeval boyars . . . and a forest of impaled people . . . the spikes are toothpick-sized . . . it's bringing back another remembrance . . .

Yes. But there's more. Can you hear it?

A train whistle somewhere in the distance. The puff of a steam engine . . . the clatter of wheels. Here it comes. It sounds almost real. Look, it's the Jupiter, the first transcontinental, a 4-4-0 engine, rushing over my papier-mâché Seven Hills of Rome and . . . what's happening? Is the train layout getting bigger somehow? Is this some kind of *Alice in Wonderland* thing where the world gets bigger and smaller after you start shrooming on the different sides of the caterpillar's throne?

The train is pulling into the station.

I know what that means.

Yes. It means that we've stepped away once more from the fabric of reality . . . and we're taking the choo-choo train into the dark forest of the soul . . . toward Vampire Junction.

To suck our souls away . . .

All aboard . . . all stations west . . . west . . . into the sunset . . . into the territory of the dead . . .

memory: 1462

The dead! The Turks are invading Wallachia, and Mehmet II, now ruler of the empire, paces in his tent, waiting for nightfall, waiting for Radu to awaken. He has made an ivory coffin for him to sleep in, and the boy travels everywhere with the sultan's baggage train, drawn by black horses, protected from sunlight by a canopy of black cloth. Nights, Mehmet has the coffin brought to his tent.

It is not for carnal pleasure – who, after all, can truly enjoy intercourse with the living dead? and the sultan always travels with a full complement of concubines and catamites – It is so that Radu can sing to him. They have been travelling for days without a battle. As the twilight begins to fade, the sounds of night begin to infiltrate the coffin, and the boy awakens.

He pushes aside the coffin lid, sits up; candlelight fills the tent; he sees the sultan pacing back and forth impatiently. He is hungry, as he always is when he first awakens. Abstractedly, Mehmet says, 'Radu, Radu. I'm sorry, but I've forgotten to order your supper.'

He claps his hands. Two guards bring in a prisoner – some serf, no doubt – his wrists bound, his demeanour abject. The boy pounces; he feeds. But he drinks only sparingly. There is a point at which the feeding alters the nature of the victim; there is no need to make more vampires. After the bloodletting, the guards untie the serf and kick him out of the tent. It has been thus, every night, for eighteen years; there must be rumours by now, for Radu is always and forever a boy of twelve.

'Shall I sing?' he asks the sultan.

'No, Radu. Today I've heard talk about a manmade forest . . . a thing awesome to behold, terrible to describe. I want you to come and see it with me.'

Mehmet calls for his horse. The stallion rears up when it senses the boy – for animals do not have the gift of illusion, which allows men to see what they want to see instead of a thing's true nature – but Radu speaks sharply to him in the language of night: *Be still.*

And the horse is still; Mehmet mounts, and he scoops up the boy vampire, and sits him in the saddle, between his knees, as though he were his own child.

They ride into the night. Behind them, the same two guardsmen. No more than two? the boy thinks. Where they are going must not hold much danger.

In a while they reach the marvel that messengers spoke of.

There is, indeed, a forest not marked on any map. It is a forest of human beings. Radu has never smelled so much blood. The air is thick with it. The men, women and children are naked, and through each one of them is a long, sharp pike planted in the earth. Many are not yet dead, but wail, moan, or stare. There are row upon row of them, and they stretch in every direction, merging with the real forest at the horizon; you cannot tell where the dead end and the trees begin. It is execution on an unimaginable scale.

More of the sultan's soldiers are there already, lighting torches; the flickering light reveals more and more of the spectacle. Mehmet and Radu dismount. Here is a row of little children, aesthetically arranged by height, each one impaled through the rectum. Here are women whose breasts have been hacked off; here are men with those breasts stuffed into their mouths. Here an assortment of limbless dwarfs; their arms and legs have been threaded together and are hanging from another pole. Some are impaled through the gut, and are spread-eagled in the air as though poised for flight. Here are women with spikes rammed into their vaginas; here are others swinging on hooks that have caught on their ribcages; here is a necklace of children's heads, and there another necklace of men's hands. There is a whole section of women who have been completely flayed; their skins hang alongside their bodies.

The stench is overpowering.

'How many?' Mehmet calls out.

One of his men, who has been doing a count, shouts back, 'More than ten thousand, your majesty . . . so far. But we haven't reached the end.'

The astonishing thing, he realizes, is that there is an art to it, this tapestry of death. Two avenues of taller pikes meet at right angles to form a cross; the land slopes uphill a little, and at the upper end of the cross, where the face of the saviour would be on an actual crucifix, are the shorter children, impaled in concentric rings; their skin catches the moonlight and forms a silvery halo. It is, in a sense, a religious icon.

I should tremble at this, thinks Radu. Am I not susceptible to the emblems of divinity, the crosses, the holy water, the consecrated host? Yet he feels only the slightest of *frissons*.

This is when he understands for the first time that the symbols are losing their power. In time, there will be no more faith. Perhaps it was my own superstition, he thinks, that gave those signifiers of God their strength.

'The voivode, your brother, did this,' says the sultan. 'Perhaps it wasn't such a good idea for you to have saved him from my dungeon. My men call him *kaziklu bey* – the impaler!'

But doesn't Mehmet remember what he did to the *real* Radu? the boy vampire thinks. Doesn't it occur to him that Dracula may have learned his ways from his Turkish captors? It is a supreme irony among mortals, he thinks, that they always decry in others the things they practise themselves.

'I swear to you, Radu,' says the sultan, 'that I'm going to dethrone this monster. I'm going to to make *you* dumnator of Wallachia!'

'But Mehmet,' Radu says softly, 'I'm a monster too.'

night

. . . and the train moved on.

And through its windows they glimpsed . . . so many worlds.

New Guinea, itself woven from the fabric of fantasy; the greenery burnished by the moon, the clarity of the starlit night, the isolated villages. Tribesmen, looking up at some unwonted sound, saw no train pass, of course; they would not have known where to look for it; for they journeyed in the rustle of the wind through the dense dank undergrowth . . . and the birds blew the whistles and the clatter of wheels was the stutter of frogs' mating calls.

Beyond the canopy of darkness there were other sights if you pressed your nose harder to the window. There was the mountain where the mage still prayed to Ahura-Mazda, and the cave where the Sibyl still prophesied; the castle of Tiffauges where Bluebeard still tortured the peasant children; the stake where he burned next to Joan of Arc; beside them, the witches of Salem swung from the branches of a mighty banyan.

'Look,' said Timmy, for there were the avenues of New York, the alleys of Thauberg, the cobbled streets of old London . . . the domes of Constantinople . . . the Carpathian Mountains.

And behind those mountains there was another mountain, too, a new mountain still thrusting its way out of the earth. Sometimes you saw it, through a gap in the many overlapping illusions. Sometimes just a funnel of smoke; sometimes a smear of red-hot lava in the blackness. They gave it different names according to the whim of the hour, Mt Doom being one of the favourites . . . but sometimes they called it Timmy's Hill, and sometimes they called it Inferno, and sometimes they called it simply Olympus, the abode of the gods.

At one point they crossed the border into Papua New Guinea. How did they know this? 'Signs are all in Pidgin,' said Levy, and the mood of the two Melanesians lightened, too. They were, according to Levy, members of a Liberation Front that was fighting for a United New Guinea, somewhere in the jungle, no one knew where; he had taken them in one day, vouching for them when they were about to be beaten up by Indonesian police.

So many untold stories! thought Timmy Valentine. And yet it must all end.

Stephen, PJ and Carla took turns sitting up with the coffin of Lady Chit . . . watching her . . . wondering if she would awaken.

She did not; yet her body was uncorrupted; it was clear that she hovered between death and undeath.

Only when they reached the end of the line would they know which way she would turn.

angel

'But what do you want me to do?' cried Lauren McCandless.

'What you do best,' said Angel Todd. 'Paint dead yellow women. There is one last one left to paint, ain't there? One final victim of my big old swathe through history.'

'What do you mean?' said Lauren. 'Who did you kill now? Not Chit,' he cried. But who else could the angel mean?

'This time, though, you'd best use more than paint. You'd best paint her with your soul. Who knows, you may cause a miracle to happen.'

'A miracle?'

'You might bring her here . . . to the brink of the abyss . . . and then we'll see if she wants to jump.'

And the angel laughed.

night

. . . and the journey continued.

night

PJ woke from a dream. He had seen Shannah Gallagher, sitting by the fireplace at their house in Junction, in the dead of winter; crept down from the bedroom, didn't know why, maybe he'd wet the bed or something and needed consoling. Reached out to touch her, whispered, 'Mommy,' but when she turned to embrace him his touch shattered her like an expensive vase that you could never glue together again and then staring into the fireplace he could see devils dancing . . .

night

He dreamed that Pamina's skin was hanging from a pike, streaming in the wind like one of Dracula's pennants . . .

memory: 1462

Tirgoviste has fallen. The final stronghold on the Arges has fallen; and Dracula, fleeing to Transylvania, has been captured by Matthias, King of Hungary.

He is once more in chains. In another dungeon – but are not all dungeons alike? – the boy vampire comes to him. Calls from the shadows: 'Dracula, Dracula.'

'No one calls me by my baby-name,' says Dracula, 'not to my face, at least. You must not mock me; I am still voivode, and my Christian name is Vlad.'

'But don't you know me?'

Dracula is pensive. In the light of the cell's lone torch, his face seems deeply furrowed. 'You sound like Radu,' he says. 'But Radu must be a young man now; your voice seems to come out of the past. It's my delirium, isn't it? I'm imagining you.'

'No,' says Radu.

'Then you must be a spirit.'

'In a way.'

'If you're a spirit, then you must have died. Well, you're better off that way. I couldn't bear to think of you and that Turk . . . I think of you each time I ram a stake up one of my recalcitrant subjects . . . or one of those Turks . . . I think of you and of how I should have fought for you. I was weak then, but no longer. Would things have been different if I had been beautiful, and you the homely one? Would I have stabbed Mehmet in his

bed when he tried to ravish me? God, I don't know. How I
loved you, brother! And how you hurt me.'

'But you screamed insults at me in the sultan's throne room
. . . called me a catamite, a whore.'

'Only because I saw how powerless I was.'

'I suppose you're no longer powerless. I've seen what your
power can do. I saw the forest of the dead.'

'Yes, yes,' says Dracula, 'there was a kind of art to it, wasn't
there? I created the spectacle in the shape of a cross, because
I'm a Christian king, and the work I do is God's will. But I didn't
think of God when I killed those people, brother . . . I thought
of you!'

So that was why twenty thousand people were put to death,
the vampire thinks. Even those murders, even the most abhor-
rent of human actions . . . it all came down to love in the end
. . . all the great horrors of the world, he thinks, are finally
domestic tragedies . . . it is love that causes death. Is there then
no meaning at all to the humans' lives, no comfort? *Vanitas
vanitatis.* Vanity of vanities, all is vanity.

Dracula weeps.

morning

At the end of the line, the sleeping car, the seats, the windows,
the curtains, the train tracks, all faded away, and they were left,
just before sunrise, at the foot of the volcano.

The forest had been cleared with machetes, and there was a
building on stilts, a teakwood house. It was, in fact, the house
from Lady Chit's estate, plucked whole from Bangkok and
brought to Irian on the wings of dream. Something familiar, PJ
thought, feeling the contrary mood lift a little: the calm, he
thought, before the grand finale.

The only difference was that there seemed to be a tower
sprouting from the carved roof, a tower with a white, winding
stair that led up through the jungle canopy to God knows
where.

People were milling about in the clearing. They were familiar
faces, many of them. But they all had a see-through quality, as

though they, like the house, were only partly there. Wasn't that
Shannah again, his mother, running through the forest in a
deerskin dress, her hair braided, her feet shod with moccasins?
And there were Terry and David Gish again . . . straight out of
childhood . . . riding their bikes uphill . . . toward the crater in
the sky. And two more friends were coming down the steps –
people he had not seen since the big fire in Junction Idaho, at
the filming of *The Motion Picture*. They had disappeared somewhere with Angel, hadn't they? Or had they been here all along,
waiting for the consummation of the story?

Now and then, the earth rumbled. The volcano was very
close. But they did not seem to mind.

'Petra,' he said.

'Brian Zottoli,' said Timmy Valentine.

The four of them embraced; in the background, Stephen Miles
and Carla Rubens stood and stared about the clearing. They
were all faint, these people, sometimes mere outlines of people,
shimmering in the half-light of the Irian dawn. He could see his
old friends, but he could barely feel their embrace; for they were
wind, all wind.

'Come up to the house,' Petra said. 'You're just in time for
breakfast.'

Joshua Levy and the silent Melanesians were carrying the
coffin upstairs. They took off their shoes and stepped into the
chamber painted with the murals of hell. There was a difference,
after all. The paint was new on these walls; there were no cracks
in the tempera; in fact, the infernal flames were so vivid they
seemed to leap forth from the plaster. In fact . . . he could hear
the crackling . . . the cries of the damned.

'Tea or coffee?' said Brian Zottoli, and it was Rudy Lydick
who served them from a silver tray.

They laid the coffin down beneath the image of the compassionate Buddha, who sat, palms folded, on the western wall,
his back to the kingdom of the dead. Was it imagination again,
or were the painted eyes blinking . . . indeed, weeping? And
were the lips, which even now were parted as though in speech,
now closed? Clearly this was no earthly place at all, but a
chamber in the labyrinth of the soul.

They chatted, they laughed, they traded stories. Nobody

mentioned that some of them were already dead, and that others might die soon. Or that this very meeting was an anomaly, taking place somewhere outside space and time, in the territory of the unconscious.

'When the sun comes up,' said Petra, 'you must go to the observation tower and look at the painting.'

'It's a lovely tower,' said Brian. 'We call it the beanstalk.'

'Where's Angel?' Timmy said, frowning.

'Asleep,' said Petra. 'We put him to bed just before you came. But we have the whole day, before the two of you do what you have to do.'

PJ downed his coffee. It was New Guinea coffee, he noted wryly, mild and a little tart. Perhaps the coffee was their only anchor to the real world.

'And Lauren?' Timmy persisted.

'Didn't he tell you in his fax?' said Petra. 'He—'

'So it's true then,' said Timmy.

The two Melanesians spoke for the first time, in an uncanny unison: '*Mistah McCandless i dai pinis.*'

'Shall we go see?' said Petra Shiloh.

The spiral staircase began in front of the room with all the Buddha images (that room was almost identical to the one in Bangkok) and Petra, who led the way, unlatched the trapdoor that led through the roof. They climbed. Tree branches swished across their faces. A monkey glared at them, then swung away. Birds sang; a serpent slithered by.

Bringing up the rear of the procession was the coffin.

They climbed and climbed. The branches thinned; at length they burst through the leafy canopy onto a deck with a railing. They leaned the coffin on the railings, facing the mountain. The sky glowed with the thousand reds of dawn . . . the white railing a neon pink, the silver clasps on the coffin bright as rubies.

And there it was: the mountain of a thousand names. It was quiet at the moment, save for a trickle of glowing scarlet that streaked its lip . . . like the lip of a vampire.

Past the stream of lava you could see an image etched into the mountain side. Was it an image? Or coloured smudges on the basalt? No. It was an image. It was somehow embedded in the rock . . . and . . . though it was far too huge to have been painted on by human hands . . . the hand of Lauren McCandless was unmistakable.

The coffin was only vaguely suggested; the lid half off, the outlines partly drawn by ridges in the rock itself. Lying in the coffin was a woman. She was nude – the part that you could see – and her long, black hair trailed down from the coffin in rivulets of obsidian, all the way down to the carpet of foliage from which the mountain sprang. It seemed that parts of the face were only half-formed, that features were being filled in even as they watched.

'Open the coffin!' PJ said suddenly.

The others hesitated to obey this odd request, so PJ undid the clasps and heaved the lid off . . . and thus he knew for certain who the image in the mountain was . . . it was an exact reflection of his dead wife, down to the parted lips, the hair that had just now tumbled out, the hair that seemed to have grown and grown since Chit's death.

'So . . . where *is* Lauren McCandless, then?' asked Timmy. 'If he's dead, where is he buried?'

And PJ suddenly saw the truth. He pointed to the painting, still forming out of the rock, and said, '*That*'s Lauren.'

21

OFF THE EDGE OF THE WORLD

flying

She is dead, but still she dreams:
 Flying. Flying on the wings of the raven.

memory: 79 A.D.

. . . brimstone . . . a child's footsteps patter on a splintering mosaic, bittertoast smell of charring feet . . . fleeing, mountain thunder, then . . .
 blood *spatter spatter spatter* bursting *spatter spatter spatter* boiling on the hot stones *spatter spatter spatter*
 . . . marble columns snapping like bones over the screaming and . . .
 . . . blood *spatter spatter spatter*
 . . . bloodgutted eyes through the sulphur-haze and the screaming and
 . . . through the ash-hail, fangs glitter blood *spatter* glitter *spatter* glitter *spatter* glitter

dusk

And up and up
 Up the mountain to the crater
 That leads to the heart of the world
 And up
 Up

flying

Look, PJ. We're inside the painting now. We can't make it out
any more. I think we're climbing up Chit's arm. There's a winding path that seems to be a pale blue vein. There's the edge of
the coffin lid. Tell the pilot to bring the chopper closer . . . closer
. . . throw down the ladder . . . look, there's a ledge, we can
get out for a moment . . .
    Kneel down. Take a look at this, PJ! There's these spots all
over the rock . . . like the dots in a printed photograph, but
magnified a millionfold . . . that's how the painting's built up,
out of these little dots . . . it's no trick of the light . . . it's real.
    Pointillism. Not Lauren's style.
    But look. Closer. That's blood, PJ. That's human blood.
Spread so thin it's maybe only one molecule thick or something
but I can still smell it. I didn't believe you before, but now I can
see that it's true . . . this monster mural is literally the body and
blood of Lauren McCandless . . . he's turned himself into one
of his own paintings . . . splayed himself all over the side of the
mountain . . . and the painting's still being painted . . . will she
get up from the coffin? And when she rises, will she be dead
or alive? In the end, it depends on what we do when we reach
the summit of the volcano.
    Let's get back in the chopper.
    Oh God, PJ, smell the brimstone . . .

flying

She dreams of the cold grey space that separates the world from
the mirrored world. That is all that she is, this virtual space,
this not-quite-being.
    She dreams of sleeping in the arms of the angel.
    She dreams of coming back to life.
    She dreams she is the world.
    She dreams of being dead forever.

memory: 1476

Restored to the throne of Wallachia by his erstwhile captor, having transferred his allegiance from Orthodoxy to Catholicism, Dracula is fighting the Turks again. But this time he cannot win. He is left with two hundred loyal Moldovans, and the Turks are as numberless as the stars.

He waits atop a hill. He is surrounded. The Moldovans are being slaughtered as they cluster around their leader. As the sun begins to set, Dracula sees that there are only ten men left. Around him, radiating out from him like the spokes of a catharine wheel, are the men, pierced through with flaming arrows, shredded by cannon, decapitated, stripped; a thousand rivers of blood seem to flow from him; it is as if the very hill is wearing a crown of thorns. He waits.

As the sun disappears beneath the horizon, Radu awakens from the chryselephantine coffin that Mehmet has had made for him: its gold clasps cunningly wrought with the Holy Name of God, its ivory panels carved with interlocking mandalas, and Radu's name etched in Arabic, Cuneiform, Latin, Greek and Egyptian.

Vlad Tepes, whom no one dares call Dracula to his face, waits.

Radu knows where he is. The hill is drenched with blood, yet that blood is all dead; Radu can hear the one heart that still beats, the heart at the heart of the flames. Dracula gives a great cry as a lance rives his back; in his tent, Radu hears, picks out his mighty voice from the death-rattles all around them, for a field of the dying surrounds the hill of the dead.

'I hear him,' he says to Mehmet.

And the sultan says, 'Then go to him.'

The boy waves to his litter-bearers, ten tall Ethiopes; he sits down on the gilded throne that Mehmet has had made for him; they hoist him up, he barks out a command, and they hurry through the field of corpses.

metaphors

This is how Joshua Levy will try to explain it on the late late show:

Maybe I should borrow a metaphor from the esoteric realm of particle physics. They tell me that reality is at its weirdest when you get down into the subatomic level of existence. Well, even the word existence has very little meaning. In the real world, something is either there or it isn't. A table, a chair, a hill, an ocean, these are all big, continuous textures that we perceive as *things*. They exist.

But start going deeper and deeper into the microscope and you realize that reality is just a bunch of coloured dots – a pointillist painting – and that between those dots, there's nothing. *Nothing*.

Or maybe there is something. But you see, it comes into being and then disappears again so fast that it can never be detected. It happens in the interstices of space and time – particles being created out of nothing, then returning to nothing before they can ever be seen – particles and antiparticles that is. They blip into being, run into each other, and self-destruct – all without us ever noticing them – and yet without these things happening every zillionth of a second, the mad scientists tell us, the entire structure of the universe could not exist.

Paradigms, it seems, are founded on paradoxes.

Get a load of that! their host will say, and the audience will laugh dutifully.

Well, I think Timmy and Angel are like that – Timmy and anti-Timmy, Angel and anti-Angel – creatures that popped into existence in the twilight of reality, doomed to annihilate each other before the world can ever detect their existence – though they can suspect it from the waves that ripple through the fabric of their perceived truth.

More laughter.

Come on, people, I'm trying to be deep here. Jeeze, the *Enquirer* took me more seriously than you guys!

fire

. . . the mountain is beginning to rumble again and . . .

fire

. . . Lauren McCandless's painting is ripping apart! And the lid flies off the coffin! A hot wind rises from clefts in the mountainside, and gusts of sulphur are scouring away the shreds of Lauren's flesh that went into his painting . . .

. . . the coffin lid is clattering as it tumbles downhill and . . .

. . . the wind, white, suffocating, and . . .

. . . Angel.

Look. He's standing on a crag over the lake of lava. He's a silhouette against the glowing crimson . . . though here and there, in the bright moon, there's a glimmer of snow-white skin . . . the only thing that covers his nakedness is the shadow of leathern wings, half-formed in the hollow air . . .

Land the chopper. Land, pilot, land.

Where?

Look . . . there. There's a basalt ledge that overlooks the crater . . . it's wide enough, I think. Let me and PJ down. Then get out while you can. All the way out. Back to Jayapura. Back to reality.

All right.

Look, PJ. He's waiting for us. Look, at the shores of the glowing sea, the souls of all the people I touched in my two thousand years of wandering. Look. There's Pamina . . . an empty skin flapping in the sulphurous wind. There's Amelia Rothstein, dressed as a Valkyrie, mounted on a skull-faced stallion, galloping over vermilion waves. There's the witch-woman, Simon Arleta, rising out of the lava like a deformed Venus. There are all my friends: Carla and Stephen, Petra and Brian. They're all waiting, PJ. Why are they waiting? Because we have a final magic to make, a magic of absolute ending.

I know. Look. The helicopter is taking off. Flying across the face of the moon.

Is it too hot for you? Can you breathe?

I don't need to breathe. I'm a contrary. What's dead is living, what's first is last.

Do you understand what this magic must be?

Yes. You and Angel are going to cancel yourselves out. These are the same conditions that created your immortality: the erupting volcano, the gathering of the dying. There's so much turmoil here . . . all the timelines running into one another . . . all the threads of fate twisting, knotting, tangling themselves up.

Just like with Vesuvius.

You can erase yourself from history if you can find just the right moment . . . and I can have Chit back . . . by reversing the light and the dark. We're going to spin the wheel of time backward. That's why the spirits made me a contrary.

There's Angel. He's calling my name. But he's not calling me Timmy Valentine, or Konrad Stolz, or Sebastian, or Wally Alvarez, or Ercole Serafino, or Jeannot, or any of the myriad names I've been called during my long journey. He's calling me by a name that I can't even say aloud. It's my true name. How can he know that name?

Because he's your shadow.

God, I'm choking, I'm choking—

Try to hold on. It won't be much longer now.

The mist is deadly.

I know.

And Chit?

I know, I know what I have to do.

angel

Angel stands on the island at the centre of the churning lava. The heat does not sear him; the sulphur fumes do not choke him. Moonlight swathes his cold pale flesh. His eyes are red, from the glow of molten rock, from the rush of blood, and from his back sprout shadowy wings, half-spread. He watches the helicopter land, take off, disgorge the two friends and the dead woman in her coffin.

The mountain rumbles. Lava fountains up around him in

glowing columns. Clouds of sulphur jet up through clefts in the rock. He feels transforming fire sweep through his veins. There is power in the volcano, power he can feed on.

He gazes across the lake. There he is, his reflection, his other self. He goes to him, walking across the burning sea, his bare feet unscarred by brimstone; the boiling rock rears up about him, touches the bitter cold of Angel's soles, and hardens to obsidian stepping stones. A rosy radiance bathes his delicate features. He is as beautiful as Jesus. Though the sun has set, the crater is like the sun, its rays the thermoluminescence of a deadly dawn.

'Timmy,' says Angel. Though the earth and the sky are roaring, he speaks in a still small voice, like a child, like God. 'You said that when we met again, you would see the one great truth that only the dying can see.'

'Hi, Angel,' Timmy says. 'Good to see you again, brother.' And Timmy smiles. Angel too smiles; their smiles are just alike, except for the fangs.

'Hello, Angel,' PJ says. But he means goodbye.

'Do you see,' says Angel, 'how all the lines of time converge here? How all the separate journeys of history, all the souls that you and I have touched, they're all right here, streaming into this infernal sea? Look at it, it's totally fucking cool.'

'Dude,' says Timmy. 'I guess you could call this place Vampire Junction.'

'Look,' says Angel.

He spreads his wings. Buildings are tumbling into the lava. Trains are flying off collapsing bridges. Rome, London, Tenochtitlán, even Atlantis itself are submerging beneath the red-hot waves – and the transfigured dead are dancing on the seething waters. There is Pamina: not an empty skin, but whole, laughing, waltzing with her Tante Amelia over the coffins that are bobbing up and down in the magma. There is Stephen Miles conducting a choir and orchestra of skeletons. There is Carla Rubens swirling in a ruby mandala, Jason Sirota strutting on a stage, and dark figures of history, seated on their glowing thrones, their dark capes billowing in the hot wind. There is Gilles de Rais at the stake, going up in smoke. Caravaggio painting . . . Kit Marlowe dying for the second time . . . the stack of corpses in the oven at Oswieçim, where they once try to burn Timmy for a gipsy.

And Vlad Tepes on his deathbed, calling for Radu the ageless, the unchanging.

fire

The hillside burning. The bodies of the Moldovans smouldering. The tents aflame. A sea of burning corpses all the way to the edge of the Turks' encampment . . .

'Radu.'

'Yes, Dracula.'

'It is you, isn't it? They are going to make you king. You haven't aged at all. Except in your eyes. They look like they've seen millennia.'

'Dracula, they have.'

'Radu, Radu – you're not my brother at all, are you? You're some kind of demon, some kind of fiendish double that the infidels have concocted with Satanic alchemy. And now they'll put you on the throne, and Wallachia will be ruled by demons . . .'

'No, Dracula,' says Radu, as they set down his litter beside the dying prince. The face of the anguished boy in the prison cell is almost unrecognizable. There are scars, blotches, furrows, and ridges around the lips that form a permanent scowl. The prince is bleeding from a dozen wounds; a doctor tends to him, but there is no way to save him; his head leans on a dented helmet, he moans, he is delirious at times; but Radu knows that in his delirium there are glimpses of the truth. 'I am no conjurer's illusion,' he tells the man he once called brother. 'I am something else altogether. Men see in me what they wish to see; they never see what I truly am. Except, perhaps, in the moment of dying.'

fire

Angel and Timmy spoke to one another.

PJ watched them, could not hear what they said over the rumble of the volcano. Sweat poured down his brow, teared up his eyes. But he had a task. The bat-spirit had given him the contrary gift, and he knew that all things can be their own opposites. Hello could be goodbye. Day could be night. Flight could be confrontation. And death could become life through the transforming power of love.

Sex is the great magic, he thought. For billions of years, in a world without sex, there had been a kind of life, for the amoeba lived, divided, lived on in other amoebas, never dying. Sex was the magic that unleased the million shapes of life. The two-leggeds and the four-leggeds, the swimming and the flying, the creatures of earth, sea, and air, all came because of sexual love; and with that love came death.

What does one do to a corpse? One turns away from it. One shoves it in the earth, gives it over to the worms. And what is the contrary thing to do? To love that corpse back from the grave.

Tenderly he lifted the woman from the coffin. Lovingly he placed her on the basalt floor that fumed with the earth's deep passion. Oh, she was cold, but the volcano's heat soon seeped into her and unfroze her blood a little. A faint putrescence clung to her. Soon it would too late. He stripped off his garments one by one and folded them inside the coffin; then – putting all his hope in the impossible – he shoved the coffin into the fiery sea.

Misdirection. That was the secret of all magic.

The mountain shook, loosing great boulders from the inner wall of the crater. Lava splashed up. It burned his arms, his thighs; he screamed with pain as he sheltered Chit from the falling rock.

I love you, he thought. And kissed the dead lips. And caressed the unyielding tissue of her breasts. Tickled the stony areolas with his tongue. Oh, she was truly dead, dead, dead. He tried to slap the blood back into her face, licked at the vampire's puncture marks, as though he could suck up and spit out the poison. Oh, dead, dead, dead, he thought. How can I feel anything for this dead flesh? He remembered her last words, spoken in the heat of anger.

And now he himself began to feel that anger. He was shaking from it. His heart was pounding. You died hating me, he thought. Maybe I should hate you too. Did you think I was some kind of savage, a performing monkey for your rich family?

And with hate came the beginning of arousal . . .

fire

'Are you ready for the leap?' Angel says.

Timmy hesitates. 'I don't know. I guess.'

'Two thousand years is a long time. You want oblivion, dude.'

'Yeah. But why do you want it? You hardly tried it, the vampire thing. You could go on for another two thousand years, until you too became too weighed down with compassion to go on.'

The red sea roars.

'Slough off that immortality,' Angel says. 'You can do it.'

'Just like that?' says Timmy. He sounds so frail and so unconfident. He is a real little boy after all, Angel thinks. On the brink of nothingness, he's finally become what he asked for. 'Rip it off me like an old skin, throw it into the abyss? But what if someone catches it?'

'Someone will. The mountain's gonna blow any minute. You can reach into any moment of the past or future. You can slip the curse to someone else, unwrite the book of time so that you and me were never here at all.'

'How do you know so much?'

'I'm you – remember?'

'Come on, already, then.'

fire

Anger fuels him. Apaches used to rape women to death, he remembers someone telling him, maybe a line from some movie. Hate you, he thinks, hate you, fucking *hate* you. Gonna split you open with my dick. Gonna fuck you in *two*. She's not even a woman anymore, not even someone he used to love, she's everything he's ever hated about the world . . . about himself . . . the fire enters into him and the fire is running in his veins and his brains are on fire and his hands are on fire and his penis is a burning torch as he rams it between her flaming legs and . . .

fire

Stop, Timmy's thinking, stop, hold on, oh this is moving so fucking fast I'm peeling open like an onion and I can't grasp anything because it slips through my fingers like liquid fire and . . .

fire

'I saw Radu thirty years ago . . . Mehmet impaled him,' Radu says.
    'But here you are—'
    'No, no. A shadow. A reflection that casts no reflection.'
    And Dracula cries out in his ecstasy of dying, 'Then I have killed all those people for nothing.'

fire

The piece of Timmy-Angel that is their joint immortality is slipping from their grasp.
    Angel embraces Timmy in his dark wings.
    Did I ever know my own mother? Timmy thinks. In the shadowy time before I came to the Sibyl's cave, who was I?
    'Too late,' says Angel.
    And the rocks, the air, the boiling sea, the chorus of the damned, all cry out as with one voice: Partake of me. Love me. Leap with me. Die with me. Love me.
    Into the flaming void—

Vanitas!
It was good to think of the emptiness. It was good to rush
toward extinction, still flushed with the joy of life.

fire

'Oh, Radu,' cries the dying prince, 'is there not one gift you can
give me to assuage this pain? How I hated Radu, Radu, how I
thought him base and unworthy! How I wanted to kill him over
and over with every thrust of that impaling stake! And now you
have told me that everything I believed in was a lie.'
'Not a lie,' says Radu. 'No one deceived you. You wore the
blinkers every human wears. The world is the confluence of
your illusions; reality is but a dream.'
'But why must the dream end now, just when I see a glimpse
of the truth? Do you now come, at the end of my hate-filled
life, that all I have achieved is *vanitas*? Oh Radu, make me a
spirit like yourself—'
Radu senses other Radus in the darkling air. Where do they
come from? Pieces of himself from other lives and times? The
other Radus gather. They are in the blood-tinged mist that
sweeps over the sea of the dead. They cry out to him: *Relinquish
your power now, and in some far-off future you will find peace.*
'I will pass on my gift to you,' he says softly, 'if you will tell
the surgeon to undo the bandages about your wounds, for I
must draw the blood from them . . .'
And kneels over the dying prince to impart the kiss of death.
'I'm sorry, Radu,' says the prince, who once ruled men but
will soon rule only the darkness.
'I love you, little dragon,' Radu says.

fire

In the same moment – though that moment is a moment far
removed in space and time, it is still the same moment—
Boy and vampire are falling into the abyss.
Fusing as they fall.

PJ is gasping as his thrusts of rage reach orgasm.
Then—

oblivion

At first there's only pain. Timmy is on fire. The sulphur is oozing
into his lungs, burning his flesh. He has never felt this kind of
pain . . . only in that other igneous moment, the moment of his
creation . . . and then the millennia have passed without pain
at all . . . and then, in the brief year of human sensations, there
were only pinprick pains, nothing like this all-consuming pain
that rives his flesh, that tears into his bloodstream, that makes
his brain boil . . . and Timmy screams . . . screams in the arms
of the boy who is also himself, the boy who can feel no pain.

But after the pain—

There comes a voice, soft, soothing, still. There comes a darkness more profound even than the darkness of the vampire
world. The universe had collapsed in on itself and sucked itself
into the black hole in its own heart. He and the angel are one.

A memory surfaces. Eyes. A smile. A mother.

Angel, too, can feel this memory. It is the mother that he
never had when he was alive; not the mother he continued to
try to kill even after he had already killed her, but something
much further back . . . into the womb and beyond it.

The twins suckle at the breasts of mother darkness. It is the
peace that passes understanding. It is nirvana.

fire

PJ's hate is spent, and the contrary trance begins to lift from
him, and he breathes in the fragrance of the woman he loves,
and he hugs her to him tight as they float on the rocky island
in the maelstrom of fire—

Dracula dies.

The boy and the vampire have rolled themselves into one
ball of fire . . . tongues of flame envelop them . . . the volcano
trembles and spits them out and they soar up, up into the night

sky and explode in a supernova of brilliant energy that drowns the moon and the stars and—

PJ kisses Chit and Chit opens her eyes.

'I feel like Sleeping Beauty,' she says.

Then the whole world is shaking and rumbling and the floating rock is fragmenting beneath them and stones are cascading down the inside of the crater and—

'We're going to die!' Chit says.

. . . the coffin, still floating in the lava . . .

'Quick. Let's get inside it.'

He lifts her, lays her gently in the coffin, climbs in beside her, pulls the lid shut. They are in darkness. The world is collapsing outside, but in the womb of death they feel a kind of peace. They kiss again. And then, full of the joy of still being alive even inside the crack of doom, they begin to make love again.

They are making love when the coffin is flung skyward by the renewed force of the volcano's eruption . . .

rebirth

A long dark silence. She did not dream at all.

When she awoke, pried loose the coffin lid, the coffin slid, settled a little; startled, she cried out, and woke PJ. They were stuck somewhere in the canopy of the forest; the branches had broken the coffin's fall and saved them from death. She pushed away the lid, heard it skittering down the branches to land with a dull plop in the moist earth below. As she sat up, she saw the volcano in the horizon, quiescent now; there was only a faint glow at the summit, and a tendril of thin smoke trailing past the rising sun.

What country were they in?

'Where is this?' she said. 'We can't be in Thailand, there aren't any volcanoes in Thailand.'

'You've been dead, Chit.'

'Oh!' It all came back then. The concert. The vampire's fangs sinking into her wrist. Her last thoughts: *I hate you, PJ.*

How could she have thought such things? 'Does this mean,'
she said, 'that now I'm – I'm—'

'The sun is rising, Chit. I don't see you burning to a crisp, so
I guess you've survived.'

'And Timmy? and Angel? and—'

'They've written themselves out of history. You'll see. We
have been granted the gift of remembrance: because there was
a time, a place, a state of being where all those vampires were
as real as you and me, and the terrible things we lived through
were all true.'

'You mean – it's all gone now?'

'Never completely, Chit . . . as long as it hasn't faded from
our memories, we'll know, I guess.'

He helped her climb down the tree. They were a man and a
woman, naked, in a primaeval forest.

'It's all very mythic,' Chit said, but then she waited primly
behind a tree trunk while PJ beat a pile of bark into a kind of
garment for her.

'We could live here forever,' PJ said. 'I've got all the survival
skills. And maybe it's about time I turned my back on the white
man side of my nature and went back to being pure injun.'

'But—'

They stumbled on a clearing. There was a geodesic tent, and
in front of it, hunched over an easel, a man was hard at work
on a canvas. It was in a familiar neo-realist style. Only the subject matter had changed.

*He stands over the lake of fire, his nudity half-draped by the shadow
of the great leathern wings. He seems no more than a boy, but his eyes
betray millennial melancholy. Around him, the brimstone fumes are
swirling. He is so pale he almost seems drained of blood; yet deep within
his eyes there smoulders a dark red flame.*

'Hi,' said the painter. 'Wow, I haven't seen another human
being in days. My name is—'

'Lauren McCandless,' Chit blurted out. 'And I'm Chit, and
this is PJ – don't you—'

A weird look crossed Lauren's face. What did he remember?
'Jesus, must be a flashback; haven't popped any pills in a fucking
week . . . I can't believe that I fled into the world's most remote
wilderness to find the only two human beings who have ever

heard of me . . . Jesus fucking Christ. Art buffs, huh. And now you're here for a piece of paradise . . . doing the Adam and Eve thing in the world's last Garden of Eden? Me, I came for the volcano. Look. This is what I see inside the crater. It haunts me in my dreams. I call it Angel, just Angel.'

'It's beautiful. It's, I don't know, so haunting, so real some-how,' PJ said softly. 'As if you'd seen it in the flesh.'

And then Chit knew that the world had slipped sideways; that Timmy and Angel, by destroying each other at the moment of the nameless volcano's eruption, had unleashed such turbu-lence in the fabric of reality that they had removed almost all traces of themselves from the cosmos.

'Shit,' said Lauren, 'I'm out of alizarin crimson, and civiliza-tion's a two-week trek away. I knew I should have packed more. Volcanoes use so much *red*: vermilion, scarlet, cadmium red; dull reds, bright reds, brash reds, neon reds, you name it, they're *in* there.'

'We could trek with you,' said PJ. 'I do know something about surviving in forests . . . even though this is kind of a different wilderness than the one I'm used to.'

'I don't think we'll need to trek—' Chit began. For she could hear, above the distant rumbling, above the chirps, croaks, squeals, and chitters of the forest, the sound of an approaching helicopter. And then, turning to PJ – as though she were making up reality as she went along – she said, 'Don't you remember, honey? Today's Sunday . . . that's when we told them to send the chopper to pick us up . . .'

'Rich explorers, huh,' said Lauren. 'Do I detect a . . . *Thai* . . . accent, Ms . . . Chit? I'm from LA originally, I should know a Thai accent when I hear one. Couple of millionaires playing at Adam and Eve – that's too cool. Sure, we'll go native. Keep the marines on standby though. Gonna offer me a ride? They say the volcano could blow a gasket any day now.'

'We'll do more than offer you a ride, Mr McCandless,' PJ said. 'You see, Chit and I, we own this art gallery in Los Angeles . . .'

'So much for "turning my back on the white man side of my nature and going back to pure injun",' Chit said, and gently prodded PJ in the ribs.

'Shut up!' said PJ. 'I love you.'

22

OVERHEARD AT ANOTHER GALLERY OPENING

vanitas

'So like, is it Satanic or what?' said the punked-out, androgynous creature with the mirror shades.

'I don't know. But those Neo-Gothic rockers sure think so . . . oh, what's that *new*est new trend called? *Darkwave*. Yeah. Heard this new group, Deep Eynde, has a Lauren McCandless painting on its CD cover.'

'Which one?'

'*That* one—'

vanitas

He stand over the lake of fire, his nudity concealed by a tongue of purple flame that erupts out of the abyss. Behind him, the outline of leathern wings can be seen against the moonlit sky. He is walking across the burning lake. Where his feet touch the fire, their coldness has crystallized the lava into stepping stones of obsidian. Though he seems no more than a boy, his eyes betray an ancient melancholy . . .

vanitas

'But like, what does it mean? Is it Latin or something?'

'I don't know. Here's let's ask someone. Hey, dude, what does *Vanitas* mean?'

'That's VAN-itas, not Van-EE-tas, you uneducated piece of shit.'

'Yeah, yeah, but what does it mean?'

'Shut up! Here comes someone. A limo. Pulling up.'

'Wow, it's Giler, head of Stupendous. I wonder what he's doing in the Valley.'

'Maybe he's here to buy a painting.'

'Everyone's buying Lauren McCandless. I hear the original of the album cover went for six figures.'

'Seven.'

'Seven? Bullshit. Who is he, Van Gogh?'

'Heard a really hot rumour last night, I was at the Phoenix, you know, with Rebecca Himot, that casting agent from Oberon? So like, Giler's just bought this *hot* new property. It's a teenage rock star vampire movie. It's like this twelve-year-old kid, you know, only he's *Dracula*! OK, sounds kind of corny, but you should have heard the way people were talking about it. It seems the writer got the idea from a Lauren McCandless painting . . . pitched it the next day . . . they've already fired him, of course, but he's set for life . . . they're getting McCandless to do the production design . . . *that's* what Giler's doing in the Valley, *if* you please.'

'Giler bought that? Jeeze . . . I had an idea just like that ten years ago, but no one would touch it.'

'I hear it's like totally gory.'

'Coolness.'

'Look . . . another limo's pulling up . . . who could it be this time?'

'Oh, it's not a limo at all. Only another news van.'

'Boring.'

vanitas

He stands on the edge of the precipice. His arms are spread wide. Behind him, the stars shine, cold and comfortless. A smashed guitar leans in the foreground against a burning rock that tastefully conceals his nudity. It is the eyes, above all, that hold the viewer's attention. They seem to send forth their magnetic radiance out of the very canvas. A single tear trickles down one cheek; but in the ruby reflection of the fiery lake, it could easily be mistaken for a smear of blood.

vanitas

'Mr McCandless, where do you get your ideas?'
  'In dreams.'
'Mr McCandless, where do you get your ideas?'
  'All right. A longer answer. Sometimes when I'm by myself – I'm by myself a lot because my hosts in Thailand have put me in this houseboat on the river – I close my eyes and seem to hear an alien music. The music steals into my mind. I don't quite recognize it, can't really characterize it. It's kind of sweet, but it has an angry edge to its harmonies . . . and its beat is the pumping of a human heart. I hear this alien music . . . there's no music yet written that sounds quite the same . . . and inter-mingled with it is a voice . . . a high, pure voice . . . the purity of a child's voice, but all the power and resonance of a grown man's . . . the way, I'm told, *castrati* used to sing in the Bad Old Days. Well, so . . . I listen hard. You got to listen hard to hear this. Because it's coming from another world. A universe almost exactly like our own, but you see, it's not. It's a universe that still has magic in it, I guess, and that alters things . . . slightly, but enough to charge everything that happens in it with a febrile energy that you and I can't even imagine. You see, after a while, I seem to fall into this other world. I'm breathing its air. *Ich spüre Luft von anderen Planeten*. You know who said that? Look it the fuck up, you uneducated television reporter person, you!'
  'Mr McCandless, where do you get your ideas?'
  'Fuck off.'
  'Mr McCandless, where do you get your ideas?'
  'I have no ideas. The paintings just paint themselves.'

vanitas

'It means *emptiness*, you airhead.'

vanitas

vanitas